The Sins of Armstrong House

A. O'CONNOR

POOLBEG

This novel is entirely a work of fiction. The names, characters and incidents portrayed in it are the work of the author's imagination. Any resemblance to actual persons, living or dead, events or localities is entirely coincidental.

Published 2025 by Poolbeg Press Ltd, 123 Grange Hill, Baldoyle, Dublin 13, Ireland

E-mail: poolbeg@poolbeg.com · www.poolbeg.com

© A. O'Connor 2025

Copyright for typesetting, layout, design, ebook and cover image.

© Poolbeg Press Ltd

The moral right of the author has been asserted.

1

A catalogue record for this book is available from the British Library.

ISBN 978-1-178199-668-3

All rights reserved. No part of this publication may be reproduced or transmitted in any form or by any means, electronic or mechanical, including photography, recording, or any information storage or retrieval system, without permission in writing from the publisher. The book is sold subject to the condition that it shall not, by way of trade or otherwise, be lent, resold or otherwise circulated without the publisher's prior consent in any form of binding or cover other than that in which it is published and without a similar condition, including this condition, being imposed on the subsequent purchaser.

www.poolbeg.com

Also by A. O'Connor

This Model Life

Exclusive

Property

Ambition

Full Circle

Talk Show

The House

The Secrets of Armstrong House

The Left-Handed Marriage

The Footman

On Sackville Street

The Legacy of Armstrong House

By Royal Appointment

A Great Beauty

A Telegram From Berlin

About the author

A graduate of the National University of Ireland Maynooth and Trinity College Dublin, A. O'Connor is the bestselling author of fifteen previous novels including *The Armstrong House* series, *The Footman*, *The Left-Handed Marriage*, *By Royal Appointment* and *A Telegram From Berlin*. He has also written children's books on Martin Luther King, James Joyce and the Irish patriot Michael Davitt. The author is a regular feature writer for publications including the *Irish Daily Mail* and the *Irish Times*.

Acknowledgements

A special thank-you to the great team at Poolbeg – Paula, Kieran, David and Lee. My sincere gratitude to my editor Gaye Shortland for her dedication and her indomitable spirit. And thank-you to the book buyers, reviewers and readers for your continued support.

Dedication

For Izabela

Prologue

Present Day

The little church in the village close to Armstrong House had been transformed for the wedding. The Victorian interior was beautifully decorated with flowers and a white carpet laid down on the aisle, covering the tired red and white tiles underneath. And as the bride and groom said "*I do*" the sun shone through the stained-glass window above the altar.

As Kate Collins watched her stepdaughter Alex exchange vows, she wondered if Lord Edward Armstrong ever envisaged that his great-great-great-granddaughter would get married in that church, when he built it in the 1840s. Nico, Kate's husband, sat in the front pew alongside his first wife Susan, Alex's mother. Kate and Nico's eleven-year-old son Cian sat between them. As Kate had been delegated to sit with relatives in the second pew, she felt strangely dissociated. As the cellist and pianist began to play the "Portuguese Love Song", she could see her husband, a man not given to showing emotion, take out his handkerchief and dab his eyes. She fought an urge to go and hug him. But she remained seated, feeling like an outsider on this special day.

Since the wedding reception was to be held at their home, Armstrong House, Kate had felt like an unofficial wedding planner these past few months as she worked tirelessly to make sure everything was perfect for Alex's big day.

She remembered the first time she had met Alex. Kate had still been married to her first husband Tony at the time, and they had just bought Nico's ancestral home, Armstrong House, from him. Little did Kate know, when she renovated the house with Tony, that her destiny would be inextricably tied to the previous owners. After Tony died and Kate and Nico married, Alex regularly stayed with them at Armstrong House. Kate had watched her grow from a precocious child to a confident young woman. As Alex was an Influencer, Kate had felt extra pressure to make sure everything ran smoothly on the day, as her seventy thousand followers would be watching every move and post.

Finally, the ceremony concluded and the congregation rose to their feet and began to applaud the newlyweds as they walked down the aisle. Kate watched as her joyous husband and his smiling ex-wife filed past her with the rest of the bridal party.

Outside, Kate didn't have time to join in as the photographs were taken. She rushed to her car and drove quickly from the village which was named after the Armstrongs who had built it in the nineteenth century. She raced through the country roads until she reached the main gateway of Armstrong House and continued up the long avenue, which stretched around the lake and through the manicured parkland, until she reached the forecourt.

They had been blessed with beautiful sunshine and the caterers were already assembled in the first terraced garden in front of the house, to greet the guests for a champagne reception. The caterer bombarded her with questions as she hurried into the house to check all was ready for the wedding banquet, which was being held in the ballroom at the back of the house.

After the garden drinks reception, the wedding party had relocated to the ballroom where they had been seated at a series of beautifully dressed round tables. As the sunshine radiated through the French windows, it reminded Kate of her own wedding reception in that same ballroom fourteen years before. She felt she had a lot to be grateful for – a caring husband, a wonderful son and a house that meant so much to her – even if she felt like a guest in her own home that day as she was not seated at the head table.

The speeches began, but she kept one eye on her phone as she was expecting a text from her agent. Kate had been a well-known actress when she was younger and had been trying to resurrect her career over the past few years. She had recently auditioned for a part in a series and had high hopes of getting it. It was a wonderful part and guaranteed work for several months.

As she listened to Nico and Alex make heartfelt speeches, she couldn't help but feel disappointed that she was not mentioned. Alex was young and could be thoughtless, so Kate was not overly surprised that she didn't mention her. She sighed as she concluded that Nico, ever the diplomat, probably didn't want to offend his ex-wife Susan by acknowledging the large part Kate had played in organising her daughter's day.

Then, as the best man cracked tasteless jokes, Kate saw a text from her agent on the phone and quickly opened it.

`Hi Kate - the casting director was very impressed by you but unfortunately decided another actress was better suited to the role. They said they will keep you in mind for anything else that comes up. I hope the wedding is going well - Joey`

Kate's heart sank when she read the rejection. She knew she should be used to rejections, but they still stung – particularly this one.

By early evening, Kate felt she could at last relax. The day had so far gone without a hitch.

She was chatting with some of the guests in the drawing room at the front of the house when Alex came to find her.

"I haven't spoken to you all day so I'm going to steal you away for a moment, Kate." Taking her arm, Alex led her to another part of the room. "You look amazing! Did the photographer take your photo yet? I want to post one of you on my Instagram."

"Not yet. I think she's been too busy photographing all these trendy young people from the worlds of fashion and media to want one of me," Kate said with a laugh, flicking back her long caramal-coloured hair.

"Oh, I think people will still be interested in seeing a photo of you, Kate. People still remember you."

"Reassuring to hear!" said Kate, not sure if she should be complimented or insulted.

"I'm sure you'll be glad when we're all gone, Kate, and you get your home back!"

"It's an honour to host your wedding, Alex. This is your home as much as ours and you will always be welcome here."

"*Ahhh* – thanks! Though I'm not sure Dad agrees! He certainly will be glad to see the back of us all."

"Well, you know your father, Alex – Nico isn't one for the limelight."

"I think he's aged this past year," said Alex with a frown.

"Really? I hadn't noticed. I think he still looks pretty good."

"Well, you see him all the time, so you wouldn't notice as much. But I worry about him."

"Why would you worry about him?"

"Just the huge responsibility of maintaining this house, the expense," sighed Alex. "I worry about you too, Kate, of course ."

"We manage, Alex. There really is no need to worry."

"But it can't be easy and then you've had to pay for the wedding on top of everything else!"

"We were very happy to do so!"

"You know … when we were seated in the ballroom I was thinking of your own wedding to Dad."

"Yes, it ran through my mind as well."

"I've never said it before, but I've often thought it must be hard for you to live here at Armstrong House."

"Why ever would it be?" asked Kate, perplexed.

Alex looked through the window, down the terraced gardens to the lake. "Because every time you look out at the lake you must be reminded of your first husband being killed in the speedboat there."

Kate was taken aback. "I rarely think about Tony. I don't dwell on the past."

"That's what Mum said about you. She said the reason you're so obsessed with the history of the house is because it stops you from having to think about your own past."

"*Alex! We need you in the ballroom!*"

Alex's new husband rushed into the drawing room, grabbed her hand and dragged her away.

Kate looked out the window at the lake and bit her lower lip.

Later, having hardly spoken to Nico all day, Kate went in search of him. One of the staff told her he had gone down the stairs at the back of the hall which led to the kitchen, the staircase known traditionally as the servants' stairs.

As she reached the little hallway at the bottom of the stairs, she could hear the voices of Nico and Alex in the kitchen.

Alex's voice was high and clear. "I really think it's time you sold Armstrong House, Dad, while the market is so good."

Kate halted and listened.

"Kate will never sell this house," said Nico. "And I don't want to sell it. It's our ancestral home and you know I want it to be yours and Cian's one day."

"Dad, I have no interest in ever living here! As soon as I inherit it I will be putting a For Sale sign up. And Cian said earlier he wants to be an astronaut so I can't see him wanting to spend too much time down here either!"

"Cian is eleven years old and doesn't know what he wants," said Nico.

"I just don't get it why you still want to live here. Your office is in Dublin and you're not getting any younger, Dad! You should sell up and move to Dublin where it would be easier for you to work and easier for Cian to go to a nice school and then university."

"As I said, Kate will never leave here. She loves it even more than I do," said Nico.

"But don't you ever think of the future? In another few years this house is going to start needing a lot of work done and you don't have the money to do that. You are just about managing to maintain the place as it is, through your work and Kate embarrassing herself by taking any acting job she can get to earn some money! I mean, did you see that part she played in that Netflix series last year! It was cringe! I felt so humiliated for her that she was reduced to doing it!"

"And you think the answer is to sell Armstrong House?"

"Yes! Joshua and I will be renting forever with the property prices in Dublin. If you sell Armstrong House, I can take my inheritance now – which will allow us to buy and you'll make so much money you can buy a beautiful house in Dublin. A house that will be suitable for you and Kate as you get older. I hate to say it, Dad, but Kate is not as young as she thinks she is – hence her still trying to get acting roles that she is clearly not suited to! She might have been a respected actress once but that was a long time ago and now she's past it!"

Kate turned and quietly made her way back up the stairs. From there she hurried down the hall and out the front door.

In the forecourt, guests were gathered in different groups, drinking and laughing. She spotted a man smoking and approached him.

"Do you mind if I ask you for a cigarette and a light?" she asked.

"Be my guest!" said the man, offering his packet and a lighter.

Kate took a cigarette and lit it.

She thanked the man and then walked quickly across the forecourt and down a flight of steps which led to the first terraced garden where more guests had gathered. She walked past them and down the next flight of steps to the next garden. She rarely smoked these days but now, confident that she was out of view of Cian or Nico, she gratefully inhaled as she tried to process Alex's hurtful words. She knew young people tended to dismiss anyone over thirty as old but, as she and Nico were still only in their mid-fifties, she found her stepdaughter's opinion stinging.

"It's a beautiful day for a wedding," said a voice behind her.

She turned around to see a tall, greying distinguished man, perhaps in his sixties, standing there.

"Isn't it?" she responded.

"And a beautiful house," he said.

"Thank you," said Kate, noting that his accent was English.

"I don't think we met earlier. Are you on the bride or groom's side?"

"Neither. I'm trespassing," he said with a little laugh.

"Sorry?"

"I thought Armstrong House was open to the public and when I saw the crowd outside I thought it was a tour and came up to buy an admission ticket!"

"Oh, no – we did use to have the house open to the public, but we haven't done that since the pandemic," said Kate.

"I see. I was misinformed. I'm sorry for intruding. It's just that I've always had a fascination with Armstrong House and since I was in the area I wanted to see it. You see, I'm a relative of the woman who used to own it."

"Who?" Kate asked, startled.

"Clara, Lady Armstrong."

"*Really?* Clara Charter, the first wife of Lord Pierce Armstrong?"

"The very woman!" said the man with a laugh.

"I'm Kate Collins," she introduced herself excitedly. "Pierce Armstrong was my husband's grandfather. When I moved here first I became very interested in Clara as we found possessions of hers – photographs and a film reel – left in the house. I even tracked down her relatives in London to give those items back to them."

"Yes, I am aware of that too. In fact, I am now in possession of those items – thank you for returning them."

"You have them! How amazing!" How did he come to have them, she wondered, and why had she not met him when she met the family in London? "Listen, I would love to talk to you some more, but it's just a bad time today with the wedding. Could we meet tomorrow perhaps?"

"I'm returning to England tomorrow unfortunately," he said.

"What a pity! I know so little about Clara and what became of her after she left Armstrong House and divorced Pierce. I would love to hear more."

"I actually have a photo of her taken here at a ball." He took out his phone and started to scroll through it.

Kate eagerly stepped forward.

He found the photo and showed it to her.

Clara was standing beside a man Kate recognised as Lord Pierce Armstrong, Nico's grandfather. They were front and centre of a large crowd dressed in black tie and evening dresses. A banner hung above them on the wall with the words: *Castlewest Hunt Ball – Armstrong House 1923.*

"Good Lord!" exclaimed Kate as she threw away her cigarette and took the phone to study the photo. "I'm confused. There must be some mistake! The house was burned down in the War of Independence in 1921 and I've always understood that Clara and Pierce divorced soon after that."

"This photograph says otherwise."

"I would love a copy of this ... sorry, I didn't get your name?"

"My name is Royce Charter. I can take your phone number, if you like, and send the photo to you?"

Kate called out her number and Royce entered it into his phone.

"*Kate!*" came a sudden shout.

Kate looked up the terraced gardens to see Nico standing at the top.

"It's my husband. I came down here for a sneaky cigarette. He'll kill me if he finds out I had one," Kate said with a grimace.

"I've detained you long enough. Please go back to your wedding. Apologies for gate-crashing."

Kate smiled at him. "Not at all, it's been lovely to meet you. If you're ever in the area again, please contact me – but, in the meantime, maybe you could text or phone with details about Clara?" She fingered the Edwardian-style brooch on her dress. "In fact, this is Clara's brooch. When I met your family in London to give back her personal possessions they kindly said I could keep it. I wear it for special occasions."

"Yes, I recognised it from photos," said Royce.

"*Kate – they are about to cut the cake! Will you come on!*" shouted Nico.

"It was nice meeting you," said Kate as she smiled and then quickly headed up the steps to Nico.

"Where have you been?" demanded Nico as she reached him and they hurried inside for the cutting of the cake.

As Kate watched Alex and her husband cut the cake in the ballroom, surrounded by the cheering guests, she thought about her strange encounter with the man in the garden.

She had wanted to ask him so much more, but it was not the right day to do so. At the same time her instinct was warning her that this man turning up like that was very strange. Her phone bleeped and she looked at it, expecting it to be from her agent, but it was from an unknown number. She opened the message and saw it was the photo of Clara and Pierce at the ball. As she studied the black-and-white photo taken in that very ballroom over a century before, she was completely baffled. The fact that Clara had been living there in 1923 with Pierce meant somebody was not telling the truth about the history of Clara, Pierce and the burning of Armstrong House.

Chapter 1

Kent, England, 1922

Since she had arrived there several months before, Clara had fallen into a routine of taking a daily walk through the parklands that surrounded Oak Trees, her grandmother's house in Kent. She valued this walk as it gave her time to think. To think mainly of the past, sometimes the present. She rarely allowed herself to think about the future. She had always loved visiting there when growing up. She had never dreamed during those halcyon days of her Edwardian childhood that she would be returning there to convalesce from a broken life and a broken marriage. That it would be her sanctuary from a hostile world and a frightening past.

Clara turned back to view the pretty Tudor house that was nestled amongst the oak trees that gave it is name. She did not know how she could have coped these past months if it were not for this place and the kindness and charity that her grandmother Louisa had shown her.

She walked back to the house, climbed the steps to the French windows and went inside. She walked through the drawing room and as she emerged into the hallway she saw the housekeeper, Mrs. Wilkens, coming down the stairs holding a silver tray.

"Good morning, Lady Armstrong," said Mrs. Wilkins with a warm smile.

"How is my grandmother this morning?"

She shook her had sadly. "She hardly ate a thing. A cup of tea and some toast was all she could manage." She nodded down at the cooked breakfast that had not been touched.

"She might have an appetite by lunchtime," Clara said.

"Hopefully," said the housekeeper and continued down the hall to the kitchens.

Upstairs, Clara knocked on her grandmother's door before entering.

"Come in!"

Clara steadied herself and then forced a big cheerful smile on her face as she entered the bedroom.

"Good morning, Granny!"

Louisa Charter was propped up in her bed against a nest of pretty pillows. Despite her fragility, her hair had been coiffured by Mrs. Wilkins and her make-up applied.

Clara approached the bed and gave her grandmother a kiss on the cheek.

"Is it a good morning? It feels like just any other one to me," said Louisa.

"I was hoping that we might go outside today, Granny. If you think you could manage the stairs, I could then take you for a spin in the wheelchair around the gardens?"

"I'm not a wheelbarrow, Clara! I felt positively seasick after that *spin* you brought me on last week!"

"Well, then, to just sit outside?"

"No – no – I'm in no mood to go outside – or go anywhere for that matter," insisted Louisa.

"Very well, in that case I shall take up reading where I left off last night," said Clara, sitting down beside the bed and reaching for the copy of *The Mysterious Affair at Styles* that was on the bedside table.

"And I'm not in the mood for Agatha Christie either! What I *am* in the mood for is to talk about *you*!" declared Louisa.

"Oh, I see!" sighed Clara as she closed the novel and placed it back on the table. "I have outstayed my welcome, have I?"

"Of course not! I love having you here. But this is not you! This is not the life that was meant for you – buried down here in the country looking after a cantankerous old woman! I have Mrs. Wilkins for that, and she does it very well, bless her!"

"This is the only life I want at the moment," insisted Clara.

"Clara – you are still a young woman."

"Hardly young at thirty-four!"

"That's still young from my perch, I can assure you! I know these past few years have been pretty awful for you. But you can't just give up!"

"I haven't given up! I just have no idea where I can go from here. And I've had to come to terms with so much that has happened to me since I married Pierce."

"Your generation has had to come to terms with many terrible things. But the loss of a marriage is the least of it compared to others dealing with grief after the war, dealing with injury, dealing with … so many things," sighed Louisa.

"So, what do you suggest, Granny?"

"I suggest you return to London and resume your life there."

Clara laughed out loud in disbelief. "Resume my life there! I have no life there. I haven't lived in London in over a decade! The Clara Charter who left London to marry Lord Pierce Armstrong and go live in Ireland no longer exists! I'm no longer that socialite from before the war! All my friends are either killed, married, or are now mad from what I hear!"

"Well, you never know until you try. From what I hear many people are asking after you," said Louisa.

"Yes, and I can imagine the questions they are asking!" said Clara bitterly. "Has she really deserted her husband? Did she really have an affair while he was fighting for King and Country in the war? Did she really help the Irish rebels?"

Lousia smiled. "Gossip. Are you telling me the once great Clara Charter who thrived on being talked about is now afraid of a little gossip?"

"That was different. That was silly stuff they talked about me before. Besides, I can hardly believe *you* are telling me all this. You – to whom reputation is everything and who was forever admonishing me for my perceived bad behaviour!"

"That's because I've changed, Clara. As I sit here day after day and think of all those who died in the war – three of your cousins – my precious grandsons – I think what was it all for? All that ambition and hard work I put into raising my family up through society for it to be cut down so cruelly by bullets in France!"

Louisa reached for a handkerchief and dabbed her eyes. It broke Clara's heart to see her grandmother like this. She remembered her always being so formidable, so controlling of her own emotions – and trying to control others.

"That is why, dear child, I do not want to see another life needlessly wasted. You have a duty to those that were killed in the war to live your life to the full. And that is why I am asking you – begging you – to make an appointment with our family solicitor when you return to London and seek a divorce from Lord Armstrong at the earliest opportunity."

Clara stared at her grandmother in shock. Never in her wildest dreams did she ever think she would hear Louisa pushing for a divorce which she had always seen as an absolute disgrace.

"I feel so guilty that I forced you back to Ireland when you came back to London to visit at Christmas in 1916 and told me how unhappy you were. I told you then divorce was out of the question and, because of that, everything that subsequently happened to you is my fault."

"You can't blame yourself for what happened to me in my marriage, Granny! You were the one who warned me in the first place that it was a bad match!"

"Be that as it may be, it is now time for you to go back to London and start building a new life."

"Well – I'll think about it," said Clara.

"Don't just think about it! I want assurances from you that you will divorce Pierce and that you will never return to Ireland or Armstrong House."

"Even if I could ever contemplate doing something so unthinkable, it would be impossible anyway, Granny ... Armstrong House burned down, remember? It no longer exists as it did."

It was always very comforting for Clara being in her parents' house in London. The three-storey white stucco townhouse in Chelsea was filled with happy memories for her. But as she looked up at the building from the taxicab as it parked outside, it did not feel like home anymore. Even though her life at Armstrong House varied from excitement and joy to disillusionment and utter desolation, it still felt like home to her. It had been the first and only house that she had been mistress of.

Before she had even reached the top step, the front door swung open, and her parents' butler stood there with a big warm smile on his face.

"Oh, welcome back, Lady Armstrong! It is such a pleasure to see you again!"

"Thank you, Burton, and it's so nice to see you also. Where are my parents?"

Clara stepped into the hall.

"In the drawing room anxiously awaiting you!" said Burton as he hurried down the steps to assist the taxi driver who was struggling with Clara's luggage.

It felt odd for Clara to be called Lady Armstrong by the staff in the house that she had been brought up in. Despite her family's position, she was the first who had become a member of the peerage. She casually wondered would she still even be able to use her title after the divorce was finalised. Or would she go back to being just plain Clara Charter? She was sure her solicitor would go through all the finer details with her.

As she entered the drawing room her parents stood up to greet her.

"Clara! You look wonderful!" said her mother Milly as she hugged her.

"Just wonderful!" agreed her father Terence as he hugged her too. Studying his daughter's fashionably cut blonde hair and blue eyes, Terance was relieved that she looked so well after the terrible experiences she had in Ireland.

It had been so long since he and Milly had seen their daughter. When she had arrived back in England she had gone straight down to her grandmother's estate in Kent and refused to see anybody since.

As Clara studied them, she saw they had aged. She felt guilty that she had been the source of so much worry which must have taken its toll on them.

Burton arrived into the drawing room.

"Your luggage has been taken up to your old room, Lady Armstrong. May I suggest tea?"

"By all means, Burton!" said Milly.

As they had tea, Milly studied her daughter. Clara looked older though she was still beautiful. But she could see she had changed. She was not the carefree girl, full of fun, who had left that house a decade ago to start her new life in Ireland. Milly had so many questions to ask but knew she had to tread carefully.

"To be honest, I only came back on Granny's insistence. She was afraid I was becoming a recluse in Kent."

"Weren't we all!" said Terence.

"All your old friends can't wait to see you," said Milly. "Since they heard you were coming back, they have been writing, asking to meet you!"

There had been a number of letters arriving at the house for Clara and she had asked her mother to open them in case there was anything important among them.

"Have you given any thought to what you might do now you are back in London?" asked her father.

"No. There's very little I'm qualified to do – nothing, in fact."

"Perhaps you could paint again? You are such a talented artist. And you even had that exhibition in Dublin," said Milly.

Clara cringed at the mention of her foray into the art world and the trouble that had led to. "One painting in a second-rate exhibition many years ago hardly constitutes being an artist, Mama," she said dismissively.

They were silent for a while as they drank their tea.

"Have you heard anything from Pierce?" Terence suddenly blurted out, causing Milly to freeze.

"No, I have not." Clara could see the confusion and unhappiness her response caused her parents. She decided to bite the bullet. "If I have to be honest with you, one of the reasons I have come back to London is to arrange a divorce from him."

"Oh!" said Milly, as tears welled up in her eyes.

"I see," said Terence.

"Granny thinks it's the right thing to do."

"Louisa thinks that! Surely not!" said Milly.

"In fact, it was Granny's urging that gave me the courage to do it."

"I can hardly believe Mama would recommend such a thing!" said Terence.

"Granny has changed considerably. She says she sees things more clearly now than she ever did all her life."

"Clara, I can understand that things have not been easy for you in Ireland, but a divorce would be scandalous," said Terence.

"I really don't want to embarrass you any further than I already have, but Granny is right – there is no other option," said Clara.

"But could you not just live your lives separately, if there is no hope of a reconciliation?" said Milly. "Surely you don't need to play the whole thing out in a courtroom and in public?"

Clara sighed. "Mama, I don't want to discuss all that now. I'm actually quite tired after the journey from Kent. I need to go to my room for a rest," she said, shutting down the conversation.

Her parents didn't know anybody who had been divorced, so Clara was grateful they were not familar enough with the process to enquire what the grounds of divorce would have to be, which would have scandalised them further.

She rose from her chair and kissed each of her parents on the cheek before leaving the room and going upstairs.

Chapter 2

Clara could hardly bear to remember the looks of disappointment and fear on her parents' faces when she had mentioned divorce. For people like Terence and Milly, with their morals and concerns for their standing in society, a divorced daughter was unthinkable.

When she arrived in her room she found a maid had already unpacked her clothes. Walking around her childhood bedroom, it felt strange being back. She felt like a failure. She had left that room ten years before to become a titled lady with a man she loved more than anything.

As she went to her dressing table she saw rows of envelopes neatly stacked on it – the correspondence she had received that her mother had mentioned. She was shocked at how many there were. She picked one up and saw the envelope had been opened as she had requested her mother to do.

She sat down at the dressing table and took the letter out of its envelope. She looked at the end of the letter and saw it was from Edwin Balfour.

"Edwin!" Clara exclaimed out loud. Edwin had been a friend of hers from before she was married. She hadn't thought of him in years although she had written to him regularly when he was at the front during the war.

She began to read.

Dearest Clara,

I've heard on the grapevine that you are back in London. I am posting this to your parents' address in the hope you will get it. If you are home I would dearly like to take you out to lunch and introduce you to my wife. I have such fond memories of the times we spent together before you married that chap and went to live in Ireland. I remember also the kindness you showed me during the war by writing to me. You'll never know what those letters meant to me. In all the horror that surrounded me on a daily basis, your letters filled with wonderful memories and funny stories lifted my spirits no end ...

Clara stood up from the dressing table and went to lie on the bed to read the rest of the letters.

They say that what you give in life you get back. And, as Clara read the letters, she believed this was true. Most of them were from friends who had served in the war or families of friends who had been killed at the front. When she had been alone in Armstrong House during those years, she had filled her time by writing letters. Pierce had never written to her or responded to her letters when he was away fighting and so she had poured all her emotion into the correspondence to her friends. As post began to trickle back from the front, she had seen that her letters were very much appreciated, which encouraged her to continue writing. Now, all these years later, her efforts were remembered and these letters sitting on her dressing table were testament to the goodwill she had created. As her correspondence to the soldiers had lifted their spirits during their darkest hours, now their letters were giving Clara hope during hers. She had made a difference.

Then she came upon a letter from Cosmo Wellesley. She was shocked. She and Cosmo had been very close before the war, to such an extent that people were expecting an announcement of an engagement. But then Clara had met Pierce and that had broken Cosmo's heart. As she quickly read through his letter, she remembered his wit and contagious positivity. He had been the polar opposite of Pierce, but it was Pierce she had fallen in love with.

Clara was having breakfast with her parents in the dining room. Terence was reading a letter from his mother.

"I really cannot understand Mama. I wrote to her saying that you and I would really like to visit her, Milly. But she has written back saying she is not up to receiving visitors right now." Terence folded the letter back into its envelope.

"She's just so stubborn!" said Milly.

"Granny was always a vain woman and so strong. She just doesn't want you to see her as she now is," said Clara.

"And yet she has had no issue with you seeing her, Clara," said Milly.

"I imagine she sees me as already broken so doesn't care about my opinion of her."

"For goodness' sake! I am her son! She shouldn't care about my opinion of her most of all!" said Terence.

"I really wouldn't worry too much about her," said Clara. "She's in the best possible care with Mrs. Wilkins."

Burton walked into the dining room.

"A telephone call for you, Lady Armstrong. Cosmo Wellesley has asked to speak to you."

"Cosmo!" exclaimed Clara.

"How lovely!" said Milly.

"Tell him I'm not here," said Clara.

"You'll do no such thing, Burton! Cosmo knows you are here. I told him you would be when I bumped into him at the Savoy last week. I insist you be polite and go speak to him!"

"Oh, Mama!" said Clara angrily as she threw her napkin on the table and stood up.

Giving her mother a filthy look, she walked out of the dining room and into the hallway. She steadied herself before she picked up the receiver.

"Hello?"

"Clara! My gosh – I'd given up hope of ever getting through to you! Did you not receive my letters?"

Cosmo sounded the exact same even though they hadn't spoken since he was a guest at her wedding ten years ago. Hearing his voice again filled her with a comforting and warm feeling.

"I'm sorry I didn't write back to you but I only read your letters last night when I got back from Kent."

"Ah – well, at least they hadn't been thrown into the fire!"

"Never that, Cosmo."

"I want to hear all your news. I'll pick you up at noon and you can tell me all over lunch at the Savoy," said Cosmo.

"What – *today*?"

"Of course, today!" insisted Cosmo.

"But it's out of the question! I have several appointments that are impossible for me to break," lied Clara.

"Perfect! I'll see then you at noon! Don't be late!" said Cosmo as he ended the call.

Clara stood in the hallway, paralysed with fear. The idea of seeing Cosmo after so many years filled her with terror. The idea of being out socially again was terrifying in itself. It had been so long since she had seen anybody socially. She looked in the mirror on the wall and groaned. If the girl she had been ten years ago could see herself now she would never have believed it. The great social butterfly who spent her life flitting from party to party reduced to a gibbering wreck over a lunch invitation.

Chapter 3

"Well, you do look swell! You really do!" said Cosmo as they sat at a table in the restaurant at the Savoy.

"Swell? I take it you picked up that expression from your travels in America?" said Clara.

"Yes. I absolutely loved it there. Have you ever been?"

Clara thought back to her plan to escape from her marriage there with her lover a few years before.

"No, I never got the opportunity. Although we did have some lively American guests staying with us at Armstrong House at one point. One was a film director – very exciting."

Clara noticed some of the other diners were looking at her and whispering to each other. She felt very self-conscious.

"I wish we had gone somewhere more discreet," she said.

"Why?"

"You *know* why, Cosmo! Unfortunately, I have gained a somewhat notorious reputation, as you well know," sighed Clara. "The scandalous Lady Armstrong who cheated on her husband while he was at the front and who betrayed her country by shielding an Irish rebel during the Easter Rising."

"Ah yes – that! I'm sure it's not all true," said Cosmo.

"It is all true – for the record."

"Then it appears you have led a very exciting life since you got married," said Cosmo.

"What you have heard is only a fraction of what has happened to me. If the truth be known, though, I have been more stupid than sinful. I wasn't unfaithful to Pierce or saved that rebel's life by design – it was more by accident."

"I can't imagine falling into somebody else's bed by accident!" said Cosmo, laughing.

Cosmo spotted two women at a nearby table who were having a hushed conversation, while one rudely pointed at Clara.

"If you prefer we can go elsewhere?" offered Cosmo.

"No. I may as well get used to it as the scandal that follows me is about to get much worse."

"How so?"

"I am going to divorce Pierce."

"I see!"

"So perhaps it is you who may prefer a more discreet venue, Cosmo. I really am not the best company for a marchioness to be seen with."

"If you remember what I am like at all, Clara, then you should know that I never did care what people thought. And – for the record – I am glad that you are divorcing Pierce. As I told you years ago, he never did deserve you."

In the three weeks since Clara returned to London her social diary had been surpringly full. She regularly met old friends and she found herself surprised by how much she was enjoying being back. She made sure to return to Oak Trees each week to spend a couple of nights with her grandmother. The person she had seen the most of was Cosmo who never said goodbye until they had organised their next meeting.

That evening she was due to meet Cosmo again. He had promised to take her to a new jazz club that everyone was seemingly raving about.

Milly was leafing through a copy of *Tatler* when Clara walked into the drawing room in a cocktail dress.

"What a lovely dress, Clara," commented Milly. "I must say I have been surprised by how many lovely dresses you have since you arrived back."

"Granny insisted on giving me a budget for my wardrobe," Clara explained.

"How kind of her … who are you meeting tonight?"

"Cosmo," said Clara as she checked her appearance in the mirror over the fire.

Milly studied her daughter and put *Tatler* aside.

"You are seeing quite a lot of Cosmo," she commented. "I hope he won't get the wrong idea."

"The wrong idea?" asked Clara, turning to face her mother.

"Well, everybody knew how much he was in love with you before you married Pierce. I just hope you're not giving him any false hope."

"Cosmo and I are friends, Mama, nothing more."

"I'm glad to hear it but please tread carefully with him, Clara, for his sake as well as yours. So many young men of his generation, who went through the war, are just – lost, for want of a better word. They're trying to make sense of the horror they witnessed and will cling on to anything to give their life some kind of meaning."

"I do know that, Mama. I have experienced it close up. Pierce is one of those young men," said Clara curtly. "And it was you who encouraged me to meet Cosmo in the first place."

"That's because he is such a lovely man. As long as both of you are clear that you can only ever just be friends, that is alright. Cosmo might seem like a harbour to you in choppy waters. But both of you should be aware that his parents would never allow a marriage between you. Never. You will be a divorced woman."

"Cosmo should be here any minute. I think I'll go out to wait for him at the door." Clara abruptly left.

"*Have a nice evening!*" Milly called after her.

The waiter brought two more Sidecar cocktails to Clara and Cosmo at their table in the jazz club.

"If I have one more of these I'll be doing the Charleston all the way home!" she said.

"Sounds like a good idea to me!" said Cosmo as he lifted his drink and chinked it against hers.

Milly's words from earlier were still racing through Clara's mind. She had to admit that Cosmo was such wonderful company that she hadn't given their relationship any thought.

"I don't mean to be intrusive," she said tentatively, "but is there anyone special in your life, Cosmo?"

"Not at the moment."

"I just wonder how somebody like you has not been snared by some lucky woman yet."

"I suppose the war got in the way. I didn't have anybody waiting here for me when I went to the front and the years when I should have been finding the love of my life were robbed from me."

"But surely you have met some wonderful girls since the war ended?"

"Well, plenty of girls but I'm not sure how wonderful they were!" He laughed before he became serious again. "Girls these days are so different from how they were before the war … but … I suppose the truth is that I never met anybody who could measure up to you, Clara."

"Me? You set the bar very low in that case!"

"I was heartbroken after you went off to marry Pierce."

"I know. I asked you at our wedding if you could ever forgive me."

"I had forgiven you. You had to marry the man that you truly loved and that was Pierce."

"My grandmother used to advise me – marry the man that loves you and not the man who you love – she said life would be much easier for me then. I often wish I had followed her advice."

"I wish you had too," said Cosmo.

As they walked through the streets of Chelsea back to Clara's parents' house, Clara tightened her fur coat around her.

"It's cold. Perhaps we should have got a taxi," she said.

"I prefer to walk – it's gives me more time with you," said Cosmo.

Clara stopped walking and turned to him.

"Cosmo, I really have felt happier with you these past three weeks than I have in years, but ..."

"I feel the same way too," said Cosmo as he reached forward and drew her towards him.

Then he began to kiss her.

After, he smiled at her.

"It's just like it used to be," he whispered.

"It's very late. I had better get home," said Clara.

Cosmo put his arm around her as they walked the rest of the way back in silence.

"Nightcap?" Clara asked as they reached the front steps of the house.

"Yes, please," said Cosmo.

They climbed the steps and Clara opened the door. They tip-toed through the darkenss of the hallway, then entered the drawing room. Clara switched on the chandelier as Cosmo closed the door behind them.

As Cosmo took off his coat and placed it over the back of the couch, Clara went to the drinks trolley, took up the decanter and poured them both a sherry.

"Thank you," said Cosmo, taking the glass from her and placing it on a side table.

Then he went to kiss Clara again, but she pulled away from him.

"Cosmo, I'm sorry. I shouldn't have allowed you to kiss me in the street." She walked over to the fireplace and stood looking at the embers in the hearth.

"But why not? We are not doing anything wrong," he said.

"I'm still a married woman," said Clara.

"But not for long," he said, walking up behind her.

She turned to face him.

"Cosmo, there is no way that we could ever have a future together – your family would never allow it."

"I told you I don't care what people think!"

"Cosmo, you said it was just like it used to be. But nothing is like how it used to be for us."

"But why not? Nothing is stopping us!"

"Time had stopped us. I am not the same girl that you were in love with. You really hardly know me anymore. You are in love with somebody who doesn't exist anymore."

"But that's not true! You are the same!"

"You want me to be the same, but I am not. My grandmother told me of a friend of hers who grew up in Australia. She met a man from London and moved here to marry him. She lived here for twenty years but pined so much for Australia that she forced her husband and children to move back there. She lasted six months before she came back to London."

"I don't understand what that has to do with us?"

"The woman wasn't pining for Australia – she had just been pining for her youth. She was mixing up her feelings and thought that going back to Australia would make her feel the way she did when she lived there when she was young. But it didn't. She said Australia had changed but it hadn't – it was she who had changed. In the same way people pine for their first love, never letting it go in their hearts. But they aren't really still in love with the person, they are in love with that time of their life – their youth before things became complicated and disappointing."

Cosmo walked to the French windows and looked out at the garden.

"You don't have feelings for me, Cosmo. You are just trying to recapture how you felt when you were young – before the war changed you and everything else. But you can't go back. Neither of us can."

"We could try," said Cosmo.

"You'll only end up disappointed and you've had enough of that in your life already. There are things about me, things you could never guess that I assure you would never make me a suitable wife for you, and not just because I will be a divorcee."

"Would you like me to go?" asked Cosmo.

"I think it would be for the best," said Clara.

Cosmo picked up his coat from the couch and put it on.

"I told you on your wedding day that I will always be here for you. I still mean it," he said.

"I appreciate that … good friends are hard to find."

She walked him to the front door and kissed his cheek before he left.

She locked the front door and stood silent in the hallway. She remembered all the nights she used to arrive home there. How she would creep up to bed in the hushed house so as not to wake anybody. As she thought back to her social diary over the past three weeks she realised she had been kidding herself. She was no longer that young free girl. A divorce would not free her either. She would always be a prisoner to her memories and the consequences of the life she had led at Armstong House.

She walked up the stairs quietly to go to bed.

Chapter 4

Seated at the top of the table in the dining room of her sprawling house in Dublin, Daphne Hatton was filled with despair as she watched her adult niece Prudence and nephew Pierce as they were served breakfast. She held her breath, waiting for the usual barrage of insults that would be directed at the maid from Prudence.

"This bacon is burnt!" Prudence said on cue as she examined her breakfast plate.

"But – but you said yesterday's was raw and to make sure it was well cooked today!" said the maid, Úna.

"I asked for it to be well cooked not cremated!" retorted Prudence.

Daphne avoided the angry glares from her son Richard and his wife Ophelia who were also seated at the table. Both had expressed their unhappiness with Richard's cousins staying with them with no end in sight.

"I'll take it back to the kitchen," said Úna as she went to pick up Prudence's plate.

"No!" said Prudence, slapping the girl's hand away. "I will suffer it! If I have to wait any longer for my breakfast I'll starve!"

"As you wish, my lady!" said Úna, rolling her eyes and beating a hasty retreat.

"I honestly don't know where you get your staff from, Aunt Daphne! My gosh, I thought our old cook at Armstrong House was hard work but, compared to your cook, Mrs Fennell should have been working at the Ritz!"

"At the rate you are treating our staff, Cousin Prudence, we will be left cooking our own breakfasts soon as they will all walk out!" said Richard through gritted teeth.

"I daresay I could do a better job than they do – if I could be bothered!" said Prudence.

Richard went to say something else but closed his mouth on seeing his mother give him a warning look.

Richard and his wife, Ophelia, had always lived at Daphne's house with their children and were at the end of their tether having Pierce and Prudence as house guests. They had visited Daphne in her rooms yesterday and warned her in no uncertain terms that the situation could not continue. They refused to stay under the same roof as Prudence and Pierce for another week and if Daphne did not ask them to leave, they would take their four children and go. It wasn't as if the Hattons' huge house in Dublin was not big enough. It was just that Prudence was insufferable and Pierce at this point not much better.

As Daphne looked at her niece and nephew, she was overcome by sadness at how this branch of their family had been reduced to this.

When Daphne had been growing up the Armstrongs were one of the richest and most powerful families in the United Kingdom. Their estate in County Mayo was thousands of acres and the main house, Armstrong House, a beacon of glamour and grandeur. Daphne wistfully remembered the balls that were held there. When her sister Gwyneth held her debutante ball, the most eligible bachelors in the country had attended in the hope of catching her eye. Daphne herself had her wedding reception in the ballroom when she married her dear departed husband Gilbert. Gilbert had been the heir to a great Dublin brewing dynasty. Nearly all of Daphne's siblings had made wonderful matches. The heir to the Armstrong House and the estate was Daphne's eldest brother Charles who also inherited the title, Lord Armstrong. And that's when things started to go wrong. Charles had always been an unpredictable, spoilt and extraordinarily selfish man, under whose stewardship the estate was reduced to a couple of hundred acres as he squandered the family fortune. Prone to making enemies, Charles's health deteriorated rapidly after he was shot by a disgruntled tenant. Pierce had inherited his father's title, what was left of the estate and Armstrong House. It was a poisoned chalice by then.

Daphne had often marvelled at how unalike the siblings were. Both in their mid-thirties, it was hard to believe Prudence was only Pierce's senior by barely a couple of years. She looked considerably older than Pierce who had always been noted for his tall dark looks and handsome appearance. Whereas Prudence almost prided herself on her dowdy image. She had never married and had been more at home tending to the farm at Armstrong House than being a debutante.

"I cannot believe it! She's in the newspaper!" Prudence suddenly blurted out.

She had an annoying habit of reading the morning newspaper over breakfast and commenting loudly on everything she read. Daphne thought the one consolation was that this meant they didn't have to engage in conversation with her.

"Who?" asked Pierce.

"Your wife!" exclaimed Prudence, holding up the newspaper to show him the article.

"Clara?" said Daphne.

"Well, he only has one wife that I know of, Aunt Daphne! Of course Clara!"

"What does it say about her?" asked Pierce, reaching over for the newspaper which Prudence wouldn't release.

"It's an interview with one Thomas Geraghty who seemingly was one of the rebels during the 1916 Rising and has now just been made a minister in the new Irish government! Quite a professional leap, don't you think!"

"But what has he got to do with Clara?" asked Daphne.

"Quite a lot, according to this article. Geraghty credits Clara for saving his life! He says that when he was on the run during the War of Independence, Lady Clara Armstrong gave him shelter *at* Armstong House and nursed him back to health! Oh, the shame! As if our beloved family home has not suffered enough indignity, it will now be known for harbouring a terrorist!"

"We know all this already, Prudence," said Pierce coldly.

"Well, *we* might have known but now everyone else does too, thanks to *this*!" said Prudence, shaking the newspaper in the air.

"Is that really such a bad thing?" asked Daphne. "We are living in a different country now, Prudence. Our kind – our class – have no option but to adapt. Pierce's involvement with the British government and military during the War of Independence made him a figure of hate, which resulted in Armstrong House being targeted by the rebels and set on fire. So if Clara –"

"It wasn't just because of me the house was attacked, Daphne!" Pierce interrupted. "They were targeting 'Big Houses' all around the country. In fact, they still are even after getting their bloody independence, during this cursed Civil War! They wanted the gentry out!"

"Of course I know that, Pierce. I'm trying to say that if Clara has now been praised for helping a 1916 rebel, that can only help rehabilitate you and your family with the Irish people. Like it or not, we all must adapt – or leave for good, like so many of our friends have done, to live in England."

"If you'll excuse me – I've lost my appetite," said Pierce as he stood up from the table. He left the room.

"It's easy for you to advise us to adapt, Aunt Daphne, when you and your family are millionaires. For the rest of us who have had our houses burned down and been left with nothing, we have no choice but rely on the charity of our relatives or move to England and get a job sweeping the streets! If you'll excuse me, I've lost my appetite too!"

Daphne, Richard and Ophelia watched as Prudence left the room.

Richard threw his napkin down on the table.

"Mother! I can't take any more of this!" he snarled.

"Really we can't!" said Ophelia. "The children are even too terrified to come out of the nursery in case they bump into Prudence at this point"

"Staying here was always supposed to be short term after they had to flee Armstrong House," said Richard. "It was supposed to be only until they got back on their feet. They have always been welcome to attend a party or spend Christmas with us – but nearly a year living under the same roof has turned into hell!"

"I know, darlings, and I do appreciate you being so patient up until now. I just feel so sorry for them. They had such a difficult upbringing, and I am their only relative still here in Ireland and so I feel a responsibility to them."

"Not that we've even got any thanks!" said Ophelia.

"I shall speak to them today, I promise," sighed Daphne.

Daphne dreaded the confrontation. Pierce and Prudence were really on the wrong side of Irish history. Although the power of their Anglo-Irish upper class had been waning, they were still seen as symbols of British power and oppression when the demand for independence erupted with the Easter Rising in 1916. Considering themselves British, Pierce and his contempories had enlisted to fight during the Great War – as indeed did many thousands of ordinary Irishmen. By the time they had returned home the political landscape had transformed with the demand to be free of British rule leading to the War of Independence in 1919. The guerilla war finally came to an end with a Treaty between the British Government and the new Irish Government, led by Éamon de Valera and Michael Collins. The country became the Irish Free State, with its own parliament but still part of the British Empire. A sizable amount of the population objected to the Treaty, particularly on the grounds that it allowed six counties in the north to choose to remain part of the United Kingdom and be named Northern Ireland. They demanded a United Ireland, and the formation of a Republic, This led to a bloody civil war between the so-called Republicans and the newly formed Free State Army, which broke out in June 1922 and was still tearing the country apart.

Old aristocratic families like the Armstrongs were deeply unpopular. Many of their houses had been attacked and set on fire, as was Armstrong House.

Daphne steadied her nerves with a stiff gin as she waited for Pierce and Prudence to come to her rooms. She stood at the window, looking out at the extensive grounds that surrounded their house in Rathgar.

She really did have great sympathy for Prudence and Pierce. Prudence had never been married and her life had been running the farm at Armstrong House. When Pierce had come of age he had been sent to London to do the season with the hope that his title and looks would snare an heiress who could revive the family fortunes. He had met and married Clara Charter, a famous and very popular beauty. But although Clara was a member of the wealthy Charter Confectioner family, it transpired she had no money of her own. When she went to live at Armstrong House, apparently she found it extremely difficult to fit in with the county set. The marriage was reputed to have been a very unhappy one and, when Pierce went to fight in the Great War, it fell apart completely. Daphne imagined Pierce would not have been an easy man to be married to under the best of circumstances. After the Great War Pierce had taken an active role on the British side during the War of Independence. At the end of the fighting, when the British military were evacuating, they advised families like the Armstrongs to leave for their own safety, for fear of reprisals. That was when Pierce and Prudence had come to stay with their aunt in Dublin. Strangely, Clara had not accompanied them. Pierce never spoke of what happened in the marriage but from Daphne's enquiries she later heard that

Clara had returned to England a broken woman after her experiences at Armstrong House.

"*Knock! Knock!*" said Prudence as she rapped on the door, then came straight into Daphne's parlour.

She was followed by Pierce who closed the door behind him.

"You wished to see us, Daphne?" said Pierce.

"Yes, please take a seat. Would you like a drink?"

"I fear from this summons I may need one! Gin, please!" requested Prudence as she sat down on one of the armchairs.

"And for me," said Pierce.

Daphne poured and handed the drinks to them.

"Thank you for coming to see me," said Daphne, taking her seat again.

Pierce went to stand by the window and looked out at the view.

"So? What is this about?" asked Prudence truculently.

"*Em* ... well, we have all so much enjoyed you stay here but ... but I think the time has come for ... for ... for ..." Daphne struggled to finish the sentence.

"For us to leave? Aunty dear, is that what you're trying to say?" said Prudence.

"Well, yes. I'm sure you want to get on with your lives at this point. You must be terribly bored here."

"Believe me, if there was anywhere else we could go – we would have gone!" said Prudence.

"But don't you want to return to the Armstrong Estate?" asked Daphne.

"Armstrong House is not habitable any more! The rebels set it on fire, in case you forgot!" said Prudence.

"Of course I know that. But you still have the dowager house, Hunter's Farm, on the estate, have you not? It was a very attractive house from what I recall."

"As you well know, Aunty Daphne, the word estate could hardly be applied to the couple of hundred acres left since the turn of the century," said Prudence.

"I say the word *estate* out of habit as that was what it was called when I grew up there. So, what about returning to live at Hunter's Farm? I mean, the War of Independence is long over by now. I'm sure it's safe for you to go back."

"With this Civil War going on they are still burning down the Big Houses, determined to get rid of our class," said Pierce. "And with my previous role in the military, I'm sure I would be still a target. Plus, Hunter's Farm is very exposed and could not offer any protection."

"And the land will have gone to rack and ruin by now," said Prudence. "I've heard all the livestock have been stolen by the locals and the place is overrun. It would need major investment to get back up and running."

"Well – what about the miliary, Pierce?" suggested Daphne. "You were a war hero! And you really came into your own during your time in the army. Have you not contemplated going to England and rejoining your regiment?"

"I may have reached the rank of colonel during the war, but I was never a career officer. My position was only ever temporary and the army decommissioned hundreds of thousands of us as soon as the war was over, and we were of no further use to them. It would be impossible for me to rejoin. I was never really one of them anyway – a proper officer, in their opinion. I only gained the rank for the war."

Daphne sighed loudly. "Look, I understand how it might seem the world has left you behind, but you have to keep your chins up!"

"As I said this morning, easy for you to say that with your millions!" said Prudence.

"I'm sure things will come good for you again. Pierce, you have everything going for you. You just need to find a role in life for yourself again."

Pierce turned to look at his aunt. "What exactly have I got going for me, Daphne?" he asked.

"Well, a title for starters. You are Lord Armstrong. You are the proud holder of a title that goes back generations."

"A title does not matter a damn anymore! It doesn't even assure you of a decent table in a restaurant since the war! The only thing that really ever meant anything to me was Armstrong House. Without it I am nothing! When those bastards torched it – they torched my future!"

Daphne said nothing for a while as she drank her gin and Prudence sat glaring at her.

"What I suggest is that – for now – you both move into the gardener's cottage here," said Daphne.

"*What! The gardener's cottage!*" cried Prudence in disgust.

"Yes, it's been vacant for some time, and I think it would make the loveliest home for both of you until you sort yourselves out."

"*The gardener's cottage!*" repeated Prudence.

"It's very cozy –" began Daphne.

"It's tiny! It's got barely two bedrooms and a sitting room you wouldn't swing the proverbial cat in!" said Prudence. "And it's packed full of all the things we managed to bring with us from Armstrong House!"

"Well, exactly – you'll be amongst your own possessions there. I'm sorry but it's the best I can do for you. We just don't have the space for you here in the main house anymore."

Prudence gestured to the grandness of Daphne's suite of rooms. "Clearly!" she said sarcastically.

Chapter 5

Clara prepared herself for some unpleasantness as she was shown into the office of Stanley Bancroft, who was seated behind his desk, looking like the perfect specimen of a solicitor. A man in his sixties, wearing a pinstriped suit with small round spectacles perched on his Roman nose, his small blue eyes were carefully studying her as he stood to greet her.

"Lady Armstrong, it is so nice to see you again," he said as she shook his hand.

Clara could only remember meeting him once before at a family christening many years before.

"Thank you for meeting me, Mr. Bancroft, at such short notice."

He retook his seat and she sat down on the other side of the desk.

"I always am available to a member of the Charter family, Lady Armstrong. As I have been your family solicitor for thirty years, I like to see our relationship as more friendship than professional at this point," he said with a small chuckle.

"Of course – my father speaks very highly of you."

Bancroft's reputation was that of a shrewd operator who had managed to secure some of the most respected families in London as his clients. Clara had heard that he was very choosy about whom he represented, and it was almost considered an honour to be his client.

"So," said Bancroft, putting his hands together and leaning towards her across his desk, "what can I do for you?"

"I have come to speak to you today about the delicate matter of a divorce."

On hearing the word *divorce* Bancroft immediately sat back and folded his arms defensively across his chest.

"And whose divorce do you wish to speak about, may I ask?"

"My own, Mr. Bancroft. I wish to be divorced from my husband."

"I see. Do your parents know that we are meeting today?"

"No, I did not inform them."

"Then I think it would be wise that we should postpone this meeting until they can be present," said Bancroft.

Clara was completely taken aback. "I don't understand what that would accomplish," she said. "It is I who am seeking the divorce, not my parents."

"Nevertheless, I would not like to be part of anything that might displease your family," said Bancroft.

Clara looked at Bancroft in amazement. He was treating her as if she were a child.

"Mr. Bancroft, I do not need my parents' permission or involvement to ask for a divorce! As the wife of a householder and over 30 years of age, I am even allowed to vote since 1918!"

Bancroft's expression became cold as he leaned forward and picked up his fountain pen.

"Very well. What are the grounds for you wishing to proceed to divorce your husband?"

"Well – that is why I have asked to meet you today. To find out what is the correct procedure and on what grounds am I entitled to a divorce."

"Adultery has to be one of the conditions for a divorce. As the law stands it is more complicated for a woman to divorce her husband than vice versa. A husband just needs to prove his wife was unfaithful to be granted a divorce, whereas a woman needs to prove not just adultery but also cruelty, desertion or another number of unpleasant activities that I would prefer not to say out loud in polite company."

"Please feel free to speak freely. I have become accustomed to company that is not very polite throughout the years," said Clara.

"Who is the young – or otherwise – woman that your husband has committed adultery with? She will need to be named and maybe even summoned in the proceedings."

"Well, there is no woman, young or otherwise, that I aware of," said Clara.

Bancroft sat back in his chair again, looking shocked. "In that case, what are you accusing your husband of?"

"Nothing, Mr. Bancroft."

"Excuse me?"

"Lord Armstrong, to the best of my knowledge, has not been unfaithful to me. I am not aware of any liaison he has had. It is I, Mr. Bancroft – I am the guilty party. It is I who have sinned. I who committed adultery."

"Lady Armstrong – are you trying to shock me?"

"No, I am not. I am just stating the facts. I had an affair while Lord Armstrong was away fighting the war."

"Well, if this be the unfortunate case, it is Lord Armstrong who must make an appointment to see me in order to sue you for divorce – not the other way round."

"Can I be frank?" Clara asked.

"I have a notion that you cannot be anything but!"

"Our marriage was a mistake. Even worse than that – it has been an unmitigated disaster. Pierce and I should never have been married. I married him against all advice."

"Lady Armstrong, that sounds like half the marriages in London. I am aware that society has become somewhat liberated since the end of the war. I even saw a young woman smoking the other morning while she waited for a bus! But make no mistake, divorce is still taboo. To make an appointment with me and to discuss a husband in the same way you might discuss how you might discard last season's fashion is reckless, dangerous and unbecoming!"

Clara felt tears sting her eyes as she fought to keep her composure. All the frustration, upset and anger built up over the past few years now threatened to explode in front of this pompous ass.

"I have not discarded Pierce. Rather he has discarded me!"

"So, are you saying your husband has deserted you? It would still be a difficult achievement to get a court to grant a divorce without your husband's accompanying adultery."

Clara suddenly stood up.

"*I did not say Pierce deserted me. I said he discarded me!*" Clara said at the top of her voice.

Bancroft looked at Clara in astonishment.

"I am baffled by your distinction, and I imagine the courts will be too!" said Bancroft.

Clara walked to the tall Georgian window in the office and stared out.

"After the Great War, after Pierce returned home he had a senior position in the military in Ireland during the War of Independence. As that war ended he was advised to leave our home, Armstrong House, as he would be a target once the British army retreated. He expected me to go with him but I refused to go and so he left and I stayed. It is as simple as that. I stayed at Armstrong House on my own and faced the rebels by myself when they arrived to set fire to the house."

"I read about the burning of Armstrong House in the papers along with the other burnings of the Big Houses in Ireland. It must have been a very frightening experience for you," said Bancroft.

"You have no idea ... I haven't seen my husband since," said Clara.

"Where is Lord Armstrong now?"

"I do not know. But I believe he intended to go to Dublin when he left Armstrong House."

"As you say, that is not actually desertion if he expected you to go with him," said Bancroft.

Clara turned to face the solicitor.

"The truth is, though I loved him very much, it became clear over the years that he never had any feelings towards me. I believe he now even despises me. To give us both the opportunity to leave this hell, I would like to offer to my husband the opportunity to divorce me on the grounds of my adultery. I believe this is the simplest and easiest way to end our marriage. As you say, a husband can divorce his wife simply on the grounds of adultery without needing to furnish further reason. Then this is the easiest route for a divorce."

"Are you quite mad? You are correct on the letter of the law, but have you realised the implications of what you are suggesting? You will be destroyed. Your name and that of your family will be ruined. There will be no going back. Your husband is a war hero, and you will be painted as the scarlet woman who was unfaithful to him while he risked life for King and Country!"

"I am fully aware of the implications."

"Where is the other party now? The man who will be named as committing adultery with you?"

"I have no idea where he is. But I believe he is in America."

"I will be honest with you, Lady Armstrong. I had heard rumours of your affair previously but chose not to believe them." He lifted his fountain pen again. "What are your instructions?"

"Pierce's solicitors are a small firm called Conways in Castlewest, County Mayo. Wherever Pierce is, I'm sure they will know. Please write to Conways and tell them I wish for Pierce to divorce me on the grounds of my adultery."

"Are you sure there is no hope for you and Lord Armstrong? No possible way for you to save your marriage and this horrendous fate that awaits you?"

"There is no going back. Thank you, Mr. Bancroft, for your time and I would be grateful if you could get the letter in the post to Conways today."

Bancroft watched as she pulled her fur coat tightly around her and then quickly exited the office.

Bancroft stood up from the desk and went to the window. He watched Clara emerge on the street below. She put her hand up to hail a taxi, got in and was driven away.

This silly young woman had left a bomb in his office that afternoon that if detonated could have far-reaching consequences.

He quickly walked out of his office.

"Make an appointment for me to meet with the Duchess of Battington urgently," he instructed his secretary.

"Shall I request her to come here?"

"Of course not! The Duchess does not visit offices! I will call on her at her London home at her earliest convenience."

Even though the Duchess of Battinton was now in her sixties, Stanley Bancroft still thought that she was the most exquisite creature he had ever seen. Her blonde hair was perfectly coiffed, her beauty still evident and her regal presence as ever impressive. He remembered she had been named Debutante of the Year when she had been presented at court. Back then her family, the Armstrongs, had been a force to be reckoned with and the Duke of Battinton had to fight off many suitors to gain her hand. How the mighty had fallen! Stanley thought of the Armstrong family's present circumstances in Ireland.

As he was shown into the drawing room by a butler at her home in Regent's Park, Gwyneth stood up and greeted him warmly.

"Stanley – so lovely to see you again!"

"And you, Your Grace," said Stanley as he bowed towards her and shook her hand.

Stanley had represented the Duke's family for forty years and they were without doubt his most important and illustrious client. Quite simply, they took precedence over anyone else.

She took her seat on an elaborate couch and gestured to an armchair opposite her.

Stanley sat down.

"Tea?" she asked.

"Thank you, yes, Your Grace."

The butler served the tea and placed milk, sugar and lemon on a side table next to Stanley who noted he obviously knew exactly how the Duchess took her tea.

"Thank you, Carter," said Gwyneth to the butler and he bowed and left them.

"Poor Carter! He has suffered the most terrible shellshock since the war. One always fears he is going to have one of his fits while pouring the tea – I can't bear to think of it if he ever did!"

"Quite!" said Stanley, thinking how kind and brave it was of the Duchess to tolerate such a situation. "*Em*, may I offer my sincere congratulations on your son's recent victory in the by-election?"

"Thank you, dear Stanley. Yes, we are very pleased that he won! He nearly got trounced by the Labour candidate, but we managed to gather just enough votes to get first past the post. Alas, they say it will only be a matter of time before there is a Labour government!"

"We live in peculiar times."

"Indeed we do! Now, Stanley, to what do I owe the pleasure of your visit?"

"I thought I should inform you that I had a visit this week from your nephew's wife. I found it so disconcerting that I thought it best to bring the matter to your attention."

"Which nephew?"

"Lord Pierce Armstrong. His wife Clara."

"Oh dear!" sighed Gwyneth. "I only met the girl once many years ago at their wedding. Very beautiful, of course, but one just knew she was going to be trouble. One's instincts are always right on these things – I've heard so many ghastly rumours about her ever since. What did she want?"

"Well, I'll not beat around the bush. Clara wants to divorce Lord Armstrong. And she is offering herself as the sacrificial lamb in order to achieve this purpose. Her own adultery is to be the grounds for the divorce."

"Good Lord! Is the girl quite mad? I've heard rumours that she may very well be. You see, this is the problem when commoners marry into the peerage. They never quite know how to conduct themselves, try as they may!"

"She has asked me to write to Lord Armstrong's solicitor in Ireland to get the ball rolling."

"You make it sound like a game of croquet, dear Stanley! Have you written to him yet?"

"Not yet as I thought it wise to discuss it with you first."

"Very wise indeed, Stanley," said Gwyneth, nodding.

"Considering His Grace's position at the palace and your son's burgeoning political career, a divorce of this nature would cause a tremendous scandal that would have repercussions for you all."

"Quite true. I can't bear to think of the scandal if they do get divorced. I really find it hard to believe that my precious family in Ireland have been reduced to this. Once my brother Charles took over, everything went to pieces. He was quite the scoundrel, for want of a better word. And his son appears to be no better at managing his affairs."

"But there is another factor in this situation that nobody knows other than I, not even Clara Armstrong. But it involves client confidentiality that cannot be broken." Stanley looked intently at Gwyneth.

"In that case, pray continue, dear Stanley. It will go no further, I assure you."

"I also act for the Charters, Clara's family."

"The confectioners?"

"Yes. I recently drew up a will for Louisa Charter, Clara's grandmother. Although Clara has no money of her own, she is the beneficiary of the bulk of Louisa's estate. She will be a very wealthy woman one day."

"Ah, I see." Gwyneth paused for a few moments. "So, as Clara has no notion of this then my nephew does not either."

"Only I and Louisa Charter know the contents of her will," said Stanley.

"That really does change everything. From what I hear Pierce hasn't a penny and, since the rebels burned down Armstrong House, no home to speak of either." She paused again. "Clara might be just the answer to all his problems."

"Indeed. But I hope you understand that I am bound to now follow my client's instructions and write to Lord Armstrong's solicitor to request the divorce," said Stanley.

"Is there any way you could ... put it off?"

"I am afraid not, Your Grace. I have already not been true to my profession by delaying matters until I spoke to you."

"I understand. Leave this with me and I shall see what I can do," said Gwyneth.

"Thank you, Your Grace."

"While you are here, I must tell you that I have been speaking with my husband about that knighthood we spoke about previously. His Grace assures me that it is only a matter of time before you receive it and not before time, in my opinion."

"Thank you most kindly, Your Grace. I do appreciate your encouragement in this matter."

"You will always have my backing, Stanley. Loyalty deserves rewards."

Chapter 6

Daphne wished her bedroom didn't have a direct view of the gardener's cottage. Every time she looked out the window she felt guilty for forcing Pierce and Prudence to move there. As she closed the curtains to block her view, the telephone in her room rang.

She answered. "Yes – hello?"

"It is the Duchess of Battinton on the telephone for you, madam," said the butler.

"Excellent! I'll take her call," said Daphne as she sat down at the desk.

She waited until the butler put down the phone before she spoke.

"Gwyneth? I am so very glad to hear from you. I have been suffering the ghastliest time with our niece and nephew," said Daphne.

"Well, as it happens Pierce is the reason that I am calling you, dear sister. I've had the most disturbing visit from our solicitor who brought tidings of trepidation with him. We need to act quickly to save us all from ruin."

Pierce felt claustrophobic as he stood in the sitting room of the gardener's cottage. It wasn't just the size of the cottage. Or that fact it seemed even smaller because it was packed with items they had managed to take with them when they had fled Armstrong House. It was his circumstances. That he would be living there with his sister with no hope of escape. It was a nightmare fate for him that he could never have envisaged. Prudence came out of the bedroom and began to move boxes. What had depressed him further was that he had received correspondence from his solicitors that morning that Clara was seeking a divorce. Pierce knew their marriage was over but it felt like another slap in the face and being further set adrift from his old life.

"I suppose we had better try to make this place liveable if it is to be our new home. It is an utter disgrace how we'e being treated! All our relatives have abandoned us in our hour of need!" said Prudence.

"That is because we are an embarrassment to them now. All Papa's brothers and sisters have moved up in the world and we have unfortunately moved down."

"As Lord Armstrong you are still head of this family and they should treat you with the respect you deserve!"

Pierce picked up a photo from a box. It was one of him and Prudence as children with their father Charles and mother Arabella. The photo was taken on the steps of Armstrong House in one of those hazy Edwardian summers that now seemed like another world.

"I don't know what Papa would say if could see us now!" said Prudence as she moved more boxes.

"Perhaps Aunty Daphne is right. Maybe we should move back to Hunter's Farm. At least we would be on our own land in our own home," sighed Prudence.

"If I cannot live in Armstrong House, I will not go back there. I grew up there and lived there as Lord of the Manor and I will not have the locals sneer and laugh at me seeing me reduced to living as we are. Everyone has their pride."

"Well, mine is on the floor – where's *yours*?" said Prudence.

"Besides, it really is too dangerous for me to go back there. Perhaps you should go back on your own?" Pierce suggested hopefully.

Prudence ignored him as she continued to sort through the items. She picked up a photo of Clara and Pierce on their wedding day at the Dorchester Hotel in London.

"This – in my opinion – is where everything went wrong! Marrying that girl caused all our trouble! If you had married an heiress, as you were supposed to, then we wouldn't be living like this now!"

Pierce spotted a toy solder that he had as a child. He took it out of the box and began to clean it with a cloth. The solider had been broken, its arm now hanging off.

"I always took my position in life for granted," he said, "I always assumed that I would live in Armstrong House forever and now I have lost everything."

"If you are looking for tea and sympathy you have come to the wrong source!" snapped Prudence.

As Pierce looked at the toy soldier he felt as broken as it was, and he tossed it back into the box.

"Well, you have made it so snug!" declared Daphne as she visited the gardener's cottage. "I always say a fire makes all the difference!"

Pierce and Prudence were seated on either side of the fireplace.

"Yes, we are so elated to be here," said Prudence, her voice dripping sarcasm.

"Now, I've come to talk to you about a matter of great importance," said Daphne.

"Pray tell! Have you found a new position for us as your gardeners, now that we are to live in the gardener's cottage?" asked Prudence.

Daphne ignored the sarcasm as she sat down on the small couch before the fire.

"I have been informed confidentially that Clara is seeking a divorce from you, Pierce. Is this true?" she asked.

"Divorce!" exclaimed Prudence. "Clara wants to get a divorce! For goodness' sake – good riddance to bad rubbish in my opinion! No doubt she has taken up with some new man who –"

"*Prudence – will you be quiet!*" Pierce commanded in a loud stern voice, causing both women to jump. "Who has informed you of this, Daphne? You must tell me."

"I cannot."

He stared at her, his brow knitted.

"Have you heard from Clara, Pierce?" she asked.

"Yes, I have. I received a letter from her solicitor this very morning saying the same."

Prudence sat forward to say something but seeing Pierce's stern expression thought better of it and remained silent.

"I expected that," said Daphne. "Obviously I do not need to tell you that a divorce would look very bad, not just for you but for our whole family."

"And for Clara even more so as she is also suggesting that I be the party to divorce her," said Pierce.

"She seems not to care about her reputation at this point. I have in my possession some other information concerning Clara and I share it with you on the understanding that it is in the strictest confidence."

"You have my word – please continue," said Pierce.

Daphne focused on her niece. "And you, Prudence?"

"I promise."

"Very well. I understand that Clara is the main beneficiary in her grandmother's will. Which means Clara is to come into a great fortune on her grandmother's passing."

"What!" Prudence exclaimed. "I always *knew* there must be a great deal of money somewhere in that family, considering the number of chocolates and toffees they have churned out over the past fifty years! Common business people of course but –" At a warning look from Pierce, she stopped speaking.

Pierce turned to Daphne. "This must be a recent arrangement as I always understood that Clara was never going to inherit anything substantial."

"I believe the will was made recently. From my enquiries I suspect Clara became Louisa's principal heir as her original heirs were killed in the Great War."

"It's an ill wind!" said Prudence.

"I also believe from my enquiries that Louisa is not very well. In fact, she doesn't have that long left to live," said Daphne.

"But what's to be done about that? Clara now wants to divorce me!" said Pierce.

"Only if you allow it, Pierce. Legally, you must be the one to demand a divorce."

"I should refuse? What good would that do?"

"Surely there must be some hope in your marriage yet?" said Daphne.

"Obviously, no. She's determined to divorce me."

"But what about you, Pierce? Do you really want to divorce Clara? Is that what you really want?" asked Daphne.

"I don't think it matters much to anybody what I want anymore," said Pierce as he looked into the fire.

Daphne looked at Prudence who gave her a firm nod.

"Pierce, there's more to the situation," said Daphne. "And I tell you this in the strictest of confidence. Clara herself has no idea that she has been made her grandmother's heir."

Pierce raised his head and stared at her as the import of this sank in.

Daphne stood up. "I'll leave you to think about it. We'll talk again."

"Thank you, Aunty Daphne! It's been a revelation!" said Prudence.

"I felt it my duty to tell you this and hopefully it will make you see sense and fix this marriage while you still can," said Daphne.

Chapter 7

Pierce had fallen into the routine of meeting old friends once a month for drinks in the Shelbourne Hotel. They were mostly from the same circle as himself and had also served as officers in the war. They would meet to lament the passing of their old life since independence was granted in Ireland and to reminisce about the war. With each meeting Pierce could see that like himself the plight of his friends was getting worse as they tried to adapt to the ways of the new country they found themselves living in. Many of them were planning to join the exodus of their class and try and start a new life in London.

It was hard times for them as without suffering an injury in the war they were not entitled to any pension from the British government for the four years they had spent fighting in the trenches. Like Pierce, many had been driven from their homes in the country by either having their houses burned down or attacked, which had only intensified during the ensuing Civil War.

"What will you do in London?" Pierce had asked his friend Kit Jones that evening after he informed them all he was emigrating at the end of the week.

"I have no idea. I'm crashing at an old school chum's house until I get myself sorted. I have nightmares that I am going to end up selling socks in Libertys!" said Kit.

Pierce shuddered at the thought. It was the indignity that his class had to suffer that was the worst to bear. They had gone from being the ruling elite in Ireland, to being the enemy, to now becoming an irrelevance.

"The latest I've heard is that this new government is setting up something called the Land Commission. Their purpose is to seize land that has been abandoned or is untenanted and redistribute it to the peasantry," said Kit.

"So they burn us out of our houses and then, when we can't live there anymore, claim our land has been abandoned and take it from us," sighed Pierce.

"There are as many Irish aristocrats roaming the streets in London now as there are Russian!" said Henry. "Titles don't matter a damn anymore. The only thing that really matters now is money. Money rules the world. If you have that, you have everything."

As the night drew to a close, Pierce waited for the porter in the hotel foyer to fetch his coat. As he waited he picked up a copy of the latest *Tatler* magazine and flicked through it. He stopped abruptly on a page when he saw a photograph of Clara. He immediately recognised the man in the photo with her as Cosmo Wellesley. As the porter arrived with his coat, Pierce tossed the magazine back on the side table and left the hotel.

Pierce walked through the streets of Dublin back to his aunt's house in Rathgar, the photo of Clara with Cosmo Wellesley burning in his mind. He had gone to boarding school in England with Cosmo and they had endured an intense rivalry that had lasted into adulthood. In fact, Pierce remembered telling Clara during one of their heated rows that the only reason he had married her was to take her away from Cosmo to whom she was expected to become engaged. He was astonished that Clara had seemingly fitted back into her old life and set so easy.

It was after midnight when Pierce walked through the door of the gardener's cottage. He was surprised to find Prudence still up and sitting by the fire.

"Did you have a good night?" she asked.

"As good as can be expected when everyone is so gloomy. Where did it all go wrong?" Pierce sighed as he looked around the small sitting room.

"There is no point dwelling on where things went wrong. We need to concentrate on how to get things right," said Prudence.

"And how can we possibly do that?" asked Pierce in despair, throwing himself into the armchair by the fire.

"Well, it's obvious, isn't it? Clara!"

"How, in God's name?"

"Did you listen to a word Aunty Daphne was saying? Your wife is going to inherit a fortune!"

"My soon to be ex-wife!"

"Only if you allow it. She has no grounds to divorce you. She's admitted that herself when she's asked you to divorce her on the grounds of her adultery." She reached for the letter Pierce had received from his solicitors concerning the divorce and waved it in the air.

"That was a private letter – you had no right to read it!" he said angrily.

"I had every right – as you had left it in plain sight in your bedroom! Now, Pierce, I've given it a lot of thought, and this is your golden opportunity to get your life back. Clara will have enough money to give you financial security. You'll even be able to rebuild Armstrong House."

"You are delusional! Even if I wanted her, she would *never* come back to our marriage. She hates me!"

"Hate is a strong word, and they say there is a fine line between love and hate. I saw Clara at Armstrong House during your marriage. She was utterly and absolutely in love with you! If you had given her the tiniest bit of love back, or even affection, she would never have left you or had that affair with Johnny Seymour."

"That was then – too much has happened since. This is bringing up a lot of bad memories. I don't wish to talk about it anymore."

"Well, we *have* to talk about it! I've come up with a plan for how you can win Clara back."

"Are you actually gone stark raving mad!"

"Not in the least. Even Aunty Daphne was clearly saying you need to get back with Clara."

"That was more for the family to avoid the scandal of a divorce and the hope it might lead us to leave her gardener's cottage!"

"Be that as it may be, don't you see? With Clara, we can leave here and go home. You can safely go home to Armstrong House."

"What do you mean? Safely? Why safely?"

"That minister in the government, Thomas Geraghty, has publicly stated that Clara saved his life! That she hid him when he was on the run from the British army during the war. It's in the papers! She is your ticket to going home as the locals will see she was on the Irish side and accept you back there. With Clara living back at Armstrong House, nobody is going to touch you. She's practically a hero for the Irish cause at this point! Do not forget how popular she was with the locals. I was always complaining about how she was fraternising with the peasantry but that is now to our advantage. You can use her money to rebuild the house and use her popularity to save your hide!"

Pierce jumped to his feet and paced the floor.

"But – but Clara would never come back to me. Never a million years!"

"She will if you follow my plan."

"Which is?"

Prudence took a deep breath.

"That you kill yourself," she said.

"*What*?"

She stood up quickly and walked to him.

"What I mean is you *pretend* to try to kill yourself. First you write a suicide note telling her how much you love her and that you simply can't live without her and for her not to blame herself for your death."

He glared at her, outraged. "You really are out of your mind!"

"No, you are. You are, if you refuse to see reason here. You write the suicide note. Then you swallow a handful of pills that I will get for you.

After you have taken them, I will call for help. You'll be rushed to a hospital where your stomach will be pumped –"

"Madness, I tell you!"

"Then, while you are still recuperating I shall deliver the suicide note to Clara in person and make her feel so guilty that you were driven to try to kill yourself when she requested a divorce. She will be on the first boat back to Dublin!"

"Clara won't even meet you!"

"Oh, she will – don't you worry about that!"

Pierce took out his cigarette holder and, with his hands shaking, extracted and lit one.

"Do you – do you actually believe she would come back?" he asked.

"I'm convinced of it! Don't forget I lived in Armstrong House with her while you were away at the front. I got to know her pretty well. I found her infuriatingly naïve and I have no doubt she still is."

"You're wrong, Prudence. You underestimate Clara. Many do, including me, and it is at one's peril do so," said Pierce.

Prudence stood over Pierce as he wrote the suicide letter, prompting him as to what to put in it. She had done her research in the British Medical Journal about what tablets would best suit her purpose and the amount that would cause fatality. She then got them from a chemist she knew who would give any prescription requested for the price of a bottle of gin.

Pierce stared at the saucer of tablets she had placed on the table in front of him.

"How many do I take?" he asked.

"All of them," said Prudence.

"Would a military man such as myself not choose to kill himself by a gunshot than an overdose?"

Prudence rolled her eyes. "Undoubtedly he would – so do you want to shoot yourself in the head instead? I thought not. Idiot."

She went into the small kitchen, returned with a large glass of water and placed it in front of him.

"Best not to think too much about it – just get it over with," she said.

"Easy for you to say. You're not the one risking ending up dead!"

"It won't come to that. As I told you, I researched it and that amount of pills won't kill you," said Prudence. "You are letting fear rule your mind. As soon as you pass out, I shall run to the main house and raise the alarm. They'll call an ambulance and have you pumped out and back in the land of the living before you know it."

Pierce began to play with the tablets in the saucer.

"For goodness' sake, Pierce! Surely a few pills can't scare you after facing constant death by German artillery fire for four years!"

Pierce started swallowing the pills one by one.

Chapter 8

Clara was in the drawing room with her parents when Burton came in.

"A telegram has just arrived for you, Lady Armstrong," said Burton, handing it to her.

"Thank you, Burton," said Clara.

"Who is it from?" asked Milly after Burton left the room.

Clara stared down at the telegram in astonishment as she read it: **Clara - will be in London this week. Need to speak to you urgently. Will call to your parents' house on Thursday at 3pm. Prudence.**

"It's from ... it's from Prudence," she said.

"Prudence!" exclaimed Milly, jumping up from her seat and taking the telegram from her daughter.

"What the hell does she want?" asked Terence.

"It must be to discuss the divorce," said Clara. "Pierce must have received the correspondence from the solicitor."

"But why does Prudence want to talk to you? Why is Pierce not making contact?" asked Milly.

"One really never knows with Pierce," sighed Clara.

"Sending his sister to do his dirty work!" said Terence.

"His crazy sister!" added Milly.

"Well, you can just telegram her back and tell her to get lost!" said Terence.

"I have no idea where she is to send her a telegram. Besides, that will not stop Prudence as she will just turn up here anyway," said Clara.

"In that case, we'll just not open the door to her!" said Terence.

"You don't know her. She will wait outside and create a racket until I do see her."

"Well, I'll call the police on her!" threatened Terence.

"I doubt that would intimidate her either," said Clara.

"Look, let us keep calm heads," said Milly. "She said she needs to speak to Clara urgently and so it might be wise to hear what she has to say. If Prudence is to be the channel that you communicate the divorce proceedings through, then it might make it more amicable than dealing with Pierce directly or through solicitors."

"Nothing is ever amicable that involves Prudence," said Clara.

Clara inhaled on a cigarette as she sat on a couch in the drawing room. She looked at the clock on the wall. It was nearly three o'clock. Prudence would be arriving any minute. Clara was very nervous about meeting her sister-in-law again, but she was determined not to show it. When she had moved first to Armstrong House, she had tried her very best to be friends with Prudence. Instead, Prudence responded with spite, hate and vengeance. Clara often wondered why Prudence seemed to hate her so much, as she had gone out of her way to please her. In the end she had to concede that Prudence, like Pierce, was just very damaged from her upbringing and that had made her angry with the world. But Clara was no longer the naïve girl who had gone to live in Armstrong House a decade ago. And she was determined that she would show Prudence the strength and grit she had gathered over the years and not be cowed by her. She would not be Prudence's victim anymore.

There was a knock on the drawing-room door and Clara hastily put out her cigarette in the glass ashtray beside her.

"Lady Prudence Armstrong!" announced Burton, stepping aside to allow Prudence to enter.

Clara tensed as Prudence strode in.

"Clara!"

Clara stood and offered her hand.

"Such formality!" said Prudence, reaching forward and kissing Clara on the cheek. Clara was taken aback. In all the years she had known her, they had never even brushed against each other, let alone kiss on the cheek.

"Shall I serve tea, my lady?" asked Burton.

"Yes, please, Burton – thank you," said Clara.

"No sugar for me – I'm sweet enough! Just lemon!" ordered Prudence.

Clara gestured to the couch opposite her, and they both sat down.

"You look remarkably well, Clara!"

"Thank you ... you look ... the same as ever."

"Yes, well, I was never one for the lipstick, my dear – I'll leave that to you. I think it's such a pity the young women of today paint their faces to such an extent. It always leads me to believe they are hiding something."

"Most of us probably are," said Clara. "You should try it sometime."

"I saw your photo in *Tatler* recently," said Prudence, ignoring Clara's snide remark.

"I never had you down as a *Tatler* reader," said Clara.

"Of course I'm not. I was using the magazine to fan a fire and then I suddenly saw your photo just as it caught fire and went up in flames."

Clara tensed at the mention of fire and going up in flames. A blatant reminder of her being at Armstrong House when it was set on fire.

"I thought when you left Armstrong House you would want to disappear into obscurity after all the excitement you had living there. But the very opposite seems true – you've become quite the celebrity! You were also mentioned in an article in the *Irish Independent* recently. That unfortunate incident when you harboured a terrorist in our beloved home."

Clara wished she could disappear into obscurity. Since her photo was taken with Cosmo for *Tatler* she'd been thinking it was a mistake to ever have left Kent.

Burtin entered with the tea.

He left the tray on the table between them.

"Shall I be Mother?" asked Prudence as Burton left the room.

"Please do. I would like to make you feel as comfortable in my family home as you made me feel in yours," said Clara cuttingly.

Prudence began to pour the tea.

"None for me, thank you," said Clara.

"As you wish," said Prudence as she poured herself a cup and then put the pot back down.

Clara took a cigarette from her cigarette case and lit it.

"So, Prudence, what has brought you to London? I take it you haven't decided to finally become a debutante and do the season at this late point in your life?"

"No, indeed! As you know I was never a debutante. Never presented at court. Unlike you, who I believe was presented so many times at court in your endless search for a suitable husband they were thinking of putting a revolving door in Buckingham Palace especially for you!"

Clara continued to smile as she dragged on her cigarette. "Well, I was a popular girl," she said.

"Too popular from what I heard."

"Something nobody could ever accuse you of being, Prudence."

"But I never strove to be popular. I've always thought people who seek popularity are doormats. Always pleasing others rather than themselves."

"Nobody could ever accuse you of that either!"

Clara sat forward and stubbed out the cigarette in the ashtray.

"So, let's get on with it, Prudence. Why did you want to see me?"

"Well, I thought that would be obvious even for you. I've come about Pierce."

"I imagine then he received the letter from my solicitor requesting a divorce?"

"Indeed he did," said Prudence.

"I imagine also that he was quite delighted to hear he would finally be getting rid of me. I'm sure you are too. So, for once, I believe we are all in agreement and know what is the best for both Pierce and me. We've brought such misery to each other."

"Pierce is in hospital, Clara."

"Oh! In hospital? Why?"

"He tried to kill himself."

"*What*?"

"He took an overdose. I found him just in the nick of time. Another five minutes and he would have been a goner."

"But why? Why would Pierce do such a terrible thing?"

"Are you really that stupid, Clara? He tried to kill himself over you!"

"*Me*?"

"After he received the letter about the divorce, he fell to pieces. I've never seen him like that before. It's heart-wrenching to see a grown man cry."

"Pierce! Crying? I do not believe it. He's incapable of displaying any emotions let alone crying!"

"Well, I think his suicide attempt demonstrates he feels much more emotion for you than you ever cared to admit."

"You mean than *he* ever cared to admit! And certainly never showed! I never in a million years thought he would try and take his own life."

"I don't want you to blame yourself, Clara, for all the pain you have caused Pierce through the years that led him to the point that he wanted to end his life."

"The pain that *I* caused *him*?" Clara exclaimed incredulously

"Well, of course! He never recovered from you having your affair!"

"But – but – the affair was only born out of the fact that he didn't love me and never did, and he made it clear we had a loveless marriage!"

"Of course he loved you! He loved you more than anything! He would never have married you if he didn't love you! We sent him to London to marry an heiress so we could maintain the upkeep of Armstrong House. But he chose to marry you who hadn't a penny!"

"But he told me later he only married me to make others envious!"

"If he wanted to make others envious then he could have married a much better proposition than you! He could have married a woman with money which could have then provided new plumbing at Armstrong House which would then indeed have made Pierce the envy of the country!"

"Only you, Prudence, could put the value of an enviable marriage as one that provided a lavatory that flushed well!"

"I know Pierce may have seemed removed and cold to you, but you know we are just beginning to understand the horrors that those poor young men suffered at the front. The war left deep psychological scars which affected Pierce badly and that coupled with you carrying on with the local idiot behind his back – well, is it any wonder he couldn't show you love and affection?"

"You are rewriting history, Prudence! That was not how it was!"

"Really? Correct me if anything I have said is not correct."

"Prudence – Pierce blackmailed me into staying with him at Armstrong House when he came back from the war and when I tried to leave him then!"

"And you say he never loved you? Would he have done that if he did not totally and utterly love you?"

"He – he just wanted me then as a trophy to show off to his new powerful friends and to avoid the shame of me leaving him. Pierce never cared about me! He was cold and aloof from the day of our marriage! He even disappeared on our honeymoon, and I had to call the police to find him!"

"Clara – Pierce's problem in life is that he could never express himself. It's come from our childhood and the problems we endured with our parents growing up. He never abandoned you. Clara – it was you who chose to stay at Armstrong House in the end while the rest of us had to evacuate. You who then chose to leave for England. I think it's just very sad that it has come to this ... Pierce told me he didn't want to live if he cannot be with you."

Clara stood up abruptly, walked quickly to the French windows and stared out at the back garden.

"He wants to see you," said Prudence.

"See me!" said Clara, swinging around to face her.

"Pierce said he wants to see you. He's at the moment in a convalescent home in Dublin for veterans of the war while he recovers from the suicide attempt."

"How – how did he try to end his life?"

"He took a quantity – a large quantity of tablets. They had to pump out his stomach. He was –"

"Please stop! I don't want to hear any more!" begged Clara.

"That was always your problem in life, Clara. You always wanted everything to be pretty – could never face the brutality. He left a suicide note. It's addressed to you. I haven't opened it but kept it when he was rushed to hospital." Prudence reached into her handbag, took out an envelope and held it out.

"Since he survived I think it might be an intrusion to read it," said Clara.

"Don't be stupid! Of course you must read it! These were to be Pierce's last words and he chose to write them to you! You have a responsibility to read it!"

Clara rose and took the envelope. She stared down at it.

"How strange that all through the war I would have done anything for one letter from Pierce to show he cared. A letter that never came. And now I would do anything not to have received this one from him."

"Read it, Clara, and take note," said Prudence as she stood up. "I'm returning to Dublin on Saturday. You can reach me at the Duchess of Battington's house in Regent's Park. Gosh, it's so long since I'd seen my aunt I'd forgotten how grand she is. I really do feel like a fish out of water there and can't wait to get back to Ireland – Civil War and all!"

Clara snapped out of the trance she was in.

"How are things in Ireland? Are things any way safe there?" she asked.

"Well, we are no longer the number one enemy so it's much safer. Once they got independence they stopped targeting us and started killing each other!"

Prudence walked to the door.

"Burton will see you out," said Clara, pressing the bell on the fireplace.

"I do hope I will hear from you before I leave London, Clara. If I don't I will wonder how you will ever be able to live with yourself if Pierce tries to kill himself again."

Burton arrived into the room and Prudence followed him out.

That night, Clara sat alone by the fire. Her parents had gone out to the theatre.

They had been as shocked as she was by Pierce's suicide attempt.

"He just doesn't seem the type," said her mother.

Clara agreed. Pierce always seemed too removed from the world, so in control of himself and his emotions, that it was very hard to believe he would have allowed things get to him so badly.

She was staring at his letter which she held in trembling hands. She still hadn't read it. She was half tempted to just throw it in the fire. It scared her. It was like a message from the grave. She was sure it would be full of hate, listing her wrongdoings and blaming her for his death. She carefully opened the envelope and took out the letter.

My darling wife Clara,

If you are reading this letter then I expect that I am no longer of this world. I am writing to you because I wanted you to know that the only true happiness I ever had was with you.

I had such a sad, lonely existence before I met you. I'll never forget the first time I met you at that ball in London. I was so totally and utterly taken with you from the moment I saw you. I know it probably didn't look like that. I know I may have appeared a little formal even. The truth is I was shy when I was in your company. I never believed a woman like you would be interested in a man like me and that is why I was so unfriendly. I was protecting myself from a rejection that I expected. But you didn't reject me. You agreed to marry me and when you came to live in Armstrong House as my wife I was the happiest man in the world. But I never believed this fairy tale. I always waited for the day it would come crashing down. I always expected you to wake up one day and be bored with me and our draughty house in the west of Ireland and go back to your glamorous life in London. So, I never let my protective walls down. And then when I went off to war I could not bear being away from you, so I shut down emotionally even further. I am sorry for how I treated you. I know I should have been able to show how much I loved you, but after my upbringing I could not express how I truly felt. I do not blame you for the affair while I was away. I want you to forgive yourself because I have long ago. In fact, I never even blamed you. It is I who drove you to it ...

Clara stopped reading and clasped the letter to her chest as the tears began streaming down her face. She couldn't read any more. Suddenly she was sobbing loudly. All the pain and frustration she had bottled up over the years came flooding out.

Burton came rushing into the room.

"Miss Clara! Whatever is the matter?" he demanded.

"I'm fine, Burton, please leave me alone!" Clara begged.

"But –"

"Please – just go!" Clara managed to say between her sobs.

It was after midnight and Clara lay in her bed, holding Pierce's letter tightly. She had read it so many times by then that she nearly knew every line off by heart. Every word, every line was an explanation of how Pierce had been, how he had treated her over the years. He wasn't excusing himself, only apologizing. If only he had been able to express himself like this during the marriage it would have made everything different.

All she ever wanted was to be shown some sign that he cared. But he never had. She racked her brain trying to think of some time, some moment that would indicate what he had written in the letter was true. And then she remembered the night she told him she was leaving him. They were in the drawing room in Armstrong House, and she had told him about her affair and that she was going to leave him. She remembered he had suddenly started shaking and dropped a glass before he quickly regained control of himself. Maybe he did actually love her all that time. How different their lives would have been if she had only known!

Chapter 9

Clara felt she had no choice but to go and see Pierce. He was still her husband, and he had tried to kill herself ... over her. Despite his urgings not to feel guilty she was crippled with guilt. She felt so confused. Had she been that blind to what he was telling her in the letter? But she had tried so hard and so many times to break through the wall that surrounded him. A wall that she could only see dark shadows escape from. She needed to see him, if for no other reason than to make sure he was no longer in such a vulnerable place that he might try to kill himself again. She had never agreed with anything that Prudence had ever said but she did agree that she could never forgive herself if he tried to kill himself again and succeeded.

Terence and Milly were equally thrown into turmoil. They had never warmed to him and were very angry over his treatment of their daughter, but they didn't wish him dead. They did ask Clara if she was doing the right thing in going to see him but understood when she said she had to.

Clara stood on the deck of the boat, looking out at the sea, as she made the journey back to Dublin. She had never expected to go to Ireland again and she was filled with conflicting emotions. She had always loved Ireland despite everything. She had loved Armstrong House. She had fallen in love with the place as soon as she had arrived there. It had been heart-breaking seeing it set on fire. She wondered what had happened to it since.

After the boat docked in Dublin, Clara got a taxi that brought her to the Shelbourne Hotel. Looking out the window as they drove through the city centre, she was shocked by how much of it had been destroyed during the Civil War. There was much construction activity as the new government had started to rebuild the new capital. As she thought of the destruction of Armstrong House along with all these fine buildings, she wondered how long it would take to rebuild the country after so much fighting.

Once she arrived at the hotel, she went to bed, exhausted. But she hardly slept as she thought about meeting Pierce the next day.

The convalescent home was in a leafy suburb in South Dublin. Prudence had said it was paid for by the British government for the keep of soldiers who had been injured in the Great War. Despite how lovely the grounds and building were, Clara felt it depressing as she walked up the steps to the main entrance. There were many young men there who had been disfigured and wounded in the war. She imagined they were incapable of living independent lives and so had been shut away in that place to be looked after. But she was beginning to understand that Pierce's mind was as broken as the other men's bodies. She suddenly had this overwhelming urge to grab him and take him away from that place. It was madness, she knew. They were on the verge of divorce, but she hated to think of him there. A man who was so proud and confident to be in such a place!

The nurse on reception directed Clara to an upper floor and a room at the end of a long corridor. The place was very white and sterile and had a smell of detergent.

As she got to Pierce's door, she steadied herself. She was terrified at the thought of meeting him again. She took a deep breath and then knocked on the door and opened it. Walking in, she saw Pierce sitting on a chair on the other side of the bed, looking out the window.

"Hello, Pierce," Clara said softly.

Pierce turned to look at her.

"Clara!" He sounded shocked.

She thought he looked as handsome as ever, but his face was deathly pale.

"What the blazes are you doing here?" he asked.

"Prudence told me you were here," she said.

"She shouldn't have done that. She had no right to," said Pierce and he coldly looked away from her out the window.

As she studied his reaction to her she thought how this behaviour always made her feel in the past. Rejected, not wanted, an inconvenience. But since reading his letter, she now knew this was just an act to cover how he really felt.

She closed the door behind her and walked towards him.

"Well, you've been very stupid from what I hear," she said in a voice that she might use to talk to a naughty child. "Very stupid indeed, you silly man!"

She sat down on the side of the bed beside his chair. He refused to look at her as he continued to stare out the window.

"You gave me quite a shock," she said.

"I didn't think you would have cared," he said, still not looking at her.

"Of course I care! We spent many years together. I can't stop caring just like that."

"I wish you hadn't come."

"I don't think I quite believe you."

"Best you go now if you know what's good for you. You're nearly out – keep running."

"Pierce – are you – are you crying?" Clara asked as she could just see a tear slipping down his cheek. "Pierce!"

Clara stood up to face him.

Pierce looked up at her and she could see the tears.

"Oh Pierce!" said Clara and she was crying too.

She knelt down on the floor and placed her head in his lap. "I'm so sorry that I hurt you."

"There really is nothing to feel sorry about, Clara. We are just who we are," said Pierce as he began to stroke her hair.

"I'm sorry."

"Don't cry, Clara. I'm really not worth your tears," whispered Pierce.

Clara had planned to stay only a couple of days in Dublin before she returned to London. She had hoped after meeting Pierce that things between them would be fixed, and she could leave with neither of them feeling guilty about the past anymore. But she quickly understood the situation was much more complicated than that. If she abandoned him now at his lowest, she feared for his future. Marriage was a strange beast, she reasoned. Even if a marriage had been a battlefield like theirs, there was still a bond that had caused two people to decide to spend the rest of their lives together in the first place. She concluded she had never grown to hate Pierce, despite how he had acted towards her. It gave her no pleasure to see him as he was now.

She could see her daily visits to him benefited him and so she deferred her return to London. As the small allowance her parents gave her did not enable her to continue her stay at the Shelbourne, she found a cheaper and smaller hotel on the north side of the city.

Each day she walked down Sackville Street to get the bus to the convalescent home. There were rumours that the street was to be soon renamed O'Connell Street after the great Irish patriot Daniel O'Connell. The name Sackville Street was just one of symbols of English rule that were quickly being erased by the new independent government. She knew that families like the Armstrongs were also seen as symbols of English rule and many wanted them erased too.

She was filled with sadness to see the city's main thoroughfare destroyed. The street had just been rebuilt after the 1916 Rising only for it to again be the scene of fierce fighting during the Civil War. She remembered having tea in the Gresham Hotel on visits to Dublin. Now only the façade of the building remained as it was the centre of fierce fighting when the anti-government forces had seized it as their headquarters before being driven out. As Clara waited for her bus, she lamented the terrible times they lived in. So much chaos and destruction unleashed by wars, and revolutions turning the world upside down. It was understandable how Cosmo and her other friends in London had had enough of it all and now just wanted to forget the past and enjoy life while living it for the moment. As she looked around the destruction of Dublin, she thought it would be so tempting to join them on their new fun-filled adventure.

Pierce was still weak and so the doctors had recommended he use a wheelchair when he left the building. Each day Clara would push him through the grounds.

"The doctors said they hope you'll be able to soon go home," said Clara.

"Back to Aunt Daphne's in other words – not exactly home," said Pierce.

Clara had avoided the subject of Armstrong House as she did not want to upset Pierce, but she felt this might be an opportunity to raise the subject.

"Have you been back to Armstrong House at all?"

"Not since that day we evacuated."

There was a moment of awkwardness as both remembered that was the day they had separated when Clara refused to evacuate with Pierce to

Dublin. Clara by then had made her mind up to leave Pierce and made the decision to separate from him.

"Conway our solicitor sent some men to secure the house as best they could after the fire to try to deter people going in or looters," said Pierce.

Clara had a flashback of standing, watching the house on fire. It felt odd that she was the last person in the family to have seen the house.

"It was mainly the east of the house that was damaged by the fire," she said. "The rebels set fire to the curtains in the dining room and that room was quickly engulfed in the blaze. The fire travelled upstairs then to the bedrooms above and, standing outside, I could see the fire come through the roof there."

"It – it must have been terrifying for you, Clara."

"It was but the main emotion I felt was sadness. Then it started to rain ... I remember it so vividly. The skies opened up and the rain poured down just as the rebels were making their escape. I watched the rain fighting against the fire and it managed to eventually quench it and stop it from spreading to the rest of the house."

"You were very brave."

"Or stupid. I should have left when the rest of you were going."

"I understand why you didn't want to leave with me," said Pierce.

"Is there any chance you can rebuild the house?" asked Clara.

"I don't have the money to do so, Clara. It's impossible."

Clara sighed as she continued to push Pierce through the grounds.

"It's cold. Can you not make the fire bigger?" snapped Prudence at the maid in the dining room of the Hattons' house. She had continued to come up to the main house each morning to have breakfast with her aunt and cousins.

"There's no more room for any more wood to go on!" said the maid, looking at the blazing fire in the hearth.

"It's this house then – the windows are too big. They let in a draught," said Prudence.

Richard gave his mother Daphne an exasperated look.

"I'm sure we could deliver your breakfast to the gardener's cottage each morning if you prefer, Prudence. It might be warmer for you there," said Daphne.

"Absolutely not! Bad enough I have to sleep in that pokey building without having to eat breakfast there as well!"

"Will you excuse me, please?" said Richard, rising abruptly from the table and throwing his napkin beside his half-finished plate.

"Me too!" said Ophelia as she followed her husband out of the room.

"I think there's something very strange about that girl Ophelia," commented Prudence. "She never seems to speak to me. I think she may have some social problem. Strange name too – Ophelia – Shakespearean – a Shakespearean tragedy in her case."

Daphne dabbed her napkin against the corners of her moth. "Prudence, I have been thinking, now that Pierce is due to be discharged I will invite him back to stay here in the main house temporarily. It will be better for him having the staff here to help and less pressure on you in the cottage to look after him."

"I see! So, I am to remain in situ while he is allowed back here! Perhaps if I took an overdose too you might show kindness to me as well and give me my old bedroom back!"

"Well, it might be a little bit crowded here because I have been thinking of inviting Clara to stay here too until she returns to London – if she returns to London."

"Clara! Oh, I see. Very well, Aunty Daphne! And quite clever! I see what you are hoping for. It's in all our best interests for Pierce and Clara to reunite and so I think that's a very good idea of yours. And I, for once, will keep out of the way!"

Clara was surprised and touched when a letter was left at the convalescent home for her by Pierce's Aunt Daphne, inviting her to stay at their home in Rathgar. She had only met Daphne once before at their wedding and remembered her as a kind and good-natured woman. As she had been kept awake each night by the rowdiness in the bar of the small hotel she had relocated to, it was a very welcome invitation.

Daphne welcomed her warmly when a taxi dropped her to the Hattons' house.

She was greeted with afternoon tea in the drawing room and was afterwards taken to her room by Daphne personally.

"This is very kind of you," said Clara as she looked around the large elegant bedroom.

"It's the least I can do. I find hotels tiresome," said Daphne. "And, besides, you are family."

Clara said nothing as she looked out the window at the beautiful grounds. She wondered how much Daphne knew about the break-up of her marriage. She knew Pierce was very private and couldn't imagine him telling his aunt or cousins too much about it. And yet, due to the long time he had been living at the Hattons' without his wife, they surely must know they had separated.

"Only the immediate family know of Pierce's suicide attempt so we would ask you not to refer to it while you are staying here," said Daphne.

"Oh yes … of course."

"We have told people he had an acute case of food poisoning. Far less embarrassing for poor Pierce for people to think that."

Clara managed to nod and smile. She was sure this story had been concocted more to save face for the Hatton family than for Pierce.

"But he's getting so much better now that you are here, and the doctors say he will be discharged by the end of the week," said Daphne. "You've really been a tonic for him. He has been so miserable without you these past months while you've been nursing your grandmother in Kent."

"Has he?" So Pierce had used this as an excuse for her absence rather than tell his relatives the truth.

"Why, of course he has, my dear! He loves you more than you'll ever know! Poor Pierce was never one to wear his heart on his sleeve."

"Yes, I'm just beginning to realise that," said Clara.

Spotting a second door in the room, she walked over, opened it and was shocked to find that it was a connecting door to another bedroom.

"Oh – whose room is this?" asked Clara, trying not to show her concern.

"Well, Pierce's, of course. I thought it would be better to give him a separate room from you as he continues his convalescing, but at the same time you can be right next door to each other," Daphne said with a smile.

Clara looked down at the lock and saw there was no key. She felt alarmed. She wanted to say something to Daphne but didn't want to scandalise her if she didn't know she and Pierce had separated. She decided not to say anything. Pierce wasn't even due to be released until the end of the week and then her intention was to return to London very quickly.

"Oh, by the way, we're having a party on Saturday night," said Daphne. "It was in our diary in any case for Christmas but I think we can combine it as a kind of welcome home party for Pierce. I think it would cheer him up, don't you?"

"Well – I suppose so."

"It's exactly what he needs. I'm inviting lots of his old friends so it will be marvellous for him – for both of you!"

"But I have nothing to wear! I didn't bring any party dresses with me from London."

"You can borrow one from Ophelia – you both look about the same size. She has so many dresses!" Daphne smiled at Clara and left the room, closing the door behind her.

Sighing, Clara closed the interconnecting door to Pierce's room. This was all getting very awkward. Obviously nobody knew about the impending divorce except Pierce and Prudence. Clara decided it was time to go home to London as soon as she could.

Chapter 10

Looking at herself in the mirror, Clara admired the sequinned fringed cocktail dress she was wearing and conceded that Daphne had been correct about one thing: she and Ophelia were the same size. Ophelia had led her to her dressing room earlier that day and kindly gave her the pick of the vast array of dresses she owned. As Clara adjusted the oversized feather on her headband, she thought she looked the epitome of a flapper.

She had got up early that morning to collect Pierce from the convalescent home. Daphne had loaned her their chauffeur to drive there and back. Clara had forgotten what the luxury of a having a chauffeur felt like. When she had first gone to live in Armstrong House, Pierce had a chauffeur called Joe. That was when they had a full staff working for them, to keep the house running smoothly. Joe was a sweet lad who drove her everywhere as she could not then drive herself. He had left for the front at the same time as Pierce. Clara had cried and cried when news came back that Joe had been killed in Flanders.

The snow that had been falling all day had stopped and Clara looked out the window and saw there was now a white blanket on the ground, glistening in the moonlight. She could hear loud music playing downstairs and, seeing it was nine in the evening, she expected the party had already started.

When she'd arrived back from the convalescent home with Pierce that morning he had gone straight to his room to rest. Clara was sure he would not be in the mood for a party that night and when a knock came on the connecting door she expected it to be him telling her that.

She went to open the door. To her surprise Pierce was standing there dressed in black tie with his dark-brown hair combed back.

"You look ... you look beautiful," he said, sounding almost surprised to see her so dressed up.

Clara was stunned at how good Pierce looked too. It reminded her of the first time she met him at a party in London when he had also been wearing black tie. She had fallen in love with him on the spot.

"Are you ready to go down?" he asked, offering her his arm.

"*Eh*, yes. I think if we leave it any later we will be the last to arrive!" said Clara as she took his arm.

He smiled down at her. "We always looked like such a wonderful couple, if I say so myself!"

"Looks aren't everything," Clara said with a small shrug.

They stood on the landing, looking down at the hall below which was filled with guests. The men were all wearing black tie and the women cocktail dresses.

As they descended the staircase, Clara asked, "Are you sure you're ready for this, Pierce?"

"I can do anything ... with you by my side," he replied.

Clara felt anxious at his reply. Now he was better, she had planned to return to London on Monday. She did not think Pierce would take the news well when she told him.

As they got to the bottom of the stairs a man approached them.

"Armstrong! My gosh!" said the man. "I'm glad to see you've recovered from your food poisoning! I heard you had a terrible time of it! To think you survived the Germans but nearly got done in by an undercooked trout!"

As faint smile hovered on Pierce's lips.

"And Clara! Wonderful to see you back on these shores! You might remember me? I met you at a few parties at Armstrong House. Dorkley – Major Dorkley."

"Yes, of course I remember you, Major Dorkley," said Clara, smiling as she shook his hand.

"Glad to see you back by this chap's side! He's been pining away for you while you minded that grandmother for so long!"

Clara continued to smile but her anxiety increased. Pierce obviously couldn't take the humiliation of people knowing his wife had left him and she was becoming very concerned about how going through the divorce would affect him.

The band in the drawing room was playing a new song that had just been a hit in America called "The Charleston". As Clara stood at the side of the room on her own she enjoyed watching the other guests trying to learn how to dance to it.

"I must admit that dress looks better on you than it ever did on me!" said Ophelia as she sidled up beside her.

"Hardly, Ophelia, but thank you for the flattery!"

"I see even *she* has made an appearance tonight!" said Ophelia, nodding over at Prudence who was on the other side of the room studying the canapés. "I don't remember her being invited but when did that ever stop Prudence? I believe you used to live in Armstrong House with her. However did you cope?"

"I'll admit it was very difficult at times," said Clara.

"You deserve a sainthood and a damehood for it! It looks like we'll be stuck with the bitch forever unless ... unless ..." Ophelia trailed off.

"Unless what?"

Ophelia turned from looking at Prudence to study Clara.

"Just be careful, Clara," she said.

"Be careful of what?" asked Clara, alarmed.

"They –"

"Clara!" interrupted Daphne, edging between the two. "I want to introduce you to the most wonderful man. He's a journalist with the *Irish Independent* and he wants to interview you."

"Interview me! Whatever for?" Clara asked incredulously.

"About your saving Thomas Geraghty's life during the Easter Rising," said Daphne.

"No! I have no notion of doing such a thing!"

"But why not? It's a wonderful way of promoting what you did. It's nothing to be ashamed of anymore and will show that you were on the side of independence all along, which will immeasurably help rehabilitate Pierce's reputation."

"No! I don't want any publicity or to draw any further attention to what I did," Clara objected.

"Clara, half the people who are in this room would not have got through the door five years ago. Half of them were rebels who have now turned into politicians, and we must make them our new friends if we are to survive in this new country. We must all adapt to the new circumstances."

"But I'm not going to be here long enough to adapt to anything!" said Clara.

"Oh, I do hope you and Pierce aren't planning on joining the exodus and moving to London? I had always hoped you might move back to the Armstrong Estate one day."

"We – I –" Clara was lost for words. As she looked at Daphne's smiling face she decided now was not the time to tell her about the divorce.

"If you'll excuse me," said Daphne as she walked away.

It had started to lightly snow again and somebody had opened the French windows and now a small group of people were dancing on the terrace outside. The girls in their flimsy dresses seemed oblivious to the cold or the falling snow as they danced furiously to the Charleston. The night sky was completely clear and a fireworks of shooting stars blazed through the heavens above them.

"Are they actually mad?" asked Prudence, looking at the dancers outside from her pivotal position beside the roaring fire.

"They could very well be!" said Clara as she took a sip from her cocktail.

"I think they are all mad!" declared Prudence as she surveyed the rest of the partygoers crammed into the drawing room around them. "All quite different from the garden parties we used to have at Armstrong House!"

"It's a different world," said Clara.

"One I lament! One hates to live in the past but I'm only happy when I think back to life at Armstrong House."

"It wasn't always happy for me," said Clara.

Prudence turned to face her. "And I know that one of the main reasons you were unhappy there was because of me. I was very cruel, and I've had time to think about it since we came here. I regret it all now."

Clara's eyes widened with astonishment.

"I treated you very badly and I am sorry for that, Clara. The truth is I was very threatened by you. I had been running things at Armstrong House before you came and then when you arrived you were – as it should be – the new the Lady of the Manor. I felt upstaged – sidelined. No longer relevant."

"I can see now how that might have affected you," said Clara, never having seen things from Prudence's point of view before.

"I was terribly jealous of you. You were so young and charming and everyone loved you, including Pierce. You were everything I wasn't, and I hated you for that. But you didn't deserve that hate or the way I acted."

Clara felt tears sting her eyes. All that hostility and bad blood she had suffered had now been explained by one word – *envy*.

"I wish you had just talked to me and explained how you felt," she said.

"Oh, my stubborn pride prevented me. I don't have much pride anymore so I can say it freely."

"I thank you for your honesty. Coming back to Ireland this past couple of weeks has made me understand so much about what happened to me in the past. It's like putting the ghosts to rest."

"Can you forgive me, Clara?"

"I can certainly try to forget."

"I'm so glad. Clean the slate! New beginnings! Because I really would like us to be friends if it's not too late."

"Although I'm planning on going back to London on Monday so it's going to be quite a short friendship," said Clara.

Prudence's face fell. "*Monday!* Does Pierce know?"

"Not yet! I plan to tell him tomorrow," said Clara.

"But you can't! You can't possibly! He's far too fragile still to lose you again!"

"Pierce doesn't *have* me to lose me anymore, Prudence!"

"But have you not realised how much he loves you? Clara, the doctors have warned me that Pierce will possibly, most probably, try to kill himself again if he hits a bump on the road! You walking out on him again – for the second time – will be more than just a bump!"

"Prudence – you can't just put all this on me!"

"Of course I can because it's true! And next time he won't be taking an overdose, he will take a gun and blow his brains out! He told me he almost did that last time but then thought he would spare us the horror of it!"

"Prudence! Don't say such a terrible thing!" pleaded Clara as she started to shake.

"That's the problem with everyone these days. We must mince our words to make sure that we say nothing – terrible! Well, I believe in calling a spade a spade!"

Clara put a shaking hand to her mouth as she put down her cocktail on the table beside her.

Prudence laid a hand on her bare shoulder. "I'm so sorry, Clara," she said in a calm voice. "I didn't mean to shock and upset you. I'm just so terrified of it happening again."

Clara looked across the room at Pierce who was standing with a group of men talking.

"You always made such a handsome couple," said Prudence. "Made for each other, that's what everyone said."

Clara suddenly found the room claustrophobic. The music seemed to be blaring so loudly and the people dancing so energetically. Beside Clara, a man holding a cocktail glass was dancing with a woman who was kicking her legs as high as they could go in the air.

Clara felt she was caught in a vortex, the heat from the blazing fire too hot on one side of her and the air from the open French window too cold on the other. She needed to get away. She suddenly pushed past the couple and through the crowd, out the French windows, past the dancers on the terrace and into the gardens.

She stood at the bottom of the pathway leading through the gardens, breathing deeply. She was shivering and she folded her arms. Prudence's words had seared her mind – *he will take a gun and blow his brains out.*

She turned and looked back at the house, the party in full swing.

There was a figure walking towards her down the pathway.

"What are you doing out here? You'll catch your death of cold!"

It was Pierce. He was holding a stole – Prudence's, she thought – and when he reached her he put it around her.

"What happened? I saw you run from the party, Did Prudence say something to upset you?"

He was standing close to her, his breath turning into fog in the cold air. She suddenly grabbed him and held him close, resting her head on the lapel of his tuxedo.

"Pierce, you must promise me you'll never do something like this again. That you'll never try to hurt yourself again! Promise me! *Promise!*" she demanded.

"I will promise anything you ask of me," he said.

"Not for me! For you! Even when I'm not here anymore!"

"Where will you be if you are not here with me?" he asked.

"Back in London! This was always meant to be a short visit. I'm going on Monday!"

His face filled with despair.

"Why couldn't you always have been like this?" she said. "All these years all I wanted was for you to be like this! Now, it's too late!"

"It's never too late. There's still time, Clara. We can make this work," he said, looking down at her.

"I can't go back to the life I had with you. It was too painful the first time to ever go through that again!"

"It will be different this time – I promise you," he said.

"I can't take that risk."

"Aren't we worth a second try – a second chance?" he asked as he put his fingers under her chin and turned her face up to him. He bent down and began to kiss her as the music continued to flow in the background.

The curtains were open in Clara's bedroom, and she could see the falling snow fluttering on the windowpanes outside. The house was in total silence, the party long over. The fire had turned into a smouldering heap in the hearth. The aroma of the turf fire brought back memories of Armstrong House. Clara could vividly remember that aroma permeating through the old manor house which she had loved.

She looked at Pierce's sleeping form beside her in the bed. Her emotions were running wild, and she suddenly had a longing for her life in Armstrong House and was filled with nostalgia. She never thought she would feel that way again about the house or Pierce.

After they had kissed in the gardens, they had slipped away from the party to her room where they had made love. Clara sat up in the bed, trying not to wake her husband. Never in a million years did she ever think she would share a bed with Pierce again. And yet it seemed so easy to be with him again. He was still her husband after all. The reasons why she had fallen in love with him in the first place had come creeping back to her over the past couple of weeks. He had become the husband she had always prayed for – but could she trust him? Were the walls that had surrounded him finally demolished after this past year of separation? Or was this past two weeks just a flash of vulnerability after his suicide attempt and he would revert back to the way he had been during their marriage?

The next afternoon Pierce and Clara walked along the pier in Dún Laoghaire. Pierce was still calling the suburb Kingston even though it had been renamed by the new government. Clara wondered how could the population ever get used to all these new names that were so rapidly being bestowed on streets, towns and even counties to eradicate the memory of British rule.

They mostly walked in silence, careful not to slip on the snow that lay across the stone pier. When they reached the end of the pier, they stood staring out at the still sea.

"I keep thinking I'm going to wake up and find out this is all a dream," said Pierce.

She turned to him.

"Pierce, you asked me last night were we worth a second chance. My answer is I can't just walk away now without finding the answer. There is too much at stake not to."

"I won't let you down," he promised.

"But what are our lives to be? Where are we to live? What are we to do?"

"Well, I thought that was obvious – we go back to Mayo," Pierce said.

"But how can we when Armstrong House has been burned down?"

"We'll live in Hunter's Farm, the dowager house, for now. I have to go back there. The farm is the only thing that I have left and I've heard rumours that land left unfarmed is going to be seized by the government and redistributed to the local farmers. If I allow that to happen then I really won't have anything."

Clara felt panicked at the thought that Pierce could lose the land so soon after losing Armstrong House.

"I'm certain the farm has gone to rack and ruin so it will take a lot of work to get it up and running again," said Pierce.

"But you've always been a gentleman farmer – you have no experience of actual farming. Will it not be a big comedown for you?"

"Many of my peers have had adapt to our new circumstances," said Pierce.

"But is it safe for you to go back there? Will you not still be a target after the role you played during the War of Independence?"

"I'm willing to face it with you by my side. The locals always loved you. I wish I had listened to you and been more friendly with them as you always had been."

Clara thought of the handsome small manor house that was known as Hunter's Farm. It had been rented out to tourists who came to the area to hunt and fish. It suddenly seemed very idyllic to her, just her and Pierce living a simple country life devoid of the trappings and social rigidity that ruled their previous life. Maybe it was what they had always needed.

"I think I would make a very bad farmer's wife, but I'm willing to give it a shot. Maybe I'll try milking cows myself!"

"Let's not get ahead of ourselves! That's not a fitting activity for a former Debutante of the Year!" said Pierce.

After returning from Dún Laoghaire, Pierce visited Prudence in the gardener's cottage.

"It's worked. Clara has agreed to meet her solicitor and call off the divorce," he said.

Prudence jumped her feet and clapped her hands. "Thank goodness for that!"

"She's still going back to London this week to tell her parents and tie up a few loose ends."

"Well, I'm glad my plan has worked out for you! A thank-you would be nice!"

"Thank you for what? I nearly died of that overdose!"

"Well, I grant you I might have misjudged how many tablets you should have taken but I never claimed to be a doctor after all! And besides it really isn't my fault it took so long to get you to hospital as the ambulance service is shocking since this country got independence! It took ages to arrive! But you are fine now so no need to grumble!"

"Easy for you to say. Well, Clara is waiting at the main house, so I'd better not keep her waiting," said Pierce.

"Yes, please continue to play the devoted husband. We want to make sure she returns from London this time!"

Chapter 11

After arriving back in London, Clara braced herself to tell her parents the news of her reunion with Pierce.

"I can hardly believe it!" said Milly.

"Nor can I!" said her father, slamming his fist on the table in the drawing room.

"One minute you are divorcing Pierce and next returning to him!" cried Milly.

"After all he put you through!" added Terence.

"He's really changed, Papa. A different man entirely."

"Oh, leopards never change their spots, Clara!" said Milly.

"But I thought you were against me divorcing Pierce!"

"We were against you going through the scandal of a divorce, yes – but that didn't mean you should return to him instead!" said Milly.

"So, what in your opinion was I meant to do for the rest of my life? You warned me, Mama, not to get involved with Cosmo. You don't want me to divorce Pierce officially, but you don't want me to return to him either. So, you expect me to live the rest of my life in this sort of limbo, never having anybody to be close to? Living here in this house with you as you get older and surviving on pocket money that you kindly give me?"

"It's not we that messed up your life, Clara!" said Terence. "You did that all by yourself! It was your choice of a bad husband in the first place that did it!"

As Clara looked at her parents, she could understand their despair. They had always been the kindest of parents. Her grandmother used to complain they were too soft on her and spoilt her. They never objected strongly when she wanted to marry Pierce, even though they had reservations.

"I understand how all this is upsetting for you," she said. "But I always did love Pierce, despite everything. I was deeply, obsessively in love with him. But I have reasons, some you don't even know about, that are forcing me to at least give my marriage another chance. I'm going in with my eyes wide open this time."

"I just hope you are not returning to Pierce out of guilt after he tried to top himself," said Terence.

"There probably is guilt on my part. I didn't see things for what they really were before."

"Well, it's your life at end of the day," sighed Milly.

"I'm going to travel to Granny's tomorrow to spend the rest of the week there before I return to Ireland. Since she was the one urging a divorce, I'm sure she'll be very upset to hear about me and Pierce getting back together."

"Oh, please don't tell her the truth, Clara! It will kill her!" urged Terence as Burton walked into the room.

"Please, Burton, not now! We are in the middle of a crisis!" said Milly.

"I am afraid this is an urgent matter. I've just had Mrs. Wilkins on the phone from Oak Trees," said Burton.

"What did she want, Burton?" asked Milly, too distracted by Clara's news to entertain her mothers-in-law's demands.

"It's Mrs. Charter – she has passed away," said Burton with tears in his eyes.

Clara wiped tears from her face as the vicar said the final words over her grandmother's grave in the churchyard. A very large crowd had turned out for the funeral. Louisa had been a very popular figure in society for many years. Clara held on to Pierce's arm tightly. He had come to London immediately when he heard the news and had been a tower of strength since. She could hardly believe how supportive he was.

Clara had gone down to Kent and made the arrangements for Lousia's body to be returned to London for the funeral. Her parents were relieved that she had taken charge as Louisa's death had hit them very hard.

The guests had been invited back to their house in Chelsea after the funeral, for refreshments.

Stanley Bancroft was in attendance and looked suitably surprised to find Pierce there too.

"Lady Armstrong, my condolences. Your grandmother was one of my favourite clients," said Bancroft.

"Thank you, Mr. Bancroft. I simply do not know what I'll do without her," said Clara.

Bancroft turned to Pierce. "Lord Armstrong, it is good to see you again. We met many years ago at your wedding."

"Did we? I can't recall," said Pierce.

"Indeed we did. If I could ask you to excuse us a moment, I would like a private word with Lady Armstrong."

Pierce looked irritated by the request but moved away to speak to other guests.

"May I enquire if Lord Armstrong's presence here today is merely to pay his respects or as your husband?" asked Stanley.

"Pierce is here to support me as my husband," said Clara.

"In that case, may I take it that you no longer wish to continue with a divorce?"

"Yes, please don't continue with that."

"I must say I am relieved to hear it. As I'm sure your grandmother would be too," said Stanley.

"No, she wouldn't," said Clara emphatically. "She would be horrified."

"Oh ... be that as it may be, I would like to see you in my office at your earliest convenience over a different matter."

"A different matter?" She frowned. "What matter is that?"

"I'm sorry but this is neither the time nor the place, Lady Armstrong."

"Very well. I'll make an appointment. Now, if you could please excuse me – I need to attend to our guests."

She walked away, irritated by his refusal to enlarge on what this "matter" was. Typical of him to be so formal and pedantic. What could he possibly want to talk to her about?

In the back garden, Clara stood at the fountain with Pierce beside her. She idly scraped the snow from the stone sculpture that sat atop it, from where the water usually spouted. It was too frozen that day for the fountain to be able to work.

"You were very brave today," said Pierce.

"I wish I had been with her. I should have stayed in Kent but it was she insisted I leave and start living my life again," said Clara.

"That was excellent advice. Now, I want to show you something," Pierce said, reaching into his inside pocket and taking out a booklet of papers.

"What is this?" she asked as he handed her the papers.

"It's the deeds to Armstrong House," he said.

"Why do you have them here?"

"Because I've added your name to them," Pierce announced.

Clara read on the first page that her name had been added to the deeds for the house and land.

"But why did you do this?" she asked.

"Because I wanted to prove to you how committed I am to you and our marriage. Armstrong House is the most important thing in the world to me and I want to share it with you. Now you own it too."

"I'm – I'm not sure what to say," said Clara. "I suppose – thank you. I never expected it. I not sure I ever even wanted it."

"You love Armstrong House as much as I do and you deserve it probably more than I do. You stayed to face the danger to it while I ran away."

Clara reached forward and held Pierce tightly, the deeds pressed between them.

Clara decided she really did not enjoy being in Stanley Bancroft's company. His condescending air was insufferable.

"Thank you for coming to see me at such short notice, Lady Armstrong," he said.

"What's all this about, Mr. Bancroft?"

"It's about your grandmother's will."

"Her wll?" Clara was puzzled. "Oh – you want to arrange a formal reading of it? But why call me here? It could be arranged over the phone."

"No, it's not about a reading."

"What then?" Clara was becoming irritated. Why all this mystification?

"Well, to put it bluntly, Lady Armstrong has named you as the chief beneficiary."

"*What?* No! There must be a mistake."

"I do not make mistakes when it comes to legal matters, Lady Armstrong. Mrs. Louisa Charter had named you as her main heir."

"But she never said anything about this to me!"

"We must assume she had her reasons to keep it confidential."

"Her main heir? What does that mean exactly?" asked Clara, becoming flustered.

"It means you are going to be a wealthy woman, Lady Armstrong. Your grandmother was a major shareholder in her late husband's business Charter Chocolates. As you are probably aware, the business was sold several years ago which brought a very large dividend for Louisa. Then her money was also invested in stocks and shares …"

As Stanley continued to list off the items of Clara's inheritance she was not even listening any more as she was frozen in shock.

"But what about other family members – cousins and my brothers?" she asked when he finally paused.

"They are all to receive a share but, as I said, you are the main beneficiary. In a conversation I had with Louisa she said all the others were already set up in life and that you would need her money more than they. I wasn't quite sure what she meant by that."

As Stanley continued discussing the legalities of the will, Clara sat back in her chair, her mind reeling.

Chapter 12

After her meeting with Stanley Bancroft, Clara met Pierce at the Café Royal and told him about the will.

They were seated at a corner table, Clara still stunned and Pierce managing to look suitably shocked.

"I continued to think Stanley Bancroft would tell me he was playing an appalling joke or made a mistake. But he is not the kind of man prone to practical jokes and he assures me he never makes mistakes."

"And you never had any notion of what your grandmother had done?"

"Never! I never imagined I would be even included in her will, apart from perhaps some small gesture to show her affection. It's the strangest sensation – I've been around wealth all my life but never had any of my own!"

"I know this! When I married you I knew you hadn't a penny."

"Which is the one thing I had always loved about you," said Clara. "Until in one of our arguments you told me you married me because I was about to marry Cosmo and you took great pleasure in taking me away from him, out of spite."

Pierce's looked down at the table. "The cruel things we say to hurt the ones we love in the heat of the moment," he whispered.

Not wanting to put a dampner on the day, Clara quickly said cheerfully, "To think this time last week I had nothing and now you've put me on the deeds of Armstrong House and I'm to come into all this money!"

"What will you do now that your circumstances have changed?"

"I really don't know! There's nothing I really want to do. But knowing I have the comfort of money behind me now is wonderful in itself."

"You aren't going to run away from me to Monte Carlo then?" said Pierce, smiling.

"No, I'll give the casino as miss, thank you! I don't want this money to change me, and I hope it never will."

"So our plan is still to return to Ireland – to Mayo?"

"Yes! That has always been our life together and that's what I want to return to – even if Armstong House is no longer an option to live in. But at least now we'll be able to afford a better lifestyle than you tilling the fields and me milking cows!"

"Well, it's a week for good news. Because I received correspondence from Conway our solicitor informing me that the new Irish government is planning to bring in a compensation scheme that we can apply for."

"What kind of scheme?"

"For damage that was inflicted to property during the War of Independence. I can claim the money from the government to rebuild the house," said Pierce.

"But that's marvellous news!" said Clara, clapping her hands together. "Do you mean we can really rebuild the house and live there again?"

"That's the plan," said Pierce with a smile.

"Oh, I think I need to order champagne! I know it's extravagant, but I don't really care!"

Clara beckoned to the waiter and ordered a bottle. Her head was dizzy with excitement at the thought of Armstrong House being restored and living there again.

"How long do you think it will be before the compensation will come through?" she asked.

"Oh, it could be months, maybe a couple of years even before the bill gets through their parliament and the application is assessed."

Clara was deep thought as the waiter opened a bottle of champagne and poured them each a glass.

"*Cheers!*" said Pierce, holding up his glass to her.

"*To Armstrong House!*" Clara chinked her glass against his and took a sip. "I think I could never live without champagne!"

"I could live without champagne but never claret!"

Clara leant forward. "Pierce – I don't want to wait that long until we can move back into Armstrong House again. I'm going to use some of Granny's money to rebuild the house."

"No, Clara! Absolutely not!" said Pierce sternly, the smile disappearing from his face.

"But why ever not? You've put me on the deeds of the house and so it's my house now too! It broke my heart seeing it being set on fire and I've carried this sadness that it has been left abandoned ever since. I love it as much as you do, as you said yourself."

"Clara – I'm not going to allow you to use your inheritance to rebuild my – *our* house!" said Pierce.

"Pierce, this is an investment into my house as well as yours now. And, besides, if it makes you feel better we can call it a loan until the government pays you the compensation."

While Pierce sat in silence, looking unsure, Clara's mind was filled with excitement at the prospect of being in Armstrong House again.

"*Clara!*" came a sudden call across the restaurant.

Clara turned around and her heart sank when she saw it was Cosmo. He came rushing over to their table.

"Clara! I was going to call to your house today. I am so sorry I missed your grandmother's funeral, but I was stuck in Scotland with the snow –" Cosmo stopped abruptly when he registered Pierce at the table.

"Hello again, Cosmo. Long time no see," said Pierce with a smile.

"Pierce!" said Cosmo, sitting down at the table in shock. "What are you doing here?"

"Well, I thought that was obvious – having lunch with my wife," said Pierce.

"But – but –" Cosmo looked at Clara, bewildered. "But you're getting divorced!"

"Wherever did you get such a notion?" asked Pierce.

"Clara – tell me this is not so! You are divorcing him – aren't you?" demanded Cosmo.

Clara cringed in discomfort. "I'm going back to Ireland with Pierce, Cosmo," she said quietly.

"Ireland! But it's not safe there. It's in the middle of a civil war!"

"The new government has managed to get the upper hand by this point. I imagine the fighting will be over soon," said Pierce.

"Clara, you can't go back to him! Not after all he put you through!" said Cosmo.

"Please, Cosmo, nobody knows what really goes on in a marriage except the two people that are in it," said Clara.

"We were just discussing the rebuilding of Armstrong House. You must visit us when the work is complete," said Pierce, with a smirk which caused Cosmo to be overcome by anger.

"I never liked you, Armstrong! I hated you in school, as everyone else did, and I see you are no different now!"

"Cosmo!" pleaded Clara.

"Well, at least it's out in the open now! Perhaps it's best you don't visit us in Armstrong House after all," said Pierce.

"For somebody with impeccable taste I cannot fathom why Clara ever chose you."

"It's called love, Cosmo," said Pierce.

"Love! You don't know the meaning of the word!"

"You really know nothing about me. Look, everyone always knew you were besotted with my wife. But I really do think it is time you now – moved on – don't you?"

"Oh, I'll move on, Armstrong, don't you worry! It's just a pity Clara can't do the same!"

Cosmo stood up abruptly and strode away.

"Cosmo!" Clara called after him.

"Oh, let him go," said Pierce.

Clara ignored Pierce and ran quickly through the restaurant after Cosmo, catching up with him in the foyer.

"Cosmo – please wait! I don't want to leave it like this with you being angry and upset."

"How could I be any other way?" he demanded.

"I was always honest with you. I told you that we couldn't have a future together. I warned you not to put me on a pedestal as I was a different woman to the one you used to know and I would only disappoint you."

"Well, you've certainly managed to do that! I told you on your wedding day that I would always be there for you but if you go back with Pierce now I won't be anymore."

"I have to do this for reasons you don't know and will never understand," said Clara.

"In that case, I wish you well," said Cosmo.

She watched as he marched out of the building into Regent Street and disappeared from view.

Chapter 13

Present Day

In the three weeks since the wedding life returned to normal at Armstrong House. Despite what she had claimed when talking to Alex, Kate was relieved to have her home back. There had been considerable work clearing up after the event and after dropping Cian to school in the nearest town, Castlewest, she was relieved there was not some wedding detail waiting for her when she arrived home.

Kate walked through the hall and down the back stairs to the kitchen where Nico was working on his latest architectural job. The nature of his job allowed him to work from home a lot, but he still had to travel to Dublin regularly to attend meetings at his office.

"I see on her Instagram that Alex and Joshua are in Capri at the moment on the last leg of their honeymoon," said Nico.

"Nice for some," said Kate as she put on the kettle and opened her laptop at the island.

"Alex told me she thinks we should sell Armstrong House," Nico said out of the blue.

Kate had known Nico would eventually broach the subject with her and was not sure how to deal with it.

"Really?" she said in a disinterested voice as she checked her emails.

"Alex says we are spending all our money maintaining the house while we would make a killing if we sold it now and we could move to Dublin which would be better for us all in the long run."

"Nico – Armstrong House has been in your family for one hundred and eighty years. Are you going to be the one who gave up the legacy?"

"That's not strictly true, Kate. I did sell it previously – to you and Tony – and only managed to buy it back after Tony died because it was going so cheap during the property crash."

"That was different. When Tony bought the house from you it had been uninhabitable for ninety years, after the fire. It was just a relic you were minding – now, since Tony's money rebuilt the house and you then had the opportunity to buy it back, it has become our home."

"Still –"

"Speaking of that fire," said Kate quickly changing the subject, "I forgot to tell you. During the wedding I met a man who had wandered up to the house and who claimed to be a relative of Clara Armstrong."

"What was he doing here?"

"He was on holiday from England and came to take a look at the house. He seemed pleasant enough. His name is Royce Charter."

"Why didn't you tell me before?"

"There was too much going on with the wedding and then I forgot," lied Kate, taking out her phone and showing him the photo Royce had sent her. "He forwarded me this photo of Clara and your grandfather Pierce at the Hunt Ball in 1923, taken here at the house."

Nico studied the photo. "She doesn't look very happy," he commented.

"Well, it was a miserable marriage from all we've heard. But the point is, when I visited Clara's relatives in London years ago to return the things we found belonging to her here, they told me the house was burned down in 1921 during the War of Independence – after which she left Pierce. And yet here is a photo of Clara with Pierce in the house in 1923, two years after the War of Independence ended!"

"So, Clara's relatives must have been mistaken, and the house was instead set on fire during the Civil War afterwards. To be honest when you asked me about the fire years ago I didn't know which war it had been burned down in. As my grandfather Pierce died when my mother was still an infant, we had no real link to the past of the Armstrongs. My mother might have inherited what was left of Armstrong House, but she was more interested in being part of the social scene in Dublin than in its past or her father's first marriage."

"Yes, that's why I've contacted Professor Donald Maguire at Maynooth university," said Kate.

"Who?"

"He's an expert on the burning of the so-called 'Big Houses' in Ireland during the War of Independence and Civil War."

Nico gave her a straight look. "So you didn't, in fact, forget about this Royce and this photo."

"*Eh*, well, I forgot to tell *you!* I'm hoping the professor will have some information when I meet him next week."

"So I am trying to discuss our future," Nico said, with some irritation, "and again you're more interested in the past of this house."

"Our future is Armstrong House, Nico, along with its present and its past. You can't have one without the other."

Kate had an audition in Dublin and, on her way back to the west, took a detour to Maynooth as she had arranged to meet the history professor at the university on the same day.

She walked through the grounds of the old campus, found the history department and was directed to Donald Maguire's office which overlooked the gardens, with the steeple of the college chapel in the background.

"I was intrigued to get your email with the photo," said Donald after they had shaken hands and Kate had sat down on the other side of his desk.

"I was fascinated to see the photograph myself," she said, "as I always believed the house had been burned down in 1921 at the end of the War of Independence. Which now was clearly not the case. There is very little about it on the internet, but the house is listed as being set on fire in 1922 by rebels, but I now assume this must be incorrect."

"Well, I've looked through my archives and your original assumption was correct. Armstrong House was attacked by masked rebels in January 1922. It was one of the 76 country mansions that were either set on fire or blown up by the IRA during the fight for Ireland's independence. Because of Lord Pierce Armstrong's position with the British military the house was heavily protected during that war but, once the British withdrew, the house was a prime target and attacked. I actually found in the archives a photograph of the morning after that fire."

Kate sat forward eagerly as Donald produced a large grainy black-and-white photograph and presented it to her. She studied the photograph of Armstrong House with policemen standing in groups in the forecourt. She could see part of the roof was missing and the windows on the left side had been destroyed.

"And this photograph is definitely from 1921?" she asked.

"Without a doubt. There was a police report filed with a statement from Clara Armstrong who said she had been alone in the house when the rebels broke in during the night. They escorted her out of the house and then set the house on fire."

Kate remembered how Clara's relatives in London had told her she had remained at Armstrong House after Pierce had fled to Dublin in the hope her lover Johnny Seymour would return for her.

"The report said that after the fire had started there had been a torrential downpour that quenched the blaze – which was fortunate as otherwise the house would have been burned to the ground like so many others at that time."

Kate continued to study the photo and cast her mind back to when she had first gone to Armstrong House with Tony to buy it. The house had been boarded up for ninety years since the fire at that point.

"There must have been a second fire," said Kate eventually.

"Sorry?"

"When I came to Armstrong House first in 2007 the house had been boarded up for decades and had been uninhabitable, but I remember the fire damage to the house was not the same as in this photograph."

"In what way?"

"This photograph shows the fire was in the east side of the house whereas that part of the house was intact and it was the west side that had been fire-damaged when my first husband Tony and I bought it."

"Are you sure?"

"Yes, absolutely. We have plenty of photos and records of the original property before we renovated and rebuilt it. But I remember clearly the damage to the house was very different from the damage shown in this photograph. And you could find no records of the house being rebuilt after this fire?"

"No, I don't have any further information. There is a strong likelihood the house might have been attacked a second time. The burning of the Big Houses in Ireland did not just stop after the War of Independence ended. In the ensuing Civil War more mansions were destroyed than in the previous war, a total of 199. That was mostly linked with an attempt to drive the old aristocracy out of the country in order that the locals could then lay claim to their land. It was called 'land hunger'. Families like the Armstrongs were no longer welcome in Ireland and if they were brave or foolish enough to move back to Armstrong House then there is a very good chance they were targeted again and the house set on fire a second time."

"But you have no record of the house being attacked during the Civil War?"

"No, and there usually would be, but the times were so chaotic with the foundation of the State that the usual reports were probably not filed. The police force were fighting a civil war and so it's not inconceivable that administration wasn't followed up. And times then were so strained that reports often weren't filed on purpose in case friends and neighbours would be exposed."

"It sounds the most awful and dangerous of times," said Kate. "I tried looking up the census to see if I could gather some information but there was none held during the early part of that decade in Ireland."

"Yes, a census should have been held in 1921 but was postponed due to the war and was not held until 1926 when things had settled down."

"I checked the 1926 one already and it showed nobody living at Armstrong House so the second fire must have happened long before that. From what I know, the Armstrong family were not particularly wealthy by the 1920s. Where would they have got the money to rebuild the house?"

"The new Irish government did begin to compensate the owners of Big Houses that were attacked in the War of Independence but often the money awarded was insufficient to rebuild the houses and most families used the money to start new lives elsewhere as they also feared repeat reprisals if they returned to their homes."

"Perhaps the Armstrongs should have done the same," mused Kate.

Later that evening Nico studied a copy of the photograph Donald had given Kate with a magnifying glass and compared it with photographs of the house before it was reconstructed in 2007.

"Yes, you're right, Kate. This photograph shows the fire damage is in a different area to where it was in the photographs before the reconstruction.

But, also, I remember from when I owned the house that the fire damage was in the drawing room and the hall and the rooms above that. This photo indicates that part of the house was left intact, and the damage is to the to the other side where the dining room and library are located."

"Donald suggested that if the house was rebuilt after the first fire then it was targeted again in the Civil War, to drive your family out once and for all."

"And look here!" said Nico as he lifted the photograph and peered at it through the magnifying glass. "There's a woman standing at the side of the building just staring up at the house."

Kate took the magnifying glass and observed the woman, who appeared to be blonde.

"That's Clara!" said Kate. "It must be! All the other people in the photograph are policemen. Donald told me the police statement said she was the only person in the house when the rebels attacked. How sad to see her standing there, looking up at her house being destroyed."

"But she came back," said Nico, pointing to the photograph of the Hunt Ball taken in 1923.

"What made her come back to a house and a life she had been so unhappy in?" Kate asked.

Chapter 14

1923

Clara had a lot to do before she left England to restart her life with Pierce. He had returned to Dublin to stay at the Hattons' house until Clara had concluded her business, and she would join him before they set off to Mayo to restart their marriage and new lives.

Clara made many visits to Stanley Bancroft to officiate Louisa's will. She found the solicitor's attitude to her had changed considerably since she had become an heiress. His condescending air had been replaced by an overly courteous one. She wasn't sure which version of the man she disliked the most. She spent most of her time at Oak Trees in Kent, sorting through her grandmother's possessions. Mrs. Wilkins was to remain on at the house, taking care of everything in Clara's absence. Clara would make frequent visits back to Oak Trees but knew she could go to Ireland with a clear mind, knowing she was leaving her charge in the safest of hands with Mrs. Wilkins.

Once everything was taken care of in England, Terence and Milly took Clara to Euston Station to get the train to Liverpool, from where she would take the night crossing to Dublin.

As the train steamed through the English countryside, Clara was filled with a mixture of excitement and trepidation. This was very different from the first time she had moved to Ireland in 1913. Back then Ireland was a very different political landscape, and she was marrying into the ruling class. Now the peace and gentility of that time had been wrecked by years of warfare and the Armstrongs were a symbol of a past that nobody wanted anymore. However, Clara believed their future was in Ireland and the country needed to be rebuilt. She was sure there was a place for them in this new country that had been declared, and she wanted the Armstrongs to be part of rebuilding that country.

The crossing over the Irish Sea was smooth and Clara was excited when she saw Pierce waiting for her when they docked in Dublin.

"I can hardly believe you are really here," Pierce said as he held her tightly on the pier and kissed her.

As she smiled at him she realised something that had not hit her before. Since the Great War she had rarely seen him out of his officer's uniform. Even after he returned from the war he wore his uniform when he took up his post for the military during the War of Independence. Pierce had been a member of the Auxillary Division, a force set up by the British Army, composed of demobilised offciers who had served in the Great War, to combat the fight for Irish Independence. She realised she never liked him wearing that uniform. He wore it with such pride, but it made him a different man. Now, in civilian clothes he seemed so much more gentle and kind.

After spending the night at the Hattons' house, Pierce and Clara loaded the car with their suitcases and other luggage the next morning, about to set off to drive to the other side of the country. With Clara's money they had bought a shiny new Model T for the journey back to Mayo and their new life there.

"I'm just so pleased for you that everything worked out!" said Daphne as she gave Pierce a kiss on the cheek.

"Thank you for all your hospitality," said Pierce.

Daphne looked across the drive at Prudence who was speaking with Clara.

"And hopefully it won't be too long until Prudence can join you back at Armstrong House, once you have it rebuilt."

"As soon as we can I'll send for her," promised Pierce.

"Oh, good boy! She's like a fish out of water here," sighed Daphne.

"I'm sure you'll miss Pierce now he'll be gone," Clara was saying to Prudence.

"Oh, I get over things quickly so I shouldn't worry. Anyway, everything is only temporary in this life, isn't it?" said Prudence with a smile.

Prudence's response caused the smile to drop from Clara's face.

"Clara! We need to get on the road if we are to reach Mayo before dark!" called Pierce.

"Yes – coming!" said Clara.

She hurried to the car and got in.

Pierce hooted the horn as they set off down the driveway with the Hatton family waving after them.

"Will you miss them?" Clara asked.

"Not in the least. I'm just happy to be going home," said Pierce.

"What of Prudence? What is she going to do now? She can't spend the rest of her life in that gardener's cottage, can she?"

"Oh, good old Pru will figure something out – she always does," said Pierce as he glanced at Clara with a smile.

Travelling through the Irish countryside was very different from the train journey Clara had taken through England. Burned cottages and bridges that were blown up were evidence of the Civil War that was still being fought outside the capital. There was a strong presence of troops from the new Irish Free State patrolling the countryside which Clara wasn't sure made her feel confident or nervous about the state of the country.

It wasn't long until they came across a roadblock manned by soldiers. Pierce slowed the car and stopped.

"Identification papers, please," said the solider who seemed to be in charge.

Pierce handed over his papers.

The soldier gave him a suspicious look as he handed them back.

"Where are you travelling to?" he asked.

"We are going home to Armstrong House in Mayo," answered Pierce.

Clara felt uncomfortable as the soldiers looked at her as if she were a peculiar curiosity.

"Very well, but you can't go through this way. The rebels blew up the bridge further down this road last night and so you'll have to take a detour through the woods." The soldier pointed in a different direction.

"Is it a long detour?" asked Pierce.

"Well, sir, it's certainly shorter than trying to drive across a river with no bridge!" said the solider, causing the others to laugh loudly.

"Thank you," said Pierce as he started the car again.

"And drive carefully as there're snipers in those woods," cautioned the soldier as he stepped out of the way to let them pass.

As Pierce drove on and turned into the road that led to the woods, Clara held her breath.

"Snipers? Maybe we should turn back?" she said.

"Nonsense! If I survived four years of snipers during the war I'll survive a drive through an Irish wood!" said Pierce as he picked up speed.

It was late afternoon before they neared their destination, having navigated several halts, roadblocks and detours.

Clara felt her heart lifting with joy as they drove through Armstrong Village where everything looked as she remembered it. They continued towards the lake and when they reached the gateway to the house Pierce stopped and unlocked the chains on the gates before pushing them open.

Driving up the long avenue that stretched around the lake, Clara was surprised to see that the land was not overgrown and run wild as they had expected. It looked to be in good shape and there were cattle and horses grazing it.

"Who owns that livestock, Pierce?" she asked.

"I have no idea."

But then the house came into view and Clara became distracted. She felt her stomach knot, dreading to see what condition it would be in by now.

Pierce drove into the forecourt and brought the motorcar to a halt. They both got out of the vehicle and stared up at the house. The windows downstairs had now been all boarded up. Rory Conway, their solicitor in the local town of Castlewest, had arranged this and secured the house as best he could.

Clara walked to the balustrade along the edge of the forecourt and looked down on the three terraced gardens leading down to the lake. The gardens were now overgrown, save for what the roaming cattle had been eating away but to Clara the view remained the same. It was the same breathtaking view across the massive lake, which was several miles wide, with a silhouette of hills framing the other side.

"Clara!" called Pierce.

Clara turned to see he had opened the front door and was about to enter. She quickly joined him, and steadied herself as they walked inside.

Her heart sank when she saw the fire damage. The huge hall inside the front door looked to be badly damaged. To the right of the hall was the grand drawing room and behind it the ballroom. Even though Clara remembered the rebels setting fire to the curtains in the drawing room when they attacked the house that night, it had not suffered the main damage. The rooms on the other side of the hall on the east side of the house – the small parlour at the front, the dining room in the middle and the library at the back – had taken the brunt of the fire. Most of the fine old books that had been shelved there since Pierce's grandfather's time had been destroyed. And the fire had carried through to the upstairs with large gaps in the ceilings. Some of the rooms were empty of furniture as it had either been destroyed in the fire or looted afterwards.

The main staircase was intact and they walked upstairs to what had been their bedroom. Clara felt emotional when she saw a lot of their old furniture was still there intact, and it almost looked as if they had never left.

Suddenly there was a banging on the front door.

They froze, staring at each other, and then hurried out onto the landing.

"*Hello!*" came a man's voice loudly from outside.

Clara looked at Pierce.

"Who is that?" she asked.

"How the hell do I know until I go out and see?" snapped Pierce.

Clara felt nervous. The place had been locked up so she couldn't imagine what business anybody would have at the house unless they were up to no good. The house felt very isolated and eerie in its dilapidated state and she couldn't help but fear that the person outside might have evil intent towards them.

She followed Pierce down the staircase and joined him at the front door.

A man was standing in the forecourt, surveying the house, holding a shotgun.

Clara recognised him as Tadgh O'Meara. He owned a small farm that adjoined the Armstrong land.

Tadhg stared at them, looking shocked to see them.

"Lord Armstrong! Is it my eyes deceiving me or is it yourself and your good lady wife?" he asked incredulously.

"Your eyes are quite correct, Mr. O'Meara," said Pierce as he walked down the steps towards him.

"But sure what in the Lord's name are you doing back here?" asked Tadgh.

"We are moving back, Mr. O'Meara, back to Armstrong House," said Pierce as Clara came down the steps and stood beside him.

"*Moving back*? But sure you couldn't move back in there! Isn't it destroyed altogether?"

"We are going to repair and rebuild it, Mr. O'Meara," said Pierce.

"I see – said the blind man and sure he couldn't see at all! And where are you going to live in the meantime?" demanded Tadgh as if it were his right to know all their plans.

"We are going to stay in Hunter's Farm until the main house is rebuilt – that's if it's still standing," said Pierce.

"Oh, it's standing alright. Well, they said you were a brave man at the front during the war and they weren't telling lies. You're very brave to be moving back here!"

"Why so, Mr. O'Meara?"

"Well, there's a civil war going on in case you didn't realise. Are you not scared the Republicans will burn down the house again and you in it this time?"

"I understand the Free State forces have the area under control and are trying to restore law and order."

"Well, they are trying alright – but trying and doing are two very different things!" said Tadgh with a harsh laugh.

"We just want to live our lives peacefully here, Mr. O'Meara. We have no quarrel with anybody," said Clara.

"Sure you might want that, but people have long memories. Some would say people here haven't forgotten Lord Armstrong working for the British government during the War of Independence," said Tadgh.

"Mistakes were made," said Clara. "But I hope people also remember I helped Thomas Geraghty during his time of need."

"I'm sure they will remember that. Of course, that probably will make some others dislike you, now you've shown you're on the side of the new government with Geraghty being one of the new ministers and all."

"Do you happen to know who owns all this livestock on my land?" asked Pierce, trying to divert the conversation from politics.

"I do surely. That's my own livestock," said Tadgh.

"*Yours*?" said Pierce.

"Well, when you left here all your own livestock was stolen and the land was going to rack and ruin so I tried to mind it for you as best I could by letting my cows graze the grass."

"I see. Well, our plan is now to farm our land again," said Pierce.

"But, sure, you wouldn't know one end of a cow from another! Now that sister of yours was different. Lady Prudence knew more about farming than any man. Is *she* back too?"

"Prudence is still in Dublin," said Pierce.

"Best place for her. She always had brains, that woman. She knows when to stay away."

"As my wife said, we don't want any trouble. I have as much right to be here as you or anybody else as my family have been on this land for two hundred years," said Pierce.

"That they have. And weren't my family tenants of your family for most of that time. My grandfather was a tenant of your grandfather Lord Lawrence, God bless his soul. And my father was a tenant of your father, Lord Charles. You'll forgive me if I don't bless his soul, but he treated us all very bad during his time. Thank the Good Lord those days of your family owing all the land in the area are long gone and we are no longer at your family's mercy."

Clara was very uncomfortable at this hostility their nearest neighbour was showing them. She hoped this was not the prevailing mood or they would never be accepted back by the community.

"It has been lovely talking to you, Mr. O' Meara, but we really must be getting on as we want to be settled into Hunter's Farm before it gets dark," she said.

"Oh, I don't mean to be delaying you, Clara," said Tadgh. "You don't mind me using your first names now, do you, Pierce? Sure, aren't we equal neighbours now and fancy titles have no worth in Ireland anymore. In fact, I heard in Germany they have done away with titles altogether. And as for Russia, so many of the aristocrats there were killed by the peasantry that a title was the last thing on their minds when they were being shot while they slept in their beds ... so I hear."

"You are welcome to call us by any name you want, Mr. O'Meara," said Clara.

"Right so! I'll try to stick to the first names so, rather than any others that come to mind. I better tend to my cows. I bid you good day and wish you good luck – you'll need it!"

Tadgh tipped his cap to them and walked away.

Pierce and Clara watched him as he walked across the forecourt and down the steps and began checking on his cattle who were munching on what used to be beautiful flower beds.

Chapter 15

After they locked up Armstrong House they drove down the long avenue. Pierce stopped the car when they passed the gates and got out to lock them.

"I'm not sure what the point was in locking that gate when O'Meara had no trouble driving his cattle in elsewhere," said Pierce, getting back into the car.

"I never had much to do with him during my time at Armstrong House. But he always struck me as insolent," said Clara.

"That he is and his whole family were insolent before him. I remember when we were selling off the estate twenty years ago after the government brought in the Land Acts. He was very difficult to deal with when we were selling him what is now his farm. It was after my father had died and my mother was trying her best to deal with the selling of the land. I was at boarding school in England and was brought back to assist her. They were trying to pressurise us into selling them more land which Mama refused to do. I'm sure O'Meara's intention now was to take the rest of our land, and he is furious we are back."

"Pierce, as you told him, you have as much right to be here as he has. This is your country too and just being a Protestant rather than a Catholic or from a different class does not change that. Now that I'm back I'm glad we are here. We've come back to stake our claim on Armstrong House before people like O'Meara claim it all. You are not just protecting your legacy but the legacy for our children and future generations."

"That was something that always astonished me about you," said Pierce as he started the car.

"What was?"

"Your innate ability to always look on the bright side of everything. I often thought it bordered on the delusional."

Clara went to say something but wasn't sure how to respond. He made something positive about her sound negative.

Pierce drove through the gates and up the short drive that led to Hunter's Farm.

Clara was relieved to see the house still standing as Tadgh O'Meara had stated. As she expected, the gardens around the small manor house were overgrown and the drive populated with weeds, but the house was intact which was the main thing.

They got out of the car and Pierce silently walked to the front door, selected a key from his ring of keys and opened the door.

There was an immediate smell of damp but as Clara walked down the corridor to the main parlour she could see the building had not been broken into or vandalised.

"Home from home," said Pierce despondently as he looked around the parlour.

There was a stack of wood and turf left beside the fireplace and Clara immediately started to set a fire in the hearth.

"We'll light fires in all the hearths in the house," she said. "Fires brings a house quickly back to life – the warmth travels through the walls."

Pierce went out to get the luggage while Clara set the fire and found some matches to set it alight.

She could hear Pierce taking the suitcases upstairs and when he returned to the parlour he said, "I left the shopping in the kitchen."

"It may be bread and cheese for dinner for a while, as I do not pretend to know how to cook – but I can learn!" said Clara.

He looked at her as she stood up from her kneeling position in front of the fire.

"This is a sorry life you have chosen when you could be over in London in the Café Royal," he said.

She came towards him and put her arms around his neck.

"Pierce – I came back here with my eyes wide open. I feel closer to you now than I ever did and that is all I ever wanted from you."

He smiled down at her and then gently moved her arms away.

"I'll fetch the sheets and blankets from the motorcar so we can make a bed for tonight," he said.

Tadgh O'Meara drove his horse and cart along the boreen that led to his cottage and angrily pulled it to a halt at the front door. Four of his five children were playing in front of the house, but he ignored them as he stormed through the door and into the kitchen where his wife Molly was busy making bread at the large table.

The interior of their cottage was very different from that of most of the farmers who lived in the west of Ireland. The cottage had been furnished by fine furniture that they had looted from Armstrong House after it had been abandoned. Tadgh threw himself on the fine Regency couch that had once graced the drawing room at Armstrong House.

"And what has you so vexed?" demanded Molly as she folded the dough on the kitchen table.

"I'll tell you what has me so vexed! I've just seen that bastard Pierce Armstrong and his English whore of a wife!" announced Tadgh.

"What? Where?" asked Molly, abandoning her work.

"Up at Armstrong House, coming out of the front door as if they had never left!"

"And what are they doing back there?" asked Molly.

"They said they're back to live there! That they're going to fix it up and move back in!"

"*Move back in?*" cried Molly, aghast. "But I thought they had broken up and she had hightailed back to England?"

"Well, clearly that wasn't true!"

"I can't believe it! Oh my God! Did they say anything about our cattle on their land?"

"They did surely. I told them we had let the livestock on the land so it would be minded," said Tadgh.

"Did they ask you to remove them?"

"No, but it will only be a matter of time until they do."

Molly kept wiping her hands on her apron in agitation as she thought about the situation. This was a shock. Their plan had been to claim the Armstrong land as their own once they had established rights on it.

"How were they to you?"

"Pierce Armstrong was the same arrogant snob he always was. The wife was pretending to be friendly. I've heard she has friends in the new government from when she was riding that artist fella and whoring around with that political crowd he was part of."

"Isn't it a wonder that Lord Armstrong ever took her back after she cheated on him?"

"Ah, sure, aren't those Protestants different from us? They wouldn't have a shred of morals about them or decency for that matter."

Molly sat down beside him.

"Now listen, Tadgh, we have to box clever. They won't be staying for long once we are finished with them but in the meantime we'll pretend to be friendly neighbours so they can't accuse us of what is to come."

"I want that land, Molly. It's mine!"

"And you'll get it, Tadgh. You just need to be patient and smart. I think I'll pay a little visit to Lady Armstrong myself tomorrow– just to welcome her back," she said with a sly smile.

It was after midnight and Clara was lying on the couch with Pierce asleep beside her. The fire was still burning in the hearth after Pierce had stacked it with more turf.

The sudden sound of gunfire in the distance made Clara suddenly sit up.

Then Pierce suddenly jumped up with his fists raised.

"What the hell?" he shouted, his whole body shaking.

Clara got up and went to him. "It must be just the Army fighting with Republicans!" she said but she could see even in the dim light that he had gone deathly pale. She realised the sound of the guns were bringing back memories from the front.

He looked around and got his bearings, remembering where he was. He sat back down on the couch and put his face in his hands.

"The fighting sounds like a long way off. We are quite safe," Clara assured him as she sat beside him and put her arms around him. She could only imagine what horrors the sound of the gunfire was conjuring up for him.

"We should never have come back to this place," he whispered.

"Everything will be fine, Pierce. This place is our home – our past, our present and our future," she said.

They went up to their bedroom and Pierce fell into a troubled sleep. As Clara lay awake, listening to the gunfire, she thought that she didn't quite believe what she had said to Pierce earlier. When she thought of the inheritance that she had come into, she knew she could be living a life of comfort somewhere else. But she loved Armstong House as much as Pierce did and their whole relationship was based around it. She didn't think their marriage could be built on real foundations anywhere else. It would always be false in any other location, built on convenience and comfort. Only here could it be truly tested, proving that it was based on love and that they really had a future together.

Chapter 16

The next morning Pierce and Clara set off to drive to Castlewest for a meeting that had been arranged with Rory Conway, their solicitor. Clara had met Conway on numerous occasions in the past and she had always found him an honest and agreeable fellow.

In Pierce's father's time the Armstrong solicitor had been a Protestant, but that practice had long since closed down. Conway was part of the new Catholic middle class who were now running most of the businesses in the town and indeed the country. Regardless of Conway being a different religion and class, he had been indispensable during their absence from Armstrong House, trying his best to make sure their interests were protected as best he could.

Instead of driving straight to Conway's office, Clara persuaded Pierce to drive to the top of the main street, for both of them to walk through the town. Clara's reasoning was that it would be better for them to make a statement to the locals by appearing in public together. She wanted to avoid numerous situations like yesterday with O'Meara and have to regularly face inquisitions from people shocked to see they were back. She felt she would prefer to get it all done by one parade through the town that would state they were back, they were together, and they were here to stay.

Clara understood why Pierce was more reluctant than she to do this. Because of his role during the War of Independence he had provoked much hatred towards him while she had gone out of her way to make friends with the locals and had got on very well with them through the years. But in her last year at Armstrong she too had been a victim of the animosity created by Pierce's position. This walk would be a test of how deep that hatred still ran with the townspeople.

Pierce parked the car at the top of the town and they stepped out. As they looked down the street, it was busy with people going about their daily business. Clara took Pierce's arm, and they began to walk down the street. She could feel that his body was so tense he felt like a statue. People began to stop and stare at them as they walked by. They looked astonished. Outside one house children were playing until a woman suddenly appeared from the doorway and ushered them inside before slamming the door shut as Pierce and Clara walked by. People moved out of their way to allow them to pass while staring after them.

Pierce flinched as one woman spat on the ground in front of them.

"This is a mistake, we should go back to the car," he whispered.

Clara held his arm more tightly, forcing him to walk on though her heart was pounding.

"I wonder how many men have passed through her hands other than Johnny Seymour?" said a woman out loud.

Clara felt tears stinging her eyes. She hadn't believed it could be as bad as this. She remembered the deference the townspeople had showed them when they were still regarded as the local aristocracy.

As they approached Cassidy's pub, she remembered how she used to pop in to while away an afternoon when Pierce was away at the front, as she was desperate for company other than the servants. Of course, normally a woman sitting on her own in a pub was frowned upon but she was the Lady of the Manor and expected to behave differently. And the fact she would usually buy everyone in the bar a drink ensured she was welcomed. It was there that she had got to know Johnny Seymour and become close to him.

Cassidy the publican appeared at the door and seemed as astonished as everyone else to see them. Clara waited for him to quickly turn and snub them. But instead, he walked out to them.

"Lord and Lady Armstrong! I heard a rumour you were back but seeing is believing!"

"Good day, Mr. Cassidy," said Clara.

Cassidy looked around at the people in the street who were watching and then he put his hand out to Pierce.

"Welcome back, Lord Armstrong," he said.

Pierce looked suspiciously down at Cassidy's hand and then cautiously reached out and shook it.

"You look well – both of you," said Cassidy, "I'm glad to say."

Clara looked into the man's face, and saw he was being genuine.

"Thank you, Mr. Cassidy. It is nice to see you again too," she said.

"Would you come in and have a drink with us on the house?" he asked.

"Thank you and we would love to," Clara said, "but we have an appointment. Perhaps another time?"

"I'll hold you to that, Lady Armstrong. You are welcome here any time."

Clara nodded to him, and they continued walking down the street.

"Good afternoon, Lady Armstrong – you're looking lovely," said a woman, smiling warmly at Clara.

"Thank you," said Clara, smiling back.

As they continued walking, some of the men raised their hats and the women smiled at them.

"Are you alright?" Clara asked Pierce when they stood at last in the solititor's reception room.

Pierce nodded to her, but she could see he was breathing heavily.

Conway emerged and shook both their hands before ushering them into his office.

They sat at his desk as he took his seat opposite them.

As they indulged in small talk, Conway seemed even more perplexed than the townspeople by Clara and Pierce's return. Of course, he was privy to the fact Clara had been seeking a divorce not that long ago.

"It's certainly nice to see you both again," he said.

"I'm not sure everyone feels the same way," said Pierce.

"Emotions are running high with the Civil War, Lord Armstrong, as I'm sure you are aware. There might be a period of adjustment as you settle in back here. On a positive note, I believe, Lady Armstrong, that you have friends in high places."

"Pardon?"

"The new government has instructed the local constabulary that you are to be assisted and looked after in any way they can. Due to the help you afforded Minister Geraghty." "I feel I owe a depth of gratitude to Mr. Thomas Geraghty for his continual promotion of my character when, if the truth were known, I hardly know him and barely helped in his time of need."

"Well, Thomas Geraghty is obviously a man who remembers kindness to him, and this will make things so much easier for you as you rebuild your lives here."

"The neighbouring farmer, O' Meara, has allowed his cattle onto my land and he appears to be trespassing for want of a better word," said Pierce. "Perhaps you could write to him and ask him to remove his livestock?"

Conway began to frown. "I'm not sure if that would be wise, Lord Armstrong. O'Meara is a stubborn man with a temper. Sending him a solicitor's letter might inflame the matter. I would suggest trying to coax him gently off the land to start with."

"But it's my land and he has no right to be on it!" said Pierce.

Conway coughed and sat forward, putting his hands together.

"There are rumours that Tadgh O'Meara is involved with the Republicans. I don't think it would be to your advantage to make an enemy of him by being heavy-handed. I remember when the Armstrong Estate was being dismantled and sold off after your father died. O'Meara wasn't content with the thirty acres your mother sold him. He put tremendous pressure on Lady Arabella to sell the rest of the farm to him, but she refused to do it, despite being of a very fragile mental state at the time. She insisted she wanted to keep the two hundred acres surrounding the house as it was your legacy."

"I know all that," said Pierce.

"Just give him some time to get used to you being back before issuing ultimata to him," advised Conway.

"When you say O'Meara is a Republican, do you mean he is actually fighting with them against the government?" asked Clara, feeling nervous.

"There are rumours. That's the trouble with this Civil War – it's hard to know what anyone is doing or thinking or even what side they are really on. There has been a lot of fighting in the woods around the lake so I would keep away from there, if I were you."

"Thank you for the advice," said Pierce. "But, moving on – we are anxious to rebuild Armstrong House as quickly as possible. My wife has graciously offered to provide the funds for the work until the compensation is paid by the government. I was hoping you might be able to recommend a local builder – somebody I can trust."

"Yes, of course I can. They will be glad of the work. I'm afraid I haven't managed to get out to inspect the place for some time, but I can imagine it is very run down."

"Yes, it was a shock to see it in that state," said Pierce.

"I wonder also, Mr. Conway," said Clara, "if you might know somebody who could help with the domestic work and cooking at Hunter's Farm until we manage to get a full staff when we move back to Armstrong House?"

"I pray that you do! Culinary skill is really not one of my wife's talents and so her cooking is quite appalling to endure!" said Pierce, making Conway laugh.

"I never claimed to be a cook," said Clara, feeling her cheeks go red.

"Just as well! One would hate to add delusion to the charge of bad cooking!" said Pierce.

"I do believe your old cook at Armstrong House still lives in the area so perhaps she may be available," said Conway.

"Mrs. Fennell?" said Clara, smiling broadly and thrilled at the thought of finding her old friend still around.

"Yes. I think she is practically retired but helps with the cooking in the hotel where her husband is the porter. Maybe you could ask her?"

"Oh, how wonderful! I can't wait to see them again!" said Clara, clapping her hands in delight.

"I'd thought I'd seen a ghost!" cried Mrs. Fennell as she nearly collapsed on a chair in the foyer of the local hotel, the Castlewest Arms.

"A ghost, I tell you!" added her husband as he fanned his wife with a newspaper to revive her.

"I thought I'd never see you again in all my life, Lady Armstrong!" cried Mrs. Fennell who then started crying.

"What are you doing back here, my lady?" asked Fennell.

"Lord Armstrong and I are back for good! We are going to move back to Armstrong House once it's repaired and are staying at Hunter's Farm in the meantime."

"After all that happened!" cried Mrs. Fennell in astonishment.

"It's so good to see you again!" said Clara. "I've missed you so much. And we want you both to come back and work for us as butler and cook and move into your old room in the attic in Armstrong House when it is ready, so things will be just as they were! And in the meantime if you could help out at Hunter's Farm?"

"Well, we were considering retiring," Mrs Fennell said, looking to her husband for guidance.

"We would be honoured to go back into service for you and Lord Armstrong, my lady," said Fennell with a huge smile.

Clara felt hopeful as they drove back to Hunter's Farm. After the initial hostility they had experienced in the town, there seemed to be many others who appeared to be welcoming to them. Perhaps, as Conway advised, they just needed for people to adjust to them being back. But Conway's warning about not knowing what anyone is really thinking or whose side they were on was also echoing in her mind.

Pierce had gone up to Armstrong House, leaving Clara alone, and she was just about to prepare something for them to eat when there was a loud knock on the front door.

As she reached the front door she felt anxious about opening it.

"*Hello?*" she called out loud.

"Hello! It's Molly O'Meara here just dropping by to say hello!" came a cheery voice on the other side of the door.

Trying to appear composed, she opened the door. She remembered the jovial-looking woman from seeing her around in the past, though they had never spoken.

"Ah, Lady Armstrong! Sure, aren't you as welcome a sight as a drop of rain in a drought!" said Molly. "You probably don't remember me at all? I live in the next farm."

"I do remember you, Mrs. O'Meara," said Clara.

"Don't be calling me by any other name but my first one – Molly. I just wanted to call to welcome you back myself and to bring you this for your supper." She handed over a basket.

Clara took it and could see there were eggs and homemade bread inside.

"Oh, that's most kind of you – Molly," said Clara, feeling relieved at the woman's friendliness.

"I made the bread myself – it's soda bread with currants in it and there's my own butter in that basket too."

"That's really too kind!"

"Well, sure, it's as I said to my husband, Lady Armstrong probably arrived down here to cupboards bare and only the mice and rats in the place to keep her company! And isn't it a wonder you ever managed to find your way here at all when they have renamed nearly every town and village along the way!"

"Yes, it can be confusing," said Clara.

"Sure, aren't they going to rename the village next, so I hear."

Clara's heart sank on hearing this. Armstrong village had been built by Pierce's great-grandfather and named after the family.

"What is it to be renamed?" asked Clara, not hiding her concern.

"Ballymucky," said Molly.

"Ballymucky! Surely not! But that's an awful name!"

"Well, what is attractive to the Irish ear might not be as attractive to the English ear," said Molly, looking amused.

"I can't imagine that name being attractive to anyone's ear!" Clara said, putting the basket on a table in the hallway behind her. She was unsure whether Molly was teasing her. "Won't you come in for a cup of tea?"

"Not at all! Sure, I'm not grand enough to take tea with a great lady such as yourself! But if you want anything – anything at all – all you have to do is ask Molly O'Meara and she'll have it done for you!"

"Well, there might be one thing, Molly. Your husband's cattle – I wonder how long he plans to leave them on our land? Not that we're rushing him off!"

"But, sure, only say the word and the cattle will be gone, Lady Armstrong! But – and you wouldn't know much about farming so take heed to what I'm saying – you would be wise to leave our cattle on the land until you get your own back on it. Otherwise, the fields will go astray and it will take years to get them back in order."

"I see," said Clara.

"Sure, we tried to be good neighbours and mind your land as best we could when you were away. And the same for Armstrong House, sure we used to watch out for it all the time and keep them looters and robbers away who wanted to break in and steal your furniture and valuables!"

"I didn't realise that you did that for us. We are very grateful to you, Molly."

"I promise you now, so I do, when the next fair is on in town we'll take His Lordship there and personally advise him what livestock to buy to get back into the farming again."

"That really is very kind of you," said Clara.

"Well, His Lordship will need all the help he can get and isn't that what Hugh and Molly O'Meara are famous for – being good neighbours and lending a helping hand to a friend! Anyway, I'll leave you in peace but rest assured I'll be seeing you very soon again, Lady Armstrong."

"Yes, I hope so and thank you again!" said Clara as she watched the woman walk away. She closed the door again and bolted it, smiling to herself. Perhaps Pierce and Conway had got it wrong about the O'Mearas. She hoped so.

Chapter 17

Wearing a white satin dressing gown, Constance Fitzgerald was brushing her luxuriant black hair as she sat at the dressing table in her room at the Dorchester in London when there was a knock on the door.

"*Come in!*" she called.

The door opened and a chambermaid called Peggy entered, carrying a silver tray.

"Your morning tea, Mrs. Fitzgerald," said Peggy.

"Thank you, Peggy, you can leave it on the table," said Constance as she continued to brush her hair.

"Will I pour it for you?" asked Peggy.

"Yes, please."

Constance had been staying at the Dorchester for a week, and she had grown fond of the young Irishwoman who tended to her room each day.

"I'm afraid I'm running late today, Peggy, and delaying you from making up the room."

"You're a busy woman, Mrs. Fitzgerald. How did the antiques show go for you yesterday?" Peggy picked up the silver teapot and poured tea into the china cup.

"Disappointing, if the truth be told, Peggy. Too many sellers and not enough buyers!"

Constance and her husband Clement were antique dealers with a shop in Dublin.

"There are just too many antiques on the market at the moment as the great houses try to sell off the family silver literally to keep them afloat!"

sighed Constance. "It's New York where the money is. I think we need to concentrate on selling there in future."

"I believe the streets are paved with gold in New York," said Peggy wistfully.

"Not quite – but there are far more gullible millionaires anxious to buy antiques to furnish their sprawling Long Island mansions with!"

"Cream or milk this morning?" asked Peggy.

"Cream, please."

"Oh, aren't you beautiful!" gasped Peggy suddenly.

"Thank you, Peggy!" said Constance as she checked her appearance in the mirror.

"Sorry, I wasn't referring to you, Mrs. Fitzgerald!"

"Oh!" said Constance in surprise and turned around to see Peggy had picked up a copy of *Tatler* that had been left open on the table.

"I was talking about *her*," said Peggy as she showed Constance a photo of a beautiful young woman.

"Who is she?" asked Constance, glancing at the photo.

"That is Lady Clara Armstrong who I used to work for as a parlour maid in their fine house, Armstrong House, in County Mayo in Ireland."

"Oh, I see," said Constance, losing interest and turning back to the mirror.

"She wasn't born into the peerage, but she was the classiest woman I ever met," said Peggy as she began to tidy up the room.

"Really?" said Constance, disinterested.

"How she put up with that fucker of a husband I'll never know. Sorry, pardon my language!"

"Pardoned!" said Constance in a sing-song voice.

"People blamed Clara for having that affair but in my opinion her husband Pierce drove her into that other man's arms!" Peggy's voice suddenly grew whimsical. "And what arms she was driven into! I can still see Johnny Seymour dressed in his gleaming white tennis clothes on the lawns at Armstrong House!"

Constance suddenly swung around.

"Johnny Seymour? As in the artist?" she asked.

"That's the one! Sure, there was never a man as charming as Mr. Johnny as we used to call him. He'd make a nun blush!"

Constance suddenly stood up and went to the table to take up the copy of *Tatler* to examine the photo of Clara.

"And how did they meet?" she asked.

"He had a house near Armstrong House called Seymour Hall and he was commissioned to paint a portrait of Clara. This is going back seven or eight years."

"A painting? I know all Johnny Seymour's work and I'm not familiar with any painting of this woman," said Constance as she scrutinised the photo. "Are you sure?"

"Oh, yes, I am! Wasn't I there every day when he was painting her in the ballroom? And the painting was then hanging in the drawing room until it had to be removed when her husband Lord Pierce came back from the war and their affair ended."

"Peggy, will you stop tidying up and come and have a cup of tea with me!" commanded Constance in a half-impatient, half-excited voice.

"I can't stop my work to have a cup of tea, Mrs. Fitzgerald!"

"Of course, you can – I'll tell the head housekeeper it was my fault you were delayed." "But there isn't a second cup anyway!" said Peggy.

"Actually – let me get you something a little stronger!" Constance went to the decanter on a side table and poured a glass of sherry.

She handed it to Peggy.

"Oh, I can't!"

"Drink up!" said Constance, pushing Peggy to sit down in a chair. "So where is this painting now?"

"Well, I don't know for sure, but I imagine it's probably still in Armstong House if it wasn't destroyed during the fire," said Peggy.

"What fire?" demanded Constance, horrified at the thought of a Johnny Seymour painting being eradicated.

"The rebels set fire to the house during the War of Independence. But I went up to the house after the fire and it was mainly one side of the house that was burnt and the painting wasn't kept there so maybe it wasn't destroyed."

"So where in the house was the painting kept?"

"Well, I have no idea because Clara hid it when His Lordship came back from the war and found out about her affair. Sure, she was lucky he didn't kill her in a jealous rage." Peggy took a gulp of her sherry and smacked her lips. "After that she couldn't have it on show as it would be a reminder to him of her lover who had painted it! How romantic is that!" Peggy took a gulp of her sherry.

"Yes, very. What happened to the house after the fire?"

"It was abandoned by the family and boarded up. And with all the wars going on in Ireland since then, there's no hope of going back to do anything about it. Sure all the gentry familes are fleeeing for their lives! So, there the house lies to this day like a heartbroken woman abandoned by her lover!"

"Tragic. So, the contents are all still there?"

"They would be surely – anything, that is, that wasn't destroyed in the fire."

"But she could have taken the painting with her."

"No, she didn't. It was big and awkward and she was seen by the locals getting the train to Dublin with just one suitcase so she hardly had the painting in that. No, it's there alright – pining for her somewhere in the dark!" said Peggy and she took another gulp of her sherry.

The Fitzgerald house was a large Victorian terraced house in Blackrock in Dublin. The taxicab pulled up to the front door and Constance got out and rushed up the steps.

"I'm home!" she called as the taxi driver followed her in and placed her suitcases in the hallway. She took out her purse and paid the driver before closing the door behind her.

She turned to see her husband Clement walk down the stairs towards her.

"Hello, darling! How was business in London?" he asked.

"I've done better but I guess I've done worse too!" she said.

"Did you manage to get rid of the George III side table?" he asked as they walked into the front parlour.

"Thankfully, I did! But I practically had to give it away for a song." She sighed as she lay down on the chaise longue.

"Oh dear!" he said as he poured them both a glass of wine.

"This new rage for art deco is not helping matters. Wealthy clients are looking to buy new stuff instead of antiques as they traditionally did. I do hope it goes out of fashion soon."

Clement was in his sixties and over thirty years older than Constance. She was used to the surprised looks and rude comments they got from people when they discovered they were married and had become accustomed to ignore them.

"Let's hope I'll do better in New York next week," said Clement.

"But I did find a nugget of information that could make us a very large sum of money," said Constance, sitting up.

"Do tell," said Clement, loving the glint in her eye that Constance always got when she sniffed an opportunity.

"There was an Irish chambermaid called Peggy in the hotel, who used to work in a place called Armstrong House in County Mayo. And the mistress of the house had an affair with Johnny Seymour before he became really famous and commissioned a painting from him. The house has been abandoned since it was attacked by the rebels and it's been boarded up and the painting is just sitting there somewhere inside!"

"How come it's not common knowledge about this painting?"

"Because it was never displayed publicly. It was a private commission and Clara hid it somewhere in the house after her husband returned. Because of the affair."

"Can you really believe this maid?"

"I've done my research since and it's all quite true. Lady Armstrong did have a well-known affair with Johnny Seymour and I have no reason to suspect Peggy was lying about the painting. She went into a lot of detail about it. Lord and Lady Armstrong have since separated, and nobody goes near the house. We can literally go there, find a way into the house and get the painting!"

"Risky!" Clement raised an eyebrow.

"It's not like we haven't taken such a chance before!"

"And we could never sell it on the open market as questions would be asked as to how it came into our possession and Lady Armstrong could find out," said Clement.

"I know this and that's why we would sell it on the black market in America. Clement, you know how much a Johnny Seymour painting is worth these days. He hardly releases any new work since he became a recluse on Long Island. If we got that painting and sold it to a private buyer who doesn't care how we got it we won't have to worry about Geroge III Regency tables for ever more!"

"I'll make enquiries when I go to New York and see what interest I can muster," said Clement.

"While I'll go down to Armstrong House and do a reconnaissance!"

"It's quite a dangerous thing for us to do, darling," said Clement.

"Faint heart never won the fair lady, Clement!" said Constance as she sat on his lap and kissed him.

Chapter 18

As Constance drove her red Packard Six Sedan towards the west of Ireland, she was filled with a new sense of vigour. She had received a telegram from Clement in New York saying he had found several parties very interested in acquiring their latest 'project', code for the Lady Armstrong portrait. Constance had no doubt that there would be considerable interest, and she could feel herself practically salivate at how much money they could sell the painting for.

Constance had made many business trips around the country during the War of Independence and the ensuing Civil War and so the journey across the war-torn country didn't faze her in the least.

The wars in Ireland had been very good for their business, releasing valuable antiques that had been in houses for generations that were now being abandoned. They had made a killing selling those items on abroad.

It was dark by the time she reached Castlewest and booked into the local hotel on the main street. She had sandwiches delivered to her room, took out local maps and got acquainted with the area, locating the route to Armstrong House. She didn't speak to any of the locals or ask any questions. Planning a robbery entailed being very discreet, even if nobody knew there was anything of value to be robbed.

Driving through the countryside, Constance felt a shiver of exhilaration as she approached Armstrong House. Sometimes she wondered was there something wrong with her. Ever since she was a child, when most other girls recoiled at the prospect of doing anything unconventional, she got a thrill and a surge of excitement from doing so. Clement had often told her she was fearless, and she liked that description of herself. He also told her it would be the cause of her downfall, though that seemed to spur her on to be even more daring in her pursuit of her goals.

When she reached the gates of Armstrong House she stopped abruptly. Peggy had told her the gates were closed and locked and she had expected to have to find a way in over a wall or ditch. But the gates were wide open. Cautiously she drove through the gateway and began to follow the long avenue around by the lake until the house came into view. She could see a number of men at the property who seemed to be carrying out building work. She was shocked to see them as Peggy had said the house had been abandoned.

She thought about turning around but decided to press on and drove into the forecourt.

"Good morning to you!" she called to a man who looked to be managing the work.

"Good morning, ma'am. Can I help you?"

"I hope you can." She pointed back behind her. "Is that the right road for Castlewest? Or have I gone astray?"

"No, you're on the right road, ma'am. Go back to the gateway, turn left and it's a straight road to the town. It's about seven miles."

"Thank you!" said Constance, looking up at the building. "What a beautiful house!"

"It will be by the time we're finished, ma'am!"

"Is it going to be up for sale? I'm looking to buy in the area," said Constance.

"No, it's Lord and Lady Armstrong's house. They're rebuilding it to move back in."

Constance hid her dismay. "Are they here now?"

"No, they're staying in the first house down the road, Hunter's Farm, until they move back in."

"Lucky them, having a house like this!" said Constance. "Thanks again and cheerio!"

Constance set off back down the avenue. When she reached the gates she turned left and looked out for the house the man had said the Armstrongs were staying in. As she passed it she saw young blonde woman tending the garden. As Constance drove on she was overwhelmed with frustration. The Armstrongs had obviously only just moved back to the area. Perhaps a month before she would have had clear access to the house to find the painting. But, as she thought of the several buyers waiting for the painting in New York, she refused to give up quite so easily.

Constance spent a few days in Castlewest, exploring the area. There were quite a few manor houses scattered around the county and, as it was not a place she had been to before, she decided there could be some business to be done with the owners if they were willing to sell the contents. As in England, many of these gentry families were now on their uppers and would probably be glad of the cash – even more so here as they were desperate to leave because of the war. Although judging by the work being carried out at Armstrong House, that family did not seem to be short of money. Intrigued about the former home of Johnny Seymour, she located Seymour Hall. When she got there she was surprised to see a sign at the gateway declaring the house was for rent. It was an attractive manor house perched on a hill, overlooking the lake. She called in to the agent in Castlewest and organised a viewing.

"Who is the owner?" asked Constance as the agent showed her around the house.

"An artist called Johnny Seymour. This house was in his family for generations and he used to stay here when he wasn't up in Dublin."

"He's not coming back?" asked Constance.

"I doubt it. He's emigrated to America, and he tried to sell this house but nobody was buying so it has been put up for rent to stop it falling into disrepair or being robbed. Nobody wants to buy houses like this in places like this anymore. Not until the Civil War is over anyway."

Constance felt excited as she examined the house. She felt it was almost an honour to be in a house that Johnny Seymour lived in and tried to imagine him painting there.

"I'll take it!" she declared.

"Are you sure? It's a big house for a woman on her own," said the agent, surprised.

"Oh, my husband will be joining me when he gets back from New York. A short-term lease if that suits to see if we like it."

"I'll take any lease I can get to shift this property!" said the agent, laughing.

"Yes, it's just perfect for us!" said Constance as she looked out the window. She could just about see Armstrong House across the lake.

Clara had done some gardening when she was staying at her grandmother's to keep her mind occupied so she put that experience to work in the gardens at Hunter's Farm. She was busy trimming rose bushes when a woman on horseback rode in through the front gate.

"Lady Armstrong, I presume!" said the woman with a wave as she dismounted.

"Yes – I'm sorry, but do I know you?" asked Clara, leaving the rose bushes and taking off her gardening gloves.

"Not yet! But I'd like you to! I'm your next-door neighbour!" said Constance with a big smile.

"Oh!"

"Well, not quite next-door neighbour. We've just moved into Seymour Hall."

Clara felt herself go stiff at the mention of Johnny's old home. As she looked at the raven-haired beauty, she felt a shiver of dread. She looked just like Johnny's type and she feared he had moved back and this was his new Muse.

"Do you know Johnny?" Clara asked, trying to keep her voice steady.

"Gosh no! We're just renting his house through the agent in Castlewest."

"Oh, I see!" said Clara, relaxing.

"We tried to buy it, but he's not interested in selling apparently," lied Constance.

Clara observed the smiling, very confident woman with growing curiosity.

"What brings you to the area – have you relatives here?"

"None at all! We've just lived in Dublin for far too long and felt the need to get out. The city is going to take years to rebuild after all the fighting, so we decided to start afresh down here."

"Well – welcome!" said Clara. "Won't you come in for tea?"

"Thank you, how kind – I would love to."

Mrs. Fennell eyed Constance suspiciously as she poured the tea in the parlour.

"My husband Clement is in New York for several weeks on business," said Constance, seated across from Clara.

"What business is he in?"

"We are antique dealers."

"How interesting!"

"We have a shop in Dublin, but it has been destroyed twice – once in the War of Independence and then again last year during the Civil War. After that we decided we needed to have a simpler, quieter life and so started looking to relocate to the country."

"I'm not sure you'll get a quieter life down here! Not with all the fighting still going on," said Mrs. Fennell.

"Thank you, Mrs. Fennell. I'll ring for you if we need anything else," said Clara.

Mrs. Fennell sniffed the air and left them alone.

"How did you find us?" asked Clara.

"I called up to Armstrong House to ask directions – I thought I'd lost my way first day I arrived and was trying to get to Castlewest – your builders told me I was on the right road and when I admired your house told me the owners were Lord and Lady Armstrong and that you were staying here until the work was finished."

"Ah – I see," said Clara, taking up her cup and sipping her tea.

"The builders seem to be very busy. When will they be finished?"

"We hope in a few weeks – they are working around the clock to get us back home," said Clara.

"Which war was it set on fire – the War of Independence or the Civil War?"

"The first one," said Clara sadly.

"Well, hopefully all this fighting will be over soon. That's all everyone wants – to get back to normal."

"Yes, it certainly is," agreed Clara.

"What about the furniture? Have you managed to find replacements for what was damaged or destroyed?"

"No – I actually haven't given it much thought. All our energy has been going on the actual rebuilding. I must start looking or else when we move back we will be sitting on the floor in some rooms!"

"Well – I must help you!" said Constance, quickly putting her teacup back on the coffee table.

"Oh no – I couldn't possibly ask you!"

"Of course you could! I'm in the business and have the contacts. I'll quickly find you exactly what you're looking for and make sure you don't get taken advantage of."

"What commission do you charge?" asked Clara.

"Oh, I wouldn't charge you anything. It would be my pleasure to help restore Armstrong House to its former glory."

"Well – it does seem a wonderful opportunity that has just landed at our door!"

"Look, it's actually a buyers' market so I have plenty of clients who will be falling over themselves to sell you whatever you want. Unless you want to refurnish with art deco or something ghastly like that?"

"Oh no, Pierce would hate that! We want to try and replicate the original furnishings as much as possible."

"I'm so glad to hear it! Why don't we meet at the house tomorrow and we can take it from there?" suggested Constance.

"Yes, if you can?"

"I can! What I would love to see is any photos of the house before the fire. That would be really helpful in finding replicas."

"Yes, we have photos. What an excellent idea!"

"I'm so glad I met you! I just know we're going to be the best of friends!" said Constance.

"I do hope so – I could do with a friend here."

At that moment the door opened, and Pierce walked in.

"I've just taken a walk through the entire estate and Tadgh O'Meara's cattle are still all over my land grazing –" He stopped abruptly when he saw Constance there.

"Oh, Pierce, this is Constance Fitzgerald. She's our new neighbour," said Clara.

"Lord Armstrong, it's a pleasure to meet you. I've heard so much about you," said Constance, standing and smiling broadly.

"Have you? From whom?" asked Pierce suspiciously.

"Well, from my business dealings around the country at the Big Houses. I am an antiques dealer and so I know many of the landed gentry families."

"I am not sure how I would come up in conversation," said Pierce.

"Oh, you are too modest, Lord Armstrong!"

"Constance has offered to help furnish Armstrong House, Pierce," said Constance.

"Oh, I see. Well, we would have to check your references," said Pierce.

Seeing Constance look taken aback, Clara rushed in. "Constance is doing so as a friend and not charging a commission," she said, giving Pierce a warning eye.

Pierce nodded but said nothing, surveying Constance with cold dark eyes.

Constance suddenly looked very uncomfortable. "Well, I had better be off!" she said quickly. "We shall be in touch, Lady Armstrong?"

"Yes, well, as we decided, let us meet tomorrow at two o'clock at Armstrong House," said Clara, standing up to show her out.

"Wonderful!" said Constance. "Lord Armstrong." She nodded at him as she passed.

Pierce nodded in return.

After Clara showed Constance to the front door she returned to the parlour.

"You could have been a little more friendly, Pierce!" In fact, he had been extremely rude.

"Why should I bother?"

"Because she's going to be our new neighbour!"

"There is something about that woman that I don't like," mused Pierce.

"Oh, you don't like anybody, Pierce!"

"That is not true. Where is she living anyway?"

Clara felt herself go rigid. "Seymour Hall," she answered.

Pierce swung around to glare at her.

"She's nothing to do with Johnny Seymour if that's what you think! She and her husband are merely renting the house through an agent in Castlewest!"

"I wish you hadn't agreed for her to do the furnishing without consulting me," he said.

"There is no agreement in place! Obviously, we will be shown what she suggests, and it will be our option whether to buy it or not!"

"She'll probably charge us a fortune," cautioned Pierce.

"Well, it is I'll be paying for it, so don't worry too much about that!"

"I wondered how long it would take you to throw your money in my face!" said Pierce.

"What? I didn't mean it like that, Pierce!"

"Really? Well, how exactly did you mean it then? When I thought you had nothing I put you on the deeds of Armstrong House out of the love I have for you, but you now try to make me feel guilty that we are using your money to rebuild it!"

"I am not trying to make you feel guilty! It was I who insisted we use my grandmother's money for the house," Clara said, becoming upset.

"Well, just remember that in future before you mention your money to me again!"

He walked over to the window and stared out.

In the past this kind of behaviour from Pierce would upset Clara so greatly that it would cause a wide chasm to grow between them. Now she knew him better. This was him being defensive, born out of a deep insecurity he felt about her.

She walked over to him and, standing behind him, put her arms around his waist and rested her head on his back.

"I am deeply grateful that you have given me Armstrong House, Pierce, and it is my absolute pleasure and desire to be able to pay for its restoration. With all the problems we had in the past, money was never one of them. Please let it not now become an issue between us."

He turned to face her.

"I just get so agitated when I hear Johnny Seymour's name," he said. "It brings all the past back to me."

"But that's exactly it, Pierce. Johnny Seymour is in the past and we can't allow him to be a shadow over our future."

Pierce put his arms around Clara and held her tightly.

Chapter 19

Constance felt a ripple of excitement as she followed Clara up the front steps of Armstrong House and entered the hall. She was trying to contain her excitement at the thought that she was about to view an unknown work by Johnny Seymour.

There was the sound of much building activity, with men carrying planks of wood up the staircase while others plastered the hallway.

"Good day, Lady Armstrong," said a builder as he came down the stairs.

"Hello – how is the work going?" asked Clara.

"We're getting there!" said the man with a laugh as he passed the women and continued out the front door.

"It's looking magnificent!" said Constance as she looked around in awe.

"Do you think so?" said Clara, delighted to hear the praise.

"Just wonderful!" said Constance as she twirled around, admiring everything, before following Clara into the drawing room.

Work on the room had now been completed and the smell of the fresh plaster and paint filled Clara with joy as she remembered the previous offensive odours of fire and water that had lingered there. The room had been fitted with new Georgian windows and French windows leading to the terrace and was filled with light.

Despite the bareness of the room, Clara's mind could transport her back to the memories she had of it. She fingered the new, oak. carved fireplace that had been installed.

"So how this was this room furnished before the fire?" asked Constance, taking out her notepad and pen.

"We used to have a Regency-style couch with matching armchairs here," said Clara as she walked around the room. "With a small table in front of it. Over there beside the French windows was a writing bureau ... in the corner there was a card table ..." Clara's eyes became misty as she continued to explain the layout of the room and the furnishings it had contained.

They proceeded to go from room to room, with Constance taking as many notes as she could. Every part of the house seemed to be bursting with memories for Clara as Constance noticed she continually digressed from the job of solely creating a furniture itinerary to recalling stories from her time living there. No mention of Johnny Seymour though.

"This was my favourite room," announced Clara as they went into the small parlour on the other side of the hallway from the drawing room. "I always found it much cosier than the main drawing room. I'd sit here and write or read with the turf fire blazing in the hearth."

Constance decided to ask what would be, after all, a normnal – even necessary – question. "*Em*, I should have thought to ask ... were there any items or furniture that survived the fire put in storage before you finally left the house? For safe keeping, I mean – under lock and key upstairs, for instance?"

"No, no. Nothing at all. As you see, we are missing a lot of furniture even from rooms that were not damaged in the fire. I can only conclude they were stolen. After the fire, I understand there was some looting," sighed Clara.

"How awful! How can people take advantage of other people's misfortune like that?" Constance was filled with dread that Johnny Seymour's painting had also been taken and was now hanging in a peasant's cottage somewhere.

"There seems to be a lot of paintings here still, though," she commented.

"Yes, well, of all the things the locals might have been interested in robbing I doubt portraits of Pierce's ancestors were high on their list! I think they mainly took practical things like a table or chairs and of course all the silver and delph from the kitchen."

"Thank goodness they were more interested in delph than paintings!" said Constance. "Delph is replaceable but family heirlooms are not!"

As the tour of the house continued, Clara showed Constance into the ballroom.

"This ballroom used to be the venue of many wonderful balls in the past but by the time I came to live here it was seldom used. Finances dictated that the great balls of Armstrong House were consigned to the history books."

"But the Armstrong fortune must be still abundant? I mean, for you to be able to rebuild the house?"

"It's my money that is rebuilding the house, not Armstrong money," said Clara.

"Oh – I didn't realise that," said Constance, intrigued.

"Yes, my grandmother bequeathed me a large fortune and so I am lending the money to Pierce until he gets compensation from the government."

"That's very generous of you," said Constance.

"Well, it's my house too," said Clara.

As Constance walked around the ballroom, she remembered Peggy saying this was where Clara had sat for the portrait.

As Clara led her through the bedrooms upstairs, there was still no sign of the portrait. She depressingly realised the house was so large, with so many nooks and crannies, she could be there a full week searching on her own and still not find the hiding place. That's if the painting was still even in the house. She feared she might be on a wild goose chase and the painting was in fact destroyed in the fire or stolen.

As she looked at Clara, who was filled with nostalgia as she toured her former and future home, she knew the answer to the painting's resting place was with her but Constance couldn't reveal she even knew of its existence. It was hugely frustrating.

"Now I think this could be of great use to you!" said Clara as they entered a bedroom at the far side of the house and she picked up a box that appeared to be filled with photo albums. "These should be actual photos of the house from before the fire here."

She sat down on a chaise longue and Constance sat beside her.

The photos were of elegant garden parties or cocktail parties inside.

"Ah, here's a photograph of the drawing room!" exclaimed Clara excitedly, handing it to Constance.

Constance took the photo and examined it. The men were all wearing black tie and the women elegant dresses. From the fashion she guessed the photograph was taken before the Great War. Clara and Pierce were amongst the people and Constance thought they both looked distinctly unhappy.

"That was a party we held just before the men went off to fight in the Great War. Half of them never returned," sighed Clara.

"*Hmm*, a photo tells more than a thousand words, they say. But I can really see what the drawing room looked like from these photos and I'm sure I can make it look the same as before." Constance jotted down descriptions of the furniture she could see in the photos.

"I hope so," said Clara.

"What's this?" asked Constance, taking up a film reel from the bottom of the box.

"Oh that ... it's just a film that was taken here."

"A film! Inside the house?"

"Yes."

"But it would be wonderful if I could actually see film footage!" said Constance.

"I'd prefer if you didn't. This is from a time I'd really not like to be reminded of."

Constance sensed this was connected to Johnny Seymour and might be her opening to discuss the affair.

"But, Clara! This is a golden opportunity! If you want the house restored to exactly how it was then, this if the key! I can get a film projector and we can view it –"

"I didn't even know this film reel was still here. I would have got rid of it if I had known."

"But why?"

"I told you. It's from a time I don't want to remember."

"Clara, I've learned as antique dealer that you must never destroy anything! What is painful or uncomfortable to have now, you may crave in years to come."

"I won't. It's from a deeply unhappy time in my marriage," said Clara.

"I know what that feels like, Clara. But I've learned you can only have a future when you have really faced the past. Perhaps looking at the film reel would help you face your past, so you can then forget it."

Clara thought as she held the film roll. She remembered the night it had been taken by an American film director friend of Johnny Seymour's. Johnny was on that film ... suddenly she became intrigued at the thought of seeing him again. She had so many mixed feelings about Johnny. She had thought she'd been in love with him but had now convinced herself that had just been an illusion. She wondered if seeing him again on this film would answer her question or would she be opening a Pandora's box?

She handed Constance the film reel.

"Very well. But Pierce must never know I have this film or allowed you to have it."

"He won't, I promise! Wonderful! We can watch it at Seymour Hall once I get the projector," said Constance.

However terrifying it would feel to watch this film again, Clara thought, it felt appropriate to watch it in Johnny's old home. It was time to put both – the film and Johnny – to rest.

Clara was stunned by Constance's diligence and speed. After their initial meeting at Armstrong House, Constance practically took over the refurnishing. The woman seemed to have contacts in the antiques trade everywhere. She could sniff out the exact furniture that Clara had described or from studying the photographs she had loaned her. Clara was very grateful that such expertise had landed on her doorstep without her even having to go looking for it. She also found Constance very engaging company and they spent much time together. Constance called to Hunter's Farm regularly and whisked Clara off to visit an antique shop in Galway or an auction.

As the builders had completed the inside of the house, and with the painting work finished, the furniture began to arrive.

As Clara walked around the house she felt elated as all traces of the fire and neglect were vanquished and it felt like the home she loved again. She stood at the window in the drawing room looking out on the forecourt. Gardeners were fetching and carrying as they worked to bring the terraced gardens beyond the forecourt back to their former glory.

Seeing Constance's motorcar arrive, Clara turned to go out to meet her. Constance had arranged to take her to an auction that afternoon in a Big House some forty miles away. Constance had said the entire contents of the house were being sold and, as it was the same vintage as the original furnishings of Armstrong House, she was confident they would find many items of interest.

The truth was, refurnishing Armstrong House was turning into a very lucrative venture for Constance. It was rare that she was asked to source so many antiques for the one house. Although Constance was not charging

Clara a direct commission, she certainly made sure she was making a profit from the purchase of furniture for Armstrong House which she then sold on to Clara at a higher price. She had made so much money in the process that that alone had made her stay at Seymour Hall more than worth it. But however beneficial the transactions had proved, she did not lose sight of her main objective – to get the portrait of Clara. What she really needed was to gain access to the house when there was nobody there so she could make a thorough search of the property.

As they reached their destination that day, Clara immediately recognised the manor house the auction was taking place in. It was the home of the Bramwells, a family who had been part of Pierce's circle. The auction had attracted much interest and there were many people milling around the front of the house.

"Oh dear, it looks like we will have stiff competition today!" sighed Constance.

"Have you any idea why the owners are selling everything?" asked Clara, curious about the fate of the Bramwells.

"I believe they are moving to England," said Constance.

Clara's heart felt heavy at the news. It was sad to think of another family fleeing the country. The inside of the house was filled with people examining and viewing furniture and other items. As Constance inspected a glass cabinet, Clara spotted the owner of the house, Nell Bramwell, seated by herself in a Queen Ann chair in the front parlour. Clara immediately went to her to make her presence known.

"Nell! How are you?" Clara greeted her with a big smile.

Nell was portly woman in her sixties who Clara remembered as having the no-nonsense approach to life that she shared with many of the women of her generation and class.

"Lady Armstrong – is that you?" asked Nell, shocked to see her.

"I certainly is!" said Clara.

"It's certainly nice to see a familiar face amongst all these – vultures!" said Nell as she gestured to the visitors poring over her possessions. "Are you here for the auction?"

"Yes, I am looking to buy some furniture for Armstrong House," said Clara.

"I had heard you were back and rebuilding your house after the fire," said Nell, lifting a handkerchief to her eyes and dabbing away tears.

Clara's heart went out to her as she realised the auction was being done out of necessity rather than choice.

"Is it true you are moving to England?" asked Clara.

"Yes, what choice do I have? Since the Major died a couple of years ago I cannot stay here on my own anymore," said Nell. "I can't afford to have servants anymore and so this place is really too big for me on my own. Our land has been grabbed by the local peasantry and I just do not have the will to fight them any longer. Perhaps if our son … perhaps then there would have been a reason to try and stay here and brazen it out. I am just hoping to raise enough money today by selling everything, so I can provide for some kind of comfort in my new life in England."

"Is there anything I can do to help?" asked Clara.

"Perhaps just sit with me for a while and hold my hand," suggested Nell, gesturing to the empty chair beside her.

Clara did as she was bid and watched the whiteness of Nell's knuckles as she gripped her hand tightly.

"It's different for you," said Nell. "You and Lord Armstrong are still young enough to have children and give Armstrong House a future."

Just before the auction was to begin, Clara found Constance upstairs examining a four-poster bed.

"Constance, if I ask you do something for me, would you do it?" asked Clara.

"Of course!"

"I would like you to bid against me for those pieces at the auction to raise the proceeds for the seller. I know the owner and I do not wish to see her being taken advantage of."

"But you aren't taking advantage! She needs to sell and you want to buy at the cheapest price!"

"Not everything is that simple in life, Constance. Nell Bramwell has lost everything. I just want to help her start again."

"The only person who ever helped me was myself and that's all any of us can rely on in this life!" Constance regretted saying those words as soon as she had uttered them. She didn't want Clara to think her ruthless, so quickly said, "Sorry! That's not true and your kindness proves it isn't. And of course I will bid against you. It's totally understandable and commendable that you wish to help your friend."

"Thank you," said Clara.

As the bell sounded, indicating the auction was about to begin, the two women made their way downstairs.

Clara's act of benevolence only seemed to heighten the resentment which had begun to fester in Constance towards her. She didn't want to have this resentment but, try as she might, it would not go away.

When the day came for them to move back into Armstrong House, it felt surreal for Clara. As Fennell served her and Pierce a dinner cooked by Mrs. Fennell it was as if they had never left.

That night as she lay in bed with Pierce everything seemed exactly as it was, except for the sound of constant gunfire in the nearby woods around the lake.

Chapter 20

Seated in the drawing room, Clara studied the young woman she was interviewing for the position of housekeeper. Her name was Asty Horan and she had been sent to her by an agency in Dublin. It had been difficult to get staff to work at Armstrong House as there was still a reluctance by the locals to come and work there. Mrs. Fennell had managed to find some local girls to work in the kitchen and to be the parlour maids but they were hopelessly inexperienced, and Clara needed an excellent housekeeper to train the staff and make sure the house ran smoothly.

Asty was a pretty girl with abundant brown hair that had been tucked neatly into a bun.

"What age are you, Asty?" asked Clara.

"Twenty-nine, my lady."

"Your references are excellent. I see you worked in the Gresham Hotel for two years before you moved into service and your last position was with Lord and Lady Kilternan."

"That I did, my lady. A grand couple. They gave me no trouble," Asty said before quickly adding, "Nor I them."

"And I believe you are local? That you are originally from Castlewest?"

"Indeed I am, my lady. My family live in the town but I left after school to go make my own way in the world. But I always wanted to come home and be close to my parents."

"Well, this is a wonderful opportunity for you to do so," said Clara. "This is a large house, Asty, and most of the staff are inexperienced. Do you think you could handle it?"

"I can handle the job, my lady, don't you worry."

"Have you any reservations about coming to work at a Protestant 'Big House'? Not everyone wants to, in the present political climate."

"Sure, didn't I see Lord and Lady Kilternan through the War of Independence and the Civil War without a bother. I'd be there still if Lord Kilternan hadn't been killed. Imagine – he survived two wars only to be done in by a faulty floorboard at the top of the stairs!"

"Yes, I did hear Lord Kilternan had an unfortunate accident."

"Shocking, it was."

"*Em*, Asty is an unusual name," said Clara.

"My mother says we are descended from the Vikings and so my full name is Astrid. It means 'divinely beautiful'!"

"I see!" said Clara with a smile. "Your accommodation would be provided for you obviously. Your bedroom would be in the staff quarters in the attics. In your position you would be in charge of the house. The cook is Mrs. Fennell and her husband is the butler. They have been with the family for many years and are delightful. They are of an age and set in their ways but I wouldn't like them to feel they are being denigrated in any way by your arrival."

"I'm sure we'll get on like a house on fire!" said Asty.

Clara stiffened at the analogy but pushed the memory away.

"If you would like the positon I would like to offer it to you," she said.

"When can I start?"

"Oh, I am pleased. You can start straight away if that suits," said Clara.

At that moment Pierce walked into the room and looked surprised to see someone with Clara.

"Oh, Pierce, this is our new housekeeper, Asty Horan. Asty, this is Lord Armstrong," said Clara.

Asty went bright red on seeing Pierce and stood up.

"Pleased to make your acquaintance, Your Lordship, I'm sure," she said as she gave a little courtesy.

"Have you seen my riding crop, Clara?" said Pierce, ignoring Asty. "Those damned parlour maids keep moving everything!"

"I'm afraid I haven't," said Clara as she went and tugged the bell-pull. "Well, if there is nothing else, Asty, I'll have Fennell come to show you around the house and introduce you to the other staff. He will also show you to your room in the attic where the staff live."

"Very good, my lady," said Asty whose eyes followed Pierce around the room as he searched for his riding crop.

A minute later Fennell arrived and led Asty away.

"That girl looks impertinent," said Pierce once the door had closed and Asty was safely out of hearing distance.

"She's perfectly fine. Besides, she's the only one the agency could find who had the proper experience," said Clara. "I really had no choice but to hire her."

"Well, if she can put some manners on those parlour maids it would be a help!" said Pierce, finding his riding crop hidden behind a curtain.

Asty followed Fennell to the back of the hall and down the servants' staircase that led to the kitchen, where Mrs. Fennell was busy plucking a goose for that night's dinner.

"Mrs. Fennell, this is Asty our new housekeeper," said Fennell.

"I see!" said Mrs. Fennell. "You look familiar."

"I should do. I'm from Castlewest."

"So, you've come home now, have you?"

"Yes, I'm back amongst my own tinkers!" said Asty.

"Indeed!" said Mrs. Fennell, looking her up and down. "Well, you are very privileged to come work for a family like the Armstrongs. They are a very distinguished and respected family, and I hope you appreciate working for them."

"Not that respectable from what I heard," said Asty.

"What does that mean?" asked Mrs. Fennell.

"Wasn't Lady Armstrong riding some fella behind her husband's back when he was at the front?"

"I never heard such a thing! You shouldn't listen to idle gossip, young lady!" snapped Mrs. Fennell.

"When I have time, we can sit down and talk about your menus, Mrs. Fennell," said Asty, walking around and inspecting the kitchen.

"My *menus*! This isn't a restaurant, young lady! And I always discuss the food requirements with Lady Armstrong herself!"

"*Hmm*, well, things are going to change around here now I'm in charge! There's no need for you to come upstairs anymore. You can stay here in the kitchen where you belong." Asty took out a box of cigarettes and lit one.

"Filthy habit in a young lady! Put that out at once in my kitchen!" demanded Mrs. Fennell.

"You just concentrate on plucking your goose and keep out of my business, Mrs. Fennell. And that goes for you too, Mr. Fennell!" said Asty as she turned to walk back up the servants' stairs.

Later that week, Asty was in Pierce and Clara's bedroom with Síle, one of the parlour maids.

"You don't fold the blankets down that way – you fold them this way!" said Asty as she demonstrated, tutting.

"I'll never get the hang of this making beds the posh way!" said Síle.

"Oh, you will – if you just pay attention!" said Asty. "Where's Lord Armstrong gone today, do you know?"

"I heard Mr. Fennell saying he was gone off fishing with his friends."

"Nice for some! He's very handsome, isn't he?"

"I suppose so. I never really look at him. I try not to cross his path if I can. He kind of scares me."

"But that's what's so attractive about him," said Asty as she opened a window and lit a cigarette. "He's kind of mysterious and you just know from looking at him he could do something unexpected – even cruel if the notion took him."

"Lady Armstrong is so nice. I would never put the two of them together," said Síle.

"Oh, I would! I could see how she couldn't resist him," said Asty wistfully as she gazed out the window.

"I could easily resist him! He's the one thing I don't like about working here," said Síle.

"So, what do we do for fun around here? I suppose we have to trek in to Castlewest for a night in Cassidys?" said Asty.

"Yes, usually. Unless there's a dance in a house nearby. There's a dance at Tadgh O'Meara's this Saturday. I'm going if you want to join me?"

"Tadgh O'Meara? He has a younger brother called Hugh?"

"He does indeed. Do you know him?"

"Sure didn't I know Hugh growing up. We played many a game behind a gooseberry bush. Is he married yet?"

"No, he lives in a cottage the other side of the Armstrong Estate and works on his brother's farm."

"*Hmm*, I might just join you at that dance. It would be nice seeing Hugh again – like old times!"

"Now – is that bed made right?" asked Síle, stepping back to look at her work.

"It will do. You head off downstairs now and clean out the fireplace in the drawing room."

"Alright," said Síle, and left the room.

Asty walked around the room, taking it all in. She picked up one of Clara's perfume bottles from the dressing table and smelled it before placing it back. She then opened the door that led into the dressing room. She walked to Pierce's suits and began to feel the fabric, smelling the scent on the material at the same time.

Chapter 21

It was a beautiful spring day as Constance and Clara rode side by side along the shingled beach of the lake.

"As I look out across the lake on a day like today, I understand why I had to come back here," said Clara. "After the fire, I went to stay at my grandmother's in Kent. She died recently, and I miss her terribly. We were very close."

Clara had by now mentioned that her grandmother had been one of the Charter Chocolate family, and so Constance realised that Clara must be now very rich indeed. She couldn't understand it – if Clara had been left a fortune and could live anywhere in the world, why would she have chosen to come back here and in the middle of a Civil War?

"You really love it here, don't you?" said Constance.

"It's almost become a part of me. While I was in England, I felt there was a part of me missing, not being here."

"And Pierce was there with you?"

"No – he stayed in Ireland," said Clara quickly, her tone aimed to close down that line of conversation.

They rode on silently for a while.

"It must be nice to have attachment to a place like that. I've never felt such an attachment to anywhere – or anyone for that matter," said Constance.

"But you must feel – attached, for want of a better word – to your husband?" asked Clara curiously.

"Oh, of course I do! I adore Clement. When I met him first I thought he was the most intelligent, knowledgeable person in the whole world!"

"How did you meet him?"

"I was in Cairo at the time and met him there. I was quite young, and Clement is much older than me. I was very impressionable, and he was very impressive!"

"How much older is he?"

"He's thirty years older than me," said Constance.

"Oh!" said Clara, startled. "That is quite a lot older!"

"Not that it has ever been a problem for us, only for other people. He taught me everything I know, not just about antiques but everything in life. I remember, when we first got to know each other, he took such joy in teaching me. And I soaked up his knowledge. How we talked and talked! He was the teacher, and I was his student. We have so much in common but, as the years have gone by, I fear I may have surpassed him in my knowledge. Now he relies on my direction."

"But you do still love him?"

"I couldn't do without him, if that answers your question! We want the same things in life, but ... well, I don't think I've ever truly, fully, been in love with anybody," said Constance sadly. She had learned that the best way to gain a person's confidence was to expose her own vulnerabilities to them. She hoped this would be the case with Clara.

"Perhaps you are happier that way. Love can be overrated and often brings misery rather than happiness," sighed Clara.

"That's sounds like the voice of experience?"

"You asked me if Pierce came to England with me after the fire and I said he stayed in Ireland. The truth is, we were on the brink of divorce when I decided to give our marriage one last try."

"I'm sorry you've had problems," said Constance.

"I married Pierce because I was deeply in love with him, but we couldn't connect. When he was away at war I had an affair with Johnny

Seymour. I don't mind telling you this because it is common knowledge unfortunately."

"Johnny Seymour, the artist?" exclaimed Constance, feigning surprise. At last Clara was going to open up about him!

"Yes, the owner of your house."

"I nearly met him once at an exhibition in New York, but he didn't show up in the end. He never goes anywhere and it's impossible to find him!" said Constance.

"Then he has changed since I knew him. The Johnny I knew was impossible to lose!"

"He is such an enigma. What was he really like?"

"Johnny was unique. When he walked into a room, literally everyone turned to see him. He was funny and charming, hugely intelligent and full of life! But Johnny bored easily and lived life at the fastest speed he could."

"He's nothing like that anymore from what I know. Why did he change, I wonder?"

"I think he changed because of me," said Clara sadly. "I changed him. Or at least getting mixed up with me and my life and my marriage and all the horrible consequences changed him. As I told you, love often leads to misery."

"How did you meet him?" asked Constance, remaining cool on the outside but getting more excited as she was getting nearer to the subject of the portrait.

"He was part of the gentry set down here when I moved into Armstrong House. He was in the same circle as Pierce. I met him first at a garden party at the house and then my grandmother commissioned him to do a portrait of me ... which led to our affair."

"How very romantic!" said Constance.

"So it seemed to me at the time. I thought I was in love with him, and I thought he was in love with me. Perhaps we were for a short time. But it wasn't real. I deeply regret our relationship for what it did to Pierce, our marriage and to Johnny."

"And whatever happened to the portrait? Was it destroyed in the fire?" asked Constance, her heart thumping as she neared getting the answer to the question that burned inside her.

"No, it escaped. It might have been better if it had been destroyed. It's still in Armstrong House. I hid it when Pierce returned from the war so that he would never have to see it as a reminder of my affair."

"I hope it's safe with all the builders going in and out of the house?" said Constance.

"Oh, they won't find it where I hid it. Nobody will," said Clara.

After bidding goodbye to Clara, Constance rode back to Seymour Hall, delighted to have it confirmed that the portrait still existed and was hidden somewhere in Armstrong House. It would appear that nobody would even miss it if she managed to find it and remove it. But the feelings of excitement were mixed with another emotion that Constance could not quite fathom. She was filled with a dissatisfaction after hearing Clara describe her life and her affair with Johnny Seymour. It seemed to her that Clara had led such an exciting life. She had been deeply in love not once, but twice. Constance had spoken the truth when she told Clara she had never truly been in love, not even with her darling Clement. She wondered what it felt like. She felt an envy that Clara had a man as talented and renowned as Johnny Seymour fall in love with her. She wondered what powers Clara had that led Johnny to fall in love with her and to have left him broken when the relationship ended.

As she dismounted in the courtyard of Seymour Hall, she begrudgingly had to accept she was nothing like Clara. But she could see that Clara had been born with a silver spoon in her mouth and every advantage a woman could have. She had never had to use her wits to succeed in the world. Clara came from a different world and would never have been driven to do the things she had done to get ahead. Of course a woman like Clara had the luxury of being in love. Love was for women like Lady Clara Armstrong not Constance Fitzgerald.

Constance opened the front door of Seymour Hall and walked through the hallway and into the drawing room. She went to the window and looked out across the lake to Armstrong House in the distance. She imagined Johnny Seymour standing at this window pining for Clara as he looked at her house across the lake. She tried to fight the jealousy she was feeling but it was threatening to overwhelm her. What she wouldn't do to spend an hour in Johnny Seymour's company! Whereas Clara had had his heart.

That night Constance set up the projector in the drawing room and put the reel of film into it. After much twiddling, bright rays streamed from the lens across the room onto the screen she had erected.

She excitedly sat down in an armchair to watch. She immediately recognised the drawing room at Armstrong House. A large group of people were attending a party. They were drinking cocktails and dressed in fine dresses and suits and pulled funny faces at the camera as it circulated around them. Suddenly Clara came into view and Constance leaned forward as she recognised the man she was standing beside as Johnny Seymour. Clara and Johnny were being very tactile with each other and seemed to be in wonderful spirits. Clara suddenly started to dance around the room on her own, clearly playing up for the camera and pretending to put on a show. Constance gasped as she spotted the portrait of Clara hanging on the wall.

As Clara continued to dance, the door into the room suddenly opened and a man walked in and stood still, staring at the scene before him. It was Pierce Armstrong, and he was dressed in an officer's uniform.

Clara stopped dancing as she and everyone else in the room turned to look at Pierce before the film abruptly ended.

Oh my God, thought Constance, guessing it had captured the moment Pierce Armstrong had arrived back from the war. He had walked in unexpectedly to find Clara and Johnny together, hosting a party at his house.

But the film had captured the portrait of Clara which Constance could see was beautiful even from the black-and-white film. But it was Clara and Johnny that had mesmerized her the most. The two seemed so suited to each other, so comfortable in each other's company.

For the rest of the evening, Constance replayed the film continuously though she felt almost like an intruder watching the film, spying on somebody else's life and relationships.

The following day she gave the film back to Clara and lied to her, saying that the quality was so bad that nothing could be seen.

Chapter 22

The full moon lit up the faces of the twenty men who had gathered in the ruined abbey hidden amongst the trees, high in the woods around the lake. Hugh O'Meara knew he could trust each of them with his life. That was a unique thing to have in recent months as the Civil War swept the country. He had many friends he had fought alongside during the War of Independence that he had trusted with his life too. Now many of those friends were on the other side since the outbreak of the Civil War. As the new government's hold on the country was becoming stronger each day, Hugh knew they had to rely on each other even more if they were ever going to win.

As he leaned against the ivy-clad wall of the old abbey, he listened intently while his brother Tadgh addressed the meeting.

"The Free State Forces raided the house of Donnie Caroll this morning and arrested him. They are keeping him in the barracks in Castlewest and I hear they are giving him a terrible beating," he said to a chorus of furious shouts from the men.

"Keep it quiet, lads! The police are out every night!" warned Hugh.

"This government's idea of law and order is rounding up anybody who doesn't agree with them," said Tadgh, "and throwing them in prison without even a trial! We need to fight now like never before!"

The lookout suddenly came rushing into the abbey.

"*Enemy is approaching!*" he hissed, causing the men to scramble in different directions.

Suddenly shots rang out as the men ran for cover.

Hugh ran down the wooded hill and onto a narrow path that led down to the lake. He knew the area like the back of his hand. He didn't look back as gunfire and shouting shattered the still night. Once he reached the lakeshore he ran as fast as he could until he couldn't hear the commotion anymore.

A sudden loud noise jolted Constance from her sleep. She sat up in the main bedroom at Seymour Hall and looked around in the darkness. She reached for the oil lamp beside the bed and lit it before climbing out of bed and putting on a dressing gown. She stood listening but everything was silent.

Then she could hear movement downstairs.

Constance had a strong constitution, she did not scare easily, but now her heart raced fearing somebody had broken into the house. She felt very isolated with the nearest neighbour some distance down the road. She came out of the bedroom, gingerly walked down the landing and peered over the bannisters to the darkness downstairs. But she couldn't see or hear anything. There was now complete silence, and she hoped she had dreamt or imagined the noise. Or that whoever had caused it was gone. But she needed to go down and make sure the windows and doors were locked. She crept down the wooden staircase, holding the oil lamp aloft.

When she got to the bottom of the stairs a man's face suddenly appeared in front of her, ignited by the flame from her lamp and she screamed at the top of her voice.

"*Shut the fuck up!*" hissed the man as he leapt forward, clasped a hand over her mouth and swung his body around her back. He took the oil lamp from her hand and placed it on a table.

Constance stood as still as a statue as the man held her tightly in the dark, so tight she could feel his heartbeat thumping in his chest.

Eventually he spoke.

"If I let you go, do you promise not to make any sound?" he whispered into her ear.

She nodded quickly and suddenly she was free from him.

She backed over to the wall and flicked on the light switch.

"*Don't turn on the light!*" he shouted but it was too late and the room was suddenly engulfed in light.

She could see the intruder standing a couple of feet in front of her.

She didn't know why but she felt relief on seeing him. He looked to be in his early thirties and didn't look dangerous or threatening. He looked as nervous as she felt.

"Take whatever you want! Then please go!" she said.

"I'm not a fucking thief, you eejit!" he snapped. "Who else is in the house?"

"Nobody – I'm here alone."

"I thought this place has been empty for years?"

"It had been. I've just recently moved in."

"I wouldn't have come in if I knew," he said, going to the window beside the front door and looking out frantically.

Constance realised that if this wasn't a robbery the man must be somehow connected with the Civil War.

"If you don't want to steal something, can you just leave, please?" Constance said.

"That's exactly what I'm about to do! Goodnight, miss, sorry for disturbing you!" He walked past her, going towards the kitchen, but then swung around. "By the way, the latch on your kitchen window is broken. You'd want to get it fixed or otherwise anyone could get in!" he said cheekily.

"Thanks for letting me know!"

Suddenly the sound of a vehicle broke the silence of the night and men were shouting as lights shone through the windows of the house.

"Oh, they're here now! I'm fucked!" said the man frantically, pulling a small gun from inside his coat.

Constance panicked when she saw the gun. She realised he must be a Republican on the run and the men who had arrived outside were the Special Infantry Corps searching for him.

She went to the window and peeped out from behind the curtain.

"There's too many of them! You won't win!" she said as a dozen men jumped out the back of the lorry outside.

"Get away from that fucking window!" hissed the man, pointing the gun at her.

"Why – would you shoot me if I tried to run outside?"

She turned and peeped out the curtain again.

"They are going around the back now so you won't escape that way," she said.

She turned to look at the man who was still pointing the gun at her but looked more scared than combative. She knew she was in in real danger if this turned into a gun battle. But also she knew if this man was caught he would certainly end up dead. She had heard the Special Infantry Corps were executing Republicans without trial. She had heard stories of how they were being tortured before being killed.

"Quick – go upstairs and hide and I will deal with them," she urged.

"What?" he asked, shocked by her suggestion.

"I said I will get rid of them. Go upstairs!" She pushed him towards the stairs.

"You're a Republican?" he asked.

"Yes," she lied.

He stared into her eyes. "How do I know I can trust you?"

"You can't know! But you have no choice!" she said as there was suddenly a loud banging on the front door.

The man turned and fled up the stairs.

Constance pulled herself together and went to the front door.

"Who is it?" she demanded.

"*Open this door!*" came the order from the other side.

Constance unbolted the door and swung it open. She found three men standing there holding guns.

"What the hell is going on?" she demanded.

The officer in charge was surprised at the sight of a beautiful woman standing there in a satin nightgown.

"Sorry to disturb you. There was a Republican meeting nearby tonight and a number of them escaped in this direction."

"Oh, how frightening!" said Constance as she glanced around outside.

"Are you alone in the house?"

"Quite alone! My husband is in America on business."

"Have you seen anybody come in this direction?"

"No, it's been very quiet until you arrived!"

One of the other soldiers arrived back to the front of the house.

"We searched the stables out the back and nobody is there, sir," said the soldier.

"I do hope you catch them wherever they are," said Constance.

"Stay inside for the rest of the night, ma'am, and make sure all your doors and windows are secure," ordered the officer.

"I most certainly will but I won't get a wink of sleep now!"

"Don't worry, ma'am, we'll catch them. There will be a strong military presence in the area for the night."

"Thank you, that's very reassuring."

The men turned and got back into the lorry.

Constance closed the door and bolted it and looked from behind the curtain of the side window as the lorry drove away. She managed to breathe easily again.

She could hear footsteps on the stairs and saw Hugh coming down.

"Thank you," he said.

"I don't know about you, but I could do with a stiff drink after that!" said Constance as she walked into the drawing room.

He followed her and she handed him a full glass of whiskey.

"I suppose we should introduce ourselves – I'm Constance Fitzgerald," she said.

"I don't think it's necessary for you to know my name," he said, taking a gulp from the glass.

"Well – Mr. Whoever-you-are – you won't be able to leave for the night. Did you hear the man say they are all over the area searching for you and your comrades?"

"Yes, I heard them. I hope the others have been as lucky as me," he said.

There was suddenly a loud sound of gunfire in the distance, causing him to jump.

"I hope they were," said Constance. "Tell me why do you do it? Put yourself in such danger?"

"You're a Republican, you know why! To get rid of this government who sold us out to the British by allowing them to keep six of our counties and not getting full independence."

"Oh, I lied about that incidentally. I only said that so you would trust me and go with my plan. I am not a Republican. I'm not on the other side either. I don't believe in causes. Life is for living not dying for some cause."

Constance sat down on an armchair and took a drink from her tumbler.

"I see! Well, then I'm doubly grateful to you for saving my life – when you don't believe in the cause," he said, sitting down opposite her and holding his glass up to her in a salute.

"You're welcome!"

"So why did you save my life in that case?"

"Well, I don't have much of a conscience, but I didn't want your death on it all the same."

"And what would you have done if they insisted on searching the house and found me hiding upstairs?"

"I would have told them you threatened to shoot me if I didn't do as you said."

"And you think they would have believed you?"

"Of course they would. I can convince anybody of anything!"

"You're pretty sure of yourself," he said with a grin.

"Lucky for you that I am."

"What are you doing here anyway?"

"I'm renting. I'm here on business. I am in antiques."

"Very fancy!" he said.

"And what do you do when you're not a freedom fighter?"

"I don't think I should be telling you anything else about myself, do you?"

"Oh, you can tell me. I'm very trustworthy!"

"You could be a spy for the government drawing me in to find out about our network."

"May I remind you it was you who broke into my house, causing us to meet, not the other way round!"

"Alright – I'm a farmer," he said.

"Well, maybe stick to picking turnips in future rather than trying to overthrow the government. Far safer an occupation, I daresay."

"I like you!" he said, laughing.

"Good! Since we are destined to be in this house together for the night, we may as well enjoy each other's company. I really think you can trust me by now with your name."

"Hugh."

"And my second question to you, Hugh, is … do you have you a wife?"

Chapter 23

The next morning Constance came downstairs and found Hugh fast asleep on the couch under the blanket she had given him. She watched him sleep for a while. They had spoken for a couple of hours during the night until he could hardly keep his eyes open. She found him intriguing. There was something about him that reminded her of herself or at least who she had been before she had met Clement and adapted herself to his world. This man had a raw energy and intelligence, and she could imagine he could make a great success of his life if he could only direct himself like she had. As it was, he was being misdirected into a cause that had already been lost.

She gently nudged him awake and he jumped up with his fists raised.

"Calm down, handsome, it's only me," she said with a smirk.

He quickly went to the window and peeped out from behind the curtains, in time to see a lorry carrying infantry men drive by on the road at the end of the of the drive.

"The place will be still crawling will soldiers. I haven't a hope of getting home without them stopping me and asking questions. And they'll be visiting all the farms and get suspicious when they don't find me at work."

Constance thought for a while before speaking.

"I'll drive you home. You can crouch in the back of the car and we'll cover you with blankets."

"But what if they stop you and search the motorcar?"

"I thought you would have learned from last night that I can deal with any situation. Trust me."

Hugh stared at Constance with a mixture of amazement and awe. He had never met a woman like her before.

"Why are you doing all this for me?" he asked.

Constance did not have an answer to the question. It occurred to her that Clara had stirred something in her. A quest for excitement and bravery. It had seemed very exciting to her that Clara had harboured the rebel Thomas Geraghty at Armstrong House after the Easter Rising. Part of Constance wanted to know how that felt when the opportunity had unexpectedly come to her. Could she be as brave and perhaps as foolish as Clara and get away with it the same way she had? Perhaps it was a boredom with her own life and marriage that had stirred her into action when this stranger had barged into her life. And she also felt Hugh could be useful to her. He would be in her debt now and that was a situation Constance always liked having with people.

"It's as I told you last night – I wouldn't like to have your death on my conscience," she said.

With Hugh hidden under blankets in the back seat, Constance drove along the country roads. There was a strong military presence around and she tried to use back roads where she could avoid being stopped. As Hugh peeked from under the blanket, she followed his directions. She turned off the road and drove down a long boreen until she reached a whitewashed thatched cottage. Stepping out of the vehicle, she took in the beautiful view down the fields and across the lake to the wooded hills on the other side.

Hugh got out of the back.

"Home safe and sound!" Constance said. "Is this your land?"

"No, it's my brother Tadgh's farm. I work for him. He lives across the hill with his wife and children."

"Is Tadgh part of your cause as well?" she asked knowingly, not expecting him to answer.

"Will you come in for a cup of tea?" asked Hugh.

"No, I had better be on my way. I have a viewing of a Regency flower-stand on the other side of the county."

Hugh watched Constance drive up the boreen and turn into the road before going into his cottage. He lit a fire in the hearth, filled the kettle with water and hung it over the flames to boil.

Sitting down at the table, he looked out the window down the fields to the lake. He would shortly go to his brother's home to see had there been any casualties from the previous night. It didn't occur to him that Tadgh might have been killed. Like Hugh, Tadgh knew the woods like the back of his hand. But it had been a close call for them all. He owed his own life to this mysterious woman who had given him shelter for the night.

Despite the fear that he had felt all night, he had been fascinated by her. She seemed so sophisticated and clever, and he was baffled that she had spent so many hours talking to him and wanting to know about his life. He felt flattered that she had taken an interest in him. Her outlook on life was so different from that of anyone he had met before, and he wanted to know more about her.

When the kettle boiled he made himself tea and had a quick breakfast before setting off to his brother's house.

"Two men down! Mícheál and Diarmuid shot in the head at point-blank range as if they were animals! Fucking bastards!" cursed Tadgh as he spat into the fire.

Hugh was seated on the couch in the O'Meara's kitchen. He was filled with sadness at hearing of the killing of his friends as they had all grown up together.

"Poor Caitlín! She'll be broken-hearted after Diarmuid and how is she going to look after their six children on her own?" said Molly.

The front door of the cottage was closed but they could hear the children playing outside.

"Sure, all they were trying to do was make their escape across the lake in a boat when they were set upon by those bastards!" said Tadgh.

"How did you get away?" asked Hugh.

"I climbed a tree and stayed up there most of the night until the coast was clear. At one point there were two soldiers stopped under the tree to have a cigarette and me looking down on them! I could hardly allow myself to breathe! What about you?"

Hugh had decided not to tell anybody about how Constance covered for him. He didn't want to draw attention to her as Tadgh would not like having a witness alive who could identify him.

"Same as you, hid up a tree for the night," he said.

"So, what do we do next?" asked Molly.

"We will kill two of them as revenge. Though I'd like a good clear shot at that bastard Sergeant Cantwell in the town myself!" said Tadgh.

"See how his stuck-up wife likes being left a widow!" said Molly.

"But the county is crawling with troops. Whoever does the assassination will hardly get away alive," said Hugh.

"We'll plan it well. But it's too risky to meet in the hills anymore to arrange our plan. We'll have the next meeting here in the top room while the dance is on here on Saturday. Nobody will suspect we're holding a meeting with all the dancing and music going on."

Chapter 24

Present Day

Kate walked down the main staircase and, seeing the door to the drawing room open, walked in to find Nico kneeling on the floor with a series of plans laid out in front of him.

"How's your project going?" she asked.

"I'll never make this deadline for the client. He keeps asking for changes and is being very unreasonable!" said Nico, standing up.

"Poor you!" She walked to him and kissed him. "I'm going to Dublin for the day. I'll be back this evening."

"Do you have an audition?"

"No, I've made an appointment to visit the Office of Public Works. Professor Maguire told me that there is a list of all the compensation claims paid out to the owners of the Big Houses held there in the National Archives. If so, I want to see if there was compensation paid to your grandfather for the attack on the house in 1921 – which would explain how he paid for the rebuilding work after the first fire. And, perhaps, if the house was attacked and burned again during the Civil War then there might be a record of that as well."

"I see!" said Nico with that look of disapproval that she had grown to hate. "Nice to see you're using your time to our financial benefit!"

"Have you no interest at all in what happened here in the 1920s?"

"I'm more interested in our future and how we're going to pay for it!"

"Nico, you have been unsettled ever since Alex started pushing you to sell Armstrong House. I am quite happy to reopen Armstrong House again to the public – it is you who are set against the idea!"

"That is because I hate to have a continuous stream of strangers traipsing through our home! I don't like living somewhere that feels like a train station! Besides, after your sister's despicable theft, followed by the pandemic, it will take years to rebuild that business again."

Kate felt herself getting upset at the mention of what her sister Valerie had done to them. Several years previously Valerie had come to stay with them uninvited for a number of months. Then she had organised the theft of a lot of the valuable antiques in the house before she fled to Brazil. Kate had never been close to her sister, but the act of betrayal had hit her hard. It had taken them years to finance the purchase of replacement antiques and furniture which had also disrupted the tours they regularly hosted at the house. By the time the house had been fully refurnished, and they were about to reopen to the public, the pandemic hit and the plans were put on hold. One thing Kate always loved about Nico was that he never brought what Valerie did to them up and the fact he did it now showed how much Alex had rattled him.

"Thank you for the reminder," whispered Kate.

"You enjoy your day at the Office of Public works while I try to finish this project," said Nico sarcastically as he knelt down and started to study the plans again.

Kate quickly turned and left the house.

The archivist Kate met at the Office of Public Works was an enthusiastic young woman named Deirdre. As she led Kate to the Reading Room, she explained the process of compensation that was paid out for the burning of the Big Houses during the 1920s.

"The Damage to Property Act was passed by the Irish government on the 20th of March 1923 and compensation could be claimed by the owners of houses that were damaged during the War of Independence and the following Civil War. The period of time covered for compensation was from July 11th 1921 to March 20th 1923 when the Civil War was drawing to a close."

"And there was compensation filed for Armstrong House under this Act?" asked Kate as they found a free desk and sat down.

"Yes," said Deirdre, opening a file she was carrying and handing Kate a document. "Lord Pierce Armstrong filed for compensation on July 11th 1923, for the burning of his house. It was for a sum of £20,000 – a huge sum in those days. The compensation claim was filed through Pierce's solicitors, a firm named Conways in Castlewest, County Mayo."

Kate studied the document. "The compensation claim states the house was attacked in January 1922 – attacked by a group of masked rebels who set the house on fire, causing extensive damage."

"Which entitled Lord Armstrong to the compensation he claimed, as it was in the time frame covered. There are eyewitness reports from the local constabulary confirming the attack and that Lady Clara Armstrong was the only one present in the house when the act of arson occurred. The claim was accepted and the compensation was paid to Lord Pierce on March 12th, 1924."

"But that makes no sense," said Kate. "I have a photograph of a ball being held at Armstrong House in 1923 and, if the compensation wasn't paid until the following year, how was the house rebuilt the previous year in order for it to be held there?"

"I see the problem," said Deirdre.

"Have you any records of the house being rebuilt?" asked Kate.

"No. There is only a record of the compensation being paid by bank draft to Lord Pierce. It lists his address as Monkstown in Dublin at that time."

"I believe Armstrong House must have suffered a second fire after it was rebuilt. Is there any record of a second compensation claim for the house?" asked Kate.

"No. But if the second fire occurred after March 20th 1923, then it would not have been liable for compensation under this Act. That's really all the information I have to offer."

"Thank you – you have been very helpful," said Kate.

After Deirdre left her alone with the file, Kate spent some time poring over it. It left her even more perplexed. She would have suspected that the 1923 photograph was fake or forged but the fact the fire damage in the photos from 1921 were in a different part of the house from when it stood derelict for decades persuaded her it was not, and Armstrong House had another chapter in its history that had been long forgotten.

In the dining room at Armstrong House, Kate grilled Nico to see if he could shed any more light on his family history.

"But your mother must have known something about her father's life before he married her mother," pressed Kate.

"You know the story," Nico said impatiently. "My mother Jacqueline never really knew her father Pierce. He died when she was still a toddler. Pierce married his second wife, my grandmother, in 1938 and there was a big age difference between them. They were only married three or four years before he was killed in the Second World War. As there was no male heir the title became extinct and my mother inherited Armstrong House or what was left of it and the twelve acres that was left of the land which I then inherited. My mother was always proud of her Armstrong heritage. Even after she married my father she referred to herself as Jacqueline Armstrong Collins."

"But was Pierce's first wife Clara ever mentioned?" pushed Kate.

"Hardly ever. It was like she was airbrushed out of history. All that was ever said about her was that she had been a bitch who cheated on my grandfather with the artist Johnny Seymour when he was fighting in the First World War."

"But clearly the affair was not the cause of the marriage ending. The First World War ended in 1918, and Clara was still living at Armstrong House when it burned down in 1921, long after Pierce had returned home to her. And there is now this photograph of the Hunt Ball in 1923 showing them still together here at Armstrong House!"

"Does any of this really matter at this point, Kate?"

"It does to me," said Kate.

"You've always had a fixation on Clara. Even years ago when you went off to track her relatives down in England."

"I'm beginning to think her relatives didn't tell me the full truth at that time for whatever reason. They told me Clara returned to England after the fire, a broken woman from her failed marriage, and went to live as a recluse in her grandmother's house in Kent for the rest of her life. Now I find out she was hosting a ball in Armstrong House two years later! I've arranged to meet the Master of the Castlewest Hunt tomorrow to see if he can help. I'm hoping he might have some information about the 1923 Hunt Ball to confirm the photograph is valid."

Kate was telling her son Cian what she had discovered about Clara as she drove him to school in Castlewest. As they drove through Armstrong village, which had once been the epicentre of the vast Armstrong Estate but was now mostly holiday homes, she detected that she didn't have his full attention. Ever since Alex had expressed zero interest in Armstrong House and was pushing to sell it, Kate had tried to foster a curiosity in Cian about his lineage.

"Do you ever think about your family's past?" she asked.

"Not as much as you," he retorted with a laugh.

"Don't you think it's fascinating that your ancestor Lord Edward built this village for the workers on his estate in the nineteenth century?"

"I guess I'd like to have his money!" said Cian.

"You should be very proud that you're descended from such a distinguished family," said Kate.

"We're doing the Great Famine at school now and I don't think there's much to be proud of coming from one of those landlord families that caused so many deaths by evicting starving tenants who couldn't pay their rent!"

"Well, that is true, Cian, but Lord Edward was not one of those cruel landlords. He was known as one of the good landlords who protected his tenants during those terrible times."

"But his son Lord Charles was a bad one, wasn't he? He got shot by one of the tenant farmers for being so cruel, didn't he?"

Kate was a little flabbergasted at this and didn't know what to say.

"Well – yes, that is unfortunately true from what we know," she conceded.

"I feel embarrassed when we're doing Irish history at school. I don't really like to think about being from one of those families who hurt so many people. I prefer to think of the other side of my family – your side who were just normal people living in Castlewest. Why don't you look into your own family's history instead? I'd say they were much kinder people."

"I don't think there is much interesting in my family's past," said Kate.

Which Kate believed was true. Her family were originally from Castlewest before they had emigrated to New York in the eighties. But, even as a child growing up in Castlewest, she had often come out to play at the abandoned Armstrong House and been fascinated with the place. She knew the house was owned by the descendants of the Armstrongs who rarely came near the place. Even as a child she had pictured who had lived there in the past and fantasised about their lives. She had never guessed that one day she would come back to live there and she felt honoured to be the custodian of the house now.

As she glanced at Cian, who was now on his phone, her heart felt heavy that her love for Armstrong House did not seem to be shared by the next generation.

Chapter 25

1923

Clara had driven to Castlewest to do some shopping. It was a Fair Day, and the main street was full of people, stalls and livestock. As she walked down the street, she stopped occasionally at a stall to inspect what they were selling.

"Fresh salmon caught in the river this morning, Lady Armstrong," said the man behind a fish stall as she smiled at him and walked by.

She had stopped at another stall that was selling flowers when she spotted a familiar figure over at a cattle pen, haggling over the price. It was Tadgh O'Meara and, as she observed him, he appeared to be buying a large number of calves. She remembered his wife's Molly promise that the next time there was a fair in the town they would bring Pierce in and assist him in buying livestock to replenish the farm at Armstrong House.

As she watched Tadgh conclude his deal, she realised it had been a false promise.

"They had no intention of assisting us with the purchase of livestock at the next fair or any fair," said Clara as she told Pierce that evening of what she had witnessed that day.

"And he has no intention of getting off my land!" said Pierce.

"So, what can we do? He can't stay on it forever."

"That's his plan unless we forcibly remove him," said Pierce. "I will call to Conway tomorrow and we will start legal proceedings against O'Meara."

"Oh, Pierce, we can't do that! You heard Conway say it would provoke him terribly. Your father was shot at the gates of Armstrong House by one of those farmers he got on the wrong side of. I don't want the same thing happening to you!"

"What else can I do?" asked Pierce in exasperation.

"We're just managing to settle back here – it's hard enough without starting another war with the locals! As I said, they shot your father, they burned down the house previously – if we are heavy-handed with O'Meara I really do fear what they will do next!"

"I'll bring back Prudence. She'll sort them out!" said Pierce.

Clara went cold at thought of Prudence coming back. "Prudence will certainly cause a war with the locals if she returns here! That's the worst thing you could do! I'll visit the O'Mearas and firmly request they leave the land."

"*You!*" guffawed Pierce.

Pierce rarely laughed, but when he did it was usually when he was being derisive.

"I don't see what is so funny about that," said Clara, becoming angry.

"Clara – these are tough people. They will just laugh at you!"

"Believe it or not, I can be tough too, Pierce. After all, it is I who stayed at Armstrong House to face the rebels while you fled to Dublin."

Pierce's smile disappeared. "As we all know, the reason you stayed was not to face the rebels but in the hope Johnny Seymour would come back to you. Which he never did, of course."

Pierce turned and strode from the room.

Constance was sitting at the desk in the parlour writing letters to her clients, informing them of the purchases she made at the latest auction, when she suddenly heard the sound of loud banging from the back of the house. She had stood up and walked down the hallway and into the kitchen where to her surprise she saw Hugh with a hammer in his hand.

"What are you doing back here?" she asked in surprise.

"What does it look like? Fixing that latch I told you was broken on the window!" he said, grinning.

"Well, I wasn't expecting that! I was just about to call the agent to send someone over to fix it."

"Well, I've saved you the bother and him the trouble," he said.

"Very conscientious of you!" said Constance. "There's a few other jobs that could be done around here if you're in the mood to do them!"

"It would be my pleasure," Hugh said with a wink.

"I'll write you a list in that case," she said, turning and going back to the drawing room.

As Constance watched Hugh cutting the hedges in the garden through a window, she was amused by his efforts to impress her. As the afternoon drew into the evening, he was still working and Constance imagined Seymour Hall had not looked so well for quite a long time.

There was a knock on the door and Constance went to answer it, to find Hugh standing there.

"Well, at least you knocked this time!" she said.

"I usually only come through kitchen windows in emergencies."

"Glad to hear it!"

"If there's nothing else, I'll be off home."

"I feel guilty about all the work you did for me today. After all, I only saved your life – there really was no need," she said.

"Do you enjoy teasing me or are you like this with everybody?"

"I think I like teasing you. I'm cooking dinner. If you have no plans perhaps you would like to join me?"

He looked surprised at her suggestion.

"Oh, please don't be coy – you're embarrassing me," she said, pretending to look demure.

"Well, I am fairly hungry and that smells good, whatever it is," he said.

"It's Channel No. 5 – oh sorry, I thought you meant me not the cooking! It's roast beef – now how could you say no to that?"

"Indeed I couldn't!" he said as he walked past her into the hallway.

Hugh looked around the dining room at Seymour Hall. He had been seated at the head of the table with Constance sitting opposite him. He looked down at the roast beef dinner in front of him and the glass of red wine beside it.

"Do you like claret?" asked Constance.

"I'm not sure that I do. I wouldn't drink much wine. Guinness is more my thing," he said, raising the glass and taking a sip.

"Well?" asked Constance.

"Very agreeable!"

"*Bon appetit!*"

"I've never eaten in such a fancy place before," said Hugh as he lifted his knife and fork and began to cut the beef. "I'm just wondering what I'm doing here."

"You know what you're doing here. You broke in and now we're old friends," she said.

"You must make friends quickly," he said.

"That I do! I couldn't be in my business if I didn't. People have to trust you when you are buying and selling them antiques and that means making friends quickly."

"I would love to be like you. In control of your own life and able to do anything you want to."

"Nothing is stopping you. You seem bright and clever. The only thing holding you back is yourself and the people around you," said Constance.

"Sure, there aren't any opportunities around here for somebody like me."

"There are opportunities for everybody if you know how to take them. The first thing you need to do is abandon this political cause and start thinking of yourself."

"My friends have died for that cause," said Hugh.

"More fool them! You could easily have been one of those men who were shot the night you escaped."

"I have been wondering lately what are we doing this for? What are we even fighting for anymore? The Civil War will be over soon and is it worth having anyone else killed for a lost cause?"

"I told you that you were clever," said Constance.

"And you really got me thinking when I was here that other night. About life and what I want out of it."

"I'm an inspiration!" she said with a laugh.

"Well, you've inspired me. I've never met anybody like you."

"That's because you've lived all your life in this backwater!" said Constance.

"I am thinking of breaking away from the cause, but my brother will go mad if I do. He'll never forgive me and, as I work for him, I'm very dependent on him."

"If your brother is putting you in harm's way then he hasn't got your best interests at heart. Perhaps it's time you stood up to him?"

"You don't know my brother," said Hugh.

"And I don't want to know him either by the sound of him."

"He's not that bad. He just believes in what he believes in and he is very loyal."

After dinner, they had drinks in the drawing room.

"When is your husband arriving back from America?" asked Hugh.

"I'm not sure. He is only supposed to be gone for six weeks but one never can tell with Clement."

"Are you not lonely without him?"

"Not overly! I'm used to him travelling and then I travel a lot myself."

"If you were my wife, I wouldn't leave you alone for a day," he said.

"Would you not indeed?"

"Not a minute, in fact."

"That could be somewhat impractical, but I'll take it as a compliment," she said.

"He must be an odd sort of man to leave his wife for so long," said Hugh.

"You've never been married, Hugh. What seems odd can suddenly seem normal once you get married – desirous even!"

Hugh looked at the clock and suddenly stood up.

"It's after midnight. I'd better be going home," he said.

"You can stay the night if you want. On the couch like last time."

"Wouldn't be right. People might talk."

"Who would know? There're no neighbours near here. And it isn't as if you haven't stayed the night here before."

"That was different. That was out of necessity, not choice."

"It might be nice if you stayed out of choice in that case," she suggested, standing up.

"Am I ... am I missing something here? Or reading something that isn't there?" he asked.

"Oh, I think we both know what has been happening since that first dramatic moment we met," she said, walking towards him.

"I can hardly believe that you would be interested in somebody like me," he said.

"I'm sure you are well used to female attention, Hugh. Don't get too excited, I'm not looking for anything important – just a nice way to pass the time."

Hugh stared into her eyes before he pulled her close and started kissing her.

Light was shining through the curtains as Constance held Hugh in her arms in her bed.

"Well, that was unexpected," he said.

"Not so unexpected. I think that's why you came back yesterday to fix my window and cut my hedges."

"I wanted to see you again but never imagined it would lead to this."

"I think I've surprised myself by it, I must admit."

Constance really was surprised by her actions. It wasn't that she had always remained loyal to Clement in the past, but she did not make a habit of having such adventures. There had been the art dealer in Paris that she got to know and ended up spending a weekend with. There was the restorer in Rome whom she had a dalliance with while furnishing a palazzo. She always made sure the liaisons were far from home and not connected to anyone in their circle. In a way, this made Hugh safe as well. Nobody in their circle would ever know him or certainly never believe it if they heard about their relationship. He was a different class, a different breed. And yet he was not that different from who she used to be before she met Clement. Like the previous two times she had cheated on Clement, she felt the initial terrible guilt. It would pass, she knew it would. In fact, she was always surprised at how quickly those guilty feelings had left her in the past. It wasn't that she was cold, but she prided herself on being practical. Life was full of transactions, and this was just another one of them. Perhaps Hugh was a desperate attempt to distract her from the emptiness she felt.

Chapter 26

As Asty and Síle walked down the drive to the O'Mearas' cottage, they could already hear the loud Irish music, indicating the dance had already begun. Asty was looking forward to enjoying a night of music and fun. She was also interested in seeing Hugh O'Meara again. It was several years since she had seen him, and she was intrigued to find out how he had turned out.

When they reached the door of the cottage, Síle opened it and Asty followed her in. The room was full of people drinking, talking and laughing. There was lively Irish music being provided by two men by the roaring fire, one playing the accordion and the other a fiddle.

On seeing bottles of poteen on the table, Asty went over and poured two glasses.

"Oh, my mammy says I'm not to touch that stuff!" objected Síle when Asty tried to hand her one of the glasses.

"Oh, your mammy will never know!" snapped Asty as she forced the glass into Síle's hand.

Asty surveyed the crowd and spotted Hugh O'Meara in the corner, laughing and joking with a group of men. She observed him as she drank her poteen.

"Isn't the music great?" said Síle, taking a sip of her drink and pulling a disgusted face.

"*Hmm*," said Asty, but her eyes didn't leave Hugh.

"I guess the men here must seem very boring compared to the men you've met on your travels," said Síle.

"I could have done without meeting some of those men! Fighting off advances from the customers in the hotels or my last employer, Lord Kilternan. Now if it was Lord Armstrong, I wouldn't mind fighting off an advance from him one little bit!"

"You're a sinful girl, Asty!" giggled Sile.

"So what if I am? Do you want to know what happens to nice girls, Síle?"

"I don't know – what?"

"Nothing!" said Asty, finishing her drink and placing the empty glass on the table. "I'll see you later!"

Asty moved quickly across the floor to Hugh and tapped him on the shoulder.

Hugh turned around and looked puzzled for a few moments until he recognised her.

"Asty Horan! And what rock did you climb out from under?"

"One that you couldn't afford, I'm sure!" said Asty.

"How long has it been?"

"Too long!"

"And what's brought you back here?" he asked curiously.

"I'm now the head housekeeper up at Armstrong House," she said proudly.

"Oh! Congratulations – although I wouldn't say that too loudly around here. My brother isn't too fond of them up at the Big House."

"That's his problem not mine!"

"I see you are still as brazen as I remember you," he said with a smirk.

"Even more so now, Hugh!" she assured him.

The crowd lined around the walls of the room as the dancing started.

"Are you still a good dancer?" Asty asked.

"There's only one way to find out," he said as he took her hand and led her out on the floor.

Asty's heart palpitated as Hugh swung her around to the music.

"Don't you dare let me go or I'll end up in that fucking fire!" she shouted at him over the music as he twirled her near the fireplace.

"Don't worry, you're in safe hands. It's just like old times!" he said as he pulled her in close to him.

Hugh opened the front door of the cottage and stepped outside. He took a deep breath then walked to the end of the building and stood looking at the full moon that was weaving its reflection across the lake. It was nearly midnight, and he knew Tadgh would be having the meeting in the top bedroom soon. He was bracing himself for what was to come. He had been having doubts about continuing fighting, but meeting Constance had left him in no doubt that he didn't want anything more to do with it.

He had been unable to get Constance out of his mind. He knew there could never be a future between them and so he had not allowed himself to think about what his feelings were for her. But even though they had known each other for such a short time she had profoundly affected him and changed him. Even though her arrogance did not allow her to think she was ever in any danger, he knew she had actually risked her life by saving him from the police. And then talking to her that night and hearing her views on life and the world had opened his eyes. It made him see how narrow his mind-set had been. And why would it not when his life training was owed to sermons once a week at Mass where he was told everything was a sin. Or to his family who conveniently forgot those sermons in their single-minded pursuit of their political and personal goals. Constance had made him realise that up to this point he had just followed orders and never really did or thought about what was best for him. Constance had shown him that doing something for yourself was not a sin. He had been flattered that she had taken an interest in him. He would never forget the night he had spent with her. He wished he could see her again but knew it was not possible.

The door to the cottage opened and Asty stepped out, closing it behind her. Seeing Hugh standing at the gable of the house, she walked over to him.

"What has you out here? You're missing all the fun," she said.

"Just taking in the air," he said, turning to face her.

"I thought you might be trying to escape me."

"And why would I want to do that?"

"Maybe I was stepping on your toes while we danced."

He studied her face. "I'm surprised you aren't married yet. I'm sure you must be fighting them off."

"Maybe I was saving myself for you," she said with a wink.

"For me? Are you mad?" he said, laughing. "Sure, we forgot about each other years ago!"

"Maybe I did and maybe I didn't," she said.

"There was nothing ever serious between us anyway."

She moved closer to him and looked up into his eyes.

"Maybe we never gave it a proper chance to get serious," she said.

He stared at her and then shook his head in bewilderment and laughed.

"What's so funny?" she asked.

"Nothing you'd understand. But all of a sudden I seem to be much in demand!"

They leaned towards each other and began to kiss passionately.

Then, as they heard the door open, they quickly pulled away from each other.

"*Hugh!*" came the loud voice of Molly. "*Tadgh wants you!*"

Hugh looked down at Asty.

"*I'm coming, Molly!*" he called.

Asty watched as Hugh sauntered away from her and back into the house.

Hugh sat in the corner of the top bedroom, looking at the group of enraged men plot a bloody revenge for the killing of their comrades Mícheál and Diarmuid. He could hear the music and laughter from the party which was in full swing, and he wished he was there. He looked at the washbowl resting on top of the mahogany dresser that Tadgh had taken from Armstrong House. All the furniture in the bedroom, from the double bed to the chairs, had been stolen from the Armstrongs. Hugh had not thought it was wrong when Tadgh had gone into the Big House after the fire to take them. Tadgh had said he was claiming the furniture as opposed to stealing it and the Armstrongs would never be coming back so they wouldn't miss it anyway. It was only when Hugh had seen Lady Armstrong driving around since she and her husband arrived back that he felt any guilt about it. He remembered Lady Armstrong from when she lived in the house before and she had always behaved nicely, always making sure to be polite.

"The problem is if we shoot two of their men in retaliation, how do we escape? There's so many soldiers in the area that we'd never get away alive," said Tommy Gilsenan.

"I know that," said Tadgh. "And that's why I think we should leave a bomb for them."

"A bomb!" exclaimed Hugh.

"That's right – a bomb! I've been in contact with our unit in Cork and they assure me that they can provide us with a bomb. We'll place it under Abbeydale Bridge and detonate it when the lorry is carrying them back to barracks. As we'll be some distance away we can make our escape and they'll be all dead and so can't come chasing us!"

"You're talking about killing a dozen at the same time!" said Hugh incredulously.

"They might think twice about shooting two of our men in the head next time then," said Tadgh.

"But that won't stop them! It will escalate the violence not frighten them off!" said Hugh. "They'll throw everything at us and won't stop till they track us all down and execute us!"

"They won't find us. We're faster and cleverer than them," said Tadgh.

"This is insane, Tadgh. What's the point? It's all going to be over soon," said Hugh.

"What are you talking about?" demanded Tadgh.

"The Civil War is lost, Tadgh, we just haven't admitted it! They are in control of nearly the whole country. All we're doing is prolonging the agony and needless killing!"

"I can't believe you're talking such defeatist talk!" said Tadgh.

"Or even traitorous!" added Tommy.

"I'm just trying to get you all to see sense! It's over, lads! The fight is over or at least it will be very soon," said Hugh.

Tadgh's face was contorted with anger as he approached his brother.

"Or maybe Tommy is right, and you are a traitor? Are you jumping to the other side?"

"I'm not jumping to any side! I just not getting involved in this anymore. Life is for living not dying for a lost cause."

"I'm ashamed of you!" spat Tadgh. "There's no point in you being part of this meeting if you aren't one of us anymore."

"I won't, so! Good luck!" said Hugh as he stood up abruptly and marched out of the room.

He walked quickly through the next bedroom and then down into the kitchen and past the dancers to the front door.

Asty who was seated beside Síle saw Hugh storm out and stood up quickly.

"Where are you going?" demanded Síle.

"I'm off to see if Hugh is alright! I'll see you tomorrow at breakfast!"

"But you can't leave me here! I don't want to walk back to Armstrong House at night on my own!"

"Ah, it's a full moon, you'll be fine! Besides, I can't see any fella being that interested in bothering you!"

Asty dashed across to the front door and into the night air.

She was just in time to see Hugh reach the top of the drive and turn onto the road.

"*Hugh! Hugh!*" she called as she raced towards him.

"What do you want?" he demanded.

"You looked upset rushing out like that. I just wanted to make sure you are alright?"

"I'm fine! Go back to the dance!"

"No, I won't if you don't mind. I'll walk along with you for a while instead on my way back to Armstrong House." She pulled her shawl around her shoulders and smiled at him.

When they reached the top of the boreen to Hugh's cottage, he stopped and turned to her.

"Will I walk you back the rest of the way to Armstrong House?" he offered.

"No, I was hoping you'd invite me in for a cup of tea instead," she said.

"Will they not miss you up at Armstrong House?"

"I have my own key and come and go as I please. So how about that cup of tea? Or something stronger if you have it."

Hugh thought of Constance and the freedom with which she lived her life. Asty could not be more different from Constance. But as he looked at her, he knew she was his equal. Constance had been no more than a strange, exhilarating excursion.

He offered her his arm and she took it, and they began to walk down the boreen.

"Not that anything will be happening between us tonight, mind you! I'm a good girl," said Asty.

"You must have changed since we used to meet behind those gooseberry bushes in that case," he said with a laugh.

Chapter 27

The servants were just finishing their morning break in the kitchen. There was a sombre mood as they had received news that a bomb had been detonated under Abbeydale Bridge the previous evening that had killed four soldiers.

"Those poor young lads!" tutted Mrs. Fennel as she began to prepare tea for Pierce.

Asty ignored the talk as she read the newspaper at the top of the table and smoked a cigarette.

"Shocking behaviour! Will the violence never stop?" sighed Mr. Fennell as he put on his coattails and got ready to go to work again.

"There will be floods of tears from their mothers," said Mrs. Fennell, wiping a tear from her own eyes.

"Síle, make sure you have Lord Armstrong's shirts ironed perfectly this morning," said Asty, putting out her cigarette and standing up.

"I will, of course," said Síle.

"And, Julie, I found dust on the mirrors in the ballroom this morning," said Asty.

"I must have missed a spot when I was cleaning yesterday," said Julie.

"More than a spot! Go back and do the job again and do it properly this time!"

The bell rang on the wall.

"That will be Lord Armstrong now looking for his tea," said Mrs. Fennell as she quickly wet the tea in a silver teapot and added it to the tray she had already prepared.

Mr. Fennell walked over to take the tray.

"I'll take the tea to Lord Armstrong this morning," said Asty.

"But Mr. Fennell always takes His Lordship his tea!" objected Mrs. Fennell.

"Well, I'm saving him a job this morning!" said Asty as she walked out of the kitchen, carrying the tray, and up the servants' stairs.

When she reached the hall, she put the tray down on a sideboard and checked her appearance in the mirror over it before knocking on the library door.

"*Come in!*" called Pierce.

Asty opened the door and then lifted up the tray and entered.

She saw Pierce at his desk, looking through paperwork.

"Your tea, sir," said Asty as she approached the desk.

Pierce barely looked up at her as he continued with his work.

"Will I pour the tea for you, sir?"

"Very well," said Pierce.

Asty picked up the teapot and poured the tea into the cup.

"Will there be anything else, sir?"

"No, you can go," said Pierce.

"I've told Síle to iron all your shirts today as a priority, sir."

Pierce looked up at her and nodded.

Asty felt herself go red.

"If you need anything – anything at all, I'd only be too willing to oblige," she said with a smile.

Clara walked into the room, holding a card.

"Pierce, we've been invited to a tennis party at the Foxes'. Good morning, Asty."

"Good morning, my lady. I was just bringing His Lordship his tea. If there is nothing else, I'll get on with my work."

And she made a hasty retreat from the library.

"Asty is so efficient, she is even doing Fennell's job now," said Clara.

"There is something peculiar about that girl," commented Pierce as he examined his tea before taking a drink.

"Well, I find her to be a treasure. The house is working like clockwork since she arrived. Síle is even making the beds perfectly now!"

Pierce said nothing as he continued looking through his paperwork.

As Clara observed him she thought there was no comparison now between him and the broken man he had been after his suicide attempt. He had regained his position in life and his pride. Pierce's self-worth and position in life was defined by being Lord of Armstrong House. She had seen how without it he quickly crumbled and became nothing. Now they just needed to get the estate up and running again for things to be back as they used to be.

As she looked out the window she saw O'Meara's cattle still on their land. Pierce had been dismissive of her idea of calling to Tadgh O'Meara and asking him to remove his livestock, but she felt it was the only option they had at this point. She was sure if she asked nicely and explained their trespassing could not continue, he would do the decent thing. She decided it would be best not to broach the subject with Pierce again as he would just be dismissive.

"So shall we attend the tennis party?" she asked.

"Of course! We always attended the Foxes' tennis parties," said Pierce.

"From what I remember their tennis parties turn into late-night parties. If we go, I would want us to be home early. I wouldn't feel safe for us to be travelling after dark after that bridge at Abbeydale was blown up."

"As you wish. If there is nothing else, I want to concentrate on my work," said Pierce.

Clara nodded and left the room.

Clara drove down the uneven boreen to the O'Mearas' cottage.

There were four children outside the cottage who stopped playing and stood in awe, staring at her.

Clara braced herself and got out of the car.

"Good afternoon," she said as she walked past them to the open front door.

"Hello!" she called as she hovered there. She saw Molly O'Meara was at the table peeling potatoes while Tadgh was reading the paper by the fire.

"Lady Armstrong!" exclaimed Molly, shocked to see her, as she put down her peeling knife.

"May I come in?" asked Clara.

"*Em* – I suppose!" said Molly, who anxiously looked at Tadgh who stood up from his chair.

"What a charming home you have! And so beautifully furnished," said Clara, stepping inside, genuinely surprised at the quality of the furniture.

"Thank you!" said Molly.

As Clara looked at the Regency-style couch and armchairs she suddenly felt confused. They looked remarkably like the ones they used to have in Armstrong House that went missing after the fire. Her heart sank as she surveyed the rest of the furniture in the room. She recognised it all from Armstrong House. As she looked at Molly and Tadgh she now realised that instead of protecting Armstrong House in their absence as they had claimed, they had robbed it. As much as she felt tempted to challenge them, she realised it was pointless. The O'Mearas would only deny they stole the goods and if they called the police Clara dreaded to think of what reprisals they would endure. She would have to remain silent.

"Can I offer you a cup of tea?" said Molly quickly.

"No, thank you, this is not a social visit," said Clara. She felt she would choke on the tea that would no doubt be served to her in china stolen from Armstrong House.

"Well, what can we do for you in that case?" asked Tadgh.

"It's about your cattle, Mr. O'Meara. They are still on our land, and we really would like you to remove them at this point," said Clara.

"I see – said the blind man and he couldn't see at all!" said Tadgh.

"I'm surprised at Lord Armstrong sending his wife to do his work for him," commented Molly.

"His dirty work at that," added Tadgh.

"It's my land as well as my husband's and this isn't dirty work that I am here for. It is merely a request for you to leave our land."

"*Merely* – she says *merely*," said Tadgh. "And where am I supposed to put all the calves I just bought at the fair if we leave that land? It's very short notice you're giving me."

"It's really not my concern where you put your calves, Mr. O'Meara. Perhaps you shouldn't have bought them if you didn't have enough land for them."

"Well, that's the fine thanks we get after minding your place all this time," said Tadgh.

"I can see now just how well you minded Armstrong House in our absence," said Clara as she looked around the room at the furniture.

Molly gave her husband a sly look.

"Ah, no need for bad feeling between us," she said. "We'll take the livestock off your land, Lady Armstrong, if that's what you want."

"It is what I want," said Clara.

"Sure, they'll be gone by the end of the week as sure as Saturday follows Friday," said Tadgh.

"We really would appreciate it," said Clara.

"As we said we were – *merely* – taking care of the land while you were gone," said Tadgh.

"Thank you. I do not want to take up your time any further so I will bid you good day," said Clara.

"Ah, sure, bid us anything you want!" said Tadgh.

"Nice to see you, Lady Armstrong," said Molly, frowning at Tadgh. "I'll bring you some more fresh eggs and bread some day soon."

The sound of a horn caused Clara to turn and walk outside where she found the four O'Meara children climbing all over the motorcar.

"*Will you get out of Lady Armstrong's motorcar, you little brats!*" shouted Molly.

"*We want to go for a ride in it!*" shouted one of the girls.

"*A long ride!*" shouted a boy.

"*Sure, Lady Armstrong doesn't have time to be giving the likes of you rides around the county!*"

"*We don't care about Lady Armstrong!*" shouted the girl.

"*Yes, we don't care about that whore Lady Armstrong!*" shouted the boy.

"*Timmy!*" roared Tadgh.

"But that's what you always call her, Dad!" Timmy retorted.

Clara turned to glare at Tadgh.

"Oh, children have such imaginations these days. I blame the schools," said Molly, smiling.

"'Tis filth they d'be teaching them in schools these days, that's all – pure filth!" spat Tadgh.

"Quite!" said Clara as she walked to the car, opened the door and shooed the children out.

"Sure, the little darlings are that excited as they were never in a motor car before," said Molly.

Clara turned the motorcar and drove back to the main road.

Tadgh and Molly folded their arms as they watched her drive away.

"I don't know about you, Molly, but I'm getting sick and tired of the mighty Lady Armstrong swanning around telling us what to do," said Tadgh.

"It's a pity she wasn't finished off the last time she lived here," said Molly.

"We'll have to make sure the job is done right this time, Molly," said Tadgh.

Hugh and Asty were in Castlewest and were walking down the main street, arm in arm. Asty was very pleased at how things were going between them. She was surprised at how Hugh had seemed so agreeable to courting her. She remembered him being wilder in his youth, with no interest in being serious with anybody. But, of course, he was older now. She had met enough men while away to know Hugh was worth holding on to. He had a good character and was reliable but fun to be with too. And he was hard-working and one day, with the right woman behind him, she was sure he could do well in business or with his own farm.

Hugh felt Asty's hand grip his arm tightly, almost as if she was frightened he would run away. It was funny going out with Asty after all these years, but she had arrived back in his life at the right time. He was getting older and needed to think about settling down. And since he had fallen out with Tadgh, it was nice to have her around. Hugh showed up for work every day at the farm, but Tadgh didn't speak to him and he was no longer welcome to have dinner with the family in the evening. He hoped Tadgh would get over it in time, but Hugh knew it was the right decision to leave the cause behind.

He was surprised when he came face to face with Constance in the street. She looked as surprised to see him and even more so to see him with Asty linking his arm.

"Good afternoon, Hugh. How are you keeping?" asked Constance.

"I'm fine, ma'am," Hugh said with a nod.

"And who's your friend?" asked Constance, looking Asty up and down.

"This is Asty, ma'am."

"Aren't you a pretty little thing!" said Constance. "You look familiar – where have I seen you before?"

"Probably up at Armstrong House. I'm the housekeeper there," said Asty.

"Ah, that must be it. I always find it hard to remember the faces of servants!"

"Well, we'll be on our way," said Hugh.

"Yes, you do that. Nice to see you again, Hugh!" said Constance with a bemused look as she walked on.

"How do you know that stuck-up bitch?" asked Asty.

"I cut her hedges for her one day," said Hugh.

"I hate that one! When she's up at Armstrong House she acts so grand you'd swear she was Lady Armstrong herself!" said Asty, tightening her grip on his arm.

"*Hmm*," said Hugh, feeling confused by the feelings seeing Constance again had stirred in him.

Constance could not get the image of Hugh and Asty walking arm in arm out of her head. When she arrived back to Seymour Hall she poured herself a stiff drink. Seeing them together made her feel sad and she did not know why. They looked so young and happy together, their whole lives ahead of them. When she compared them to herself and Clement it made her feel old and weary. She knew she was being ridiculous. There was nothing to be envious of and she would be appalled at the very notion of swapping her life for theirs. And yet she had to admit she liked Hugh and felt jealous that she had lost that power over him that she had briefly enjoyed.

Chapter 28

Clara was sitting with Emily Foxe, watching Pierce playing tennis on the lawn tennis court at the Foxes'.

Emily and George Foxe lived in the nearest Big House to Armstrong House and had been the first friends Clara had made when she had moved there after marrying Pierce. The Foxes had lived in the area as long as the Armstrongs and had weathered many storms over the previous decade. Their son Felix had been killed in the Great War but they had remained stoic and stayed at their manor throughout the War of Independence. A nephew and his wife had now become their heirs since their son's death – they had moved in with them and were running their estate.

"More sandwiches, Clara?" asked Emily, lifting up a plate of cucumber sandwiches.

"Oh, no thank you, Mrs. Foxe. I must keep some room for that delicious Victoria Sponge I have my eye on," said Clara.

"Pierce is looking so well. I can't tell you how wonderful it is to have you and Lord Armstrong back here. We are just so thrilled!"

"And we are happy to be home."

"It's funny to hear you call it home. When you moved here first we thought you would never last," Emily confessed.

"Really?"

"Well, we thought you could never fit into our world. You couldn't shoot, fish or hunt and all you seemed interested in was art!" said Emily.

Clara laughed though the remark stung a little.

"But you were very kind to me when Felix was killed and you must have had your own worries with Pierce away at the front."

Clara knew that Emily and her husband would have no idea that Pierce and she were actually separated for a year.

"We must get on with life now," said Emily. "The bad times are over, and we must build our futures here."

"That's what I hope for too," said Clara.

Emily leaned forward and whispered, "Families like ours were never liked and now there is Independence we must fight to maintain and protect our way of life."

"*Game, set and match to Lord Armstrong!*" announced the umpire and the crowd around the tennis court applauded loudly.

Pierce gave a small bow and walked over to Clara and Emily.

"Bravo, Pierce!" said Emily as she clapped.

"Thank you," said Pierce as he sat down.

Emily stood up and went to speak to some other guests.

"Well done," Clara said as Pierce reached over and put some sandwiches on a plate.

"I was speaking to Conway earlier," said Pierce.

"What about?"

"About Tadgh O'Meara. I've arranged to meet Conway next week so he can write to him insisting he removes the cattle from my land."

It had been two weeks since Clara's visit to the O'Mearas and their cattle were still grazing on the Armstrong Estate.

"But O'Meara will just laugh when he receives Conway's letter," said Clara.

"As he did when you visited him and asked him to remove them," said Pierce.

"Well, I had to try!"

"Perhaps you need to stay out of the farm business and concentrate on the running of the house from now on."

"Pierce," said Clara, looking around nervously, "this is neither the time nor the place for this discussion."

Pierce shrugged. "If the O'Mearas choose to ignore Conway's correspondence I will get a court order and have the police forcibly remove the cattle."

Clara sat up quickly in fear. "But, Pierce, you can't do that! It will enrage them, and they will wreak revenge on us!"

"What can they do to us?" asked Pierce arrogantly.

"Are you really asking that question? You know what they can do to us!" Clara had to made an effort to lower her voice when she spoke again. "Your father was shot at the gates of Armstrong House after he consistently made enemies of the locals!"

"We never had any evidence it was the locals who shot my father," said Pierce.

"Of course it was the locals! He acted ruthlessly towards them and that's what happened back then – they shot ruthless landlords!"

"I've always felt there was more to the shooting of my father than agrarian agitation. My father was a complicated man who had made many enemies."

"And ended up being shot! I do not want the same thing to happen to you!"

Pierce stared at her across the table. "I have no choice but to go down this route. Now we are back at Armstrong House I am going to bring Prudence back as well to run the farm. She knows how to, and she will keep manners on the locals and sort out Tadgh O'Meara."

"*No!*" cried Clara and noticed a group of guests look in her direction. Tears sprang to her eyes. She forced herself to speak quietly. "Pierce – I do not want Prudence back at Armstrong House."

"She doesn't have to live in the house – she can live in Hunter's Farm where she did before," said Pierce.

"I don't want her anywhere near us, Pierce!" Clara hissed. "It was Prudence ruined our marriage the last time by mounting a campaign against me and spying on me and reporting everything I did back to you when you were at the front."

"If you had been behaving yourself appropriately then there would have been nothing for Prudence to report! As it was you were fucking Johnny Seymour," Pierce stated coldly.

Clara's mouth opened in shock. "Do you need to remind me of Johnny every time we have a discussion?" she demanded.

"*Johnny* might be in America, but he is still like a ghost between us, hovering around us," said Pierce.

"He is only a ghost because you allow him to be," said Clara.

Clara was walking through the gardens at Armstrong House with Constance.

"I fear Pierce is going to use force to remove the O'Mearas' cattle from our land and it will set off a chain of events that there might be no coming back from," said Clara.

"Sometimes the best way to deal with force is with force!" said Constance.

"Which only results in war, and I just want to live in peace," said Clara.

"I understand your predicament," said Constance.

"And the very idea of Prudence returning here is abhorrent to me!"

"But why don't you just drive the cattle off your land?" asked Constance as she looked at O'Meara's cattle grazing on the parkland leading up to the house.

"Well, we have nobody to do it," said Clara. "I can't see Pierce out in his wellingtons trying to herd them. He'd consider it beneath him"

A plan began to formulate in Constance's mind.

"Pierce has this – implacability – for want of a better word," said Clara. "There is something in him that cannot back away from a fight, even if he knows he is going to lose it. I'm sure it was what made him a war hero. Some would call it bravery, others stupidity. I saw it when he returned from the war and became so involved in the War of Independence. It is as if he thrives in a hostile environment."

"What a difficult way to choose to live your life!" said Constance.

"He will destroy himself before he gives in and admits defeat. If I tell you something, do you promise not to tell anyone?"

"Of course!"

"Pierce tried to kill himself not that long ago."

"How terrible! He strikes me as somebody far too self-assured to do such a thing," said Constance.

"But he thought he had lost everything, and he had too much pride to live that way. But that is what I mean – he is almost self-destructive. Oh, I don't blame him. He had a very difficult upbringing and is damaged from it. That's why I came back to him – not just to try and save our marriage but to save Pierce from himself as well."

"I can see how you must try everything then to avoid any more conflict for him with these neighbouring farmers."

"I am due to travel back to England next week to see to my grandmother's affairs in Kent and I am terrified to leave Pierce here on his own … I don't know what he might do in my absence. Thank you for listening to me, Constance. There's nobody here I can talk to about Pierce."

"Clara, I think I may have a solution to your problem. If you can't win them, then join them!"

"I don't follow?"

"If you are frightened of the locals and any repercussions then you must employ a local to run your farm," said Constance.

"But no local will come to work on the land while O'Meara is here. They would be too frightened to make an enemy of him," said Clara.

"He sounds like a terrible bully. But I think I might know just the man who will not be frightened of him and would take the position of farm manager if you offered it to him." "Who is this gifted person?"

"Hugh O'Meara," said Constance with a bright smile.

"O'Meara?"

"Yes, he is Tadgh's younger brother. I know him as he has been doing work around Seymour Hall for me. He is presently working for Tadgh but he's terribly ambitious and I would say he'd jump at an opportunity to manage your farm. Just think – Tadgh will not take on his own brother. Hugh is a very strong character and will not be frightened to challenge Tadgh if need be – and if the price is right, of course."

"I would certainly pay him well if he could solve this dilemma and run our estate for us," said Clara.

"He's also excellent at maintenance. Armstrong House will need a maintenance man for fixing anything you need," said Constance.

Clara became excited at the thought. If she employed this man, it would mean they would have peace with the locals and also there would be no need for Prudence to come and manage the farm. Having him there would keep them and Armstrong House safe. What was more, it would impress Pierce if she managed to solve their problems.

"Constance – you are a treasure! Would you mind awfully if I ask you to enquire of Hugh if would he like to meet with me to discuss the position?"

"I'll do it this evening," Constance assured her.

Constance drove down the long boreen to Hugh's cottage and parked in front of it. Climbing out of the motorcar, she walked to the front door which was open and called out "Hello?"

Hugh was reading the newspaper inside and stood up, looking surprised to see her.

"Can I come in?" she asked, not waiting for an answer but walking inside.

"I didn't expect to see you again," he said, moving towards her.

"Your friend isn't here?" Constance asked, looking around.

She was desperate to ask him questions about Asty but did not want to appear obvious.

"No, Asty is working up at Armstrong House."

"Ah, of course – she's probably busy making beds!"

"What do you want?" he asked bluntly.

"Well, I have a proposition for you, a very lucrative one."

"I'm all ears," he said.

"I think I've got you a job as the estate manager at Armstrong House," she announced.

"*What?*"

"My friend Lady Armstrong is looking for somebody to run their estate and I recommended you."

Hugh ran his hands through his hair in amazement.

"It's basically doing what you do for your brother, but you get paid a lot more!"

"I don't know what to say."

"Just say yes and I'll arrange an interview with Lady Armstrong," urged Constance.

"But there's a lot of politics going on between my brother and the Armstrongs. He would never forgive me if I went to work for them," said Hugh.

"Hugh – this is an opportunity to turn your life around! Do you want to be working for your brother and living in this cottage forever or do you want to put yourself first and try to make something of your life?"

Hugh looked up at the thatched roof. Tadgh really would never forgive him if he took that job, but then could he ever forgive himself if he didn't? He looked at Constance and at her motorcar parked outside. She'd had a profound impact on him since he met her by completely changing how he saw the world. And now she was presenting him with an opportunity to change his life.

"Why would you do this for me?" he asked.

"Because I like you and I want to see you making a success of your life," she said.

He was quiet for a while before he nodded.

"I'll meet Lady Armstrong and I'll take the job if she offers it to me," he said.

Chapter 29

Clara was excited about Constance's suggestion about hiring Hugh. It made perfect sense. The one person who could stand up to Tadgh O'Meara without fear of retaliation would be his brother. She did not inform Pierce of her plan to meet Hugh. She knew he would forbid it. Pierce never countenanced any idea that was not his own. He always dismissed any suggestion Clara had and never gave her credit, even if it was for his own benefit.

Clara had waited until Pierce was gone for the day fishing, to meet Hugh. She had grown to trust Constance. She had seen how she dealt with people while furnishing Armstrong House and Clara believed she would only recommend Hugh if he was honest and right for the job.

Fennell opened the door to the drawing room and announced, "Mr. Hugh O'Meara, my lady."

Clara stood up from the couch and smiled at the young man who walked into the room.

"Thank you for coming – may I call you Hugh?" said Clara as she held her hand out to him.

"You can call me anything you please, ma'am," said Hugh as he took her hand and shook it.

Clara did a quick observation of the man. He stood in front of her with his cap in his hands and seemed confident in an understated way. He was fair-haired and very strong-looking and did not look like his brother or show any of his arrogance. Clara judged him to be one who knew his own mind and was nobody's fool. As he looked around the drawing room, she could tell he was uncomfortable being in such grand surroundings, but he was not intimidated either.

"Is anything the matter?" asked Clara.

"It's just I expected to meet Lord Armstrong as well as you," said Hugh.

"I'm afraid you are stuck with me," said Clara.

"Oh – I can assure you that I'm not complaining. You have a nicer smile than him!"

"I believe Constance already informed you about the position I am interviewing you for – that of manager of the estate here," said Clara.

"She did."

"Constance told me a little about your work history. How long have you been working on your brother's farm?"

"Since I left school."

"You won't miss it?"

"What's there to miss? Hard work and poor pay?"

"I'm sure you must be aware of the situation that has arisen between us and your brother about his livestock on our estate. Are you prepared to deal with that?"

"You make me manager of this estate and you won't have any problems from Tadgh or anybody else," promised Hugh.

"That *is* reassuring. I am afraid we must build the farming up from nothing. We have no livestock as it stands," said Clara.

"I'm already familiar with your estate, ma'am, as I've been farming it with my brother's cattle for the past couple of years."

"Ah, I expect you have been," acknowledged Clara, raising her eyes. "Then I don't need to show you around?"

"No, ma'am," said Hugh.

"Your brother doesn't like me much, Hugh, and I expect he will like me even less when he finds out I've poached you."

"He never could recognise class when he saw it," said Hugh.

"Unlike you?" she said with a smile. "I'll double the wages your brother pays you and when can you start work?"

"Tomorrow morning if it suits."

"That will be fine. The first job is to remove your brother's cattle if you are ready for the challenge?"

"Ready and able," he confirmed.

"You can report to the kitchen in the morning," said Clara as she sat down.

"Thank you, ma'am." Hugh nodded at her and then turned to leave.

But, before he reached the door, he turned around.

"There's just one other thing you should probably know, ma'am."

"Yes? What is that?"

"I'm courting your housekeeper, Asty."

"Oh! I see!" said Clara, surprised.

"Is that a problem?" asked Hugh.

"Not at all. If you are as good a worker as she then I am to be doubly blessed," said Clara.

Hugh smiled and nodded and then opened the door and left.

Clara got up and walked to the window. She watched as Hugh walked across the forecourt and got into a buggy.

Shaking the horse's reins, he set off down the avenue.

When Asty called to Hugh's cottage that evening she was shocked to hear about his new job.

"But why didn't you tell me you were going for an interview?" she demanded.

"Well, I didn't want to say anything in case I didn't get the job. Are you unhappy I'll be working there?"

"Unhappy? I'm thrilled!" Asty said, grabbing him and kissing him. "Sure, you were going nowhere working for your brother. With this job, Hugh, we can really go places. We'll have enough money to be married in no time!"

"Let's not get ahead of ourselves!" said Hugh, removing her arms from around his neck.

"Well, at least engaged! But how did you even hear about the job?"

"The lady I did some work for around her house, Constance Fitzgerald, is friends with Lady Armstrong and she put in a good word for me."

"Well, you owe her a big thank-you!"

"Indeed I owe her a lot," agreed Hugh as he went to the open door and looked out at the lake down the fields.

"I'm so proud of you!" said Asty, coming behind him and resting her head on his back while she put her arms around his waist.

"What's she like – this Lady Armstrong?" he asked.

"Dull as ditchwater! Born with a silver spoon in her mouth and always has an expression on her face as if she has a red-hot poker up her arse!"

She didn't seem like that at all, thought Hugh, as he watched the sun going down over the hills across the lake.

"What are your plans for tomorrow?" asked Clara as Pierce came out of the bathroom and climbed into bed beside her.

"I'm seeing Philly Scott in the morning as she is having problems with a horse," said Pierce.

Clara raised her eyebrows as she closed the *Tatler* she had been reading and put it on her bedside table. "Does that woman have any horses that do not have problems? She constantly needs your help." Why, she didn't know as Philly supposedly had some veterinary training. She pushed that thought out of her mind, turned to Pierce and laid her head on his chest.

"Are you jealous?" he asked.

"Not anymore," she sighed. "When I arrived here first after getting married I used to be enraged with jealousy when these girls fought for your attention. But now I realise that you have no feelings for them, and they are just friends. I can live with that."

He looked down curiously at her. "*Hmm*," he said.

Clara thought about telling Pierce about hiring Hugh O'Meara but she knew he would be furious and she didn't want to ruin the night. She would wait until Hugh had proven himself the next day after he had removed all Tadgh's livestock and they were back in control of their own land. Surely even Pierce could not be angry with her then, when she had finally got rid of Tadgh O'Meara and his trespassing cattle.

Chapter 30

The next morning, with Pierce safely out of the way visiting Philly Scott and her bothersome horse, Clara met Hugh at the stables at the back of Armstrong House as he set about his work. She rode her horse across the estate in the late May sunshine and watched Hugh round up livestock with impressive speed and drive them off Armstrong land and back through a gap leading into Tadgh's.

Clara felt a huge sense of relief.

She rode around the estate for a short while and then returned to find Hugh putting the finishing touches to a wooden fence which now blocked the gap in the ditch that Tadgh had created and used to access the Armstrong land. Hugh had told her that he would check all the boundaries around the estate to make sure the cattle could not break through or be driven in by Tadgh again.

Clara felt a huge sense of pride that she had solved the problem without it escalating any further.

Then, just as Hugh drove in the last nail and stood back to admire his work, Tadgh O'Meara arrived on the scene.

"What the *fuck* do you think you are doing?" shouted Tadgh.

"What does it look like to you? I'm fixing this gap that you made," said Hugh.

"And why the fuck are you doing that?" demanded Tadgh. "And what the fuck are my cattle doing back on my land!"

"Because that's where your cattle belong – on your land."

Tadgh's eyes bulged with anger. "You have two seconds to explain to me what the fuck is going on or I'm going to jump over this fancy new fence and thump you!"

"I'm not working for you anymore, Tadgh. I've taken the job of estate manager here at Armstrong House and the first thing that meant was freeing the land of your cattle so we can put our own herd on it."

Tadgh's mouth dropped open. "I can't believe it! You treacherous son of a bitch!"

"Now, now – Ma wasn't a sweetheart, but I wouldn't be calling her that either."

"When did all this happen?"

"I was offered the job yesterday by Lady Armstrong," said Hugh.

"And you couldn't even have the decency to come and tell me!"

"Sure, you're not talking to me since I left the cause so I didn't see much point?"

"*You traitorous, conniving, wretched fucker!*" shouted Tadgh.

"I'm a busy man so I don't have time to stop and trade insults with you. I need to get on with my work and make sure the fences are secure so none of your cattle break in again."

Hugh turned and walked away.

Consumed with rage, Tadgh jumped over the fence and ran at Hugh, hitting him on the back of his head.

Hugh fell to the ground, then quickly turned over, a look of shock on his face.

"*Not so brave now are you, sonny!*" shouted Tadgh.

Hugh scrambled to his feet. Tadgh rushed at him and Hugh punched him in the face.

Clara looked on, horrified, as she saw a vicious fight break out between the two men.

"*Stop! Stop that at once!*" Clara shouted as she rode quickly towards them.

"*I'll teach you to cross me!*" roared Tadgh as he fought his brother.

The two men fell to the ground fighting.

"*Please stop!*" Clara shouted as she jumped off her horse.

Then, as Tadgh was pinned to the ground, he reached out, grabbed a stone and hit his brother in the forehead. Blood spurted from the wound as Hugh fell sideways and Tadgh flipped him over and held him captive.

Seeing blood pouring from Hugh's forehead, Clara raised her riding crop and struck Tadgh with it across his back.

"*Get off him! Get off, you brute!*" screamed Clara as she continued to hit him with all her might.

Tadgh jumped to his feet and rushed in fury at Clara. He raised his fist in the air but stopped short of striking her.

She had raised her arms to protect herself, but Tadgh quickly stepped back from her. He stared at her venomously.

"You've made an enemy of me, and you'll regret this day for as long as you live, Lady Armstrong," he said in a quiet but threatening voice.

Then he suddenly turned, spat at his brother who was splayed out on the ground before jumping over the fence back to his own land.

As Tadgh strode away, Clara rushed to Hugh and helped him up from the ground.

"Can you walk?" she asked.

"Yes, I'm fine."

But as he leant against her Clara realised he was far from it.

"Can you get up on the horse and ride with me?" she asked.

He nodded and Clara ran to lead the horse over to him.

She mounted and he managed to clamber up behind her.

"Hold tight," she said.

He put his arms awkwardly around her waist and she turned the horse in the direction of Armstrong House.

Pierce and Philly Scott rode into the forecourt of Armstrong House and dismounted. Pierce had known Philly since childhood and had always been impressed by her no-nonsense approach to life. She maintained her appearance in a practical way too, shying away from the latest hair styles of the 1920s and perfering to tie her thick brown hair back the way she always had.

"Are you sure Clara won't mind me dropping by unexpectedly?" asked Philly as she tied her horse to a balustrade.

"No, she'll be delighted to see you. She was always very fond of you," lied Pierce.

"Glory, Glory, Alleluia!" exclaimed Philly as she looked up at the house. "You've done a spiffing job rebuilding the place. It looks as good as new!"

"Yes, it's wonderful to be home," said Pierce with pride as he led her up to the front door.

"Is Clara as pretty as ever?" asked Philly as she entered the hallway and admired the house.

"Yes. A little aged but haven't we all?" said Pierce as he led her into the drawing room.

"We were damned lucky the rebels didn't target us!" said Philly, surveying the refurbishment. "Of course, Papa said that if the bastards had tried to burn our house down they would never have succeeded as it's so damp it would never have caught fire!"

At Armstrong House Clara and Hugh walked to the back door with his arm around her shoulders. Entering the kitchen they found Mrs. Fennell making pastry at the main table while Fennell polished silverware.

"Lady Armstrong! Whatever happened?" Mrs. Fennell stood, hand to her heart, in shock at the sight of them.

"Fetch a clean towel, Mrs. Fennell," commanded Clara as she led Hugh to the table and he sat down.

Mrs. Fennell got a clean towel and started wiping the blood off Clara's face.

"Mrs. Fennell! What are you doing? It's Hugh who is injured!" said Clara, grabbing the towel and pressing it on Hugh's wound. "Fennell, call a doctor and the police!"

"*No! No police!*" said Hugh urgently.

At that moment Asty and Síle came down the servants' stairs and entered the kitchen. Síle screamed at the top of her voice when she saw Hugh covered in blood.

"What on earth is that?" asked Philly in the drawing room, on hearing the scream.

"I have no idea," said Pierce who had been pouring two glasses of sherry.

"It sounded like a strangled cat!" said Philly.

Pierce put down the decanter of sherry and walked out of the room into the hallway, followed by Philly. They could hear a commotion coming from the kitchen downstairs.

"Whatever now?" sighed Pierce.

They walked to the end of the hallway and down the steps to the kitchen where they were greeted by the sight of the household staff gathered around a bloodied Hugh while Clara tended to his wound.

"What the blazes is going on? Who is this man?" demanded Pierce.

"Oh, Pierce – this is Hugh O'Meara. I employed him as the estate manager and his brother Tadgh attacked him when Hugh drove the cattle off our land this morning," explained Clara in a panicked voice.

Pierce looked Clara, covered in blood, up and down in shock.

"Have you lost your mind?" he demanded.

"Fennell – I told you – call the doctor!" said Clara.

"I'm fine! I don't need any doctor!" snarled Hugh.

Philly marched across the kitchen and pushed Clara and the servants out of the way while she inspected Hugh's injury.

"Nothing life-threatening here," she announced. "He'll just need a couple of stiches. No need to fuss. Mrs. Fennell, bring me boiling water and a needle and thread. Oh, and a bottle of whiskey for the both of us!"

"But you can hardly do the surgery, Philly!" Clara objected.

"Of course I can! Didn't I study for a year at the Royal Veterinary College in Dublin?"

"Lord help us!" said Síle as she blessed herself.

"And I would have graduated as a vet too had I not failed the exams!" added Philly.

"Clara – what on earth did you think you were doing hiring this man?" demanded Pierce.

"Well, I didn't want to go to England with the problem unsolved!" said Clara. "And this seemed the simplest way!"

"Simple! *Simple*? The only thing that is simple here is you! You've made everything a hundred times worse, you stupid woman!"

Despite their long and tempestuous marriage, Clara had never really seen Pierce lose his temper before. It was not his style to get angry. He never needed to. He could either silence someone with those cold dark eyes of his or subdue them with a cutting remark. It was quite a shock for Clara to see him look as if he was about explode in rage. And it shocked her that he was speaking to her like that in front of the servants.

"You had no right to interfere in the running of this estate! No right at all!"

"I was only trying to help," said Clara lamely.

"You of all people should know from when you harboured that terrorist during the Easter Rising that the road to hell is paved with good intentions!" barked Pierce.

Clara was humiliated as she felt the servants and Philly's embarrassment and sympathy. As tears stung her eyes, Clara left the table and rushed past Pierce up the stairs.

"Golly, she's still the delicate flower, I see!" said Philly. "Now – where's that boiling water and needle and thread, Mrs. Fennell? We don't want this man bleeding to death!"

In the drawing-room, Clara stood at the window while she tried to catch her breath. The whole morning had shocked and upset her – from seeing Tadgh O'Meara attack Hugh, to the ensuing fight to Pierce's shouting at her. She wiped away the tears that were falling down her face. She knew Pierce would be coming any second and she did not want to show weakness to him. When she came back to Pierce and Armstrong House she was determined to never be weak again. She was here and with him on her terms this time.

The drawing-room door opened and slammed shut and Clara turned around to see a still angry Pierce.

"How did you even meet the man to employ him in the first place?" demanded Pierce.

"Constance recommended him. He did some work for her."

"I might have known she was involved in this!"

"It was excellent idea, Pierce! And it's worked! The cattle are finally off our land!"

"I could have had that done any day without setting two brothers at each other's throats, you stupid woman! But I wanted to do it with legal backing!"

"Well, it's done now."

"At what cost? A stranger being stitched up by Philly down in the kitchen and you looking like you work in a butcher's shop!"

"I prefer that to what might have come otherwise. Pierce, I've seen how nasty and violent Tadgh O'Meara is. He could have turned that violence on you had you brought him to court."

"Oh, I imagine this is not the end of him, Clara! And you are even more naïve than I took you for if you believe it is! You have made things much worse by enraging O'Meara by employing his brother."

"On the contrary. I saw how Hugh is not afraid to stand up to him," said Clara.

"Shall I tell – Hugh – he is no longer required or will you?" asked Pierce.

"What do you mean?"

"We can't have O'Meara's brother here. I want him gone."

"No – no! Absolutely not! Hugh is staying! He has fallen out with his family over this job and suffered injury. He has also got our land back for us. I refuse to fire him now! It would be reprehensible!"

"I didn't employ him and I don't want him here. Get rid of him, Clara!"

"I refuse to do so! Perhaps I was wrong not to speak to you about it beforehand, but I knew you would object –"

"For good reason! I don't trust those O'Mearas and I don't want one of them working for us. For all we know he might have been one of the hoodlums that burned down Armstrong House!"

"Pierce – I am not allowing Hugh O'Meara to be fired. And, at the end of the day, it is my land too and I am the one paying for everything!"

"Well, thank you for reminding me again!" snapped Pierce. "I'll never be in charge here as long as you are here pulling the purse-strings!"

The door opened and Philly walked in.

"All done! He's as good as a shiny new shilling!" she said.

Pierce gave Clara a filthy look and picked up the glass of sherry he had poured for Philly earlier and handed it to her.

"Well done, Philly," he said.

"I don't mind if I do!" she said, taking a gulp. "I sent the young man home to rest for the day. He's quite inebriated from the bottle of whiskey I forced him to drink anyway so I doubt he would be much use to anyone."

"Thank you, Philly," said Clara, avoiding Pierce's cold gaze.

"Quite sturdy, some of these peasants! He didn't flinch once during the operation." Philly looked Clara up and down in her bloodied clothes. "You do look a sight, Clara!"

"I should go and bathe and change," said Clara. "Thank you again for putting Hugh back together and it was nice to see you again."

"Oh – have I outstayed my welcome? I had been promised dejeuner!" said Philly.

"I'd invited Philly to Armstrong House for lunch, Clara. So, make sure you are ready to join us in the dining room for one o'clock sharp," said Pierce.

Clara paused for a moment and clenched her fists together. She hated when Pierce issued orders to her like that. She knew he was angry and stressed over what had occurred, but when he spoke to her like that it reminded her of the last couple of years of the marriage when he had all the power, and she had none.

"I'm quite famished! What is Mrs. Fennell conjuring up for us for lunch?" asked Philly.

Clara didn't answer.

"Philly asked you a question, Clara. What is for lunch?" asked Pierce in a cold and commanding voice.

"Pheasant," Clara whispered.

"Excellent! I've missed Mrs. Fennell's cooking while you were away. Jolly good to have her back at Armstrong House!"

"I cannot believe that Hugh would do this to us!" said Molly, throwing her arms in the air, after Tadgh told her what had happened. "And he attacked you as well!"

"Came up behind me and punched me in the back of my head!" said Tadgh.

"His own brother! After all you did for him over the years!"

"I had to hit him with a stone to defend myself!"

"He's changed, Tadgh! I'd hardly recognise him. Abandoning the cause for the other side and then going working for the enemy and turning his own brother's cattle off the land!"

"It must be the influence of that hussy he's started seeing, Asty Horan. Sure isn't she working up at Armstrong House herself. She must have talked him into taking the job." "The little tramp! I'd like to cut her hair off and march her through the streets of Castlewest!" said Molly.

At that moment their colleague Tommy Gilsenan came rushing through the front door.

"Tommy, what has got into you?" demanded Molly, seeing the look of panic on his face and tears in his eyes.

"You didn't hear the news yet?" asked Tommy.

"What news?" asked Tadgh.

"The war is over! The high command has called a truce with immediate effect!"

"There must be a mistake!" cried Molly.

"No mistake, Molly, the order came from De Valera himself. All fighting units are to cease activity immediately. We are not to surrender arms to the National Army, but orders are given to dump them."

"We've lost!" said Molly as she sank down into an armchair.

"We've given in! We should have kept fighting!" said Tadgh.

"It's over, Tadgh. You may as well accept it like we all have to," said Tommy.

"I'll never accept it," said Tadgh.

He stood up and went to the cabinet which had a number of photos. He picked up the photo frame that contained a photograph of him and Hugh. He took the photo from the frame and threw it on the fire and watched it burn.

Chapter 31

The next morning Clara was due to travel to England and Constance had offered to give her a lift to the train station. Clara was glad she had as Pierce was ignoring her since he'd found out she'd hired Hugh O'Meara.

When Constance arrived at Armstrong House she was disturbed to learn of the fight that had occurred the previous day.

"I say – I do feel terribly guilty. It's all my fault in a way," she said as Fennell placed Clara's suitcase in the back of the motorcar.

"There is nothing for you to apologise for!" insisted Clara. "It was a wonderful suggestion to hire Hugh and, although it has been a baptism of fire, I just know it's going to work out wonderfully."

Clara looked up at the house and saw Pierce looking down at her from an upstairs window. She gave him a smile and waved up at him, but he turned and disappeared.

"Oh – one thing," Constance said as Fennell opened the door of the motorcar for Clara. "While you're in England, Clara, I'm expecting the last pieces to arrive for Armstrong House. Is it alright if I have them delivered here and put in place?"

"Of course! Just ring the front bell and Fennell will let you in. Won't you, Fennell?"

"Of course, my lady," said Fennell.

"I really don't want to get in the way of Lord Armstrong," said Constance.

"Oh, he's off with his friends nearly all the time, so you won't disturb him nor he you."

"Thank you," said Constance, overjoyed at having unrestricted access to the house.

"Have a safe journey, my lady," said Fennell, stepping back from the car.

"Thank you, Fennell. Please take good care of His Lordship while I am away!"

As they drove down the driveway, Clara felt relieved to see the parkland was now free of O'Meara's cattle.

"I should not have gone behind Pierce's back, I suppose, and now I fear this has set us back just when we were managing to put the past behind us," she sighed.

As she glanced at Clara in her furs, Constance couldn't help but feel pleasure that her perfect life had been disrupted. But she also felt guilty for being pleased.

"Perhaps this might be a good thing? I mean your reunion with Pierce has not really been tested, due to your grandmother's money."

"What do you mean?" asked Clara, puzzled.

"Any marriage can work when there's no financial pressure. As my grandmother used to say, when money worries come through the front door love goes out the back door. But, apart from that complication, if Pierce can't allow you to make decisions, then can you really trust him?"

Clara frowned as she digested Constance's comments.

That evening, Constance drove down the boreen to Hugh's cottage and parked there. She hopped out and walked up to the front half-door, the top half of which was open.

"Hugh?" she called. She could see him lying down on the bed beside the fireplace.

He stood up, startled to see her.

"I heard about the incident with your brother and I wanted to see how you are," she said, going in.

"You're all heart!" said Hugh with a half-smile.

Constance walked up to him and inspected the cut on his forehead.

"That looks nasty!" she said, wincing.

"I'll live," Hugh said.

"You look dreadful!"

"I think that's more from the hangover from the bottle of whiskey the surgeon made me drink before she got to work," said Hugh.

"Your brother is an absolute monster! Why would he do this to you?"

"I guess he had his reasons – good reasons to his mind."

"Well, you can't give in to him now! You've broken free of him so keep running."

"I doubt he would want me back even if I wanted to go."

"Well, Lady Armstrong thinks you are a hero!" said Constance.

"Does she indeed? Her husband didn't look too pleased."

"Oh, don't mind Pierce. It's Clara who has the money not Pierce, so he really has very little power up at Armstrong House anymore."

"Interesting. Has anyone bothered to tell him that?"

"You just continue with your work and show them you are the best estate manager in the country," urged Constance.

"That's the plan but at the same time maybe I should be a bit wary of taking advice from you in future. It seems to lead me into a lot of trouble."

"Hugh – you said you wanted to be just like me and now's your chance," said Constance.

"Right. I'll bear that in mind. *Um,* I was just going to have some supper if you care to join me?"

"That's the best offer I've had all day! What's cooking?"

"Just bacon and potatoes and onions. Nothing fancy like you're used to," said Hugh.

"I don't mind. I like a bit of rough!"

"As I well know."

It was dark outside as they sat down to have dinner. The room was lit by oil lamps and the blazing fire.

"This looks quite romantic. Are you sure your girlfriend won't mind us eating together like this?" said Constance.

"What she doesn't know won't bother her," said Hugh.

"She seems a sweet girl."

"I could think of many words to call Asty, but sweet isn't one of them," said Hugh.

"You make a nice couple. I had no idea she was the housekeeper at Armstrong House when I recommended you for the position."

"Would it have stopped you if you knew?"

"No ... in fact, it's rather ... sweet. Both of you working there. As the years go by you can become like Mr. and Mrs. Fennell, a life of servitude to the Armstrongs."

"Well, now that I've become a man of ambition I think I'll aim a little higher than just that."

"I'm delighted to hear it. But I fear I have unleashed a beast in you!" said Constance with a chuckle.

"Maybe one day I'll own a house like Armstrong House myself."

"Let's not get ahead of ourselves! Or perhaps you really do aim to make your fortune? I'm not sure Asty will fit in the role of Lady of the Manor though, do you?"

"I haven't quite decided," said Hugh.

"I think *she* has! It's clear from looking at her she's in love with you. I have to confess I felt jealous seeing the two of you together. Full of young love and your future ahead of you."

"There is no need for you to be jealous of Asty and me," Hugh assured her.

"Why?"

"Because you should only be jealous of something you can't have and you can have me anytime you want," said Hugh, staring into her eyes.

Constance felt comforted by his words. She had needed to hear them. In her mind, his words indicated she meant more to him than Asty.

"Is that an invitation to stay?" she asked.

"It's an invitation to anything you want," said Hugh as began to stroke her hand.

It was after midnight when Tadgh made his way through the woods until he came to the place where a number of guns were stored, hidden in the hollow of a tree. He made several journeys carrying the arms to a boat that was moored nearby on the lake. When all the guns were loaded he got into the boat and began to row out towards the middle of the lake. As he rowed, he thought of all the years of fighting he had taken part in, only for his dream of a fully free and independent Ireland now to be thwarted. When he reached the middle of the lake he began to throw the guns over the side of the boat. When he got to the last gun he held it close and instead of throwing it into the water he put it inside his jacket before he started to row back to shore.

Constance awoke in the bed beside the fire in Hugh's cottage, to what sounded like thousands of birds singing in the nearby woods. She looked at the clock ticking on the wall and saw it was six in the morning, and it was already light outside.

"Good morning," said Hugh, already awake in the bed beside her.

"I had the most glorious sleep," she said, stretching. "I can't remember when I slept so well before."

"Who'd have thought you would sleep better in my little cottage than you do in Seymour Hall!"

"Indeed – who would have?" said Constance, putting her arm across his naked chest.

"I better get up and get going," said Hugh. "I've a busy day today. I'm going to the fair in Castlewest to buy livestock for the estate."

"A man with a purpose," she chuckled then paused before speaking again. "I need a favour from you, Hugh."

"Name it."

"I've agreed to go to Armstrong House while Clara is away to finish arranging the furnishings. I'd rather not be there when Pierce is. I don't think he likes me much."

"He doesn't strike me as the most sociable man," said Hugh.

"Could you find out from Asty which times he would not be there, so I don't have to see him?"

"She'd be like a spy?" he said with a grin. "I'm sure I could manage that."

"I would be grateful," said Constance.

"So ... I guess that two of us are cheating now. You on your husband and me on Asty."

"That kind of evens things out somewhat, don't you think?"

"*What's sauce for the goose is sauce for the gander*," said Hugh.

Chapter 32

Present Day

Kate knocked on the door of a small manor house that was located outside Castlewest and, soon after, a distinguished-looking man in his sixties answered.

"Hi, I'm Kate Collins – I'm here to see Liam Berill," she said with a smile.

"That's me! Nice to meet you, Kate – come on in!" he said, stepping out of the way and gesturing for her to come inside.

She looked around the narrow hallway, which was lined with photographs of fox hunts. Liam being the Master of the Castlewest Fox Hunt, Kate felt uncomfortable in his company. She could not understand people's enjoyment of the sport.

"Would you care for some tea?" he asked.

"Oh – no, thank you," she said.

"In that case, come into my study and we'll take a look at what you were requesting."

She followed him into a room at the front of the house, which was laden with books and files.

"I wasn't sure if you could find anything from that 1923 hunt – it is so long ago," she said.

"Well, as it happens, you are the second person to enquire about that hunt in the past few weeks, so when you asked for it I already had the file to hand."

"Oh?"

"Yes, we get so few enquiries about hunts in the distant past that when I got two enquiries for the same hunt it was quite a coincidence."

"Indeed – who else was enquiring, if you don't mind me asking?"

"An English chap – what was his name? Royce – Royce Charter, that was it."

The man who had introduced himself at the wedding and had given her the photograph of the Hunt Ball.

"Did he mention why he was looking for information?" asked Kate.

"He said he was related to somebody involved in the hunt and was trying to do some research," said Liam as he opened a file on the desk. "Curiously, he didn't mention who and I didn't pry." He cast a glance at Kate.

"That is odd. Well, in my case, I'm trying to confirm that there was a Hunt Ball held at Armstrong House in 1923," said Kate.

"To answer your question – yes, there was! The Armstrongs were very involved in the Hunt Club here throughout the nineteenth and early twentieth centuries." He handed her a large black-and-white photograph.

It was the same as the one Royce had sent to her.

"Did this man – Royce Charter – get a copy of this photograph from you?" asked Kate.

"Yes, and he asked for a copy of the whole file for that year."

Kate nodded. That explained how Royce had got the photograph. It had not been in the Charter family all these years but rather Royce had got it here from Liam recently.

Liam fingered through the papers in the file.

"I can see from the records that Lord Pierce Armstrong offered Armstrong House as a venue for that year's Hunt Ball in September 1923 – which was then held on the 10th of December of that year. Then there was a hunt that took place the following day, with the meet – or starting point – being at Armstrong House as well. And I have here a photograph of that meet." Liam handed Kate another large black-and-white photograph.

It was taken in the forecourt of Armstrong House with the house in the background and in front men and women on horseback, in their jackets and riding clothes, while the pack of hounds swarmed around.

"The Hunt Ball was often hosted at Armstrong House during those years. Ah, those were the days! It was the highlight of the year," sighed Liam. "Not like now – we haven't had a new recruit in several years. Are you interested in joining the club, Kate?"

"Ah, no thank you, Liam," she said firmly. "Is there any other information about how the hunt went that day or who was in attendance at the ball the night before?"

"Yes, here is a list of the participants in the hunt," said Liam, handing her a page.

Kate looked at the list of names and saw Pierce and Clara's names at the top.

"Thank you, Liam, this is all very useful." So that confirmed the fact that Armstrong House was rebuilt after the fire in the War of Independence, and that Pierce and Clara were still married and living together there by the end of 1923 ... She just needed to find out what happened after that. She turned to Liam.

"You mentioned that the Hunt Ball was often held at Armstrong House. Would you have the file from 1924 to see if it might have been held there that year too?"

"Well, I can go and see if you have time to wait?"

"Take all the time you need," said Kate.

He gave her the file and she sat down on the wine-coloured Chesterfield couch to study it.

Left alone, she tried to piece everything together. The compensation claim paid in March 1924 listed Pierce as living in Monkstown, Dublin, by then and so presumably the second fire must have occurred sometime between December 1923 and March 1924.

Eventually Liam returned to the study, carrying another file.

"Here we are – the Hunt Club's file from 1924," he declared as he put it down on the desk and flicked open the cover.

Kate stood and joined him to examine it.

"There was usually a club meeting every January, outlining the aims and ambitions for the year ahead and a roundup of the previous year's achievements," he informed her as he looked through the file and took out some papers. "Ah, here are the minutes of that meeting held in January 1924."

As Liam scanned the minutes he suddenly frowned and handed a page to Kate.

"You might want to take a read of this," he said.

Kate began to read.

The Castlewest Foxhunting Club would like to express their sympathy to Lord and Lady Armstrong regarding the fire that occurred at their home on December 11th last. After hosting a specular Hunt Ball at Armstrong House the previous night, members were shocked and saddened by the fire that broke out the following day during the hunt and the ensuing tragedy. As many of our members know, this is the second fire to befall Armstrong House in as many years and Sergeant Cantwell of the Castlewest Police has asked for anybody with information that could assist with their enquiries to make contact with him and be assured of confidentiality.

"There is a photograph here too," said Liam, handing it to her.

Kate looked at the photograph which showed members of the hunt gathered in front of Armstrong House as the fire raged.

"The fire broke out during the hunt so, as there was a photographer present, he took this photograph," said Liam.

That evening Kate hurried in through the front door of Armstrong House, carrying a copy of the files from the Hunt Club. She could hear laughter in the drawing room and went in to find Cian there with some of his friends.

"Hi, Cian, where's your dad?" she asked as she waved to his friends.

"He's down in the kitchen and he's not in a good mood," said Cian.

"Oh dear. I guess your friends are staying for dinner?"

"Only if Dad is cooking – we don't like your cooking!" said Cian.

"Well, I can't argue with that!" said Kate as she left the room.

She walked to the end of the hall and down the stairs to the kitchen. Cian was correct – Nico did not look in good form as he sat at the island reading through documents.

"I had the most interesting meeting with Liam Berill, the Master of the Castlewest Hunt Club," she said. "So, it's confirmed! The house did suffer another fire at the end of 1923 –"

"Look at this!" demanded Nico as he handed Kate the paperwork he had been reading.

"What is it?"

"I received it in the post today. It's from a firm of solicitors in London representing a Royce Charter. Wasn't that the name of the man who turned up at the wedding and sent you that photo?"

"Yes – but what do they want?" asked Kate, getting a bad feeling on hearing Royce's name for the second time that day.

"They are writing to put me on notice that this Royce Charter is the rightful heir of Clara Charter and as such he has a claim on Armstrong House."

"*What*? But – *how*?"

"They claim that Clara Charter, Lady Armstrong, was the half owner of Armstrong House from when her husband Pierce put her on the deeds in January 1923 and that, by a will she subsequently made in 1929, all her possessions – which included her share of Armstrong House – were to be inherited by her natural heirs which this Royce Charter claims to be. They've even sent a copy of the deeds and Clara's will."

Kate looked at the deeds with Clara's name on them in shock.

"They have also forwarded a file of evidence that Clara was living in the house in 1923 and still married to my grandfather at the time the deed of transfer was made – including that photograph from the Hunt Ball in 1923 with Clara and Pierce together!"

"It all makes sense now," said Kate. "That man Royce came up here to check out the house. And when I met Liam Berill today he told me Royce had been there a few weeks ago and asked to see the same 1923 file. Royce was going around looking for evidence to back up his claim that these deeds are legitimate."

"The solicitors are also claiming that Clara paid for the reconstruction of the house after it suffered the fire in the War of Independence and have forwarded evidence of the payments she made, paid from her bank account, which they claim show she was living in the house during the time she was added to the deeds! I don't know anything about this – it must be bullshit!"

Kate sat down at the island and put her face in her hands.

Then she looked up at her husband.

"I'm afraid it's not. The research I've been doing shows this is all true. Pierce did get compensation from the government after the first fire but it wasn't paid until 1924. I couldn't figure out how they could afford to rebuild the house the year before, but this answers that question. Clara was a member of the Charter Chocolate family and so must have had the money to rebuild the house in 1923 and Pierce must have put her on the deeds in exchange."

"Whose side are you on?" demanded Nico, suddenly angry.

"Our side, of course! I'm just stating what I already know. But surely this doesn't give this man any rights to our home because of a will that was made a hundred years ago?"

"I need to speak to my solicitor as soon as possible," said Nico, suddenly getting up from the island and marching upstairs.

Chapter 33

1923

Clara walked through the grounds of her grandmother's house in Kent. It was now June and her mind dwelt on the past few months since she had last been there. Pierce appeared to be fully recovered from his suicide bid. So much so it was hard to believe he had ever sunk so low that he had wanted to end his life. But she knew she must not forget that he had tried to kill himself and, no matter how arrogant he could sometimes appear, it masked a fragility that she had never known existed. Sometimes at Armstrong House she felt she was stepping on thin ice around him, frightened that fragility would reappear. Things were certainly different than they were before in their marriage. He didn't show the cruelty he had before. But Constance's remarks worried her. Did the fact she was now wealthy make their marriage easy? Did it make Pierce treat her differently? There were still regular moments when he expressed casual maliciousness towards her. But she was stronger now, so that did not affect her as it had done before. She did not regret going back to him and to Armstrong House but she still felt she could not fully trust him. Pierce was still an enigma.

She looked back at the house where her parents were seated on the terrace. They waved at her, and she waved back. They had agreed to stay at Oak Trees to take care of everything for her for the time being and that gave her great comfort before she returned to Armstrong House. The Civil War had finally been brought to a close in Ireland and she dearly hoped that the troubled years for the country were now in the past.

As she walked back to Oak Trees, she knew she would not be able to feel secure until she had opened her heart to Pierce. With the Civil War over, she decided it was now a safe time to trust him fully with the truth.

Constance took full advantage of Clara's absence to try and find the portrait. Hugh kept her informed of Pierce's activities so that she made sure to only visit when he was not there. Unknown to herself, Asty proved to be quite the useful spy.

Constance would always take an artefact or objet d'art with her on the pretext it was for the house, as her cover. Fennell even offered her tea every time she called, which she would politely decline saying she was too busy. The staff were too focused on their work to pay her much attention as she purposefully walked around the house, looking official.

She had already made a thorough search of the downstairs when she was furnishing it and was confident the portrait was not there. After again making sure it wasn't hidden in the library, the ballroom or the dining room, she had switched her attention to upstairs. Day after day, when she arrived at the house she would slip upstairs and begin searching the bedrooms. She left no stone unturned in her pursuit of her prize but the house as so big and there were so many nooks and crannies, she sometimes feared she was looking for a needle in a haystack.

She now moved her search to the attic which housed the servants' bedrooms. She imagined Pierce would never go up there so she reasoned it might be the most likely place for Clara to have hidden the portrait. As in the past there had been many more servants in the house than at present, there were a number of unoccupied bedrooms there. Ignoring the few that were occupied, reasoning that Clara would never leave the painting in one of them, she made a thorough search of the unoccupied ones, from looking under beds to searching old trunks to checking for loose floorboards and scanning the roof and rafters.

The last room was now being used as a storeroom and Constance made an exhaustive search of the boxes being kept there but could find nothing more interesting than a bed pan and a large brass urn.

Constance flounced down on the bed and with resignation at last conceded defeat. She was forced to admit to herself that unless Clara told her where the painting was then she would never find it. And she could never broach that subject with Clara without pointing the finger at herself as the guilty party if the painting was then discovered missing.

She stood up and looked out the window that jutted from under the roof. The room was at the front of the house and offered a view down the terraced gardens and across the lake. In the nearby fields she spotted Hugh busy tending the cattle that he had bought at a recent fair. She sighed as she began to return the boxes to where they had been originally placed.

Then, as she moved a box back against the knee wall that ran across the little room, supporting the sloping roof and timber rafters, her eyes were suddenly drawn to a fine line that ran down the three-foot-high wall. She pushed the box out of the way, got down on her knees and traced her finger down along the little crevice. In doing so, she realised the knee wall was made of painted wood rather than bricks and painted plaster. At one point there was a small indentation on both sides of the crevice, a slightly damaged spot less than half an inch long. Then she noticed another vertical crevice further along the wall.

She knew that behind the knee wall there would be an empty space.

Her breath came short as she went and opened one of the boxes and took a knife from the cutlery set inside it. She slipped the top of the knife into the crevice where the indentation was and made a levering motion. An entire panel of plywood fell forward.

She peered into the small attic space and saw something large and rectangular wrapped in brown paper. Reaching in, she pulled the object out into the room. She hastily ripped off the paper. Her eyes widened as she saw she was holding Johnny Seymour's portrait of Clara. Her heart thumped with excitement as she moved quickly to the light of the window to view the painting properly.

"Oh – you beauty!" she whispered as she took in the full glory of the painting.

Familiar with Seymour's work, her hands started to tremble as she realised that this was his greatest painting. If possible, the painting made Clara even more beautiful than she was and the detail and care the artist had put into the portrait shone through. Constance could tell the artist had indeed been in love with his subject when he painted her.

Slowly, she went to sit down on the bed while she continued to gaze at Clara's portrait.

"Whose motorcar is that, Fennell?" asked Pierce as he came through the front door and found the butler arranging flowers in a vase on the sideboard in the hallway. "Is it not Constance Fitzgerald's?"

"It is, my lord," answered Fennell.

"What is she doing here?"

"Mrs. Fitzgerald has been coming while Lady Armstrong is away to finish her work furnishing the house, sir," said Fennell.

"Has she indeed? And where is she now?"

"I am not certain. I have not seen her downstairs so she must be upstairs, my lord."

Pierce looked up the staircase and then went and ascended it.

As he walked down the corridor towards the master bedroom he could hear Asty and Síle talking.

"And that's where they found her, by the fireplace as dead as a dodo with her knitting still in her hands!" said Asty.

"Mrs. Reilly was always a great knitter. Didn't she die doing something she loved? What more could she ask for?" said Síle.

Pierce rolled his eyes on hearing the servants' idle gossip as he walked into the bedroom. Asty was folding sheets as Síle cleaned out the hearth.

Both women jumped to attention when they saw him.

"Have you seen Constance – Mrs. Fitzgerald?" asked Pierce.

"No, sir. Not since yesterday," said Asty.

"She was here yesterday as well?"

"Yes, sir. Most days since Her Ladyship has been away," answered Asty.

"For pity's sake! Wretched woman! This is a house not a railway station to be passed through!" snapped Pierce as he turned and left the room.

He walked down the corridor and began to open the doors to all the bedrooms, but Constance was nowhere to be found. He turned the corner at the end of the corridor and glanced inside the old nursery which still brought back bad memories of mind-numbingly boring afternoons being taught by governess after governess. Prudence used to scare away the governesses with alarming speed, so there was a constant array of young women being hired for the position.

At the end of the corridor was the servants' staircase that led down to the kitchen and another that went up to the attic. Thinking Fennel must be wrong and Constance must be on the ground floor, Pierce had turned to go back downstairs when he thought he heard a noise from the attic rooms.

He silently climbed the stairs into the attic and listened intently before quietly opening each door to check the other side. When he reached the final door he swung it open in a dramatic fashion.

"Pierce!" exclaimed Constance who was standing there, holding a brass urn.

"Constance! What exactly are you doing up here?" demanded Pierce.

"Well, I was just wondering where would be the right spot to place this!" said Constance with a big smile, holding up the urn. "I just found it in one of the boxes here. I remembered Clara saying there were some ornaments stored up here and I thought I might take a look to see if there was anything here that could be displayed downstairs."

"And all you managed to find was that urn? I imagine the reason it was put up here in storage is because it is so ugly!" said Pierce.

"Well, beauty is in the eye of the beholder!" said Constance, surveying the urn.

"I really think my wife has inconvenienced you far too much in her endless pursuit of restoring Armstrong House to its former glory," said Pierce.

"But it has been my pleasure!"

"Still – I wouldn't like Clara to take advantage of you so perhaps you should consider your work to be finished here at this point," said Pierce.

"But Clara has not taken advantage of me in the least!"

As Pierce's cold dark eyes stared at her, Constance suddenly felt a shiver run through her. It was as if he could look into her soul. She felt trapped and felt the need to rush away from him. And she could suddenly see why Clara could not escape from this man. He had a power, a dark mysterious attraction that she imagined could be as dangerous as it was intoxicating. She always believed nobody could get the better of her. But maybe this man could.

"As I said, it has been my pleasure," she whispered and for some reason that she could not understand her eyes filled with tears.

"Good day, Constance," said Pierce, stepping back and by doing so indicating she should leave.

"Good day, Pierce," said Constance as she walked past him and out of the room.

Pierce looked around the room and then went to the windows and waited, brooding, until he saw Constance walk quickly across the forecourt to her motor car and drive away.

That evening Pierce was seated in the dining room, having dinner on his own.

"Mr. and Mrs. Fennell have left for the evening, your lordship," said Asty as she served dessert. "They have gone to visit relatives for the night."

He ignored her as she poured custard on his apple crumble.

"I was wondering if I could meet you tomorrow to go through the menus for the following week, as Lady Armstrong is away," said Asty.

Pierce looked at her as if she were mad.

"No – I don't have the time for that! Just repeat whatever was on the menu for this week."

"As you wish, sir. *Hmm* – just so you know, I gave permission for Síle to go and stay with her family in Castlewest tonight as her mother has been poorly," said Asty.

"Why does that concern me?"

"It doesn't – but just so you are aware that it is only you and me in the house tonight. I'll be just upstairs from you if you need anything – anything at all."

Asty smiled at him and Pierce watched her walk from the room, holding the custard jug.

Chapter 34

At Mass on Sunday morning Hugh was seated beside Asty as he listened to the priest give his sermon. Hugh kept his eyes fixed on the altar. Tadgh, Molly and their children were seated in the bench directly across the aisle from him. When arriving at the church, on seeing Hugh one of Tadgh's children had made to rush to greet him but Molly had quickly restrained the boy and held him back from doing so. Hugh thought it very sad that he had been so close to his family and now they were divided and enemies. He knew that Tadgh must be even more infuriated that he had got the Armstrong Estate up and running at such speed. Lady Armstrong had left funds with Conway, their solicitor, for Hugh to buy livestock and now the land was being grazed by their own livestock again. But then everyone knew that Hugh was a better farmer than his brother. Hugh knew that Tadgh's anger wasn't just because he had taken the job at Armstrong House but because he had abandoned the cause and in Tadgh's mind gone to the other side. Hugh knew the reality was that leaving the cause had facilitated taking the job at Armstrong House. He couldn't have done one without another.

As Hugh looked around the packed church, he knew his was not the only family there torn apart by the civil war. There was now a deep divide in the community, a bitterness created with one half now enemies of the other. Hugh remembered that two years previously, when there was a truce in the War of Independence, there had been a glorious summer when people started to live life to the full again. There had been parties and fun and people could travel again as the hostilities ended. That was not happening with the end of the Civil War. Now the country was divided in two and there was mistrust. Even though the command had been given to down arms, many people felt unsafe and there were scores to be settled and much anger.

Hugh glanced at Asty who smiled adoringly at him.

Ignoring the fact that half his congregation hated the other half, the priest was concentrating his sermon on the safe subject of the sins of the flesh. His voice rose to an alarming volume as he warned about giving in to temptation. Hugh started fidgeting with his hands as he thought of the mortal sin he was guilty of. As the priest expanded his sermon to vehemently condemn the sin of adultery, Hugh felt a moment of shame that he had been the cause of Constance committing this mortal sin. Everybody would be shocked beyond belief if they knew he was having an affair with the married lady renting Seymour Manor. He felt guilty over Constance's husband and Asty but he knew he could not help himself. Meeting Constance had been the turning point of his life. He never dreamt he would meet somebody like her or that such a woman would be remotely interested in him. He knew Asty was the type of girl everyone expected him to marry but Constance was a woman he could not resist. All he could think about now was seeing her when he called to Seymour Hall that night. He knew there could be no future between them, but it did not stop him from fantasising about a very different destiny they could have together.

After the Mass was over Hugh and Asty filed out of the church with everyone else and thanked the priest who was positioned at the front door.

"Well, isn't that a lovely sight? I'd heard the two of you were courting and it's about time this fella settled down," said the priest as he slapped Hugh on the shoulder.

"Isn't that what I'm always telling him, Father?" said Asty, smiling.

"It took a girl like you to snare him, Asty!" said the priest. "When can I expect a visit to discuss the wedding?"

"Any time you want, Father!" said Asty.

"Let's say next Saturday at two. I'll put you in my diary for then."

"Perfect! We'll see you then!" said Asty as she smiled up at Hugh.

"Hold on – I'll be busy on the estate next Saturday!" said Hugh, bewildered by the conversation he had been the subject of but had no part in.

"Sure you can slip away for an hour or two and nobody will miss you! Good day, Father, and thank you for the lovely sermon," said Asty as she tugged Hugh down the path to the road.

As the train neared Castlewest, Clara was gazing out at the countryside they passed through. She had been very sad leaving Oak Trees but was looking forward to being back at Armstrong House.

Her mind was much clearer now on what were the next steps she must take for the future. With the Civil War now over and her marriage on more solid ground, she felt the time was right to trust Pierce fully. But, before she had left for England she had upset Pierce by going behind his back in hiring Hugh and the first thing she must do was make amends for that.

The train pulled into the station at Castlewest and she was thrilled to see Pierce waiting on the platform to greet her. She had feared he might have sent one of the staff to collect her. That would have been his usual reaction after they had a disagreement. His walls would come up and he would become more distant. But the fact he was waiting for her proved how their relationship had grown. She opened the carriage door and stepped out onto the platform, then rushed to him, embraced and kissed him.

"Clara – please! It's not becoming for Lady Armstrong to make such public shows of affection," said Pierce, removing her arms from around his neck as he looked at the other passengers disembarking from the train.

"Oh, I don't care about them! I missed you!"

"Well, you might not care but I do. Let's fetch your luggage." He moved towards her carriage in the train to retrieve her suitcase.

As Pierce drove them back to Armstrong House, he listened to Clara speak about her visit to England until she eventually asked, "So what has been happening here? Has there been any more trouble from O'Meara?"

"We haven't seen him," said Pierce.

"Then it's all worked out well, hasn't it? Employing Hugh and putting him in charge. I knew it would."

"Aren't you clever?" said Pierce in a bored voice.

"Pierce, I'm sorry I went behind your back hiring Hugh," said Clara.

Pierce didn't respond.

Nevertheless, as they journeyed up the avenue towards the house, she felt elated to see the livestock Hugh had bought grazing the land.

"Now they'll never be able to say we are not farming the land and claim it," she said with satisfaction.

They drove into the forecourt and parked outside the house.

"Welcome home, Lady Armstrong," said Fennell as he opened the door for her.

"Oh, thank you, Fennell," said Clara.

"Can you take Lady Armstrong's suitcase to her room and have tea brought to us, Fennell," said Pierce as they took off their hats and coats in the hall.

"Certainly, sir," said Fennell.

In the drawing room, Clara twirled around as Pierce closed the door. Everything looked so perfect now compared to when they arrived there a few short months before.

She went to him and kissed him intimately.

"I missed you," she whispered.

"Yes, the place was certainly quieter without you too," he said.

She smiled at him and shook her head.

"Oh – you! Do you think you could ever remove that mask and show what is really going on in that heart of yours?" she said, putting her hand on his chest.

"Maybe you might not like what is really going on in my heart," he replied.

"Stop pretending you don't care about anything, Pierce. When I know you really do," she said, taking his hand and leading him to the couch.

They sat and Clara turned to him.

"Pierce, I need to tell you something. I'll expect you'll be angry with me, but I hope you'll understand my reasons –"

Before she could continue, the door opened, and Prudence walked in.

"Oh, you are back, are you? Trains running on time – who would ever have thought with this lot running the country," said Prudence.

Clara looked at Prudence incredulously.

"Prudence! What are you doing here?" she demanded.

"What does it look like? I've come back to live here. It is my home too," said Prudence.

Clara's eyes shot to Pierce in disbelief.

"With the estate back running I thought best we bring Prudence back to oversee things. Nobody knows this farm better than her," he said.

"But – but – you should have discussed this with me first!" said Clara.

"Like you discussed hiring O'Meara with me?" asked Pierce, raising an eyebrow.

"That's completely different. Hugh was a simple case of hiring staff, Prudence is – Prudence!" said Clara, horrified at the thought of her sister-in-law being back in their lives.

"Oh, I'll keep out of your way, don't worry about that!" said Prudence. "I won't even be living at Armstrong House – I'll be down at Hunter's Farm."

"You were living in Hunter's Farm previously when you made my life hell, Prudence!" said Clara, standing up abruptly.

"Well, I have apologised for all that misunderstanding," said Prudence. "I mean, Pierce is quite correct that you cannot leave the running of the entire estate in the hands of Hugh O'Meara. His brother is a thug, his father was a thug and is grandfather was a thug too from what I remember. They gave Papa the most beastly time during the Land War."

"Pierce, I would like to speak to you privately," said Clara.

"Anything you want to say you can say in front of Prudence," he replied.

"No, I can't, and I don't want to!"

"Clara, I just don't understand this hostility," said Prudence. "Is it not I who came to London to rescue your marriage? Is it not I who told you how much Pierce was in love with you when you were ready to divorce him? In fact, I should open a matchmaking agency – I'm quite the Cupid!"

"And was it not you who tried to drive us apart in the past, Prudence? You who spied on me and reported everything back to Pierce!"

"I love the fact you are blaming me for trying to destroy your marriage when you were the one cheating on your husband! Don't shoot the messenger! But that's all in the past and best forgotten. I must say the house is looking amazing. You've both done a marvellous job getting it back in order. The plumbing is even working like a dream now for the first time ever."

The door opened and Fennell entered, carrying a silver tray.

"Ah, tea – just what the doctor ordered. Well done, Fennell!" said Prudence. "Amazing how you even managed to get the old staff back. Although I don't like the look of that new girl you engaged as a housekeeper. She looks like trouble, if you ask me."

"Nobody is asking you, Prudence!" snapped Clara as she rushed past her out of the room.

"I'll pour, Fennell, you may go," said Prudence.

Fennell retreated from the room and closed the door behind him.

"Poor Clara, she is always so out of her depth, isn't she?" said Prudence, pouring two cups of tea. "Poor deluded creature actually thinks you are in love with her."

"Well, why would she not after the plan you concocted to get her back?"

"Well, she has served her purpose now. Armstrong House is back to its former glory, the Civil War is over and we are quite safe."

"What are you suggesting?"

"Do I need to spell it out? When are you going to give Clara her marching orders?"

"Perhaps you don't really know me. Perhaps I like having her around," said Pierce.

"Oh, I know you, Pierce, more than anyone and you don't like having Clara around. It may afford you some amusement to persecute her but that's as far as it goes. Most of the time she just irritates you."

"Maybe I have changed."

"And maybe you haven't!"

"Perhaps it's quite nice being married to an heiress. She pays for everything."

"That's her money, not yours. Once we have the estate up and running again you won't need her money. You've got what you need out of her to rebuild the house. Now it's time to end this sad charade of a marriage."

"Firstly, you have no idea what my feelings for Clara are. Nobody does, except for me, not even Clara. Secondly, I would be rather foolish to get rid of a wife who had just come into a large inheritance. One never knows what the future might hold. And her money allows me to have a very nice life – and I never want to see the inside of a gardener's cottage again!"

"So, you plan to keep her here as a kind of insurance policy?" asked Prudence, surprised. "And I thought I was cynical!"

Pierce rose from his seat and walked out.

Pierce walked into their bedroom to find Clara staring out one of the front windows.

She turned to face him.

"How could you, Pierce? How could you bring that woman back into our lives?" she demanded.

"That woman is my sister, and I couldn't leave her destitute in Dublin forever. And, besides, she speaks the truth. If it were not for her we would not be back together."

"But I don't want her here, Pierce! Even if she lives at Hunter's Farm she will come into the house as she likes and treats it as her home!"

"But it *has* been her home all her life. Surely you can see that?"

"This is you trying to keep control. You hate when I try to do something independently!"

"Do what you want, Clara, it is no concern of mine. What I object to is when you try to make decisions about Armstrong House that are mine to make. Prudence will make sure you are kept in your place."

Clara stared at him disbelievingly.

"Armstrong House is mine too! You've put me on the deeds! And how can you say it's no concern of yours what I do?" she demanded.

"Don't put me in a predicament where you force me to choose you or my family, Clara. If you love me as you claim you do, then you would honour my decision."

"I was so looking forward to seeing you when I came back from England. I felt our marriage was stronger than it ever had been before. I felt I finally trusted you, but you've just proved that I can't."

"Nor I you, Clara. Perhaps we are two people who must just live with that."

Chapter 35

Clara was in the drawing room with Asty as they went through the arrangements for the garden party on the coming Saturday.

"Have Mrs Fennell prepare beef, chicken, salmon and of course cucumber sandwiches, Asty – oh, and devilled eggs," said Clara.

"Yes, my lady."

"Also have her bake scones to be served with cream and raspberry and strawberry jam."

"And for dessert?"

"Apple tart and rhubarb tarts served with cream," said Clara.

"Very good, my lady," said Asty.

"That's all for the moment, Asty. I'll talk to again later."

"One other thing, my lady. I have to go to a funeral in Castlewest in the morning. My second cousin once removed has died."

"I am sorry to hear that, Asty. Of course you may go."

"It's hit us all very badly that she died. It came as terrible shock to us."

"I'm sure. How old was she?"

"Ninety-three, my lady," said Asty.

"Oh – I see!" said Clara.

"If there's nothing else, I'll get on with my work," said Asty.

She stood up

"One other thing, my lady," she said.

"Yes?"

"Since Lady Prudence arrived back she's in the house all the time telling me what to do which is usually contrary to your instructions and what makes sense to do!"

"You have my full authority to ignore her, Asty. I know that is easier said than done but don't let her get in the way of your work."

"I hoped you'd say that," said Asty with a smile and a nod.

Once Asty left, Clara went to the French windows, opened them and stepped onto the terrace. Down the fields she spotted Prudence with Hugh, having some kind of a disagreement which resulted in Hugh storming off.

Clara sighed as she watched Prudence march after Hugh, berating him.

She knew Prudence was Pierce's sister, but she could not understand why he had brought her back when he knew she upset her so much and she was destined to be a thorn in everyone's side.

Asty was coming down the servants' stairs and could hear Fennell and Mrs. Fennell speaking in the kitchen. She didn't make her presence known as she cocked an ear and listened into their conversation.

"I don't know what Lord Armstrong was thinking bringing Lady Prudence back here. Whatever chance their marriage has of working this time will be ruined with her around," sighed Mrs. Fennell.

"That poor girl went through enough in the past with the two of them ganging up on her. I had hoped Lord Armstrong had changed his ways but does a leopard ever change its spots, Mrs. Fennell?"

"Indeed, it doesn't. We'll have to look after Lady Clara as best we can, like we always did before. I can't imagine what life would be like here without her – with just him."

"Don't you worry, Mrs. Fennell. Lady Clara won't be going anywhere – not now she is an heiress. Lord Armstrong knows what side his bread is buttered on, and he won't lose the goose that is laying the golden egg!"

"I suppose you're right, Mr. Fennell. Remember when he blackmailed her to stay last time and that was before she had money. The only way Lady Clara will be leaving Armstrong House next time is in a box, I daresay."

Asty digested what she had heard as she turned and went back up the stairs.

In the courtyard at the back of the house, Clara waited as Hugh led her mare out from the stables. She was dressed casually for her ride, in a white shirt with a blue cravat and a black divided skirt, a black brimmed hat low on her brow. Pierce would no doubt frown if he saw her without jacket and gloves, even though she was riding on their own land.

"It's a nice day for a ride, ma'am," said Hugh.

"Yes, I feel like having a long relaxing ride to clear my mind ... Hugh ... I need to ask you ..."

"Yes, ma'am?"

"I saw you having an argument with Lady Prudence the other day. I hope she wasn't upsetting you but I fear she was."

"Well, she's a difficult character, ma'am. Always thinks she knows best and interfering, but don't you worry – I can handle her."

Clara smiled, relieved. "I am so pleased you came to work here. You run everything so smoothly and never a word of complaint out of you."

"I'm not here to complain, I'm here to work, ma'am."

"Asty is a very lucky girl," said Clara.

Hugh assisted her to mount astride.

Then the horse let out a shriek and reared onto its hind legs.

"*Steady! Steady!*" shouted Hugh as he tried to grab the reins from Clara, but the horse suddenly bolted out of the courtyard.

Clara screamed as the horse raced furiously through the parklands.

Asty had been watching from the kitchen window and came rushing out.

"What's happened?" she demanded.

Hugh raced to fetch the fastest horse in the stables and jumped up on it bareback.

"Something's wrong with Lady Armstrong's horse!" he shouted as he raced out of the courtyard after them.

Asty grabbed a bicycle and went in pursuit.

Clara desperately tried to regain control of the horse as it raced across the parklands and jumped across a ditch into a field.

"*Stop! Stop!*" she commanded but the mare continued to race as fast as she could.

Clara hung on and put all her energy into remaining in the saddle. Her head was spinning as the trees and bushes whizzed past her. The horse was so out of control she knew it would not stop and if she fell she could be killed at this speed.

Suddenly Hugh galloped up beside her.

"*Hang on! I'm going to try to slow her down!*" he shouted.

He reached over, grabbed the reins on the nearest side and, pulling tightly, tried to force the mare's head to the side and down. "*Whoa! Whoa! Steady, girl!*" he shouted as he used all his strength to pull on the reins while keeping his seat on his own racing horse.

Then the mare began to slow down and at last she ground to a halt.

Hugh quickly slid off his horse and pulled Clara off the saddle just before her horse raced off again.

"Oh, Hugh! I thought I was finished!" gasped Clara as he held her tightly.

She was shaking uncontrollably as he soothed her.

"You're safe now, Clara. You're safe now," said Hugh.

He continued to hold her tightly as he calmed her down and stroked her hair.

Asty had abandoned her bicycle and run through the fields.

When she at last caught sight of Hugh and Clara, she stopped abruptly. She observed them as they held each other tightly and Hugh stroked Clara's hair.

"A terrible shock for you, poor Clara!" said Prudence in the drawing room.

"I just don't know what happened! The mare has never acted like that before," said Clara, seated on the couch, grasping Pierce's hand while she sipped a brandy.

"Of course, you are not a natural horsewoman, Clara. You never even rode a horse until you came to live here," said Prudence. "Horses can sense that and take advantage."

"It was nothing to do with not being a good horsewoman," said Hugh who suddenly appeared in the doorway, holding a saddle.

"There was a time when servants waited to be announced rather than just marched in when they wanted to!" said Prudence.

Hugh ignored her and walked into the room, holding up something small, green and prickly in his hand.

"What is that?" asked Clara.

"A chestnut burr. I caught the mare down by the lake and I found it under her saddle."

Clara reached out and took the burr, the spikes of which were sharp.

"When Lady Armstrong sat on the saddle, the spikes drove into the mare's back and that is what set her off," said Hugh.

"But – but how did it get there?" demanded Clara.

"Well, the horse hardly put it there itself!" said Prudence.

"I saddled the horse myself this morning and rode her out to tend to the cattle. There was no burr there then," said Hugh.

"Are you sure?" asked Pierce.

"Of course I'm fucking sure!" snapped Hugh.

"Manners, young man! You may be the hero of the day but that does not give you permission to be insolent!" said Prudence.

"But how did it get there?" asked a bewildered Clara.

"Somebody must have put it there, ma'am," said Hugh.

"But who would do such a thing?" demanded Clara.

"I could hazard a guess," said Pierce, giving Hugh a cold look.

"Did you see anybody hanging around the stables, Hugh?" asked Clara.

"Not a soul and I've asked the staff downstairs, and the farm hands and they saw nobody either," said Hugh.

"Quite the detective, aren't you?" said Prudence.

"Clearly it must be your brother, Tadgh O'Meara," said Pierce.

"There's no evidence of that, Lord Armstrong," said Hugh.

"Do we need evidence? He already attacked you with a stone and threatened my wife."

"He wouldn't hurt a woman," said Hugh.

"Oh, don't be so ridiculous!" said Prudence, laughing.

"Thank you, Hugh. You may leave us now," said Clara.

Hugh left.

"Should we not call the police? This is tantamount to attempted murder," said Clara.

"Well, as your boy says, there is no evidence so I'm not sure how much good that would do," said Prudence.

"Pierce – I was so scared!" said Clara as she gripped his hands tightly.

"There – there. You are quite safe now," said Pierce as he put an arm around her and patted her head.

Fennell opened the door and announced, "Mrs. Constance Fitzgerald."

Constance hurried into the room. "Clara, I was just calling for a visit and Hugh told me what happened. Are you alright?" she said as she sat beside her on the couch.

"Oh, I'm quite unharmed, Constance, thanks to Hugh, but it gave me a terrible fright."

"Of course it did! Hugh said it was some kind of sabotage?" said Constance.

"It certainly looks like it. My money is on Tadgh O'Meara," said Pierce.

Prudence was scanning Constance head to foot in a contemptuous fashion.

"Prudence, this is my friend, Constance Fitzgerald," said Clara. "Constance – Pierce's sister, Prudence."

"I'm so pleased to meet you. I've heard so much about you," said Constance, standing and approaching Prudence with a smile.

"Can't say I've heard anything about you! Who exactly are you?" asked Prudence.

"Constance is renting Seymour Hall and refurnished this whole house for us," said Clara.

"Well, I'm sure any friend of Clara's is a friend of mine," said Prudence with a false smile as she shook Constance's hand.

Chapter 36

In the kitchen Mrs. Fennell waved Asty's cigarette smoke from in front of her face.

"For goodness' sake, Asty, I've told you before the kitchen is not the place for your smoke!"

"Well, I don't think anybody notices the difference with the amount of smoke from your charred cooking!" retorted Asty.

"I have had no complaints from those that matter, those upstairs!" said Mrs. Fennell.

All the staff were seated around the kitchen table and having tea and crumpets for their eleven o'clock break.

While Asty smoked she was avidly reading that morning's newspaper.

"Mrs. O'Reilly in Castlewest passed away on Thursday. She's left six children behind her and a husband who is more interested in the pub than child-rearing, from what I hear. Can you imagine?"

"I don't know why you are so interested in the obituaries in the paper each day, Asty. It's morbid!" said Mrs. Fennell.

"It's not morbid at all. I just liked to keep up with who has deceased – there's no harm in that, is there?"

"I certainly think it's unusual that a young girl such as yourself has such interest in who is dead. You should be more interested in the living."

Asty folded away the newspaper and put out her cigarette.

"Now – are you happy?" she asked, standing up.

"Has anyone seen Lady Armstrong this morning? How is she doing after her scare?" asked Mrs. Fennell.

"She seemed fine when I served breakfast this morning. But I'm sure it was a terrible shock to her," said Mr. Fennell.

"We must all keep alert, to watch out for any unsavoury characters hanging around," said Mrs. Fennell. "To make sure nobody is up to any mischief again. That includes you, Síle!"

"I will to be sure, Mrs. Fennell," said Síle as she blessed herself.

"I'll get on with my work. The crumpets were alright, Mrs. Fennell, but in future they need to be less overcooked," said Asty as she left the kitchen and walked up the servants' stairs.

"The cheek of that girl!" said Mrs. Fennell.

"She may be good at her job, but she is a madam," said Mr. Fennell.

"I pity that poor boy Hugh O'Meara getting mixed up with the likes of her. She'll only bring him misery!" said Mrs. Fennell.

Clara was in the terraced gardens in front of the house with Hugh as they prepared for the garden party. Hugh was following her instructions as he trimmed the hedges.

"With the terrible scare I got with the horse bolting, I don't know if I actually thanked you, Hugh, for saving me," said Clara. "I don't know what would have happened if you had not been there."

"Ah, no need for thanks, ma'am. Isn't that what I'm here for?" said Hugh as he continued to trim.

"It was a lucky day for me when Constance sent you to seek work here," said Clara.

"More lucky for me. I love it here."

"Do you? I am so glad as you have sacrificed a lot to come here. I do feel guilty about it damaging your relationship with your family."

"That's not for you to concern yourself with, ma'am. I made the decision and if my brother can't accept it that's his problem not mine."

She admired his spirt. Hugh seemed a very self-contained person who didn't feel the need to answer to anyone.

"I hear rumours from the staff that you are soon to be engaged," she said.

"You shouldn't listen to rumours, they are not to be believed," said Hugh.

"I hope you're not going to break Asty's heart, Hugh!"

"I think Asty's heart is quite unbreakable so don't lose any sleep over that, Lady Armstrong."

"How I wish I could be like you, free as a bird," she said.

He turned to her and started to laugh.

"Why in God's name would you like to be like me? You're living in a house like this with the life you have – do you know how lucky you are?"

"Yes – of course I know that I'm very lucky," she said, smiling.

She knew if Pierce or Prudence could hear her talking to Hugh in such a familiar way they would be furious. But she had prided herself on always making friends with the staff. It might not be the acceptable norm for the people of her class but she had often found the staff her only source of support at times over the years.

Asty walked into the master bedroom and closed the door behind her. She walked around the room and sat down on the unmade bed. As she imagined Clara and Pierce sleeping there the previous night, she rolled herself on the sheets. She then stood up, walked into the dressing room and traced her fingers across Pierce's suits. She took out a shirt he had worn and held it close to her, wrapping the arms of the material around her as she inhaled his scent. She walked back into the bedroom, holding the shirt, lay down on the bed and began to roll around, squeezing the material close to her. She lay like that for a while before getting up to put the shirt back in its rightful place. As she passed the window she spotted Hugh with Clara in the garden, standing close to one another as they laughed and spoke. She dropped the shirt to the ground as she studied them.

It was evening as Constance drove Hugh to Seymour Hall.

"I feel I need to let Asty know that we aren't having a future together," said Hugh. "It's not fair on her, stringing her along."

Despite Constance feeling a satisfaction that Hugh had little or no feelings for Asty, she felt it was useful to have a contact inside Armstrong House for gaining access when the coast was clear.

"But you make such a handsome couple, Hugh. Imagine the children!" she teased.

"Seriously – she's talking about marriage, Constance!"

"Well, you could do worse," said Constance.

"So, it wouldn't bother you if I married her then?"

"Hugh, my darling, of course it would bother me but I won't be here forever, and I don't want to deny you happiness with somebody else."

"Is that all this is to you then – all that I am to you? An entertainment while you are staying down here?"

She parked the car in the drive of Seymour Hall and turned to face him.

"Of course you mean so much more than that. But we both need to protect ourselves from being hurt. Keep control of your heart, Hugh. Hearts are not easy to fix after they get broken."

"Don't flatter yourself that much, Constance. I never said anything about getting a broken heart," said Hugh as he jumped out of the motorcar.

They walked to the front door and went inside.

"I could do with a drink! I've had to listen to Clara's woes for the past two hours!" said Constance. "It's hard to have sympathy for a woman who has everything!"

"I've been thinking the same thing – that she's a woman who has everything. But there's something sad about her. I think she's not happy in her marriage and she's trying to force herself to be," said Hugh as he followed her into the drawing room.

"Clement!" Constance exclaimed.

Her husband was seated on an armchair there.

"Surprise!" said Clement, standing up and coming to kiss her.

"What the hell are you doing here?" demanded Constance, stunned.

"Well, I was finished my work in America and so came back early, and I thought I'd come down to surprise you," said Clement, turning his attention to Hugh and stretching out his hand to him. "I'm Clement Fitzgerald, Constance's husband."

"So I gathered," said Hugh, shaking his hand.

"This is Hugh, Clement. He's the estate manager at Armstrong House and helps me move furniture."

"Yes, he looks to be a big strong lad. I'm sure he's very capable of moving things," said Clement.

"Hugh – as I said, that dresser I want you to take away is in the stable out the back. If you could go ahead?" said Constance. "Take the cart but do return it."

"Sure, ma'am," said Hugh. "Nice to meet you, Mr. Fitzgerald."

"Likewise," said Clement, watching Hugh turn around and leave.

"Making friends with the locals, Constance?" said Clement with a smirk.

"I really do need a drink now," said Constance as she went to the drinks cabinet. "Clement – you should have told me you were coming! How did you get into the house?"

"You left the kitchen door unlocked."

"Silly me!"

"So – have you got the portrait yet?"

"No! I can hardly just walk in and take it! So near and yet so far! Nobody would even miss it but getting it out of the house is the problem."

"I have a buyer waiting, Constance. It will make us rich. How do we get the damned thing?"

"I'm trying to figure that out! There are servants there all the time. And Pierce Armstrong doesn't trust me – with good reason, I guess – and keeps a close eye on me whenever I am there. The key to getting the portrait is Clara. She trusts me completely and tells me intimate details of her life. She's feeling quite vulnerable and so I'm exploiting that until I get an opportunity to snatch the painting."

"I did miss you! Did you miss me?" He walked to her and put his arms around her.

"Of course I did! Do you know how boring it is down here? Nothing to do!" she said with a laugh. Then she kissed him and wrapped her arms around him.

She rolled her eyes as she realised she'd had a lucky escape – that she and Hugh had not said or done anything to expose their affair.

Chapter 37

All Hugh could think about was the arrival of Constance's husband. In a strange way he had put the fact she was married out of his mind and it was a shock to see Clement actually existed. Constance had mentioned that Clement was older that her, but Hugh was taken aback by how much older. Clement looked old enough to be her father. They made an unlikely couple. But then Hugh knew that he and Constance made an even more unlikely couple. As he already knew, Constance certainly did not live her life by what people thought of her or expected her to do. He imagined she had been attracted by Clement's sophistication and experience but, for a woman who could have anyone, he was bewildered why she was with Clement.

And now that her husband was back, Hugh's biggest fear was that their relationship was over, and she would not be able to see him again.

"What is wrong with you?" asked Asty, cutting into his thoughts.

It was evening, and they were in his cottage, cuddled up on the bed beside the fire.

"Nothing," he said.

"Something is wrong with you. You're distracted these past few days," she said.

"Ah, I'm just tired from working."

"Aren't we all! Slaving away for that high and mighty Clara Armstrong so she doesn't have to get off her skinny arse to do anything for herself!"

"Don't speak about Lady Armstrong like that – she is one of the nicest people I've ever met," snapped Hugh angrily.

Asty sat up, taken aback. Hugh was always so laid back it gave her a shock to hear him lose his temper.

"Is she indeed?"

"Yes, she is. She's very kind to me and makes me feel important. She talks to me like an equal."

"Well, you're not her equal! You're just her servant like the rest of us so get yourself off that cloud and back down to earth, Hugh O'Meara!"

"Don't worry, Asty, I have my feet on the ground."

"All you ever talk about is that bitch! Lady Armstrong this – Lady Armstrong that! You've gone cuckoo over her!"

"Are you out of your tiny pea-sized mind? I don't talk about her that much."

She leaned forward and started tapping her finger against his temple as her eyes squinted meanly.

"I know – I know – I *know* what goes on in that head of yours, Hugh O'Meara! And I don't like it one little bit!"

"It's getting late, Asty – isn't it time you made your way back to Armstrong House before Fennell locks up for the night!" said Hugh, stepping off the bed and beginning to put on his shirt.

"I have my own key, remember? And Fennell can fuck off! I've just about had enough of the lot of ye!" She buttoned up her blouse furiously. "Everyone taking me for granted!"

"What are you talking about, you mad cow?" asked Hugh and started to laugh which only made her angrier.

"You'll get yours!" she shouted as she threw on her coat and then held up her fist to him. "And if you miss the appointment with the priest this Sunday to discuss our wedding like you did the last time, I'll rearrange your face so badly that no woman will ever look at you again – you vain bastard!"

She swung out the front door, grabbed her bicycle which was lying against the wall and cycled up the boreen.

As Asty turned off the boreen and began to cycle in the direction of Armstrong House, her temper was out of control. Hugh might joke and dismiss what she was saying, but she *did* know. She knew when a man had somebody else on his mind, and she knew Hugh had somebody on his. She knew it was ridiculous to even imagine that Lady Armstrong would have any attachment to the likes of Hugh, but that didn't stop Asty from hurting that her fiancée was in love with somebody else. Even if he didn't admit to it himself.

Constance had arranged to visit Clara and, as she drove up the avenue to Armstrong House, she saw Hugh working in a field in the September sunshine. She stopped and walked towards him.

"*Constance!*" he called when he saw her and strode towards her. He was about to embrace her when he stopped abruptly and looked around, fearing somebody might see them.

"I wanted to call to your cottage to speak with you, but it's been impossible to get away from Clement," she said.

"Well, that was a shock finding your husband there!"

"I know! I nearly dropped dead when I saw him! Clement was always full of surprises!"

"Did he suspect anything?"

"Of course not! I'm a very good actress."

"So, what happens now? Between us?" asked Hugh, afraid to hear her answer.

"We're going to have to be very careful. Obviously you can't come to Seymour Hall anymore. So, I'll come to you when I can."

Hugh visibly relaxed on hearing this.

"I thought you were going to say you couldn't see me anymore," he said.

"Oh, my darling!" she said, reaching forward and putting her hand on his cheek briefly. "You're the sweetest thing that ever happened to me. How could I give you up now?"

"I want to hold you and –"

"I'd better go. We might be spotted. I'll call to your cottage when I get the first chance." She blew him a kiss and quickly walked away.

"It's such a nice day for a walk. I'm glad you suggested it," said Constance as she and Clara walked down through the terraced gardens to the lakeshore.

"Yes, but it's not just because of the weather that I suggested the walk. I wanted to get out of the house and away from prying eyes and ears which are everywhere – especially since Prudence arrived back."

"Is she proving difficult?"

"The word *difficult* was invented for Prudence! She's supposed to be living at Hunter's Farm but comes and goes to the house as she pleases," sighed Clara.

"Why not just ban her from coming?" suggested Constance as they reached the lakeshore and began to walk along the shingled beach.

"I cannot ban her from what is her family home and, besides, I learned a long time ago that there is no point in trying to control Prudence. It's a pointless exercise."

"And Pierce cannot ask her to stay away from the house as much as possible?"

"Like everything in life, she simply does not bother him. I swear the skies could come crashing down and Pierce would simply look on with a kind of aloof disinterest."

"May I ask? How are you and Pierce getting along?"

"Fine ... if you consider him looking on me and our marriage with a kind of aloof disinterest could be described as fine. I really felt when we came back here we had found a new connection, after he had tried to kill himself, but now he seems to be slipping away from me again. I understand now that this is him protecting himself but sometimes it is just so damned hard to love a man who appears like ice. But I must keep trying to break down his walls. I really believe that one day I will and we will be the soulmates we are meant to be."

"Do you really believe in soulmates?" asked Constance as her thoughts drifted to Hugh.

"I actually do. That is why I married Pierce. He wasn't the man I expected to marry or anyone else expected me to, but I felt this affinity. I still do but I can't trust him yet to tell him about ..." Clara stopped talking.

"Tell him about what?" asked Constance.

"Oh, never mind. All I do is talk about me and my life and I haven't even asked about you and your husband now that he is here."

"That's what I'm here for, Clara. I'm the friend that I hope you can tell anything to, knowing you can trust me implicitly."

"You don't know how important that is to me. You've made my time back at Armstrong House so much easier and nicer, knowing I have you to rely on whenever I need support."

"I'm always here for you, Clara."

"Well, at least I have you since I seem to have someone out there who hates me enough to try and kill me," said Clara.

"They still haven't found the culprit?"

"No. I doubt they ever will," said Clara. "Anyway, I really must insist we talk about you for a while. Do tell – how is your husband?"

After Constance had left to attend an auction, Clara chose to continue walking along the lakeshore on her own. She had always enjoyed that. It was so peaceful and quiet there it allowed her to get lost in her thoughts.

Suddenly there was loud plop in the water, disturbing the tranquillity but also her thoughts. She looked out across the still water, imagining it must have been a fish leaping. Suddenly there was another plop in the water ... and another. Then a stone went whizzing past her and into the water. She turned quickly around but there were trees trailing all along the shingled lakeshore and she couldn't see anybody.

"*Hello?*" she called.

There was no answer, only silence. She suddenly felt very isolated and realised she had come a long way from Armstong House. As she turned to walk back in the direction of the house another stone came hurtling from behind the trees, narrowly missing her and landing in the water.

"*Hello – who is there?*" she called in a stern voice but was still only met by an eerie silence.

She began to walk quickly but the shingled beach slowed down her pace. When another stone was thrown, she began to panic. And suddenly there were several stones being thrown at her from somebody in the cover of the trees. Then one stone hit her head and she fell to the ground. As she lay there feeling dizzy, terror overcame her. She realised she was in huge danger where she was but she'd be an open target if she tried to make her way along the beach. She pulled herself up and managed to scramble up the beach and take cover in the trees. She rested against a tree while her hand felt the side of her head. She saw blood on her fingers.

There was suddenly a rustling sound as she heard somebody move through the bushes.

She leapt away from the tree and began to run through the woods in the direction of home. As the trees were so dense, her speed was constantly slowed down as she scrambled through the thick foliage. She could hear that whoever was in the woods with her was moving too, chasing her, scrambling after her. She turned around several times to try and see who was pursuing her but could see nobody. The wood was dank and dark, the sun being blocked by the treetops.

She felt the briars tear at her legs and heard her dress rip on some barbed wire. The wound on her head was throbbing but she pushed on. When she tripped on a bramble she went flying to the ground but pulled herself up and forced herself to keep going. At last she reached the end of the woods and entered the Armstrong Estate.

She started screaming as she raced across the fields to the house. As she neared it she saw Hugh running towards her.

"Clara! What's wrong? What happened to your head?"

"There was somebody chasing me! Throwing stones at me!" she said as she fell into his arms. She turned her head and looked behind her but there was nobody there.

"I thought he was going to kill me!" she said and began to cry hysterically.

"You're with me now, Clara. Nobody is going to harm you while I'm here," said Hugh as he began to lead her back to Armstrong House, an arm supporting her.

"And you didn't see who threw the stone at you?" asked Sergeant Cantwell from the Castlewest police station who was interviewing Clara in the drawing room.

"No! Of course I didn't or I would tell you! And it wasn't one stone, it was many stones, and they were trying to hit me! Hit my head and kill me!" said Clara.

A doctor had been called, and Clara lay on the couch in the drawing room with a bandage around her head while Pierce, Prudence and Hugh stood around her with the policeman.

"It must have been a terrible shock for you," said Prudence. "It will be the peasants trying to kill us like they always do."

"Prudence!" snapped Pierce.

"Well, I only speak the truth! They shot Papa, they burned down the house and now they're trying to kill Clara. They won't stop until they do!"

"I imagine it was Tadgh O'Meara, Sergeant," said Pierce. "He already attacked our estate manager and went to attack my wife but stopped himself when she was driving his cattle off our land."

"I've told you before that my brother wouldn't harm a woman!" said Hugh angrily.

"Such loyalty!" mocked Prudence.

"You may go, O'Meara. The police have your statement," said Pierce.

Clara reached out and took Hugh's hand.

"Thank you, Hugh, for helping me today."

Hugh nodded and left the room.

"He's a regular knight in shining armour!" said Prudence.

"This is the second attempt on Clara's life – somebody also placed a chestnut burr under her saddle, Sergeant," said Pierce.

"I will interview Tadgh O'Meara but there really is no evidence against him," said Cantwell.

Clara stood up. "Sergeant, I thought there was an order from Minister Thomas Geraghty that we were to be protected at Armstrong House – and this is the second attempt on my life!"

"The order was for protection during the Civil War which is now over," said the Sergeant.

"The hatred and the violence has not stopped just because the war is over and I think it will take many years for it to stop," said Prudence.

"I will send one of my men to come to the house each day to check how you are but I can't have somebody here all the time now the war is over. I don't have the manpower. I suggest you shouldn't go for any walks or rides on your own, Lady Armstrong, and for everyone to be vigilant. Good night."

"Well, he is about as useful as a chocolate teapot!" said Prudence after he left.

Hugh held Constance close to him in the bed beside the fire in the cottage.

"Poor Lady Armstrong was badly shaken after the attack," he said.

"Have you any idea who it could be? Did you see anybody lurking around?" asked Constance.

"Only the family and the staff were there. The only visitor that day was yourself. But anyone could have slipped on the estate without being seen."

"I think from everything I know, Hugh, that you are going to have to look closer to home. Clearly it must be Tadgh. It's even the same weapon he used when he was attacking you – a stone!"

"I know my brother and it's not his style. I've told the Armstrongs the same as I'm telling you. He wouldn't hurt a woman."

"But perhaps he only means to scare her so she and Pierce will move away from Armstrong House? Perhaps he only hit her with the stone by accident."

Hugh started to get angry. "My brother is many things, but he wouldn't do anything that could cause somebody to be killed!"

"Really? Are you telling me that your brother never killed anybody during his time fighting for independence or during the Civil War?" demanded Constance.

"That was different. That was combat!"

"We all have committed sins, Hugh. Sometimes we don't want to admit to ourselves what we are capable of when we really want something."

"Including you, Constance," accused Hugh. "Where did you tell your husband you are tonight?"

Constance sighed loudly. "I told him I was going to an evening auction in Galway and would stay overnight. I was banking on him choosing to have a quiet night at home rather than accompanying me. He did."

"What would he say if he knew the truth?"

"I don't want to even think about it," admitted Constance. "He'll have to go back to Dublin soon on business so I will be freer to meet you. But it's best we continue to meet here instead of you coming to Seymour Hall. I don't want to slip up and leave any evidence there that might hang me."

"I get so filled with jealousy when I think of you with him. Why did you ever marry him? He's an old man!"

"I – I – we do things when we are younger out of necessity. And Clement is good to me. I don't know where I would be without him."

"So now you get the best of both worlds. Security with him and love with me," he said cynically.

"For now," she said as she kissed him.

Chapter 38

Present Day

Kate and Nico had made an appointment to see his solicitor and were seated across the desk from him in his office in Castlewest.

As Kate watched Geoffrey go through the correspondence they had received from the solicitors in London, she didn't have much faith in him. Geoffrey was now in his early seventies and still operated from the same building the family firm had occupied for well over a hundred years. Nico didn't normally have much need for a solicitor but, as the Conways had been the family solicitors since before his mother's time, they were his first port of call now. They had represented Nico in his divorce from Susan nearly twenty years before but, as Kate looked at Geoffrey, she wondered whether he was the cause of Nico coming off the worst in it.

"Surely this man can't have any claim to Armstrong House?" said Nico, his face tense.

"We hold the deeds to Armstrong House here at the firm as we always have," said Geoffrey as he held them up. "I fished them out when you emailed about this issue. These deeds do not show Clara, Lady Armstrong, as an owner of Armstrong House. They are for Armstrong House itself and the twelve acres attached to it. Your grandfather, Lord Pierce Armstrong, was the sole owner, having inherited the place from his father Lord Charles. As you know, Nico, the Armstrong Estate during Lord Charles' time stretched to several thousand acres but it was dismantled and sold off under the Land Acts of the early twentieth century. This left only Armstrong Estate and two-hundred and fifty acres of land. After the Armstrongs left the area, that abandoned land was seized by the Land Commission in 1925 and sold to a neighbouring farmer, Tadgh O'Meara."

"Where would the deeds for that land be now?" asked Kate.

"I imagine with the O'Meara family or their solicitor if they still own the land. When your grandfather was killed in 1940 the house was then inherited by your mother Jacqueline, Nico. She was but a child at the time and on her death you inherited Armstrong House."

"In that case these deeds that were posted to me from Royce Charter's solicitors, showing Clara as an owner in 1923, are fake since the real deeds are on the desk in front of us?" said Nico, visibly relaxing.

"Perhaps but perhaps not. There might have been a second set of deeds that were not left with our office but were in the possession of the Charter family who have now decided to stake their claim."

"But surely you can't come knocking at the door one hundred years later saying you should be the owner, or part owner!" said Kate in shock.

"People can do anything they want in a free country, I'm afraid. I'm not too sure how far they could get in court but they could make things very difficult for you. If the deeds that the Charter family have are proven real, you could certainly claim adverse possession – that is, to claim your home on the grounds you have lived there so long – but that could be a costly and lengthy business."

"Are you trying to tell me that if we want to sell Armstrong House this Royce could hold things up?" asked Nico.

Kate's head swivelled to look at Nico at his suggestion of selling their home.

"That's certainly where things could become difficult. Royce Charter could, and probably would, scupper and delay any sale with his claim on the property."

"Would all this not have been sorted out at the time of Pierce and Clara's divorce?" asked Kate.

"One would like to think it was but if the second deeds are true deeds and did not come to light for some reason at the time, then Clara's interest in Armstrong House was never resolved."

"But we don't even know who this man is!" exclaimed Nico. "They don't even explain his connection to Clara!"

"They are being very clever," said Kate. "He did his research before he made contact. Showing that Clara was still with Pierce and living at Armstrong House when the deed of transfer was made and that she paid for the rebuilding work. If he couldn't prove all that and it was as we originally thought – that Clara and Pierce separated when the house originally burned down in 1921 and she lived in England from then on – this claim on the house and the second set of deeds would be easily dismissed by any court."

Geoffrey nodded at Kate. "I can see you have grasped the tactics and strategy being put in place," he said.

Kate gathered that he was implying Nico had not and was in denial.

"Very well," Geoffrey said. "I will write to Mr. Charter's solicitor and tell him that we have the original deeds and do not accept the deeds they have as valid and hence we reject their claim. The onus is then on Royce Charter to prove his claim but I doubt that it will be the last we hear from him."

Kate and Nico drove home in silence. Kate was well used to the expression Nico had on his face. He adopted it when he was so deep in thought and trying to control his emotions that his mouth was clamped shut in a tight line. The claim on Armstrong House was affecting him deeply and Kate knew he hated trouble like this.

He parked the car in the forecourt, and she followed him up the steps and through the front door. Nico headed straight into the drawing room and poured himself a stiff drink.

"I'm sure there is nothing to worry about," said Kate, trying to soothe his nerves.

"How can you say that? You heard what Geoffrey said. Even if Royce Charter cannot claim ownership after so long, it's going to cost us a fortune to defend ourselves – or we may have to just pay him off to stop being a nuisance."

"Why did you ask Geoffrey if Royce Charter's claim could affect the sale of Armstrong House?" asked Kate.

"Because I wanted to know!"

"But why would that be your chief concern? We have no plans to sell – have we?"

"I've told you before that it has crossed my mind recently that it might be the right thing to do."

Kate rolled her eyes and nodded her head knowingly as she went to pour herself a gin and tonic.

"So, Alex has got to you, has she?" she said.

"I wouldn't put like that. As I told you, she just said she thinks we should sell."

"That is not true, Nico. I heard you talking down in the kitchen the day the wedding. Alex was pushing you to sell the house."

"So you were snooping on us?" said Nico angrily.

"I was trying to find my husband who had been ignoring me all day!"

"That's completely untrue!"

"No, it isn't, Nico! I was made feel like the unwanted relative! I was demoted to the second pew in the church, and not at the head table at the reception."

"Well, if you felt so strongly about it you should have made your point when planning the wedding."

"How could I without upsetting the bride who clearly didn't want me to be up front! I understand how she and you didn't want to upset your ex-wife – but what about me? Did anyone think how it made me feel?"

"We thanked you in the speeches for all you did, planning the wedding," said Nico.

Kate looked at him, momentarily speechless. "*You did not!* Neither of you did! Look at the video if you don't believe me! I didn't get one mention!"

"It was not intentional in that case, just a silly omission," said Nico.

"Oh, Nico, you could never lie so don't try to start now! I know that as always you were trying to not upset anybody by mentioning me. And I get it – Susan is Alex's mother and so she deserved not to be upstaged on her daughter's wedding day. But did you ever think how it made me feel – I felt invisible."

"You should have said something sooner if you were so upset."

"The day was so perfect I didn't want to taint it by expressing my hurt afterwards," said Kate.

"I am sorry, Kate, if I did hurt you. That was never my intention."

"Whether it was your intention or not it is what you – and Alex – did. And now you are contemplating selling our beautiful home because Alex wants her inheritance now so she can buy a house in Dublin."

"It's not the only reason. What Alex suggested makes a lot of sense. In another few years Cian will be gone away to university and making his own life and what will we do then? The two of us rattling around this huge house on our own, growing old together?"

"That was the plan. I was looking forward to it – it's sad to learn that you aren't," said Kate.

She finished her drink in one go and walked out of the room.

Chapter 39

1923

Asty was serving Clara breakfast in the dining room.

"Will you want more marmalade brought up from the kitchen, my lady?" asked Asty.

"No, this is fine, Asty," said Clara.

Asty began to clear away the plates.

"Terrible trouble in Castlewest last night, my lady, so I hear."

"Really? What happened?"

"A man killed his wife."

"How awful! Whatever possessed him?"

"Drink, my lady, drink! And I understand the deceased was carrying on with another man and her husband found out and it drove him into a ferocious rage the likes of which was never seen before!"

"I see!"

"Slit her throat as if she were a prize pig!" Asty suddenly let out a cackle of laughter.

Clara stopped spreading marmalade on her toast, startled by Asty's reaction to the violence.

Pierce walked into the room.

Asty curtsied to him and quickly left.

"How are you feeling?" asked Pierce.

"Physically, I am fine but I'm scared, Pierce." Clara stood up, going to him and putting her arms around him for comfort.

"It's probably best you don't go off on your own any more around the estate, Clara."

"So, I am to be a prisoner in my own home?"

"Your safety must come first if, as you suspect, somebody means you harm. I personally think the culprit is right under your nose and you are too blind to see it."

"Who?" she asked, drawing back from him and looking into his face.

"Hugh O'Meara. He's the one who saddled your horse and he was working in the vicinity of the lake when you were attacked by the stones. He's the obvious culprit. And I think he is working in tandem with his brother to scare us away so they can claim our land again."

"It isn't Hugh, Pierce! He's gone against his brother to come work here and I saw how angry Tadgh was with him and how he attacked him!"

Pierce rolled his eyes.

"I don't know why you hold such faith in this peasant. It is almost irritating," he said as he sat down to breakfast.

Hugh and Asty were walking back to his cottage at night, returning from a dance in a neighbour's cottage. Asty had her arm around his waist, holding him tight, almost as if she feared he would slip away from her. Every time she met Hugh, she felt he was more distant from her, and she was terrified that he was losing interest in her.

"Now, Hugh, I know you have been very busy with your work in the estate but we can't delay our plans forever," she said.

"What do you mean?" he asked, irritated that she was going to bring the subject of marriage up again.

"Well, I spoke to Lady Armstrong and she said she had no problem with you moving into Armstrong House once we were married," lied Asty.

"You did *what*?" demanded Hugh.

"Well, Fennell and Mrs. Fennell have lived there nearly all their lives, so they are used to married couples living there. Also, I think Lady Armstrong would like another man living there, as it would make her feel more secure with everything going on with her."

"You had no right to discuss this with Lady Armstrong without talking to me first!" said Hugh angrily.

"If you prefer to live at your cottage then we could do that too. I'm sure the Armstrongs wouldn't mind me moving out and living nearby," said Asty.

"Are you losing your fucking mind?" said Hugh. "In case you haven't realised, I have not asked you to marry me!"

"Well, that's only what's called a technicality! Can't you get down on one knee now and do the deed?"

"Look, Asty, this is going way too quickly for me. You're a nice girl and everything but I'm not ready for marriage."

"But you said we would get married!" cried Asty.

"I never said such a thing! You did!"

"But sure why are you going out with me if you don't want to marry me?"

"We've only been going out a very short while! I like you, Asty. But marriage is a big step. And I want so much more in life than just living up in Armstrong House in the attic or in this cottage."

"You want more than me, is what you are trying to say!" said Asty as they reached his front door.

Then suddenly she burst out crying.

"Ah, now Asty!" sighed Hugh as he watched her bawling. "Will you whist with your tears! You'll upset the cows!"

"You've made a fool of me!" she said between sobs. "You used me and took my virtue along the way!"

"Ah, sure your virtue was lost long before you met me, darling," said Hugh.

"I hate you!" she spat and then she cried louder. "But I love you too!"

"You only hate me because I don't love you," said Hugh.

"*Ahhhhh!*" shrieked Asty at the top of her voice.

"Will you get in before you wake the whole fucking county!" said High as he opened the door and pushed her into the cottage.

"You'll never find another like me, Hugh O'Meara!" she said between sobs as she slouched down on a chair at the table.

"I daresay that's true if nothing else is," said Hugh.

"Nobody can make a bed better than me!"

"Stay there and I'll get you a drink. You'll think more clearly with a whiskey inside you," said Hugh as he walked into the back kitchen.

Asty sat at the kitchen table and grabbed a handkerchief that was on the table and began to mop up her tears. She sat there glumly, twisting the handkerchief in her hands. Suddenly she started sniffing the air. She could smell a perfume. A very expensive woman's perfume. She looked down at the handkerchief and saw it was a very expensive woman's lace handkerchief. Her mouth dropped open as realisation flashed through her mind. She stood up and walked over to the bed beside the hearth and saw the sheets and blankets were completely in disarray as if somebody had made mad passionate love there the previous night and the bed hadn't been made since.

Hugh came back from the kitchen, holding two glasses and a bottle of whiskey.

Asty quickly stuffed the handkerchief up her sleeve.

"Don't bother pouring one for me," she said.

"Are you sure?" he asked, hovering the open bottle over a glass.

"I'd better be getting back, it's getting late," she said as she walked to the door.

"I'm sorry, Asty," he said.

"Let's keep the door open with us, Hugh. You might change your mind. People change their minds all the time." And she walked out.

Asty was clearing out the hearth in the library when Pierce walked in.

"Are you not finished in here yet? I have paperwork to do," he said.

"I'll be out of your way very quickly, Your Lordship. Don't let me stop you from your work."

Pierce sat down at the desk, opened his fountain pen and began to write.

"Isn't the weather lovely, your lordship?" said Asty.

"*Mmm*," said Pierce.

"It would be a lovely day for a walk by the lake," she said as she shovelled the ashes into a tin bucket.

"*Hmm*."

"Like lovers do. I always think how love blossoms in the summer, don't you agree?"

"I never gave it much thought," said Pierce.

"When a young man's fancy turns to love, isn't that what they say?" she said, standing up and going to fix the curtains. Through the window she could see Clara with Hugh in the side gardens. They were standing close together as he spoke to her.

"That expression applies to spring not summer," Pierce corrected her.

"Oh, is it? Well, love can blossom in any season if the conditions are right!" She looked out the window again. "Isn't it lovely that Lady Armstrong gets on so – so *very* well with Hugh?"

"Who?" asked Pierce irritably as he looked up at her.

Asty stood out of the way of the window so that he could see Clara and Hugh together.

"Isn't he your young man?" asked Pierce.

"He was surely but it's over now. He confessed he was seeing somebody else and was in love with her. Some posh married lady from what I hear. Heartbroken I am, but sure what can I do? You can't stand in the way of true love."

Asty picked up the bucket of ashes and walked out.

Pierce stood up and went to the window where he stood, observing Clara with Hugh.

Chapter 40

As the sun shone down, Clara finished styling her hair, got up from the dressing table and walked to the window to look out at the terraced gardens which were filling up with guests for the garden party. The forecourt below had a number of motorcars and horse-traps parked there, and she could see Pierce greeting their guests. She was very much looking forward to the day and seeing old friends again. It was the first social occasion they had hosted since moving back to Armstrong House and she was filled with nostalgia for times past. It would also take her mind off the two sinister events that had befallen her. It was the not knowing that caused her the most anxiety. The not knowing who exactly hated her so much that they wished her serious harm.

Before she left the bedroom she picked up the new bottle of perfume that she had bought that week and sprayed herself liberally before leaving the room.

She walked down the corridor and, as she descended the stairs, she could see the staff working frantically below, bringing trays of food out to the gardens.

"Isn't it wonderful to be entertaining back at Armstrong House again, my lady?" said Mrs. Fennell, carrying a silver tray of sandwiches.

"It certainly is, Mrs. Fennell."

"I thought I'd never see the day again! A garden party in July like we always used to have!" Mrs. Fennell teared up as she continued out to the gardens.

Clara followed her out and, walking across the forecourt, stood at the top of the steps leading down to the first terraced garden. As she stood there she remembered the first garden party she attended after she arrived as a bride. Pierce's friends and neighbours had viewed her as a curiosity then. But now, as she walked down the steps and people rushed to greet her, she felt one of them. As she chatted away, she saw Pierce at the other end of the terrace, as ever at a social event surrounded by an adoring group of women whom he had known all his life. In the first years of their marriage the attention he got used to make her feel insecure. Then she had learned that this was something Pierce had had all his life and for him it was like sunshine to a flower. Even though those women who idolised him were aging it did not matter to him as it was the attention he enjoyed. She wondered how he would cope when he aged and that attention was gone. Then she realised she'd already witnessed how he would cope, seeing what happened when he had to move from Armstrong House to become a relative nobody in Dublin. The answer was he couldn't cope. The only things that would compensate Pierce for losing his looks in the future were her money and living at Armstrong House. Without that, he would revert to being nobody.

Clara was standing with Prudence and some guests when Constance approached them with Clement.

"Clara, may I introduce you to my husband, Clement," said Constance.

"I am so pleased to meet you," said Clara as she shook his hand. "I've heard so much about you!"

"And I you, Lady Armstrong," said Clement. "Thank you for inviting us today."

"But Constance simply had to be here! If it were not for her we would still be living in bare rooms!" said Clara.

Although Constance had prepared Clara for the age difference between her and her husband, Clara had to hide her surprise at how big the gap was.

"This is my sister-in-law, Prudence," said Clara.

"So pleased to meet you, madam. If you are ever looking for anything in the line of antiques I am your man," said Clement with a bow.

"You're a bit of an antique yourself, aren't you?" said Prudence.

"Prudence!" Clara chastised her. "I am sorry. My sister-in-law is not known for her social graces."

"Whilst my sister-in-law is known for far too many!" retorted Prudence.

"Fear not. I am always flattered when people point out my wife's youth and beauty," said Clement.

"I wasn't pointing out her youth and beauty, I was pointing out your lack of it!" said Prudence.

"Please, let us circulate!" said Clara quickly, going between Constance and Clement and taking them each by the arm, leading them away.

Clement and Constance stood at the end of the terrace watching Pierce play tennis, while at the same time observing Clara as she held court with a group of people around her.

"I cannot understand why everyone makes such a fuss of her," said Constance.

"Does not the fact that she is beautiful, charming and gracious not sway your opinion?" asked Clement.

"But those are only superficial qualities. Look beyond them and there really is very little there. I should know, I have spent enough time in her company. She's actually quite dull."

"Is she indeed?"

"Yes, I can't imagine why a man of Johnny Seymour's talent became involved with her."

"You should know how fickle people are. Often the more talented they are, the more they are impressed by superficiality. I imagine Seymour saw it as an accolade to have conquered her."

"Seemingly she broke his heart," said Constance. "And yet she is back here desperate to prove to herself that her husband is in love with her when he clearly isn't."

"*Game set and match, Lord Armstrong!*" announced the umpire as people rushed to Pierce to congratulate him.

"Of course he had to win!" said Constance.

"You seem to have become very envious of our latest target, Constance. Never a wise move to let emotions get involved when it comes to business."

"It's not so much envy as anger. Anger at Clara's failure to realise how fortunate she is while she wastes her life on the one man who does not want to have her," said Constance.

"Perhaps that is why she cannot give him up. For the woman who has been given everything, of course she wants the one thing she cannot have ... now can we focus on business? Will there be any opportunity to get the portrait today?"

"We shall see how the day pans out," said Constance.

"I'm not sure how much longer my buyer in New York will be patient," said Clement.

"Do not fret, Clement. Everything is in hand for me to swoop at the right opportunity to seize our prize," Constance assured him.

As the sun became stronger during the afternoon, Clara began to develop a headache. What had started as a small pain began to throb. She felt like lying down but did not want to abandon her guests. She was seated at a garden table with Pierce and other guests as she tried to concentrate on their conversation.

"You did such a wonderful job restoring the house, Clara. Pierce, you must be so proud of your wife," said Emily Fox.

"I think she is quite proud enough of herself, so she doesn't need any further endorsement from me," said Pierce, who was growing irritated by the praise everyone was lavishing on Clara all afternoon.

"And I understand it's thanks to you that the estate is back up and running, Clara. We made a farmer out of you eventually!" joked George Foxe.

"I really did hardly anything," said Clara who was beginning to feel quite ill.

"Except hire the man who with his family probably set Armstrong House on fire in the first place!" snapped Pierce.

"That's an outrageous thing to say, Pierce!" said Clara.

"Why? You said yourself when the rebels came they were wearing masks, so they were unidentifiable. The man you put in charge of the estate could very well be one of them. Hugh O'Meara's family have a reputation, everyone knows that."

Constance stiffened on hearing Hugh's name.

"Hugh does a lot of work for me, and I find him very agreeable," said Constance, leaping to Hugh's defence. Although, as she remembered how she first encountered Hugh, she realised the possibility of him being one of the culprits Pierce referred to was very real.

"Well, you'll forgive me if I do not take a character reference from you, Mrs. Fitzgerald, as we know nothing really about you," said Pierce.

"Pierce! If it were not for Constance, Armstrong House would not be as it is today," Clara ptotested.

"Oh, I'm sure if Constance hadn't come knocking on the door, some other tradesperson would have done the job," said Pierce.

Constance went to say something but stopped herself. She remembered Clement's exhortation not to forget what their purpose was and not to let emotion take her over. But there was something so undeniably arrogant about Pierce Armstrong, and she would have loved to take him down.

"The problem with my wife, although she has so many fine qualities that everyone is always praising, is that she is extremely gullible when it comes to people," said Pierce.

"Does that include you, Lord Armstrong?" asked Constance.

As soon as she had said it, Constance regretted it. The was a sharp intake of breath from the people around the table and Clement rolled his eyes in frustration at his wife's blunder.

Pierce's eyes went very dark as he stared at her from across the table. Constance felt herself involuntarily shiver as his eyes bored through her. She was just about to apologise when Clara stood up from the table. She was deathly white and swaying.

"I'm afraid I need to go and lie down," she said.

"Are you alright?" asked Emily with concern.

"No ... I feel ..." said Clara as she began to stumble. As she fell to the ground she grabbed the tablecloth, pulling the plates and the cups down with her.

"*Clara!*" cried Emily.

As Clara lay unconscious on the ground, the guests gathered around her in a panic.

"Clara! Clara!" said Pierce as he knelt beside her, trying to revive her.

"*Make way! Make way! I'm a trained vet – almost!*" shouted Philly Scott as she pushed her way through the crowd.

She knelt down beside Clara. She took her pulse and checked her heart.

"We need to get this woman to the hospital without delay. She seems to be slipping into a coma!" she said.

Pierce was looking down at Clara.

"Pierce! Did you hear me? This is beyond my capabilities – I think she is dying. She needs a hospital as soon as possible!"

Pierce scooped Clara up in his arms and carried her across the lawn, quickly followed by Philly. He climbed the steps to the forecourt and climbed into the passenger seat, cradling Clara on his lap.

Philly sat in and drove quickly out of the forecourt and down the avenue.

Pierce and Philly stood in the corridor of the infirmary in Castlewest with Dr. O'Brien.

"Has your wife been using weed-killer in the last twenty-four hours, Lord Armstrong?" asked the doctor.

"Highly unlikely, but she is in the gardens regularly. And has been spending a lot of time involving herself in the running of the estate which is really none of her concern."

"Why do you ask?" asked Philly.

"Lady Armstrong has inhaled arsenic which is generally used for weed-killing in domestic situations," said the doctor.

"Arsenic!" exclaimed Philly.

Pierce shook his head in dismay. "Clearly then she must have been using it! I despair of her, I really do!"

A nurse came rushing out of the room.

"Doctor – the patient is coming round!"

Dr. O'Brien turned and walked quickly into the room, closing the door firmly behind him.

"She probably didn't wear a mask when she was using the weed-killer," sighed Pierce.

"As egalitarian as Clara pretends to be, I really can't see her weeding her own shrubs, Pierce!" said Philly.

"What happened?" whispered Clara as she tried to sit up, too weak to do so.

"You have inhaled a chemical, Lady Armstrong, which has resulted in you becoming very ill," said the doctor.

"A chemical? What chemical?"

"It's one sometimes used in killing weeds. Your husband informs me that you spend much time in the gardens at Armstrong House. Did you come into close contact with any weed-killer this morning?"

"No ... none at all."

"We will continue to do tests and we will keep you informed," said the doctor as he patted her hand.

"Is my husband here?"

"Yes, he's in the corridor. Are you strong enough to see him?"

"Yes, please. I want to see Pierce."

The doctor walked to the door and a minute later Pierce walked in.

"You gave us all a terrible scare, Clara. How are you feeling now?" he asked as he sat down beside his wife and took her hand.

"Very weak. The doctor says I've inhaled some sort of chemical," said Clara.

"Yes, arsenic," said Pierce.

"Arsenic!"

"You really must be more careful, Clara. I've told you before to stop interfering with the estate. Now you've come into contact with some dangerous weed-killer containing arsenic that could have killed you!"

"But I haven't been near any weed-killer, Pierce."

"Unbeknownst to yourself."

"I would know if I was near weed-killer, Pierce! I am not stupid! Can't you see what's happened! Somebody has poisoned me!" said Clara, becoming very distressed.

"You don't know that –"

"I do! It makes perfect sense! First the horse, then the stones and now somebody has somehow got to me and poisoned me! They are trying to kill me!"

"Calm yourself down, Clara! This is not good for your nerves!" soothed Pierce.

Chapter 41

As the days went by in the infirmary, Clara began to recover but her mind was consumed with wondering how she had managed to be poisoned.

Constance came to visit.

"You really don't need to visit me every day, Constance. I am sure Clement is not amused that you are spending so much time with me."

"Nonsense! Clement is glad to be free of me for a couple of hours! When do you think you can go home?"

"The doctor said I will be fit to go home on Friday. But, as much as I dislike it here, I am very fearful of going back to Armstrong House."

"That's very understandable," said Constance.

"Pierce doesn't believe I was deliberately poisoned but I know I was," said Clara.

"I have a suggestion. Why don't I come and stay at Armstrong House while you are recuperating? It would make you feel so much better knowing that I was there."

"I could not possibly ask you to do such a thing, Constance. Your husband would be very unhappy at the prospect."

"Clement goes away on long business trips constantly and never gives me a second thought. He wouldn't mind me staying a short while with you as you recuperate."

"If you're sure?"

"I am. Clara, have you *any* idea who might be persecuting you like this?"

"Yes, I do but I think it's going to be very hard to prove it," said Clara.

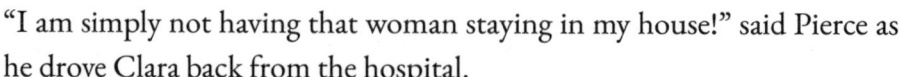

"I am simply not having that woman staying in my house!" said Pierce as he drove Clara back from the hospital.

"But I want Constance there. It would make me feel safer."

"That is what your husband is for, not this woman who has bludgeoned her way into our lives uninvited!"

"She has not come into our lives invited. I invited her and if a husband's role is to make me feel safe then you are monumentally falling down on your duties, Pierce."

"I honestly think you are losing your mind, Clara. It is you who started this war with Tadgh O'Meara and you who then hired his brother and gave him access to our house and our estate. If you do not feel safe then it is because you let the enemy in!"

"I believe the enemy was always there at Armstrong House," said Clara.

"What do you mean?"

"It's obvious to me that it is Prudence who is trying to drive me away from here. This would not be the first time she launched a campaign against me. All these strange happenings only started when she came back here."

The motor car pulled into the forecourt and came to a halt.

Pierce turned and stared at her. "That's crazy. Why would she have gone to so much trouble to bring you back here only to now drive you away?"

Clara stepped out of the motorcar and sighed. That was the one thing that did not make sense. Why would Prudence have come to London and urged her to go back to Pierce, only to drive her away now?

"Welcome home, Lady Armstrong. It is so good to see you back!" said Fennell as he quickly came down the steps from the front door.

"It's good to see you, Fennell," Clara said with a smile.

"Mrs. Fitzgerald is in the drawing room awaiting you."

"Good Lord! Has that woman no home of her own to go to?" snapped Pierce as he followed Clara up the steps and into the house.

"Clara! You look so much better!" said Constance, standing up from the couch as Clara entered the drawing room.

"I still feel quite weak, Constance, but much better than I was," said Clara.

"Well, I'm sure Mrs. Fennell's cooking will have you fighting fit in no time and I am here to look after you for as long as you need," said Constance, giving her a hug.

"Very kind of you, Mrs. Fitzgerald, but we couldn't possibly impose on you," said Pierce.

"But I've already told Clara it's no imposition in the least," said Constance.

"It's really quite out of the question. Clara needs peace and quiet," insisted Pierce.

"But I will give her all the peace and quiet she needs and just be on hand for whenever she needs me –"

"Constance – no!" said Pierce firmly.

Constance went to say something but closed her mouth on seeing Pierce's stern look.

Clara held on to the back of an armchair as she felt herself become dizzy.

"I think I need to lie down," she whispered.

"Of course you do. I'll take you to your bed. Fennell can show you out, Mrs. Fitzgerald," said Pierce as he tugged the bell-pull.

Constance watched Pierce escort Clara out of the room as she seethed with frustration.

"I really must apologise for Pierce's rudeness, Constance," said Clara the following week when Constance was visiting her.

"I don't think he likes me much," mused Constance.

"I shouldn't take it personally. He doesn't seem to like anybody much," said Clara. "I really do appreciate all you do for me, even if Pierce does not."

"It's my pleasure. I should head back to Seymour Hall as I walked over and it will take me an age to get back," said Constance.

"Why did you not drive?"

"Clement has taken the motorcar to go back to Dublin on business."

"Then you must borrow my motorcar until he returns," said Clara.

"I couldn't possibly –"

"I won't be needing it until I recover fully. And Pierce goes everywhere on horseback so he won't mind," said Clara.

"Well, if you are sure? It would help me a lot. I have to attend an auction on the other side of the county tomorrow."

"I insist," said Clara.

Constance was glad that Clement was away on business as it gave her more time to spend with Hugh. That night, as she drove from Seymour Hall in Clara's motorcar to his cottage, she looked forward to being able to spend a full night with him without rushing back home.

It was Asty's weekend off work and she was spending it at her parents' house in Castlewest. Seated in the snug of Cassidy's pub in town, having drinks with a few women friends, she could not get Hugh out of her mind. She wondered had she been too pushy with him, talking about marriage too soon. She missed him terribly. She knew something was going on that was stopping him from loving her back. She just needed to spend more time with him so that he could realise how much he loved her.

She looked at the clock on the wall and saw it was ten o'clock. On impulse, she stood up quickly, said goodbye to her friends and left the pub. She grabbed her bicycle which was resting against the wall outside. If she hurried she could be at Hugh's cottage to surprise him in an hour.

As she cycled down the boreen to Hugh's cottage she stopped suddenly. There was a motorcar parked outside it. Dismounting from her bicycle, she left it against a hedge and approached the house carefully. She was stunned to recognise the motorcar as Clara's. All the windows had the curtains drawn but there was light on inside. She stole up to the kitchen window and crouched down, listening. She could hear whispering and giggling and then her mouth dropped open in shock as she heard the loud sounds of love-making from inside the cottage. She listened until she could bear it no longer and then, with tears of anger streaming down her face, she went to fetch her bicycle.

Chapter 42

As the time went by, Clara felt better each day. She spent her time reading books and magazines that Mrs. Fennell got for her in Castlewest. One morning she went to her dressing table, brushed her hair and reached for her perfume bottle to spray herself. She was surprised to find the bottle was not there. She looked all around the dressing table and floor in case it had fallen but could not find it. After making a thorough search of the bedroom, her bathroom and dressing room, she tugged the bell-pull and waited for Síle to arrive.

"Síle, where did you put my perfume?" she asked.

"I didn't put it anywhere, my lady."

"But it's missing from its usual place on the dressing table," said Clara.

"I know. I thought you had taken it and put it away somewhere, my lady."

"But when did you notice it missing?"

"It was gone the day after the garden party, my lady. I thought you might have taken it to the hospital," said Síle.

"I was unconscious, Síle, hardly in a fit state to go fetch my perfume while I was being rushed to the infirmary!" snapped Clara.

"Yes, miss, I mean no, miss. I mean I don't know, my lady!" said Síle who started tearing up at being spoken to so harshly.

"Ask the other staff immediately if they have seen it or know of its whereabouts," commanded Clara.

None of the staff knew where the missing perfume was. Clara remembered distinctly when she had last used it. She had sprayed herself liberally with it before she went down to meet the guests at the garden party.

A horrible notion passed through her mind as she remembered that she had taken ill a couple of hours later.

Clara went to her dressing room and took out the dress she had worn the day of the garden party. She had not worn it since or had it cleaned. She put the dress carefully into a bag and then went downstairs to phone the police.

Sergeant Cantwell stood in the drawing room as he listened to Clara.

"The doctors say I inhaled arsenic, Sergeant, and I am positive that I did not come into any contact with any chemicals. But I did fall ill soon after I sprayed myself with my perfume and now I believe somebody put arsenic into the perfume as the perfume is conveniently missing."

"But who would do such a thing?" asked the Sergeant.

"The same person who put the burr under my horse's saddle and threw stones and chased me through the woods, Sergeant! I sprayed the perfume on the dress I was wearing that day and I would like you to do a test on the material to see if it contains arsenic."

"It would have to be sent to a laboratory in Dublin and it would cost a lot of money which is tight under the new government. Sure, they hardly have enough money to keep the country running at all."

"I will pay for the test myself, Sergeant. I insist it's tested," said Clara.

"Well, in that case I will fulfil your request," said Cantwell as he took the bag containing the dress from her. "I'll be back in contact with you as soon as we get the results."

Once Sergeant Cantwell received the results from the laboratory he requested to meet Pierce and Clara. They received him in the library and Clara listened intently as he spoke.

"You were quite correct in your suspicions, Lady Armstrong. The results of the toxicology examination have returned from the laboratory in Dublin and a considerable amount of arsenic was found on the material of your dress, mixed in with the perfume that you sprayed on it."

Clara closed her eyes and breathed in deeply.

"It's as I feared," she whispered.

Pierce looked at Clara in alarm. She hadn't told him what she had done.

"Could somebody explain to me what is going on?" he demanded.

"My perfume bottle was missing when I returned from the infirmary and I remembered spraying myself with it before I became ill and I asked the Sergeant to test my dress material for any sign of arsenic."

"And you did this without discussing it with me first?" said Pierce disbelievingly.

"I knew you would dismiss my suspicions without any evidence," said Clara.

"I will need to interview everybody who had access to your room," said Cantwell.

"That would be a narrow group of people – the staff in the house, my husband and I – and my sister-in-law," said Clara.

"But there were plenty of guests here that day, using the bathroom facilities upstairs," said Pierce.

"I used the perfume before any of the guests came into the house," said Clara.

"As you have suggested, Lady Armstrong, whoever put the arsenic in your perfume most probably is the same person who attacked you by the lake and who interfered with your saddle in the hope of causing you injury," said Cantwell.

"Yes, and with the other two events that could have been somebody from outside but now, with my perfume bottle being poisoned, I must face the indisputable fact that it is somebody from inside Armstrong House or who at least has access to the house." Clara started shivering.

"I will need all those names and I would like to interview them without delay," said Cantwell.

Síle sat crying loudly in the drawing room while Cantwell questioned her, as Clara and Pierce looked on.

"Lord save us, I would never try to harm Lady Armstrong or anybody else! Sure, hasn't she been so good to me since I started to work here? Why would I want to destroy her perfume?" said Síle as she wiped her eyes with a handkerchief.

"Nobody is accusing you of anything, Síle! We are just asking you if you saw anybody acting suspiciously?" said Clara, trying to calm her down.

"Sure, I am too busy with my work to notice anything, my lady," said Síle as she descended again into tears.

"Oh for goodness sake!" snapped Pierce.

"Can I get back to the kitchen and Mrs. Fennell?" asked Síle.

"Of course you can and please don't fret, Síle."

Clara watched the girl leave the room.

"We're wasting our time even speaking to that girl. She's far too simple to try to kill anybody," said Pierce.

"It is also a waste of time interviewing Mr. and Mrs. Fennell. They have been with the family for years and are devoted to us," said Clara.

"But I need to speak to them in case they have noticed anything irregular," said Cantwell.

"No, we didn't see anything irregular, did we, Mr. Fennell?" said Mrs. Fennell as they were interviewed in the drawing room.

"Nothing at all," confirmed Mr. Fennell. "I would have brought it to His Lordship's attention immediately if I had."

"I don't doubt that for a moment, Fennell," said Clara.

"And we can vouch for all the staff that I employed on Lady Armstrong's behalf – Síle and Máire and Julia. They are good girls as a rule," said Mrs. Fennell.

"What about the housekeeper?" asked Cantwell.

"Well, Asty is … well, she's very good at her job – nobody could take that away from her," said Mrs. Fennell.

"But …?" asked Cantwell.

Mr. and Mrs. Fennell exchanged looks.

"Well, she does seem to have an unhealthy obsession with death!" said Mrs. Fennell.

"I have noticed that myself," said Clara as she thought back.

"And she's very miserable since Hugh O'Meara broke it off with her – but that's no reason to try to kill Her Ladyship!" said Mrs. Fennell.

Hugh stood in the drawing room with his cap in his hands.

"I understand you were fixing a leaking pipe in the upstairs of the house the day before Lady Armstrong became ill?" said Cantwell.

"I was," said Hugh.

"Although Hugh is our estate manager he comes into the house to fix any maintenance issues we have as well," explained Clara.

"Alright, Clara! Let the Sergeant do his job without any interference from you!" snapped Pierce.

"Did you go into Lady Armstrong's bedroom while you were upstairs?" asked Cantwell.

"I don't know where Lady Armstrong's bedroom is located but I didn't go into any bedroom as the leak was in the bathroom, if that answers your question," said Hugh.

"But you did saddle the horse with the saddle that had been interfered with?" said Cantwell.

"I did but there was no chestnut burr under it after I saddled it," said Hugh. "I rode the horse myself before Lady Armstrong came for it."

"And your brother has sworn vengeance on Lady Armstrong due an earlier disagreement?" said Cantwell.

"You'll have to ask my brother that as we no longer talk," said Hugh. "But he has no access to the house in any case."

"But you do," said Pierce.

"I never touch Lady Armstrong's dressing table as that is Síle's job," said Asty.

"Síle has said she noticed the bottle of perfume missing the day after the garden party. Did you notice it gone?" asked Cantwell.

"I didn't because, as I said, the dressing table is not my domain," said Asty.

"As the housekeeper in charge of this house you are in the best position to see everything. You have access to all areas and have considerable freedom to do as you wish, is that not right?" asked the Sergeant.

"Which also means I am run off my feet." Asty stood up abruptly. "Now, if you'll excuse me, I have a list of jobs to do as long as your arm!"

Asty walked out and slammed the door behind her.

"Are you just going to let her go?" asked Pierce.

"I can't detain her, Lord Armstrong! There is no evidence against any of the people we have interviewed today," said Cantwell. "And what reason would the housekeeper have to harm Lady Armstrong?"

Pierce looked at Clara. "I don't know. Can you think of any reason, Clara? Any reason she may have a personal grudge against you?"

"No, I certainly can't. Sergeant, there is one more person I would like you interview. My sister-in-law Prudence."

"Clara! Have you lost your mind?" demanded Pierce.

"No – in fact I am thinking very clearly. You see, Sergeant, Prudence does have a grudge against me. She has never liked me and has form. While my husband was away at war, Prudence secretly launched a campaign against me to try and drive me away. Many strange things were happening to me that I could not understand and only came to light when Fennell reported it to me. You can ask Fennell, and he will confirm what I say."

"Prudence admitted what she did in the past and apologised and there was nothing life-threatening in what she did – just silly pranks," said Pierce.

"That made me think I was losing my mind. Prudence had access to the house and could easily have been behind all these attacks on me. She has also a most a most singularly cold nature, the likes of which I have never encountered in my life before."

"Clara, you are actually bringing disgrace on the family by suggesting Prudence is behind what has been happening to you!" said Pierce.

"It's a price we must pay for finding out the truth. I will ring for Fennell and ask him to fetch Prudence from Hunter's Farm," said Clara as she stood up and went to the wall to tug the bell-pull.

"Well, I have been accused of many things in the past but never attempted murder!" said Prudence with a loud laugh.

"I am sorry to have to question you, but Lady Armstrong insisted," said Sergeant Cantwell, feeling embarrassed to have called Prudence Armstrong in.

"I bet she did! Really, Clara, I had hoped you might learn some sense since coming back to Armstrong House but you have just got more delusional!"

"Nobody is accusing you of anything, Prudence," said Pierce.

"*She* is! And you, dear brother, are allowing her to do so after all I have done for you!"

"Well, you keep telling me my life is in danger and I should run away!" said Clara.

"That is out of concern for your welfare! I just think you and Armstrong House are not a good combination and you would be happier elsewhere," said Prudence.

"Do you see what I mean?" said Clara, turning around. "She does not want me here!"

"It's the locals who don't want you here, my dear! I've told you've made an enemy of Tadgh O'Meara and he won't stop until you get shot just like they shot Papa!"

"How am I supposed to live in my own home when I have you terrifying me like this all the time?" demanded Clara.

"Anything I could say is the least you have to worry about with your latest experiences with a horse saddle, stones and arsenic!" said Prudence.

"I will interview Tadgh O'Meara, Lady Prudence, but he hardly had access to Lady Armstrong's bedroom," said the Sergeant.

"I wouldn't be so sure – many have!" said Prudence.

"I think you'd better go, Prudence," said Clara angrily as she stood up, "and until we find out who has been doing this I am banning you from coming into the house, do you understand?"

"Perfectly!" said Prudence, standing up and turning to the Sergeant, laughing. "Am I free to leave or would you like to cuff me now, gov'nor!"

"Quite free to leave, Lady Prudence, and I do apologise for any inconvenience," said the Sergeant.

Prudence walked to the door and then stopped and turned to address Clara.

"Clara, if I wanted to kill you then you'd be dead by now, I can assure you of that. But if you have narrowed the suspects down to those that only have access to the house then you have omitted one prominent person," said Prudence.

"And who is that?" asked Clara.

"I thought that would be obvious. Your husband – Pierce," said Prudence as she continued out of the room.

Pierce stood by the fireplace momentarily before he quickly walked after Prudence.

Chapter 43

Hugh was working in a field building a fence when Síle came to find him.

"Lord Armstrong wants to see you, Hugh. You'd better not delay!"

"What does he want?" asked Hugh.

"How would I know? Mr. Fennell just sent me to get you," said Síle as she turned and hurried back to the house.

Hugh put down his tools and followed her.

When he entered the kitchen he found Mrs. Fennell there preparing that evening's dinner and Asty who was sewing in a chair beside the stove.

"You'd better get yourself straight up to His Lordship, Hugh. He's waiting for you in the library and he's not in good form," said Mrs. Fennell.

"Is he ever in good form?" asked Hugh as he looked over at Asty. "How are you, Asty?"

"Not any better from seeing you, Hugh O'Meara!" she said, glaring at him.

"I thought we were going to try and be friends," said Hugh.

"You can think what you like. My friends don't treat me like shit, and I look forward to seeing the day when you get yours! There's a special place in hell saved for a man who leads a girl on the way you did with me! I've told the priest to cancel any wedding plans he had for us and the next time you need a priest I hope it's for your own funeral!"

Mrs. Fennell gave Hugh a concerned look and gestured for him to go upstairs without further delay.

At the library door, he prepared himself and then knocked.

"Come in!"

Hugh went in and closed the dor behind him.

Pierce was seated behind his desk.

"You wanted to see me, sir?"

"Well, I didn't want to see you, but I needed to. I am afraid I will no longer be requiring your services as of today. You can collect your last pay from Fennell."

Hugh's eyes widened. "You're firing me?"

"Yes, if you would prefer to phrase it like that," said Pierce.

"Can I ask why?"

"I thought that was obvious. With everything that has been happening to Lady Armstrong, I do not want you around her anymore."

"You think I did all that stuff to her?"

"I certainly have my suspicions but of course I can't prove anything," said Pierce.

"Does Lady Armstrong know?"

"Not yet but I'll inform her this evening. It is my decision not hers. I make the decisions here. You are not to go near Lady Armstrong again, is that understood?"

"I would like to say goodbye to her," said Hugh.

Pierce stood up abruptly.

"I don't want you near my wife again, O'Meara. You will not speak to her, go near her or touch her again – understood?" said Pierce.

"Touch her? What are you talking about?" asked Hugh, bewildered.

"Get out of my house and stay away from my wife!"

Hugh stared back at Pierce and then quickly turned and marched out of the library and down the servants' stairs.

"Hugh – what's the matter?" asked Mrs. Fennell as he strode through the kitchen.

"He's been let go, Mrs. Fennell," said Fennell as he came down the servants' stairs.

"Couldn't happen to a nicer fella," said Asty, smiling as she sewed.

"I can't see why you're so upset," said Pierce in their bedroom that evening after he told Clara about firing Hugh.

"Because you had no right to do it without consulting me!"

"Clara, because you have money does not make you the ruler of this house and estate."

"But we are both the owners! You put me on the deeds!"

"I've fired him for you, Clara. I don't want to see anything else bad happen to you and that must mean we get rid of any likely suspects."

"Poor Hugh! He has done so much for me. If it weren't for him I'd have been killed that day on the horse! And he is now feuding with his family because he took this job. That was a very ruthless thing to do, Pierce."

"You need to be ruthless with these peasants or else they run roughshod over you," said Pierce.

"That was your father's approach, and he got shot dead! And who is going to run the estate?"

"Prudence, of course, as she always has."

Clara sat down on the bed in despair.

"So, you are disregarding my fears of Prudence," she said.

Pierce sat beside her and put his arm around her.

"I'm only doing this because I love you, Clara. And you are so fragile at the moment with all this going on. I just want to protect you."

Clara immediately felt comforted, feeling his arm around her, and rested her head on his shoulder.

"I do feel very confused – I've been so worried. The doctor did warn me I may be confused for some time after inhaling the arsenic."

"Exactly. You're not in the right state of mind to make decisions so you just leave everything to me. That's what a husband is for – to protect his wife."

"I just feel so sorry for Hugh."

Pierce's expression stiffened. "Put him out of your mind for good. And tomorrow, darling, we must get rid of Asty."

"Asty!" said Clara, pulling away from him and looking at him in shock.

"I'm afraid so. She must go. We can't trust her either. She was courting O'Meara and she's the only member of staff that we really don't know that well. Fennell and Mrs. Fennell are hardly guilty, and the other staff are just too stupid."

"But who will run the house?"

"Oh, Fennell and the others will manage. Síle can even make a bed properly now!"

"If you think it's for the best," said Clara.

Asty stayed sitting on the couch after Pierce told her she was being dismissed.

"It has nothing to with the quality of your work, Asty, which is exemplary," said Clara.

"Well, what has it got to do with then?" demanded Asty.

"We are just reorganising the staff and so there is no longer a place for you here," said Clara.

"Really? I know what this is really about," said Asty.

Clara stiffened. Asty was no fool and Clara knew she would accuse them of letting her go because they didn't trust her, with everything that had been happening.

"I know what you've been up to, Lady High and Mighty Armstrong," said Asty.

"Up to? Whatever are you talking about, Asty?" said Clara.

"You want me out of the way so you can have Hugh all to yourself!"

Clara stared at Asty in astonished silence. She glanced at Pierce who was now standing by the fireplace but his faced remained expressionless.

"Are you insane?" asked Clara.

"I know you've been carrying on with Hugh behind my back and behind Lord Armstrong's back!"

"I have no idea what you are talking about. Please explain yourself!" demanded Clara.

"I know you're riding Hugh! I've seen you together – laughing and joking, touching, sharing lovers' secrets! Can't keep your hands off him! And I've seen you at his cottage staying the night, you floozie!"

"Have you lost your mind?" said Clara, shaking her head in disbelief.

"Oh, I think you know exactly what I'm talking about! I smelt your perfume in his cottage and found your handkerchief there and saw the bed rumpled to bits from your mad lovemaking!"

"You *are* actually insane!" cried Clara. She looked over to Pierce in appeal but he remained impassive.

"What's more, I've heard you! I saw your motorcar outside his cottage at night and listened outside to the laughter and giggling from the two of you and then the sounds of shocking throes of passion that would make a whore blush!"

"What kind of blatant lying is that? I have never been to his cottage!" Clara stood and pointed to the door. "I think you need to leave now!"

"*Whore!* That's what your wife is, Lord Armstrong – a *whore*! Sure, she's long since been known as one since she was riding that artist fella and she didn't stop there! Oh, no! She had to go and seduce my fiancée and she just using him for her own sinful pleasures!"

"It's best you go to your room now and pack and leave first thing in the morning," said Pierce.

"Don't worry! I wouldn't stay here in this brothel another day! I will be gone first thing in the morning before I am contaminated with the *filth* that surrounds me here," Asty said, standing up and storming to the door.

Before she opened the door, she turned to face them.

"You might have the title of a lady, but you have the morals of a tinker! You'll get yours!" Then she swung the door open and marched out, slamming the door behind her.

Clara was frozen in shock as she tried to comprehend Asty's accusations.

"I have never heard such outrageous rantings in all my life!" she said eventually.

Pierce walked to the cabinet and poured a glass of port.

"Pierce! Did you hear the girl? She is quite delusional!"

"I heard her. How could I not?"

"Why are you taking it so calmly?"

"Because she has implied as much to me previously," answered Pierce.

"*What*? Why didn't you tell me?"

"Well, this is what happens when you get too close to staff, Clara. I've warned you enough times before," said Pierce, taking a sip from his port.

"Oh my God! Please tell me this is not why you dismissed Hugh? You didn't dismiss him because of this girl's ridiculous delusions?"

"But are they delusions? She seems quite certain she heard your lovemaking with O'Meara and witnessed your motorcar outside his cottage."

"*What?* You cannot seriously think for a moment that I would – that I could – with a member of staff!"

"Well, as the girl said it wouldn't be the first time you went with another man during our marriage," said Pierce.

"But Johnny was different! Johnny was a gentleman, Hugh is just a farm boy!"

"*Ahhh*, so there is a snob well hidden inside you after all! So, the only reason that I should believe that you did not sleep with O'Meara is that he is not of the right class?"

"That's not what I'm saying at all! How could you believe I would sleep with any man other than you?"

"How?" Pierce laughed a bitter laugh. "Because you have done so previously, Clara!"

Clara sank down on the couch and put her face in her hands.

Asty frantically puffed on a cigarette at the table in the kitchen, the rest of the staff gathered round her.

"What will you do now, Asty?" asked Mrs. Fennell.

"I'll go to America which is what I should have done in the first place instead of coming here! I'll go work in one of those fancy mansions on Fifth Avenue where they will appreciate my expertise!"

"Did they give you a reason why they let you go?" asked Fennell.

"They told me they were re-organising the staff, but I told them I knew the real reason was because Lady Armstrong is having it off with Hugh O'Meara!"

All their mouths dropped open.

"You shouldn't tell such wicked lies, Asty!" said Mrs. Fennell. "Go at once and tell Lord Armstrong that's not true. Then get yourself down to Confession tomorrow and beg for forgiveness!"

"It's not me who should be going to Confession but her upstairs! That's why Lord Armstrong fired Hugh as well – because he was sleeping with his wife!"

"It can't be!" said Mrs. Fennell.

"I saw them together in his cottage and I heard them!" stated Asty as she angrily stubbed out her cigarette and lit another. "That's why Hugh dumped me – because his head is turned with her! Lady Armstrong stole my fiancée!"

"Strictly speaking, Hugh was not your fiancée," said Fennell.

"Strictly speaking, I don't give a flying fuck what you call him! But I'll tell you this – if I ever see that fucker again I'll kill him!" spat Asty.

"Asty, please! I know you are emotional, but can you please not swear in front of Mrs. Fennell?" said Fennell.

"Mrs. Fennell can kiss my lily-white arse!"

"Oh, Lord save us, that we are not all struck down with all these profanities flying around us!" said Síle as she blessed herself.

"You may well bless yourself, Síle, when you sleep each night under the roof of a harlot!" said Asty.

"Well, I think it's time we all should be going to bed!" said Mrs. Fennell, rising from the table.

"Wise words, Mrs. Fennell," said Fennell.

"And come on to bed with you, Síle, Máire and Julia! You can do what you please, Asty – as you always do!" said Mrs. Fennell.

Asty looked in a world of her own, consumed by her anger, as the others left her and climbed the servants' stairs.

When they reached the landing upstairs, Fennell and Mrs. Fennell could hear shouting and instead of continuing up to the attic rooms with the others they paused in the corridor.

"I've never seen such venom in a living being as I just saw in Asty," said Mrs. Fennell.

"She's out of control," said Fennell.

"I, for one, will be glad when she's gone. I don't feel safe sleeping in the house with her here anymore."

"But she can't be telling the truth about Lady Armstrong and Hugh! It's unimaginable," said Fennell.

"It is – but if it's not true why then are Lord and Lady Armstrong shouting the house down?"

"You will just never forgive me for my affair with Johnny, will you?" demanded Clara, her voice raised.

"Oh, I can forgive you, I just can't forget! I've told you before, Clara, I really don't care what you do – I really don't. Just do not make a fool of me in front of everybody while you do it."

"But you do care!" shouted Clara. "Why can't you be honest about your feelings after everything that has happened! You tried to kill yourself when you thought you lost me before. And now you have fired Hugh because you suspect something is going on between us! Why can't you admit your feelings for me? I am here ready to love you – only you – but you have to let me in, Pierce! You are reacting the exact same way you always have – pretending not to care. You are reacting the same vindictive way with Hugh as you did with Johnny when you had him arrested on that trumped-up charge when you found out about our affair! You are eliminating the perceived enemy in the same ruthless way you did the Germans during the war. You don't need to do that. All you need to do is tell me – show me – that you love me, and you'll have me for life – forever!"

She rushed to him, put her arms around him and kissed him.

"This marriage is ... difficult," said Pierce. "I want to love you, and I want to destroy you at the same time."

"But why would you want to destroy something you love?" she demanded.

"I do not know the answer to that. If I, for once, am being honest with you then I will say that you should never have come back to me, for your own sake!"

"Why?"

"I will end up destroying you – one way or the other. It is our destiny," he whispered.

"I refuse to believe that, Pierce! If you didn't love me you would never have tried to kill yourself. And if I didn't love you I would never have come back. We do not need to destroy each other. We have everything in the world to live for now – more than you know."

Chapter 44

The next morning early, Asty finished packing her suitcase. She went to pull back the curtains on the window and as she looked outside she was surprised to see a policeman seated in a motorcar in the forecourt. She left the room and crept downstairs to find out what was going on.

Clara and Pierce listened intently to the Sergeant in the library. He had arrived unannounced and asked to speak to them urgently.

"Following the incidents that have occurred to Lady Armstrong, I looked into your staff here at Armstrong House and my enquiries have thrown up some dubious and unsettling revelations about your housekeeper," said Cantwell.

"What kind of revelations?" asked Clara.

"Some of her previous employers have died from mysterious accidents. Lord Kilternan tripped over a floorboard and fell to his death down the stairs. The floorboard had somehow come loose and had been raised, causing the trip. The previous employer, a fragile older woman drowned in her fountain – it is believed she slipped into the water while sitting on the surround of the fountain but the coroner left an open verdict. There have also been a couple of unsettling incidents of guests staying at hotels she previously worked at."

"Are you saying Asty was behind those deaths?" asked Pierce.

"There are a lot of coincidences, and I really need to bring her into the barracks to question her," said Cantwell.

"By all means, Sergeant!" agreed Clara. "What a terrifying prospect! But after her performance here last night I do believe she is quite capable of anything!"

"What performance?" asked Cantwell.

"In light of everything going on we gave her notice and she acted in the most extraordinary fashion. It was quite frightening to behold!" said Clara.

"Where is the girl now?" asked Cantwell.

"In her room packing, I believe." said Pierce. "I shall ring for Fennell to fetch her for you now." He went to the bell-pull and tugged it.

Outside the door, Asty's mouth had dropped open as she listened in to their conversation. She turned and raced up the stairs.

"I'm afraid Asty is nowhere to be found. She is not in her room and all her clothes are gone," announced Fennell.

"None of servants saw her this morning. She was last seen in the kitchen last night, smoking profusely and in a highly agitated state."

"Have all the staff do a thorough search of the house to make sure she is gone, Fennell," instructed Pierce.

"I will at once, Your Lordship."

"Her family live in Castleswest. I will go there now to see if she is there or if they know of her whereabouts," said Cantwell.

"I am just relieved that she's gone," said Clara. "I hope to never see her again!"

"I very much hope to the contrary, Lady Armstrong. It appears she is quite dangerous," said Cantwell.

"Please keep us informed of any developments, Sergeant," said Clara.

"I most certainly will," said Cantwell. "Good morning to you."

He turned and left.

"It appears we have been living under the same roof as a psychopath!" said Clara.

"I think you owe Prudence an apology for accusing her, don't you think?" said Pierce.

"Yes, of course. I will apologise to her this morning."

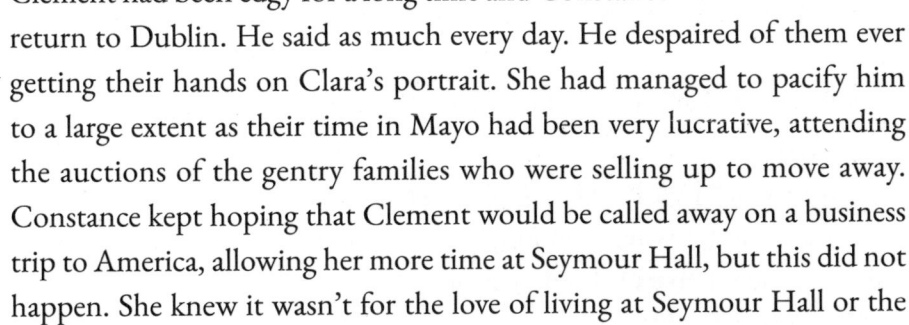

Clement had been edgy for a long time and Constance knew he wanted to return to Dublin. He said as much every day. He despaired of them ever getting their hands on Clara's portrait. She had managed to pacify him to a large extent as their time in Mayo had been very lucrative, attending the auctions of the gentry families who were selling up to move away. Constance kept hoping that Clement would be called away on a business trip to America, allowing her more time at Seymour Hall, but this did not happen. She knew it wasn't for the love of living at Seymour Hall or the scenery that she was in no rush back to Dublin. It was that she could not stand the thought of losing Hugh. And yet she knew this time would come and when Clement announced over breakfast that he had contacted the agent in Castlewest and cancelled the lease on Seymour Hall, telling him they were leaving at the end of the week, that time had come.

Constance was stunned by her own attachment to Hugh. It was only supposed to be a holiday romance. She didn't think she had it in her to actually start to care for anybody. Especially somebody like Hugh who was no advantage to her in the world whatsoever. She had learned from her childhood in Dublin and her life in Cairo as a younger woman that she should only form attachments to people who could be advantageous to her. She had briefly abandoned this rule and, as the dread of telling Hugh she was leaving beckoned, she was determined to never do it again.

Constance drove down the boreen to Hugh's cottage and parked outside the open door.

When she walked in, she found him looking morose.

"What's wrong, Hugh?" she asked.

"Lord Armstrong dismissed me from the job," he said.

He lifted the bottle of whiskey up to her. "Do you care to celebrate my new freedom with me?"

"Whiskey is not the answer, Hugh!" she said, taking the bottle from him and putting it on the dresser.

"I forgot that you have all the answers," said Hugh as he took a drink from his glass.

"Oh, Hugh, I am sorry," she said, sitting down beside him and holding his hand.

"From what I gather, Lord Armstrong appears to be jealous of me getting close to his wife," said Hugh. "The man who has everything being jealous of me – I guess I should take it as a compliment."

"But why would Pierce think such a thing?"

"Because Asty is going around telling everybody I'm sleeping with her! Asty is not as stupid as she looks. She knew I was seeing somebody behind her back – I guess she just suspected the wrong lady."

"I guess she did."

"I don't suppose you want to admit the truth to the Armstrongs?" said Hugh.

"Of course I can't, Hugh! I'd be destroyed – Clement would kill me and divorce me! Divorce me first and then kill me, I should say!"

"I know and I never would expect you to do that for me," said Hugh as he put his arms around her.

"I'm sorry it hasn't all turned out better for you," said Constance, laying her head against his chest. "And I'm afraid I have some other news for you. We are leaving Seymour Hall and returning to live in Dublin."

"What?" Hugh grabbed her shoulders and pushed her back from him.

"It was always going to happen eventually. We were only ever visitors here and the time has come to go home. Clement says he will go mad if he has to spend another week down here."

"And what about you?" demanded Hugh.

"I go wherever Clement goes."

"Even if you don't love him?"

"I never said I didn't love him."

"And you never said you loved me."

"You know how much I care for you, Hugh. But we are from two different worlds, and we could never fit into each other's."

"And I am guilty of dreaming that we could. You made me dream I could be better than I was – but it was a fool's dream."

"No! Hugh – I still believe in you. You can still do anything you want with your life!"

"Just not with you by my side?"

"That was never going to happen. You know that," she whispered.

"Of course I did. How things can change. Not so long ago I had a girlfriend, a big job and a woman I loved – now it's all gone except for this cottage," he said with a resigned sigh.

"But soon who knows where you'll be? Somewhere better, I bet," she said.

"I somehow doubt that."

"*Hugh*!" came a man's voice from outside.

Constance and Hugh gave a startled look at each other and jumped apart just before Tadgh arrived at the door.

"Sorry – I didn't realise you had visitors," said Tadgh.

"I would have thought the motorcar parked outside might have given you a clue!" said Hugh.

"I was just about to go," said Constance as she looked at Hugh and then walked to the door.

"Don't let me be delaying you in that case!" said Tadgh, stepping out of her way.

She stopped at the door and turned back to Hugh.

"Thank you all your help, Hugh. I wish you nothing but good luck."

"Same to you, Mrs. Fitzgerald – you take care," said Hugh.

Constance walked out the door and Tadgh closed it behind her.

But, instead of going to the motorcar, Constance stayed by the door to listen.

"What did she want?" asked Tadgh.

"Just came to pay me for some work I did for her before she returns to Dublin. So, to what do I owe the pleasure of your visit?"

"Sure, didn't I hear the news that you got fired from the Big House," said Tadgh.

"So, you came to gloat?"

"I came to offer you your job back on my farm, you eejit! And if you have any sense you'll take it!"

"You'd take me back even after everything that happened between us?"

"You're my brother at the end of the day. All families have disagreements and, sure, isn't blood thicker than water, as they say?"

"You certainly drew blood when you hit my head with that stone!"

"You're always such a smart arse! Come back to the farm where you belong, Hugh, and have no more of this messing! Sure, the children are crying from missing you every day and Molly has the place set at the table every night for you for dinner, hoping you'll come through the door!"

"Well, I'm glad somebody wants me at least," said Hugh.

"You never belonged up at Armstrong House with those posh bastards! I don't know what took hold of you that had your head filled with such fancy notions to better yourself!"

"I'm beginning to ask myself the same question," said Hugh.

As Constance continued to listen she was filled with sadness that Hugh was going to end up back where she had found him.

After leaving Hugh's cottage, Constance drove straight to Armstrong House where she met Clara who invited her to lunch.

"How absolutely awful for you!" Constance said as Clara informed her of the events that had taken place since she had seen her last.

"It's very unsettling to think we had this potential killer under our roof," said Clara.

"And you say the police have not managed to find her?" Constance asked.

"She seems to have disappeared into thin air. She'd told the servants that she planned to go to America so perhaps she is already on her way there."

"Let us hope so! An ocean is the very least you would like to put between you and that girl!"

"She also made the most outrageous claim to Pierce that I was having an affair with Hugh O'Meara!"

Constance feigned shock.

"She claimed I was in a relationship with him and that she had heard us having sexual relations while listening at the door of his cottage!"

"Have you ever even been to his cottage?"

"Of course not! What reason would I have to go there?"

"What a barefaced liar!"

"Clearly, but she had the audacity to also tell all the servants, according to Fennell, and you know how servants gossip! What's more Pierce has dismissed Hugh over it which is most unfair."

"Pierce surely doesn't believe her?"

"I would like to think it's too ridiculous for him to believe. Hugh is lovely lad, but he is farm boy – what lady is ever going to go to his bed? But, alas, people like to think the worse so perhaps it is a good thing that Hugh no longer works here. His presence might feed unwelcome scandalmongering."

"Yes – indeed. But, Clara, I have some news of my own."

"Oh?"

"We are leaving Seymour Hall. We have decided to return to Dublin."

"*No!* But I thought you had moved here permanently," said Clara.

"So did I. But it's turning out to be impractical. We need to be in Dublin for the shop and I'm afraid country living is not to Clement's taste."

"But I don't know what I'll do without you, Constance! You've been such a good friend to me. What will I do without my confidante?" Clara began to tear up.

Constance reached over and took her hand.

"But we can still see each other all the time. You can visit me in Dublin, and I can visit you here – that is, if I am welcome?"

"Of course you'll be welcome! You're always welcome here," said Clara as she wiped away her tears. "But I shall miss you terribly in the meantime."

A knock sounded on the door and a few moments later Mrs. Fennell walked in, carrying a tray with the desserts.

Clara was surprised to see Fennell's wife carrying out his duties.

"Is anything the matter downstairs, Mrs. Fennell?" asked Clara, seeing how flustered the cook looked as she placed the tray on the table.

"Everything is the matter downstairs, Lady Armstrong! Mr. Fennell has taken poorly and I sent him to bed. He came down with a fever and stomach trouble. And then Síle said she was feeling sick, so I packed her off home to her family to care for her. Though I told her to let us know if she got much worse and needed a doctor. I can't be looking after Mr. Fennell and her at the same time!"

"I hope there isn't a flu going around," said Constance, taking a napkin and covering her nose and mouth as Mrs. Fennell placed a bowl of sherry trifle in front of her.

"I hope so too!" said Mrs. Fennell. "And all this on the day that wretched girl Asty has left us too! You can tell His Lordship there will be no bed made for him tonight!"

"I am sure His Lordship will understand," said Clara.

"He'd still expect his bed made!" huffed Mrs. Fennell and she walked out and closed the door.

Chapter 45

"That was a rather meagre meal served to us this evening," said Pierce as he lit his cigar from the fire in the hearth in the drawing room. "Luckily, I didn't much feel like eating, my stomach being rather unsettled."

"Poor Mrs. Fennell is rushed off her feet, Pierce. She is holding the fort after Julia had to take to the bed this afternoon. Julia seems to have the same complaint as Fennell and Síle," said Clara. "I'm waiting to hear how they're feeling this evening and if they're not better I shall call the doctor."

"Oh, I'm sure they'll be fine," said Pierce dismissively.

Clara knew Pierce never had any interest in talk about the servants.

"Well, I for one won't miss Constance," said Pierce, moving the conversation on quickly.

"That's because you have so many friends here. But I don't. Acquaintances, yes, but no close friends, being as I am still a newcomer in the eyes of the local gentry – as Constance was too. I don't know how I would have got through the past few months without her."

"Oh, I'm sure you would have managed just fine. It is that woman brought Hugh O'Meara into our lives if you remember correctly," Pierce said irritably.

"Hugh who has been treated very unfairly by you and now has lost his position here over that stupid girl's fanciful lies!" snapped Clara.

"Well, I shouldn't worry too much. Prudence has now taken over the running of the estate," said Pierce.

"I'm sure she has!"

"And is running it as it should be."

"We have used poor Hugh to get rid of his brother and now have sent him packing once his usefulness is over. Shameful!"

Pierce moved away from the fire.

"Is it very warm this evening?" he said as he wiped his brow with his hand.

"Not particularly," said Clara.

Pierce went to the French windows, opened them and stepped out onto the terrace.

"Pierce – close the French windows – you are letting a draft in!"

Pierce came back inside and Clara could see he was shivering. He locked the French windows.

"It's so damned cold!" he exclaimed as he went to warm his hands to the flames.

"I thought you were complaining of being too hot a few minutes ago?"

He turned to face her, and she saw he was deathly white with a film of sweat covering his face.

"Pierce? What's wrong?" she demanded as she hurried over to him.

"I'm not sure ... I feel I have a fever," he mumbled as she helped him to an armchair by the fire.

She felt his forehead. "You're burning up! Oh, good Lord – you must have picked up the same flu as the staff!"

"I feel dreadful!" he said as he began retching into the hearth.

Out of habit Clara raced to tug the bell-pull but then, remembering Fennell was sick in bed and Mrs. Fennell would take an eternity to answer the call, she ran out into the hallway.

"*Mrs. Fennell!*" she called at the top of her voice.

At that moment she saw Mrs. Fennell appearing at the top of the staircase, groaning loudly.

Clara rushed down the hallway to her.

"Get a doctor!" begged Mrs. Fennell as Clara helped her to a chair.

Clara turned and rushed to the telephone in the library.

An hour later an ambulance was parked in the forecourt as all the staff were helped into it.

Dr. O'Brien had insisted that the whole household should be transported to hospital immediately and an ambulance was called from the infirmary in Castlewest.

"What is wrong with them?" asked Clara as he examined Pierce in the drawing room.

"I really can't say at this point," said the doctor. "I can drive him to the infirmary. There won't be room in the ambulance for him."

"Thank you, Doctor, I shall go with you," said Clara.

At the infirmary Clara waited patiently for news.

"What is wrong with my husband? Is it a flu?" Clara asked anxiously as the doctor appeared.

"It's not a flu. My first impression is acute food poisoning,"

"Food poisoning? I can hardly believe it, Doctor! Mrs. Fennell does all the cooking at the house and food poisoning would never happen on her watch! Besides, why am I not ill in that case? I ate the same food as my husband."

"I am a doctor, Lady Armstrong, not a clairvoyant. At this stage, I can only tell you what their symptoms suggest."

"How is Pierce now?"

"He seemed to have escaped the worst. Your staff are in a much worse condition. But I am going to keep him here for the night and we shall see how he is doing tomorrow."

"May I see him?"

"Yes, but he is in foul form. He is furious at being in a public ward but we have no private room available to put him in."

"Never mind about that! Just make him better!" said Clara.

Pierce was in bed in the middle of the ward that contained twenty male patients. Clara sat on the empty chair beside him.

"Pierce – the doctor said –"

"I know what the bloody doctor said! That bloody servant girl Asty must have done something to poison everyone before she absconded!"

Clara did not want to talk about it there but that thought had crossed her mind.

"I want to go home now and out of this infernal hellhole!" said Pierce.

"Pierce – please – the doctor says you must remain here for the night," said Clara.

"I refuse to be stuck in this room with these men!" seethed Pierce.

"I'm sure if you could cope with the trenches for four years during the war a night at the local infirmary is not too much of an inconvenience!" said Clara. "The main thing is you get well. The doctor says you are not as bad as the servants, and you should be able to be released tomorrow."

"Do not leave me here, Clara! Take me home at once!" ordered Pierce as he struggled to sit up.

Clara pushed him back down and kissed his forehead.

"You just relax and try and get some sleep," she urged.

"Damned chance of that in here!" said Pierce as the man in the next bed groaned.

After visiting all the servants Dr. O'Brien gave Clara a lift back to Armstrong House. It was nearly midnight when he delivered her to the forecourt. Realising she would be alone in the house, he had earlier expressed concern but she insisted she would be fine.

Now she thanked him profusely and waved him off.

As Pierce had said, it must have been Asty who did something to the well before she left. That well had been there since the 1840s and there had never been any incident with it previously that she was aware of. Asty must have committed one final act of maliciousness before she fled. But the well was outside the house so anyone could have had access to it and Clara could not help thinking about Tadgh O'Meara's threat of revenge.

She put the key in the front door and stepped inside. Moonlight shone through the windows either side of the door and Clara walked to the light switch to turn it on. The house remained in darkness. Clara tried the light switch again several times but the light from the chandelier above her did not ignite. She made her way into the drawing room and tried the light switch there to no effect. In frustration Clara realised that since Hugh had been dismissed there must have been no gasoline put into the outside generator, which had been one of his jobs. The generator had now run dry, leaving them without electricity.

Clara walked over to the fireplace. She felt along the mantelpiece until she found a taper and lit it from the cinders in the fire, then lit one of the candles on the mantelpiece.

After all that had happened that day the last thing she needed was to be without electricity, but she felt so tired all she wanted to do was sleep. She used the light from the candle to guide her out of the drawing room and up the stairs. She then made her way to the master bedroom where the fire in the hearth was still throwing out some light. She placed the candlestick on the table beside the bed and then undressed and put on her nightdress.

With the light flickering from the candle and the fire, she went to the window and looked out at the half moon weaving its light across the lake. It felt strange to be in Armstrong House on her own and at the same time normal. While Pierce was away at war she had spent four years on her own there, with only a few servants for company. And she remembered Christmases when they had all gone to be with their families, and she had been there on her own.

Of course, there was that one Christmas that she had invited Johnny to be there with her. The two of them had been in romantic isolation in the house as the snow fell outside, separating them from the rest of the world. It had been beautiful. As Clara thought of Pierce suffering in the hospital she quickly dismissed all memories of Johnny from her mind and, climbing into the bed, extinguished the candle and fell into a deep sleep.

In the infirmary, Pierce raised his eyes to heaven as he listened to the incessant snoring and groaning from the other men in the ward. He suddenly pulled himself out of the bed and began to get dressed.

"Lord Armstrong – what do you think you are doing?" asked the nurse on duty as she came into the ward.

"I would have thought that was obvious! I am leaving this zoo!"

"You get back into that bed immediately, Lord Armstrong, if you know what is good for you!"

"I will not spend another moment in this cesspit. Order me a cab to take me back to Armstrong House," ordered Pierce.

"A cab, is it? Where do you think you are – Piccadilly Circus?" said the nurse with a cackle of a laugh.

"Then get me a horse and cart, you wretched woman, or a donkey or whatever mode of transport you can possibly find. Otherwise, I will walk every step of the way back home rather than stay another minute in this asylum!"

Chapter 46

Something woke Clara from her sleep. She sat up in bed and looked around in the darkness. As she listened intently she could hear movement coming from somewhere in the house. She quickly got out of bed, pulled on her satin dressing gown and slippers. She tried the light switch on the wall but there was still no electricity. The fire in the hearth had now gone out and she couldn't find matches to light a candle. She opened the bedroom door and stepped out into the corridor. As clouds were crossing the path of the moon, the light from the Georgian window on the landing was dim. She looked over the bannisters to the hall below but could see nothing in the darkness. But she could hear somebody down there. She was filled with panic. She was about to call out to whoever was there but stopped herself. There was somebody who had tried to cause her harm, kill her even. And now she was isolated in the house alone and there was a strong likelihood whoever was downstairs was that malicious person come to get her.

The clouds cleared in the night sky, allowing the moonlight from the window behind her to temporarily light the hall downstairs. A figure was hurrying across the hall towards the staircase.

Clara dropped to her hands and knees and quickly crawled back along the landing. Then she stood up and, heart pounding, swiftly made her way to the end of the corridor, and down the narrow servants' staircase until she reached the small hallway that led to the kitchen. She knew Fennell kept the key for the back door hanging on the wall beside the stove. She found it, rushed to the door and unlocked it. Then she ran out into the courtyard, around the house and raced down the avenue to the road as fast as her flimsy slippers would allow.

She was panting when she reached the main gateway and only then allowed herself to look behind to make sure she wasn't being followed. There was no-one in sight.

She continued running down the road until she reached Hunter's Farm which was in darkness. She reached its front door and was about to bang on it to wake Prudence, but suddenly stopped. Prudence was her enemy and always had been. As much as Prudence pretended to have turned over a new leaf, she did not trust her. For all she knew it might be Prudence in the house. She had a key so could easily come in.

Clara turned and ran back to the road.

The next house she came to was Tadgh O'Meara's. He was the last person she could call on for help as Pierce was convinced he was behind everything that had happened to her. But Hugh lived close to his brother, down a nearby boreen. She knew she could trust Hugh, though after his treatment from Pierce he might no longer want to help her.

With no other choice, she made her way quickly down the boreen until she reached his cottage.

She hammered on his door. A light came on inside the cottage.

"Who in the name of God is that at this time of the night?" demanded Hugh from the other side of the door.

"Hugh – it's Clara! Lady Armstrong! I need your help!"

She could hear the door being quickly unbolted and when Hugh swung it open she rushed into his arms.

"Clara! Lady Armstrong! What is wrong with you?" demanded Hugh.

"Hugh – somebody has broken into Armstrong House. I was alone there as everyone else – the staff and Pierce – are in the hospital in Castlewest from some kind of poisoning. Somebody broke in! I saw someone crossing the hall to come up the stairs. The generator isn't working so there was no light and I couldn't see who it was!"

Hugh led her inside, closed the door and sat her down at the table.

"I'm terrified it was the same person who did those other things to me. Hugh – it could be Asty since she was fired – I don't know –"

"Asty!"

"The police are looking for her!"

"Why?"

"Because some of her previous employers have died under mysterious circumstances." "Ah, Asty is half cracked but she would never do anybody any harm!" said Hugh.

He took the bottle of whiskey from the dresser and poured some into a glass.

"Drink this!" he ordered.

"I don't know what to think anymore, Hugh. I didn't know who to trust so I came to you and I have no right to after the despicable way you have been treated." Clara gulped back the whiskey.

"Don't worry, you came to the right place. You're safe here, Clara," he said reassuringly.

He quickly got dressed and put on a coat.

"Can you take me to the barracks for the police?" she asked.

"I will but I must go up and check on Armstrong House first."

"No, Hugh! You can't go up there on your own! It could be anybody there!"

"By the time we get into Castlewest and get the police Armstrong House could be robbed blind and whoever is there gone with your valuables," said Hugh as he strode to the door.

"Hugh, it's not safe! And don't leave me here on my own!"

"I'll put gasoline in the generator before I enter the house to make sure there's light when I go in. You bolt the door after me and don't answer it to anybody until I return."

She watched as he pushed a bicycle from a shed, mounted it and rode up the boreen at speed. Then she closed the door and bolted it.

Clara paced the floor as she anxiously waited for him to return. She kept looking at the clock on the wall and watched the hours tick by – 3 o'clock, 4 o'clock, 5 o'clock and there was still no sign of him. She repeatedly looked out past the curtains on the window, hoping to see him walking down the boreen.

Sitting down on the bed beside the fire, she threw some more turf on it and set it alight with paraffin, to keep warm. She curled up on the bed and waited.

As the sun began to rise and the morning birds started to sing their chorus, announcing the dawning of the day, Clara became seriously concerned that something bad had happened to Hugh.

Eventually she unbolted the door, stepped into the brisk morning air, and walked up the boreen and back to Armstrong House.

Clara made her way up the avenue to Armstrong House and was filled with dread when she saw two police motorcars parked in the forecourt. She ran the rest of the way.

There was a policeman positioned at the door. He looked at her, obviously astonished at her attire and dishevelled state.

"What has happened?" she demanded.

"Lady Armstrong – you can't go in. There has been an accident. Your husband came back during the middle of the night and –"

"Pierce! Pierce is here?" Clara pushed past the policeman, bolted up the steps and in the front door.

Sergeant Cantwell was in the hall under the landing, with three other policemen. They were standing over what was clearly a body covered with a blanket.

"*Pierce!*" screamed Clara as she rushed to the body on the floor.

At that moment Pierce walked out of the drawing room with another policeman.

"Pierce!" cried Clara as she rushed to him and embraced him. "I thought – I thought it was you under that blanket!"

Pierce held her away from him and looked her up and down, from her wild hair to her ruined slippers. "Where the *hell* have you been, Clara? In your night attire?"

Just then Cantwell joined them and indicated that they should move into the drawing room.

When they were seated, he addressed Clara.

"Lady Armstrong – we need to question you urgently. Where have you been all night?"

"Who – who is that in the hall?" demanded Clara, her voice shaking.

"It's Hugh O'Meara," said Pierce. "I discharged myself from the hospital during the night and when I arrived back here I found him dead. He seems to have fallen over the bannisters from the landing."

"*Hugh! Oh no! No! This is my fault!*" Clara burst into tears.

"*Your fault?*" said Pierce. "What do you mean?"

"I asked him for help! There was somebody in the house when he came here! Someone who must have pushed him over the bannisters!"

Chapter 47

Present Day

As they anxiously waited for further correspondence from Royce Charter, Kate racked her brains, trying to think of some way of disproving his claim. One thing that Geoffrey Conway had said offered a little hope – or at any rate should be followed up. The farmland was seized by the Land Commission and sold to the O'Meara family in 1925. The O'Mearas still occupied the neighbouring farm. Kate and Nico had little to do with them, but she always found them friendly when she bumped into them. The O'Mearas would have the original deeds of the land bought in 1925 and they might shed light on the present predicament.

Kate went on the internet and researched the Land Commission which Geoffrey had said had overseen the sale. She learned that the Land Commission was a department set up by the Irish government and under the Land Act of 1923, they had the authority to seize land that was unused and untenanted. They then provided loans to local farmers who bought the land from the original owners. Kate understood it was basically a compulsory sale. Piecing together the chain of events, she realised that after the fire at Armstrong House in December 1923, Pierce was no longer living there to farm the land, and so it had been seized by the Land Commission and sold to the O'Mearas.

Kate remembered learning, when she'd met Professor Maguire at Maynooth University, that the Big Houses were often set on fire to drive the families out so local farmers could then claim the land. He had called it land hunger. It crossed Kate's mind that the second fire at Armstrong House had served the O'Meara family well.

She looked up the O'Mearas' phone number.

Kate drove up the long avenue that led to the O'Mearas' house. It was a modern white house that reminded her slightly of Southfork from *Dallas*. Judging by the flash cars parked outside their house, she guessed the O'Mearas were doing very well from their farming business.

Barry O'Meara was still the owner of the farm, but his son had taken over the day-to-day running of the business. When Kate had phoned their house, Barry's wife Aoife had answered and seemed very happy for her to call over. Now, as Kate got out of her car, Aoife was already at the door waiting for her with a big smile and a wave.

"You're very welcome, Kate. I can't believe in all these years as neighbours it's the first time you've called to us," said Aoife.

"That's my fault, I have no excuse," said Kate.

"Well, you are here now. Come through to the sitting room where Barry is waiting for you."

As Kate walked after her she could see the interior of the house was as flash as the outside. When she walked into the sitting room, Barry was standing there with a big smile to greet her. Kate guessed they were both in their mid-seventies and looked to be very fit and happy with life.

"Kate! Wasn't I only watching one of your old films the other night and I thought aren't we honoured to be living beside a movie star!" said Barry as he clasped her hand and shook it warmly.

"I think you flatter me, Barry! I may have been an actress but never a star!" said Kate, laughing.

"Well, you look like one to me!" said Barry, gesturing for her to sit down on the couch.

"Is he always this charming?" asked Kate with a smile to Aoife.

"He has his moments!" said Aoife. "I'll go and make tea."

"And don't be shy with the cake!" Barry called after her.

Kate found them so warm she regretted not having made their acquaintance beforehand.

"How are you, Barry? Life is treating you well?" asked Kate.

"Can't complain, Kate. My son has taken over the running of the farm and he and his wife are expecting a baby, so I can take a back seat now and look forward to being a grandfather again."

Kate felt envious of them. Their lives seemed so complete and content and so different from the bleak picture of loneliness Nico had painted of their own future at Armstrong House. They chatted some more until Aoife returned with tea and a feast of fruit cake for them.

Kate finally broached the topic she had called to discuss.

"The reason I asked to see you, Barry, was I thought you might be able to help me with some information."

"If I can I will," said Barry.

"I understand your family bought the land at Armstrong House from Nico's grandfather, Pierce, back in the 1920s."

"Yes, that's correct. My grandfather Tadgh bought it from Lord Armstrong."

"Well, we have been contacted by a relative of Pierce's first wife Clara who seems to think he has a claim on Armstrong House."

"Oh my God!" Aoife exclaimed while Barry's eyes widened.

"I am trying to think of anything that could disprove his claim and I'm wondering if there is anything on the deeds of that land you bought that could help us," said Kate.

"The purchase of the land was all above board," said Barry, looking concerned. "The sale was overseen by the Land Commission so they would have been very thorough and made sure that there was nothing untoward."

"I don't doubt it, Barry. There is no suggestion of that."

"After Armstrong House was set on fire the Armstrongs left the area for good, and the land was abandoned. The Land Commission then took the land and sold it to my grandfather Tadgh, and we've farmed it ever since."

"I understand that but I thought there might be something on the deeds of the land you bought that might help us," said Kate. "I'm probably clutching at straws here but we're desperate,"

"I'll contact my solicitor and ask him to look and see if that helps you in any way," said Barry.

"I would very much appreciate that," said Kate.

"That's terrible for ye – someone claiming the house," said Aoife.

"It is, Aoife," said Kate.

"Clara Armstrong – that's a name I haven't heard in many years," said Barry.

"Do you know anything about her?" asked Kate.

"I heard my grandparents talk about her when I was a child. She was not liked by our family."

"Was there a particular reason why?"

"She caused a lot of division and trouble in my family. My grandfather Tadgh had a brother called Hugh and they fell out badly over her. It was the time of the Civil War and Tadgh was a well-known Republican but apparently Hugh switched to the other side, causing a lot of bitterness – there was a lot of that going on at the time. Neighbours, friends and even brothers falling out."

"But what has that to do with Clara?"

"Clara, or Lady Armstrong as she was called, employed Hugh as manager of the Armstrong Estate. Well, for Tadgh, this was a terrible betrayal. He had fought in the War of Independence and the Civil War to rid us of British rule and families like the Armstrongs – no offence – and then for his own brother to go work for them! Caused a lot of bitterness."

"I can imagine it would!" said Kate, sitting forward to express her eagerness to hear more.

"Then ... there were rumours that Lady Armstrong and Hugh were having an affair." "*What*?"

"That's what people said. That she would go to his cottage at night or sneak him into Armstrong House when her husband was away. It was the talk of the place locally."

"I can hardly believe it! Though perhaps I shouldn't be surprised as Clara already had a well-known affair with the artist Johnny Seymour," said Kate. "What happened to Hugh?"

"He was killed – young," said Barry.

"How was he killed?"

"I don't really know the facts as my grandfather refused to discuss it after it happened. All I know was that Hugh died up at Armstrong House while he was working there – they said it was an accident, others said there was more to it than that. As I said, my grandfather wouldn't talk about it. It clearly upset Tadgh greatly as Hugh went to the grave without them ever resolving their issues."

"With my own children, I never allow them to argue or fall out," said Aoife. "I tell them if we don't learn from the past we can never have a future."

"Hugh is buried up in the graveyard past the Armstrong village. Poor fella – I guess he just got mixed up with the wrong woman," sighed Barry.

Kate was stunned after leaving the O'Mearas. Instead of driving back to Armstrong House, she turned her car towards the village and parked outside the graveyard. Locking her car, she opened the rusty gates and entered. The graveyard had not been used for burials for decades and was now rather neglected and overgrown. Kate began to search the gravestones, looking for Hugh's while she tried to make sense of what Barry had told her. If Clara had an affair with their estate manager, as Barry had said, then her marriage to Pierce had never really been repaired after they had moved back to Armstrong House after the first fire.

When Kate had first moved to Armstrong House and wanted to return the items she found belonging to Clara to her family, she had tracked down and met a relative called Amanda Charter in London. This relative had painted a picture of a very unhappy marriage between Clara and Pierce. She had told Kate about Clara's affair with Johnny Seymour but had said nothing about a second affair. She had portrayed Clara as a victim who had been driven to have an affair with Seymour by her husband's cruelty. She'd said that Clara had returned to live as a sad recluse in her grandmother's house in Kent after Armstrong House had been set on fire, and her marriage to Pierce had ended in divorce. Now it seemed there were two sides to this story. Perhaps it was Pierce who was the wronged party.

However, Kate could not understand why Clara had returned to her marriage and Armstrong House after the first fire if she had been so unhappy there. And then when she returned she'd ended up having an affair with a local farmer who she employed to run the estate? It didn't make sense. As she searched the headstones, she wondered if Pierce had some hold or some spell over Clara that she could not break.

She paused at a headstone that was mostly covered with moss when she spotted the first name of the inscription: *Hugh*.

She began to scrape the moss off the small headstone until she could read it fully.

Hugh O'Meara
Died August 1923
You Will Have Vengeance

Kate shivered at those chilling words, so strange on a gravestone. Barry had said there were rumours that Hugh's death had not been an accident. The inscription on his gravestone implied the same. Now she wondered if Tadgh O'Meara was behind the burning of Armstrong House – just four months after Hugh's death. Not only was he the beneficiary through gaining the Armstrong land, but he also may have had another motive – revenge – if he believed the Armstrongs were somehow responsible for Hugh's death.

A sudden wind rustled through the weeds beside Kate. She stood up quickly and made her way back to her car, closing the rusty gate behind her. Then she drove quickly back to Armstrong House.

Chapter 48

1923

After Clara had been given some brandy and had calmed down somewhat, she recounted how she was woken from her sleep and, looking down into the dark hall, saw someone making for the staircase and had fled the house.

"There is no evidence of a break-in," said Cantwell, "but a window of the dining room was left open and the intruder must have come in through that, knocking over a crystal lamp while doing so. That must have been what woke you."

"I was terrified! So I fled down the servants' stairs and out the back," said Clara.

"And can you describe this person?" asked Cantwell.

"No – the house was in pitch darkness. There was no electricity when I got home."

"But the electricity was on when I arrived," said Pierce. "When I came through the front door the light was already on and then I saw O'Meara's body on the ground."

"Before he left the cottage, I told Hugh the generator wasn't working, probably because the gasoline hadn't been replenished since he was dismissed. He said he would put gasoline into the generator and have the electricity working before he entered the house."

"You didn't see or hear anybody else in the house when you arrived, Lord Armstrong?" asked the Sergeant.

"Not a one. After I saw O'Meara's body, I feared something had also happened to Clara and searched the house for her, and when I couldn't find her I phoned the police straight away."

"As there appears to be nothing stolen, you must have disturbed the intruder, Lord Armstrong," said Cantwell.

"Or the intruder was not here to steal but to harm me but found Hugh instead!" said Clara.

"There is a possibility that Hugh O'Meara fell over the banisters by accident but that seems highly unlikely. You say the electricity was back on so O'Meara was not in darkness. Also, judging by the height of the banisters, even if he stumbled for some reason, it is very unlikely he would have toppled over them."

A policeman came into the room.

"Sir, we noticed the cover of the well supplying the house was disturbed and when we opened it there was a dead fox in the water. A very decomposed fox, that is, sir."

"Which is clearly the source of the poisoning of your staff and yourself, Lord Armstrong," said Cantwell. "Contact Dublin and put an urgent appeal out to find Asty Horan. Notify all the ports to be on a look-out for her in case she is trying to flee the country. Provide them with the description we have back at the station."

Clara thought back over the past couple of days and realised she had not drunk any water except that in the large jug normally left in her bedroom – that must have been filled before the well was poisoned.

"Do you really think Asty poisoned the well and then broke into the house, Sergeant?" asked Clara.

"She has to be the main suspect, considering her history and that she now had a vendetta against this family and also against Hugh O'Meara since he ended his relationship with her. If he found her here when he came into the house there is every likelihood they entered into a confrontation which resulted in Hugh O'Meara's death."

Constance walked into the post office on the main street in Castlewest and stood behind a woman being served by the postmistress.

"Did you hear the latest – what happened up at Armstrong House?" the postmistress asked the customer.

"No, Fidelma, what happened?"

"Hugh O'Meara was killed there last night!"

"Killed, is it? How?" said the customer, aghast.

"Nobody knows yet. But I heard from my cousin who is a Guard that it was murder!"

"But sure who would want to kill poor young Hugh?"

"Isn't that what the Guards are trying to find out! What was he doing up in the house in the middle of the night with just Lady Armstrong for company – while the rest of them were in hospital sick as dogs after being poisoned, that's what I want to know! Didn't Lord Armstrong discover the body when he arrived back at the house – I wonder if that was the only thing he discovered when he got there!" The postmistress gave a knowing wink.

Constance turned and slowly walked out of the post office.

Two days later Clara drove into the driveway at Seymour Hall. She went to the front door and knocked loudly.

A few moments later Clement answered the door.

"Clara! We weren't expecting you – were we?"

"Is Constance home? I need to see her," said Clara.

"Of course – come in. She's in the drawing room packing," said Clement, beckoning her in.

There were a number of boxes stacked in the hallway.

"Forgive the appearance of the place but we are moving back to Dublin tomorrow."

Clara nodded and walked quickly into the drawing room where she found Constance putting books into a box.

"Constance!" cried Clara as she rushed to her and enveloped her in a hug. "Have you heard the dreadful news?"

"Yes ... I heard it when I was in the post office in Castlewest. It's the talk of the town," said Constance who did not hug Clara back.

Clara released Constance and saw her eyes were red – she had obviously been crying.

"Why didn't you come to see me when you heard?" asked Clara.

"I didn't want to intrude. I know how Pierce dislikes my presence at Armstrong House at the best of times, let alone when somebody has been killed there."

Clement was standing at the door.

"I'll leave you two ladies alone," he said.

"Thank you, Clement," said Clara.

Constance sat down in an armchair, and gestured for Clara to sit on the couch opposite her.

"I've heard so many rumours it's hard to know which is true," said Constance.

"There was an intruder at Armstrong House and then I ran to Hugh for help and that's why he went to the house," said Clara.

"And Pierce discovered the body, I heard?"

"Yes. Oh, Constance, when I returned to the house the next morning and saw the dead body covered with a blanket I thought it might be Pierce!"

"Oh, you should know by now it's never the lords that get killed, Clara, it's always the little people," said Constance.

"The police believe the intruder was our former housekeeper and that she returned to get vengeance on us and killed Hugh when he confronted her. The police say he must have been pushed with considerable force to have fallen over the banisters on the landing like that."

"It doesn't bear thinking about," whispered Constance.

"I just feel so guilty. I feel responsible!"

"Well – yes, you are responsible, aren't you?" snapped Constance.

"Sorry?" asked Clara, taken aback.

"Why did you go to Hugh's cottage, Clara? Why involve him in your mess?"

"I – I – I guess he was the only one I trusted," said Clara.

Constance looked down at the floor and wiped away tears with a handkerchief.

"I'm sorry," said Constance. "I'm feeling very guilty myself."

"But why should you feel guilty?"

"It is I who recommended Hugh for the job with you. If it weren't for me he would never have got involved with the politics at Armstrong House. If it weren't for me he would still be working on a farm, content with his little cottage and life."

"You can't blame yourself," said Clara.

"I wish I'd never met Hugh," said Constance as she stared out the window. "I filled his head with dreams and ideas that brought him to a different world that was never meant for him."

"I didn't realise how fond of him you were," said Clara, clasping her hands together.

"He was the sweetest man I ever knew," whispered Constance.

"I'm sorry. I've just been thinking of my loss and how much I liked Hugh. I never realised you two were that close."

Constance suddenly sat up, looked at Clara and cleared her voice.

"He was very helpful with my business, that is all. Of course, you've heard by now the other rumours that are circulating?"

"What rumours?"

"Well, after that Asty girl accused you of having an affair with Hugh, the fact you were in his cottage that fateful night is confirming to many that you were."

"But that's insane!"

"They say you took advantage of everyone at Armstrong House being in the hospital and went to Hugh's cottage that night because you were sleeping with him and he only went up to Armstrong House to fetch you something."

"To fetch me something? Nonsense! And why in heaven's name would I go to Hugh's cottage wearing only a satin dressing gown and slippers, if it wasn't an emergency?"

"Oh, no doubt there are theories too about that."

"How can people be so cruel in the face of such a tragedy?"

"No doubt Pierce has heard the rumours too, as everyone else has," said Constance.

"Scandal seems to follow me like shadow," sighed Clara.

Chapter 49

As the autumn weeks crept by, a quietness descended on Armstrong House after that fateful night of Hugh's killing. With the departure of Asty, the drama that occurred throughout the summer seemed to leave with her. But that did not bring Clara any kind of peace. The police seemed convinced that it was Asty who had come back to the house that night after poisoning the well, to rob it, and Clara hoped that to be true. What scared her most was that if she hadn't escaped from the house that night it would most likely have been her that was killed rather than Hugh. But that did not alleviate her guilt over what had happened.

As nothing further sinister had occurred to her since Asty's departure, she realised she must concur that the vindictive campaign that had been launched against her was simply the psychotic actions of an unhinged housekeeper.

Pierce did not seem that bothered by the occurrences. It played on Clara's mind how little her husband seemed to be bothered by Hugh's death or Asty's conduct.

"You must have got a terrible shock when you arrived back from the hospital that night to find Hugh dead," said Clara one night as she lay with him in bed.

"Well, I was more concerned that you weren't lying dead somewhere also," said Pierce.

"But the shock of seeing a dead body like that – did it not traumatize you?"

"Clara – have you any idea how many dead bodies I saw during the war?" asked Pierce coolly. "However unfortunate it is to find a dead body in one's hall – it is hardly going to send me into a spin, or traumatise me."

"How many of those dead bodies during the war did you kill?"

Pierce looked at her in surprise. "Do you really want to know the answer to that?"

"No, it is better I do not know ... It's chilling to think of so many men with no military background who were trained to kill during the war and now have slipped back into their ordinary lives as husbands, fathers ..." Clara turned on her side away from Pierce.

"I met with the Master of the Castlewest Hunt today. I have offered Armstrong House as the venue for the Hunt Ball this year," said Pierce.

Clara remembered the Hunt Balls that had been hosted at Armstrong House in the past. They had always been glamorous affairs which were the highlight of Pierce's year as he could shine as Lord of the Manor.

"You know I hate blood sports, Pierce," said Clara.

"Ah yes, but how you love a ball! And I think it is time to show everybody that the Armstrongs are back where we should be – not just in our house, on our estate but at the top of society."

As Clara thought how this time last year Pierce had no means of survival but to rely on the charity of his aunt, she could understand how he wanted to show the world he was back on top. She wondered did it occur to him that the only reason he was back on top was because she had come back to him and that she had come back as a wealthy woman.

"I'll start to organise the Hunt Ball once I return from England," promised Clara. She was due to go to England the following week for a long holiday to see her family and attend to her business affairs.

"Good girl – and make it the most spectacular one that the county has ever seen," said Pierce. "I want nobody to ever forget this ball."

As Clara had promised, as soon as she returned from her visit to England she threw herself into the organising of the Hunt Ball. Seated at the table in the small parlour at the front of the house she finalised her invitations. She always came to this room to write her correspondence. It was situated across the hall from the main drawing room, and it offered her an oasis where she could concentrate. The Castlewest Hunt Ball was traditionally held in December and for that year it was being held on the night of the twelfth. The hunt would then take place the following day with the meet starting at Armstrong House at noon. Pierce had said he wanted it to be a ball to remember, and she was determined not to disappoint him. As well as the gentry from the county, Clara had invited many dignitaries from Dublin, including Pierce's Aunt Daphne and the rest of the Hatton family. They would accommodate as many of the guests as they could at Armstrong House and neighbouring families such as the Foxes and other members of the Hunt Club had offered their houses for other guests to stay.

Constance crossed her mind as she finalised her guest list. Constance had proved to be a true friend, and she missed having her to confide in.

Clara took an invitation from the table and on it inscribed –

Mr. & Mrs. Clement Fitzgerald.

Then she took a sheet of paper to pen a letter to Constance.

In their house in Dublin, Constance sat at the window, staring out. She wished with all her heart that she had never heard about Clara and Armstrong House from that maid at the Dorchester. It had set her off on a relentless pursuit for that damned painting that had resulted in tragedy. Every time she thought of Hugh, she had to fight the tears from falling.

Clement walked into the room with that morning's post.

"Ah – we have been invited to a ball at Armstrong House," said Clement as he took a card from an envelope.

"What?" said Constance.

She stood up quickly and took the invitation from Clement to study it.

"There is a letter as well – addressed to you from Lady Armstrong," said Clement.

Constance grabbed the letter from him and read it quickly.

"Clara has invited us to stay at Armstrong House for the ball," she said.

"I think we'll give that one a miss – never wise to return to the scene of a crime," he advised.

"What do you mean by that?"

"I meant nothing by it – you are so sensitive these days."

"I want to go to the ball. I want to go back to Armstrong House," Constance declared.

"Then you must go on your own, my dear. I never want to see that place again."

Constance went to the writing bureau and began to pen a letter to Clara, accepting her invitation to the ball.

Chapter 50

The day before the Hunt Ball a flurry of snow began to fall, and the house was a flurry of excitement as preparations were being made.

"My girls are run off their feet, but I have everything under control for tomorrow night," Mrs. Fennell assured Clara in the drawing room.

"I have every faith in you, Mrs. Fennell," said Clara as she looked over the food that would be served on the night.

"And the alcohol is due for delivery first thing in the morning," said Mrs. Fennell. "I'm so glad that you're borrowing the footmen from the Foxes to assist Mr. Fennell instead of hiring them from an agency!"

"Yes, well, I believe we have all learned about hiring staff through an agency after our encounter with Asty," said Clara.

"Quite!" agreed Mrs. Fennell as she left the room.

"I hope this snow doesn't interfere with the actual hunt," said Pierce who was standing at the French windows beside the Christmas tree with Prudence, looking out at the falling snow.

"A good layer of snow on the ground will make the hunt easier – easier to spot the fox," said Prudence.

"As long as it has actually stopped snowing by then," said Pierce. "And here are the first of our guests arriving."

A motorcar was coming up the avenue.

"Oh, dear, it's the relatives! Dearest Aunt Daphne, dreary Cousin Richard and awful Ophelia," said Prudence. "Was it necessary to invite them?"

"Of course it was," said Pierce. "I want them to see that I am back on top of the world."

"Something tells me this whole ball is a vanity project for you, Pierce. As everything in your life always is."

"There is no need for you to attend if you would prefer not to," said Pierce.

"I wouldn't miss it for the world! Nothing I love more than blood sports!" said Prudence.

Clara went to Pierce and put her arm around his waist as she looked out the window at Fennell who was assisting the visitors with their luggage.

"I'd better go out and help Fennell! I really don't know why you keep him at this point – he's really not up to the job!" said Prudence and she left.

"I don't blame you for wanting your relatives here," said Clara. "After seeing you at your worst this time last year, you deserve for them to see how you have come on so well."

"I wasn't that bad, for goodness' sake, Clara! I wish you wouldn't keep harping on about it!" snapped Pierce.

"Pierce – I know those are dreadful memories for you – you did nearly kill yourself things were so bad and I am just so happy to see you fully recovered."

"And I suppose you think I owe it all to you," he said with a slight sneer.

"Of course not! But I really wasn't sure if trying to make our marriage work again was the right thing to do. But now I finally believe it was." And it was time she told him what she needed to. But not with the house full of guests.

"Oh, for goodness' sake!" said Pierce as he saw Fennell slip in the snow outside while carrying luggage. "That's all we need – a butler with a broken leg for the ball!"

Pierce hurried out of the room. Clara watched as Pierce joined Prudence and they both lifted Fennell off the ground and dusted him down.

"Well, you are looking well, Pierce! So handsome! Looking again like you always did!" said Daphne as they finished dinner in the dining room that evening.

"Thank you, Aunt Daphne," said Pierce.

"And you too, Clara," continued Daphne. "And you have done such a wonderful job of restoring Armstrong House. It is simply delightful to be back in the house that I grew up in and love so much – I feared I never would be here again after the fire. You've even put me in the blue room for my stay, which was mine as a girl!"

"Only the best for you, dear Aunty," said Prudence.

"Now that you have restored the house to its former glory you need to think about providing an heir," said Daphne.

"Steady on! They are just back together from the brink of divorce!" said Prudence.

"I don't think any of us need to be reminded of that, Prudence!" said Richard.

"Besides, a child is the best thing in the world to cement a marriage, I always say," said Daphne.

"The only reason you went to the effort, Aunty," said Prudence.

"Prudence, do you ever change?" snapped Richard irritably.

"No – and why should I ever?"

"Shall we retire to the drawing room?" suggested Clara quickly as she stood up from the table.

"Yes, please. I could do with a lovely glass of port," said Daphne.

"Couldn't we all!" added Prudence.

They all rose and followed Clara across the hall to the drawing room.

"What time are your other guests arriving tomorrow?" asked Ophelia as Clara tugged the bell-pull for Fennell.

"I expect early enough if they are not delayed by the snow," said Pierce.

"I cannot wait to be at a ball here at Armstrong House again," said Daphne. "I met my dear husband here at one. All my brothers and sisters met their husbands and wives at various balls here over the years – including your own parents, Charles and Arabella, Pierce."

"Under rather dubious circumstances," Ophelia whispered to Clara.

"Papa was such a wonderful host – the best in the country," said Daphne.

"Well, that's when the Armstrongs were hugely wealthy in their own right and didn't have to marry for money," said Prudence.

Just as Fennell arrived into the room there was a very loud knock at the front door.

"Whoever can that be at this time and in this weather?" asked Clara.

"I shall go and see, my lady," said Fennell and he departed.

"We'll die of thirst at this rate! I'll serve the bloody drinks myself," said Prudence, going to the drinks cabinet. She opened a bottle, poured port into glasses and began to distribute them.

"Aren't you so versatile, Prudence!" said Daphne, taking a glass from her.

"I'm well used to serving myself. They won't even pay for one servant at Hunter's Farm for me. I have to do everything myself."

"You mostly still invite yourself to eat here at the main house, so you have no need of a servant, Prudence," snapped Clara.

"Yes – I mustn't grumble. It certainly beats the gardener's cottage you exiled me to when staying with you, Aunty," said Prudence.

"Life is so hard for a woman without a husband. She must always rely on the charity of relatives," said Daphne, smiling acidly at Prudence.

"Inspector Cantwell, my lady. He says that it is urgent," announced Fennell, opening the door to the room and standing aside to allow the hassled-looking policeman in.

"Inspector Cantwell – whatever brings you out here on a night like this?" said Clara.

"If I could speak to you and Lord Armstrong in private, ma'am?"

"You may speak freely in front of us all – there are no secrets here," said Prudence.

Cantwell looked at Pierce for confirmation.

"Please continue," said Pierce.

"We have found your former housekeeper, Asty Horan. She was arrested while trying to board a ship in Cork that was about to set sail for New York."

"Oh well done, Sergeant!" said Clara, clapping her hands together. "We may sleep easy in our beds tonight."

"However, I have interviewed the young woman, and she has denied all knowledge of the incidents that took place at Armstrong House," said Cantwell.

"Well, she would, wouldn't she?" said Prudence.

"I think there is some truth in her protestations of innocence. She informed us that later in the day, after she left Armstrong House, she began to feel very unwell. By the time she reached Dublin she was so sick she was admitted to hospital where it was found she had been poisoned. She had the same symptoms as the rest of the people here at Armstrong House that day and so she must have drunk the water that morning before she left. So, clearly she is not responsible for putting the decomposed fox in the well. If she had, she would not have drunk water from it that morning herself."

"But she must be lying," said Pierce.

"She isn't. I've checked with the hospital authorities in Dublin who confirm she was admitted that night with the same symptoms as the rest of you and was extremely ill. And, since we now know that Asty was in the hospital in Dublin, she cannot have been the person who broke into Armstrong House that night and could not have had any involvement in Hugh O'Meara's death."

"But what about the other incidents that occurred to me – the attempts on my life?" asked Clara.

"She denies all knowledge of them. Also, she flatly denies any involvement in her former employers' untimely deaths before she came to work at Armstrong House and after vigorous investigation we can find no evidence strong enough to charge her. We have had to release her."

"But if it wasn't Asty who in God's name has been behind these acts?" demanded Pierce.

"That, I'm afraid, we do not know," said Cantwell.

"But the incidents stopped as soon as Asty left," said Clara. "Surely that cannot be just coincidence?"

"We couldn't convict a person on coincidence, ma'am," said Cantwell.

"Could somebody please explain to me what on earth has been going on?" demanded Daphne.

"Patience, Daphne!" snapped Pierce.

"If there are any further developments I will of course inform you," said Cantwell as he turned to leave.

"I will call Fennell to show you out," said Clara.

"No need, I know the way out myself by now. Have a pleasant night," said Cantwell and left the room.

Pierce and Clara looked at each other in dismay.

"Pray tell us what has been happening at Armstrong House?" asked Ophelia, her face full of concern.

That night Ophelia felt extremely anxious as she put on her face cream at the dressing table in their bedroom.

Richard came from the bathroom and climbed into bed.

"Had you any idea of these ghastly occurrences, Richard?" demanded Ophelia as she rose and walked towards the bed.

"Of course I didn't! I would have told you if I had," said Richard.

"One never knows with your family and the secrets you keep! Did you see the look of terror on Clara's face when the policeman told them the housekeeper wasn't responsible? I feel terribly guilty."

"Why should you feel guilty? It's nothing to do with us!" said Richard.

"We let her come back here without voicing our concerns," said Ophelia.

"It's nothing to do with us, Ophelia. She's a grown woman who can make her own decisions," insisted Richard as he rolled over to go to sleep.

Chapter 51

The next morning the snow had stopped falling as Clara looked out the bedroom window at the white coat blanketing the countryside. Pierce was already up and had gone down for breakfast without her. He had seemed unaffected by the news about Asty when she had tried to discuss it the previous night. He seemed more preoccupied with the upcoming ball. But news of Asty's innocence had panicked Clara so much she was now dreading the ball. She was in no mood to entertain a full house of people when the person who wished them harm – who wished her harm – was still unknown and still free.

Then she felt a little better when she realised Constance would be arriving later that day. She had missed her confidante and could not wait to see her again.

Constance stood in the small graveyard near Armstrong village and looked down at the grave. There was just a meagre stone placed at the head of it with Hugh's name engraved and the month he died: August 1923. Then at the bottom of the stone was inscribed – *You Will Have Vengeance.*

Constance shivered on seeing these words. She realised the gravestone must have been erected by Hugh's family and they clearly held somebody accountable for his death.

"You deserved so much more than this, my love. I'm so sorry, Hugh," she whispered. She then turned and walked out of the graveyard and drove away.

As she arrived at Armstrong Estate, she was filled with trepidation. If she hadn't come back here on a mission, she would never have wanted to see the place again. She turned off the road and through the main gates into the estate and journeyed up the snow-covered avenue, past the parklands and onto the forecourt of Armstrong House.

Before she had even got out of the vehicle, the front door opened, and Clara came rushing down the steps towards her.

"I spotted you coming up the avenue!" said Clara as she threw her arms around Constance. "Oh, I have missed you!"

"Yes, it's nice to be back," said Constance. "Although I'd like to get in out of this cold!"

"Fennell will fetch your luggage," said Clara.

"No need – I only have a small suitcase," said Constance, retrieving it herself.

Constance locked the motorcar and the two women walked inside the house. In the hall there was a huge fire blazing in the fireplace with a Christmas tree beside it and the house was lovely and warm compared to the brisk air outside. The servants were rushing around, putting the last touches in place for the ball that evening.

"It's such a pity Clement couldn't come," said Clara.

"Yes, unfortunately he is just too busy."

"All Pierce's relatives are in the drawing room with him. Let us go up to your room where we can talk privately," said Clara, taking Constance's arm and leading her towards the stairs.

As Constance unpacked and hung up her clothes in the wardrobe, she listened intently as Clara told her of the latest developments with Asty.

"I really believed it was Asty behind everything and Asty who broke in here the night Hugh died. I mean, she even threatened to kill Hugh if she ever saw him again, according to the servants."

"She did sound the likely culprit," agreed Constance.

"Now we are back to square one. It's terrifying to think that whoever was trying to harm me is still on the loose," said Clara.

There was suddenly a knock on the door.

"*Come in!*" called Clara.

The door opened and Síle walked in.

"The other guests staying the night have started to arrive and Lord Armstrong says you are to come down to greet them – *at once* – those were his words."

"I'll come down now, Síle," said Clara.

"Alright, my lady," Síle said and left.

Clara stood up with a sigh rose and made a face. "Duty calls, I'm afraid!"

"We can talk later," said Constance with a smile.

Clara reached forward and kissed her cheek before disappearing from the room. Constance took out a cigarette packet, lit one and opened a window which offered a view of the forecourt. There were now several motorcars parked there. Constance watched as Clara walked out into the forecourt and started hugging and kissing the latest guests who had arrived.

"All you care about is yourself, Clara. *Terrified* for your own wellbeing with not a thought about poor Hugh being killed because of you!" she whispered bitterly.

All the guests who would be staying at Armstrong House that night had arrived and Constance watched from the window as a steady stream of motorcars and carriages delivered the rest of the invitees. She observed them make their way to the front door, the men dressed in black tie and the women decked out in glamorous dresses and furs. It was eight o'clock and, as music began to play downstairs, she knew the party had started

She took a final look at herself in the full-length mirror. She was wearing a slinky eye-catching yellow satin gown and had her hair piled up on her head. As she left the room and walked down the corridor she was dreading the evening. Having to make polite conversation with all these toffs she did not know and was sure she had little in common with. Reaching the top of the stairs, she saw the hall below was filled with people chattering and laughing as the servants circulated amongst them with trays of champagne glasses. She descended the stairs, took a glass of bubbles and smiled at the nearest guests. She was about to make her way into the ballroom where the band was playing when Fennell rang a loud bell and a hush descended.

"My lords, ladies and Master of the Hunt, may I present your hosts for tonight – Lord and Lady Armstrong," said Fennell in a loud clear voice.

At the top of stairs stood Clara and Pierce, arm in arm. Constance thought they looked resplendent, Pierce in black tie and Clara in a cream dress. As they walked down the stairs and the guests started to clap Constance felt herself consumed with anger and envy behind her smile.

The ballroom was filled with couples dancing as the band played that year's biggest hit "The One I Love Belongs to Somebody Else".

Clara was talking to guests when she heard a loud cough beside her and she turned to see Conway, their solicitor, standing there.

"Pardon me, Lady Armstrong – if I could be so bold as to ask for s dance?"

"Oh, Rory! Yes, of course – I'd be delighted," said Clara with a smile.

Looking very chuffed with himself, Conway led Clara out to the dance floor.

"You look very dashing, Rory. I've never seen you outside your office until now," said Clara.

"Well, this is my first Hunt Ball! I've been applying to be a member of the Castlewest Hunt for years, but I was always turned down until this year. I suppose they didn't want Catholics or people who were not a part of the gentry before."

"Well, I'm sure they're very pleased to have you now, Rory, considering how their usual membership has diminished since independence," said Clara with a smile.

"They'll be letting in shopkeepers next!" said Rory with a laugh.

"You never know!" said Clara, laughing too.

"I really am pleased for you and Lord Armstrong, after these difficult past few years, that everything has worked out so well for you," he said with genuine smile.

"Thank you, Rory and your help was much appreciated," said Clara.

"And my reward is an invitation to the ball! And now that the compensation for the burning of the house will be due shortly from the new government, that will assure the estate's future, independent of your financial backing."

"I hadn't realised the compensation had been applied for," said Clara.

"Oh, perhaps I shouldn't have spoiled Lord Armstrong's surprise," said Conway.

"But – did you not need to have my signature for the paperwork to apply for the compensation?" asked Clara.

"No – why would your signature be needed?"

"As the joint owner of Armstrong House," she said.

"But Lord Armstrong is the owner, not you," said Conway, embarrassed.

"But you are mistaken, Rory. Pierce put me on the deeds of the house and estate." said Clara.

"I'm sorry, Lady Armstrong, Lord Armstrong remains the sole owner and the deeds are in my office, I assure you."

"But I've seen the deeds. They were amended when I was added as a joint owner earlier this year," insisted Clara. "They are now in my parents' safe in London,"

"The deeds are in my safe where they have always been kept and I can assure you Pierce is the sole owner since he inherited the estate and house from his father some twenty years ago."

Conway stopped dancing amd made a little bow.

"Thank you for the dance, Lady Armstrong."

With that, looking very serious, he turned and walked quickly away.

After what Conway had told her Clara was bewildered and distracted as Ophelia approached her and began to chat. Clara's eyes searched the crowded ballroom, but she could not see Pierce anywhere.

"Are you alright, Clara?" asked Ophelia eventually.

"Yes, I'm sorry, Ophelia. I'm just wondering where Pierce has got to."

Ophelia glanced around the ballroom and shrugged. "Clara," she said, "I was quite alarmed to hear about what has been happening here. It's not my place to say but I do hope you did the right thing coming back to Armstrong House."

"Whatever do you mean?"

"Well, with all these unfortunate events that have happened to you, I hope you are safe here ... with Prudence."

"Prudence? Why would you say that?"

"It's just when I heard that somebody was trying to hurt you or drive you away it did cross my mind that Prudence might be responsible. She really is quite dangerous, you know."

"Well, I've always known what Prudence is like. She made my life hell in the past and it did cross my mind she might be behind it all but then it makes no sense that it is her."

"Why?"

"Because Prudence is the one who brought me and Pierce back together. She came to London specifically to try and mend our marriage and practically forced me to come to Dublin to meet Pierce after he tried to kill himself. She wouldn't have done all that and then try to split us up again, would she?"

"But she has what she wants now. She got your money to rebuild Armstrong House and get the estate back farming. Prudence has got what she wants from you and has no further need of you."

"But I had no money when Prudence came to see me. My grandmother was still alive and nobody had any idea that I was her heir, including me!"

"But they did know, Clara. Pierce and Prudence did know you were going to come into huge wealth," said Ophelia.

"Sorry, Ophelia, but that was not the case. Nobody knew the contents of my grandmother's will until after she died. And that was after Pierce and I got back together."

"The Armstrongs knew, I assure you, Clara. We all knew. Some indiscreet lawyer had told Pierce's aunt in England and word got back to Dublin. And that was before Prudence went to London to meet you to try and mend your marriage."

Clara looked at Ophelia in horror.

"I am sorry, Clara. I was going to warn you when you were visiting at our house in Dublin before you moved back here. But I had very selfish reasons that stopped me from telling you. I'm so sorry now."

"And what were they?" demanded Clara.

"I felt we were going to be stuck with Pierce and Prudence forever! This way they could go back to Armstrong House and we could be rid of them! Our children were literally terrified of Prudence!"

"You should have told me, Ophelia!"

"I know and I am deeply sorry! But of course I didn't expect that you would end up in a life-threatening situation!"

"I know what Prudence is, but you can't seriously suggest she wants me dead?" said Clara, aghast.

"I wouldn't put anything past her. Clara, this family is very good at hiding secrets. And I fear there is something very big and sinister being hidden in Prudence's past."

"Such as?"

"That she was somehow involved in the shooting of her father," said Ophelia, her eyes tearing up in fear.

"Lord Charles? But you are mistaken, Ophelia. Everyone knows – even the locals talk about it freely – that Pierce's father was shot by some disgruntled tenant farmer during the land war!"

"I do not know the details but, from what I've heard, that was a cover-up to protect the family name. Prudence will do anything to have control of Armstrong House and that is why I now believe you are in terrible danger while you remain here."

"What are you two ladies talking about?" asked Richard as he suddenly appeared at their side.

"Oh, nothing – just catching up on family news," said Ophelia as she gave Clara a concerned look.

Chapter 52

It was nearly midnight as Clara walked through the crowd at Armstrong House, still trying to find Pierce who had seemed to disappear. Suddenly she spotted Prudence was outside on the terrace outside the ballroom. Clara walked to the French window and stepped outside, her heels scrunching on the snow beneath her.

Prudence was speaking with two men on the veranda.

"At that point it was a fight to the finish between the fisherman and the salmon and the boat was rocking with the battle between the two – and I shouted if you don't pull that damned salmon on board soon he'll bloody well pull you into the lake! Alas, the salmon won in the end!"

The two men guffawed with laughter.

"I apologise for interrupting the joviality," said Clara, "but I would like to speak to my sister-in-law in private, so if I could ask you gentlemen to leave us?"

"Oh, of course, Clara. Excuse us, Prudence," said one of the men as he and his friend headed towards the French window.

"Don't drink too many, boys, remember the hunt starts tomorrow at noon sharp!" Prudence called after them.

Clara stared at Prudence.

"Clara – are you not going to catch your death of cold out here without a shawl?" asked Prudence.

"I'm sure you are not too concerned if I do," said Clara.

"How can I help you, Clara?"

"Did you and Pierce know that I was an heiress before you came to visit me in London and asked me to go back to him?" demanded Clara.

"Oh, I see – somebody has been telling tales outside school, have they? Well, I've never believed in beating around the bush. Since you ask – yes. We knew you were to inherit your grandmother's fortune."

Clara said nothing for a while as she digested the information.

"And that is the sole reason you came to see me and wanted me to go back to Pierce?"

"Since it is a night for honesty – yes. Guilty as charged. I guess the truth always comes out in the end."

"You could never know anything about truth, Prudence."

"And since it is a night for honesty, you may as well know the whole truth ... Pierce's suicide was a deliberate attempt to get you back."

"What do you mean?"

"We staged his suicide attempt. I, as the brains in the family, came up with the plan. I knew that if he was seen to try and kill himself over you, you would feel so guilty that you would not be able to resist coming rushing back to him, with your inheritance waiting in the wings. When I say 'staged', of course he did actually take an overdose to make it convincing and was rushed off to hospital, as you know."

Clara began to shake uncontrollably but said nothing as she tried to comprehend what she just heard.

It began to snow again as they stood there.

"You really should get a shawl, Clara."

"I have been duped, utterly duped," said Clara. "And I have been an utter fool."

"Well, nothing new there," said Prudence.

"I expect then you were behind everything that happened this year? The attacks on me, the poisoning of the well, the break-in that night?"

"No. That was not me – Scout's honour! I might not have wanted you here, but somebody obviously wants you here even less than I do. Perhaps you need to look a little closer to home to find the criminal behind all those actions."

"Explain yourself," demanded Clara.

"As I told you before, if I wanted you dead then you'd be dead by now. But Pierce – he can never do things right. He always messes up. If it weren't for me he would be lost years ago. I keep him afloat, not that he will ever admit it."

"Well, I'm going to give you an early Christmas present, Prudence. I am going to leave Armstrong House, and you will never have to see me again."

"Well, that is good news," said Prudence.

"I just ask you for one final thing and that is you do not tell Pierce of my plans. If he knows he will try to stop me, like he did last time after he learned of my affair with Johnny Seymour – and that is not what either of us want, is it?"

"Absolutely not. Be assured I will not say anything to Pierce. That's how you made your mistake last time with Johnny Seymour. You told Pierce you were leaving and the warning allowed him to stop you from eloping. This time just go before he even notices you are gone."

"And that – for once – is good advice, Prudence."

With the falling snow resting on Clara's soft blonde hair, she turned and walked back inside to the ball.

Clara was in a trance as she tried to comprehend everything she had heard. When Pierce suddenly came into the ballroom with a posse of adoring females around him, she froze. Suddenly the band stopped playing and the Master of the Hunt made an announcement.

"Ladies and gentlemen, it is time for the official photograph for this year's Hunt Ball. And so, could I ask you all to gather here – and if Lord and Lady Armstrong could take centre place as our hosts?"

Pierce walked towards Clara as the photographer began to position the guests under the giant banner hung at the end of the ballroom that read: *Castlewest Hunt Ball 1923.*

"You heard the man, Clara," said Pierce, offering his arm to his wife.

Clara paused before taking his arm and allowing herself to be led over to the crowd gathered under the banner.

"What a handsome group of people!" announced the photographer as he assembled his camera in front of the guests, causing them all to laugh.

Pierce glanced at Clara as they stood at the front of the group.

"Clara – smile! You look like you have seen a ghost!" he hissed at her.

But Clara was unable to smile as the flash of the camera captured them for posterity.

As soon as the photographer had finished his work, the band started playing again. Clara discreetly slipped away. She went straight upstairs to their bedroom and, going to her dressing room, she took out a suitcase and began to pack. She knew what she must do. Tomorrow she would join the hunt as was expected and during the day she would slip away and come back to Armstrong House, take her luggage and then drive to Dublin before leaving for good for England. She would only have to endure one more night at Armstrong House with Pierce and then never have to see either of them again. She had come back there with hope in her heart that things had changed, but now she knew they never had, and they never would. She didn't want to confront Pierce with what she had found out. She would give him no more chances. Besides, she really didn't trust him. She now feared him, as she had discovered what he was capable of. She really did have to consider the possibility that he wanted her dead. If he was willing to risk his own life by taking an overdose to get her money, then surely he was capable of taking hers? She even believed he was capable of drinking some of the poisoned water to give him an alibi to then discharge himself from the hospital and come back to get her when she was isolated and alone in Armstrong House.

As the music played on until the early hours of the morning, she looked out the window at the soft snow falling on the moonlit lake. She imagined Pierce would be the last to bed as he shone in the glory of being the host.

Clara changed into her nightdress, climbed into bed and turned off the light when the music finally stopped.

Not long after, she heard Pierce come into the room.

"Clara, are you awake?"

She said nothing and kept her eyes shut. She heard him go into the bathroom and then change into his nightclothes in his dressing room. When he got into the bed beside her, she tried to keep as far away from him as possible.

Chapter 53

Present Day

Sitting at the desk in the library, Kate scrolled through the archives of the local newspaper, the *Connaught Telegraph*, from 1923 on her laptop. She was trying to find if the death of Hugh O'Meara might have been reported. As she knew the month he died it narrowed down the search.

She came across a news item from the 15th of August 1923.

Suspicious Death at Armstrong House

The death has occurred of popular local man Hugh O'Meara. Hugh, who had been working as the manager at the estate of Lord Armstrong, was found dead in the house in the early hours of last Saturday night. It is believed he had fallen from the first floor to his death in the hall of the main house. Most of the household, apart from Lady Clara Armstrong, had been afflicted by food poisoning earlier that day and were in the infirmary at Castlewest at the time. Police are investigating the suspicious circumstances of Mr. O'Meara's death and have asked anybody with information to contact Sergeant O'Meara at Castlewest Garda Station.

Kate's eyes opened wide as she read and reread the report. She searched the newspaper for any further details but could not find any. She closed down her search, stood up from the desk and walked out into the hall, looking up at the bannisters that surrounded the first floor.

"What the hell was going on here, Clara?" she whispered.

As Hugh O'Meara's death had been viewed as suspicious, Kate hoped there might be a file kept on it with the local police. As the newspaper had not reported any further developments on his death, she imagined it had never been solved or resolved. She put in a request to the National Archives of Ireland where the historical records from the Criminal Investigations Department were stored and was excited when they emailed her back to say they had a file on the case.

Kate travelled to Dublin and met with the archivist who presented her with the file in the library of the building.

"1923 was a year of change for the police force," said the archivist, a serious-looking woman in her forties. "The police force was called the Civic Guards up until then but was renamed the Garda Síochána from August 8th that year."

"1923 seemed to be a year of change for the whole country from what I've seen," said Kate.

"It was the year the Civil War ended. The years of fighting were finally over and the new government was setting up the institutions and policies that would shape and govern the new independent country."

Kate looked at the file the archivist was holding which seemed rather large.

"Is that the file on Hugh O'Meara's death?" she asked, surprised.

"No, there was no file on his death specifically. But it was mentioned in relation to another investigation, that of Tadgh O'Meara, Hugh's brother."

Kate remembered from talking with Barry O'Meara that this was the name of his grandfather.

"Why would there be a file on Tadgh O'Meara?" she asked.

"The Criminal Investigations Department, or CID, were mainly involved in tracking and arresting anti-treaty IRA members who were a threat to the new state. Tadgh O'Meara was a prominent member of that organisation and so the authorities kept a close eye on him. To be honest, if it weren't for the fact that Hugh was Tadgh's brother, there probably wouldn't be anything on his death."

"I see!" said Kate as she was handed the file.

"Let me know if I can be of any other assistance," said the woman before she left Kate alone.

Kate held the file tightly before she sat down at a desk to study it.

As she read, it became evident that the local police force, led by a Sergeant Cantwell, was keeping a very close eye on Tadgh O'Meara. They knew he was the leader of a local IRA unit in the Civil War but were unable to pin anything on him.

Kate's interest was piqued when Armstrong House began to feature in the reports. After the first fire during the War of Independence when the estate was abandoned, Tadgh trespassed onto the land and began to use it for his own livestock. With the breakdown of law and order at the time there was nobody to stop him. It was only after the return of Lord Armstrong to the estate that the situation imploded, when Tadgh's livestock was forcibly removed from the Armstrong Estate. It was noted in the file that Lady Clara Armstrong had a connection in the new Irish government, namely a minister called Thomas Geraghty who had given the order that the local constabulary do everything in its power to protect Armstrong House from any local hostility. But this order was not enough to protect the Armstrongs, particularly Clara. Kate was horrified as she read the reports filed by Sergeant Cantwell during the summer of 1923. He was called to the house on three separate occasions as there had been three violent incidents involving Clara. Firstly, somebody had interfered with her saddle to cause her horse to bolt and she had only been spared injury by the intervention of the estate manager, Hugh O'Meara. Secondly, she had been attacked and injured by stones thrown at her by an unknown assailant while walking alone by the lake. And thirdly she had been admitted to hospital after her perfume bottle had been laced with weed-killer, causing her to asphyxiate. Cantwell had taken statements from the different members of the household. Kate read through the statements which all seem to suggest different culprits but it was Cantwell's opinion that Tadgh O'Meara was responsible as he had most to gain by driving the Armstrongs away again, so he could lay claim to their land.

Kate paused and steadied herself as she reached the report concerning the night of August 15th, 1923, the night of Hugh O'Meara's death.

I was awoken at three o'clock in the morning by the telephone ringing in the station. When I answered it, a panicked Lord Pierce Armstrong asked me to come to Armstrong House urgently as there had been an accident. When I arrived at Armstrong House I was greeted by a shaken Lord Armstrong who said he had discharged himself earlier in the night from the infirmary in Castlewest. There had been an incident of food poisoning that day which resulted in all the household, with the exception of Lady Clara Armstrong, being admitted to the hospital. Lord Armstrong informed me that when he arrived back at the house during the night he found the former estate manager Hugh O'Meara dead on the floor of the hall. It seems that Mr. O'Meara had met his death by falling over the banisters surrounding the first-floor landing. Lord Armstrong was extremely distressed as his wife was missing. We searched the house but there was no sign of Lady Armstrong. There was evidence of a possible break-in that night as a window in the dining room had not been fully closed and a crystal lamp lay smashed on the floor near the window, broken probably when someone entered the house through the window.

As we were about to start a search in the area for Lady Armstrong, she appeared in the early hours of the morning, wearing a dressing gown and slippers. She stated that she had been in the house alone when she heard somebody break in and she had fled out the back door and run to Hugh O'Meara's cottage to seek help. She said Mr. O'Meara then went to Armstrong House alone to investigate and had not returned to the cottage. Lady Armstrong was very distraught to find that Mr. O'Meara had been killed.

There had been a problem with the generator earlier in that night. Lady Armstrong had found the house without electricity when she returned to it from the infirmary. She had been driven home by Dr. O'Brien. The problem had been fixed by the time Lord Armstrong arrived. Hugh O'Meara intended to replenish the gas on his arrival, according to Lady Armstrong.

The case remains open. There is the very unlikely possibility that Hugh O'Meara lost his balance and fell over the bannisters but considering there is evidence of a break-in there is the strong possibility of a crime having been committed.

Kate gave an involuntary shiver at the thought that Hugh O'Meara's death in her home had been the result of a crime. Having learned from Barry that there were rumours of an affair between Clara and Hugh O'Meara, she also thought the police report gave further evidence of it. The fact that Clara had arrived back from Hugh's cottage while the rest of the household including her husband were in the hospital would indicate that there was a relationship between the two. But, on the other hand, in her dressing gown? Surely not?

Kate continued to look through the rest of the file which was mainly concerned with observations about Tadgh O'Meara. She squinted and peered closer when she came across a handwritten note referring to the fire in December 1923. But there was no report filed on the incident, just the note stating that Sergeant Cantwell was assisting a firm called the Royal

Ireland Insurance Company with an investigation into the crime and his file had been sent to their Dublin office. There were no further reports or information about the fire. The case went cold.

The Armstrongs had left the area after the house was destroyed and that was the end of the agitation that had surrounded them. Kate realised that this was when the marriage of Pierce and Clara finally broke down. But was the marriage breakdown a result of the fire, or was the fire a result of the marriage breakdown?

Chapter 54

1923

"*Clara! You're going to be late for breakfast!*" Pierce shouted through the bathroom door to her the morning after the Hunt Ball.

"*I'm not that hungry – you go down without me!*" she called back.

"*Very rude of you not to have breakfast with our guests!*" he said.

She said nothing.

"*Make sure you're not late for the meet of the hunt! Noon sharp!*" he demanded.

Hearing him leave, Clara allowed herself to breathe easy again.

Constance had chosen not to go to breakfast downstairs that morning. She had endured enough of the Armstrongs and their world, and exchanging any more pleasantries with them was more than she could endure. As she dressed in her riding outfit she could not wait to have finished her business and returned to Dublin. She had found out the house would be empty that afternoon. Even the servants would not be there as they would be in Armstrong village to serve refreshments to the hunt at three o'clock. She felt nervous of what she had to do that afternoon, but she had been in stickier situations in the past and always came out on top. Looking out the window of the bedroom, she could see the hunt already gathering in the forecourt as noon approached. She picked up her riding hat from the dressing table and walked out of her room and down the corridor.

She met Clara coming out of her room.

"What a wonderful ball last night, Clara!" said Constance with a big smile.

"Oh, I hoped you enjoyed it, Constance."

"Very much so! And I'm very much looking forward to the hunt today."

As they reached the top of the stairs, Clara considered telling Constance of her plan to leave. She was such a good friend she felt she needed to confide in her and perhaps she could help her.

"Constance – I need to tell you something. I know I can trust you," she whispered.

"Yes, of course you can. You can trust me with anything, Clara," said Constance.

"*Clara!*" shouted Pierce from the bottom of the stairs. "*Could you actually hurry up and get your bottom down here! We are about to start the hunt!*"

"*Yes, Pierce!*" With a shrug and an apologetic look thrown at Constance, she quickly walked down the stairs.

As Constance followed her down, she wondered what Clara was about to confide in her.

By noon, the forecourt was filled with riders on horseback as the pack of foxhounds scurried excitedly around, waiting for the hunt to begin. Fennell and the borrowed footmen were circulating with silver trays of hot ports and offering them up to the riders.

Clara steadied her horse beneath her as its breath created a fog in the cold air.

"Spiffing day for a hunt!" said Philly Scott as she rode up beside Clara.

"Yes," agreed Clara as she looked out at the snow-covered countryside.

"Just enough snow to make the fox more visible but not enough to slow down the horses!" said Philly.

Clara felt sympathy for the fox. She always did but that day even more. She felt that day she was trying to escape these awful people as much as the fox was.

Prudence was on horseback near her and nodded to Clara with a knowing smile.

"Now remember – we will be at the village for refreshments at three o'clock sharp!" Pierce instructed Fennell.

"Do not fret, my lord, we will be waiting for you," confirmed Fennell.

"And don't forget to bring fried bacon sandwiches – and whiskey!" called Philly to much laughter.

As Clara looked at Pierce in his riding outfit she still understood why she had fallen so much in love with him. But she never knew him and still didn't. He was a stranger, and she was so glad she never let down her guard to him fully since returning to Armstrong House.

Ophelia avoided Clara and did not even look at her once. Clara suspected she regretted telling her the family secrets the previous night. Ophelia would be in a lot of trouble with the family if she was revealed as the mole.

"A toast to a successful hunt!" called the Master of the Hunt and everyone raised their glasses and there was a mighty cheer before the port was drunk.

Fennell and the servants quickly gathered the empty glasses as a wave of excitement swept through the crowd.

Then the Master of the Hunt blew his horn, and the pack of hounds flew out of the forecourt followed by the riders.

As the hunt raced across the countryside, Clara bided her time. She didn't want to arouse any suspicion in Pierce. As Pierce was an excellent horseman he usually was in the first field of hunters, ahead of everyone else. Clara, an unenthusiastic huntswoman, usually lagged behind. She expected this would give her the perfect opportunity to fall back and then make her way back to the house. But that day, Pierce remained frustratingly close to Clara. She imagined this was because he had drunk too much at the ball the previous night and was suffering from a hangover. It was a couple of hours before Clara could seize the opportunity to leave, as they raced by a wood. With Pierce now in the lead, she slowed down, allowing the rest of the hunt to race on, and then she directed her horse into the wood and remained hidden there until the hunt had disappeared over a hill.

Then Clara rode back to Armstrong House.

Constance kept a close look at the time on her watch as she rode. She had to time it perfectly. Refreshments would be served at 3 o'clock in the village by the Armstrong House staff which meant there would be nobody in the house at that time. As the time approached for her to return to the house, she held her horse back and allowed the hunt to continue without her.

Once Clara reached the house she rode around the back and tethered it inside a stable.

"Is everything alright, Lady Armstrong?" asked Mrs. Fennell as she came out of the back door with the rest of the servants, all carrying baskets of refreshments for the hunt.

"Yes, I just have a headache so came back for a lie-down," said Clara.

"Well, I'll stay behind and bring you up a nice cup of tea," offered Mrs. Fennell, turning to go back inside.

"No! There is absolutely no need! You go to the village with everyone else, Mrs. Fennell. I insist!"

"Well, if you're sure?"

"I am. I'll be fine."

Mrs. Fennell climbed onto one of the traps and Clara watched the traps and carts leave the courtyard. She then walked into the kitchen, made her way up the servants' stairs to the hall and continued up the main staircase to her bedroom. She took a minute to steady her nerves and then went to her dressing room and took out her suitcase to finish her packing. She placed her suitcase on the bed and gathered her jewellery from the dressing table and placed it amongst the rest of the items she was taking with her. As she looked at the photo of herself and Pierce on a side table she picked it up and wiped away a tear. She put the photograph in the suitcase along with everything else.

The, passing the window, Clara stopped in her tracks when she saw a horsewoman ride into the forecourt. Peering out, she saw her dismount and, as the horse wandered off to eat the grass, the woman dashed over to Constance's motorcar. Then she took off her riding hat and Clara saw that it was Constance.

Clara was baffled when she saw Constance take a large rectangular object that was covered with a blanket from the back of her motorcar and carry it towards the front door of the house. Clara was about to go downstairs and make her presence known but as she opened her bedroom door she could hear Constance walk up the main staircase. Clara held back and, keeping the door slightly ajar, watched as Constance walked by and down the corridor, carrying what looked to be a painting.

Chapter 55

Constance hurried to the end of the corridor, then turned the corner and walked up the servants' stairs to the attic. She continued to the room at the end of the corridor and opened the door into the bedroom where the portrait of Clara had originally been stored.

She was filled with relief, as her job was nearly done. She put the portrait on the bed and admired it for one final time. Clement had told her she had an unhealthy obsession with the painting. If only he knew how unhealthy that obsession had been! All she had wanted was to get her hands on it. But once she got it in her possession on that horrible night, the night Hugh had died, it haunted her dreams when she slept and every waking moment of her days. She had become a different person, distracted and full of gloom. She was consumed with guilt and wanted to be rid of the portrait as soon as she could. She believed that if she returned the portrait to Armstrong House, it would alleviate the guilt. If she and Clement had sold the painting to their New York buyer as they had planned, it would have been blood money. She wanted nothing more to do with the painting and so she had come to give it back. She felt the painting was cursed.

She moved the boxes from the knee wall, uncovering the panel behind which the painting had been hidden.

"What do you think you're doing?" demanded a voice behind her.

Constance turned around to see Clara standing in the doorway.

The two women stared at each other in shock.

"What are you doing with my portrait?" asked Clara as she walked into the room and looked down at Johnny Seymour's painting lying on the bed.

Constance's heart was palpitating as she frantically tried to think of a believable explanation. She stood up from her kneeling position.

"*I'm not going to ask you again, Constance!*" Clara suddenly shouted, making Constance jump.

With the portrait on the bed Constance knew it looked like she was in the process of stealing it.

"I wasn't taking the portrait – I was returning it," she said lamely.

"Returning it from where, in God's name!" demanded Clara.

"I had just borrowed it to get it valued," said Constance.

"Borrowed it! Stole it more like!"

A hundred thoughts went through Constance's head but none of them offered a believable explanation, except the truth.

"If you don't tell me truth right now I am going to call the police and report you for theft. And, believe me, I will know if you are lying."

As Constance looked at Clara it was as if she was seeing the real her for the first time. That behind that elegant and soft exterior was steel when she was pushed too far. An excellent poker player, Constance knew when she had lost the game.

She sighed loudly and sat on the bed, looking down at the portrait.

"The painting is exquisite, isn't it? As soon as I learned of its existence I knew it would be," she said.

Constance began to explain her obsession with the painting as Clara listened in astonishment. How she had learned about the painting from a chambermaid in the Dorchester Hotel who used to work at Armstrong House. How this had brought her to Armstrong House to steal it and sell it on the black market in America. How, when she found the house was being reconstructed, she played the long game and befriended Clara to get access to the house. And how, while working on the refurnishing of the house, she finally found the painting and then waited for the right opportunity to take it to sell it to a buyer Clement had found in New York.

"You're a monster," Clara said quietly.

"Perhaps I am. I never had enough time to give who I am much thought. You'd never know that, Clara, with your privileged upbringing and life. You would never know what it was like to be a very young woman who was won in a poker game in Cairo by your future husband."

"Whatever your past, that is no excuse for how you behaved with me. I thought you were my friend. I trusted you."

"Oh, Clara – only women in your position can enjoy the luxury of having friends. The rest of us have to fight for anything we can get, wherever we can get it, whoever we can get it from."

"And whatever the cost to others around you?"

"And whatever the cost," confirmed Constance. "And the more I got to know you, the more I resented you. Resented that you tiptoed through life, married to a lord, living in this house, having the great Johnny Seymour fall in love with you and have you as a Muse for this damned painting. And you were rich without having ever to do a day's work in your privileged lazy life."

"You don't know anything about my life. You have no idea of the suffering I have had to endure."

"*Oh, boo hoo!* You entitled fool, feeling sorry for yourself when you have everything any woman could dream of!" spat Constance.

Clara stared at her but didn't react to her venom.

"So, tell me," she said then. "How did you finally steal my painting?"

"Do you really want to know the truth, Clara? You won't like the truth, I can assure you."

"I want to know everything," said Clara.

"It was the night of the poisoning of the household here. The night Hugh was killed," said Constance.

Clara listened intently as Constance began to tell her what unfolded that fateful night.

Earlier that day Constance had visited Hugh at his cottage to tell him she and Clement were leaving Seymour Hall to return to Dublin and to say goodbye. She explained to Hugh their relationship had no future. Both of them knew it. She had acted as coolly as she could as she bade him farewell, not wanting to compound the sorrow she felt by showing it to either of them. She had known Hugh would act casually as well and put on a show that it did not matter to him that their relationship was over. She knew Hugh had too much pride to behave otherwise. She was glad when his brother Tadgh had suddenly shown up at Hugh's door. It had meant she could leave without prolonging the goodbye, risking that her true emotions would flood out, which might overwhelm both of them.

After she left Hugh's cottage and Tadgh had closed the door, she had waited outside to listen in to their conversation which could be clearly heard through the partially open window. Feeling saddened, she heard Tadgh offer his brother his old job back and Hugh accept it. She didn't blame Hugh for accepting as he really had very little choice after being fired from Armstrong House. Hugh was also vulnerable, having his relationships with both Asty and her end – and being welcomed back to his family must have been comforting for him.

However, as she continued to listen she could understand that Hugh was committing himself to being controlled by his brother again. With a heavy heart she realised that Hugh would spend the rest of his life working and being under the thumb of Tadgh.

Just as she was about to turn and leave, she heard Tadgh begin to rant about the Armstrongs and his hatred for them.

"Those bastards think they've got the better of us, but I won't rest until I've got rid of them and taken back that land! They have no idea what's in store for them tonight!"

"What do you mean?" asked Hugh.

There was a silence before Hugh spoke again.

"What are you planning to do, Tadgh?" he demanded.

"It's already done. I put a fox down their well last night."

"*A fox?*"

"That's right – a dead fox I found in the wood," said Tadgh.

"But – they'll all get sick," said Hugh.

"Of course they will, isn't that why I did it! And it was fairly decomposed so it will hit them quickly too! A little trick I learned fighting the enemy during the War of Independence. I put many an army barracks out of action with a dead animal down their wells!"

"But the servants as well, Tadgh! They'll drink the same water!"

"Good! They shouldn't be working for them! Didn't we fight the War of Independence to get rid of British rule and the Anglo-Irish – the likes of the Armstrongs? And there is no room for people in our new country who are ready to go back to being their servants and slaves!"

"But, Tadgh – Fennell and Mrs. Fennell are not young. Poisoning them like that could kill them!"

"Pity it wouldn't! You've gone soft, Hugh. It's people like you that lost us the cause. Look what the Government forces did to us during the Civil War, and you gave in rather than fight on!"

"Never mind the politics now! I can't allow that to happen to the innocent people at Armstrong House."

"Don't you think about going to warn them! As I said, the fox was put in the well last night so they will have drunk the water all day today already and there's nothing you can do about it now! They'll all be spending the next few days in hospital!"

"You're insane. I want you to go, Tadgh – now! Get out of my house and I won't be going back to work for you or want anything to do with you from now on."

"You're turning your back on me again after I offer you the hand of friendship!"

"I don't want anything more to do with you – or the Armstrongs for that matter. As far as I'm concerned you deserve each other. I'll leave this place tomorrow and I'll never return. Better for me to be on my own than walk with any of you!"

As the argument continued, Constance left.

When she arrived back at Seymour House, her mind was whirling as she thought about what she had overheard. She'd had nothing to do with Tadgh, but she had heard he could be a nasty piece of work. And now she had heard it with her own ears. She thought about the people at Armstrong House going about their daily work, none of them realising they were being poisoned as they drank the water through the day. She believed Hugh would not warn them. He owed the Armstrongs nothing after the way they had treated him but, what was more, she knew he would never betray his brother despite how much he opposed what he had done.

And she knew she could not warn them either without exposing her affair with Hugh and so she would have to remain silent.

Then a plan began to formulate in Constance's mind. She had given up on ever having unobserved access to Armstrong House, to take the painting. She and Clement had accepted it was an impossible task and hence they were returning to Dublin empty-handed. But, if what Tadgh had said was true, and the household was poisoned and all of them had to go to hospital? Then there was every possibility that the house would be empty that night. At the eleventh hour, Fate had delivered the perfect opportunity.

Constance had called to Armstrong House that afternoon to say goodbye to Clara and tell her they were returning to live in Dublin. While they were having lunch, Mrs. Fennell had announced that two of the staff had got sick and Constance realised Tadgh's plan was already delivering the desired results.

While Clara was later distracted, Constance had gone to the window in the dining room and wedged it so that it would not close properly.

Later that evening, she drove near to the Armstrong Estate and parked in a discreet location off the main road. She then entered the estate and made her way through the trees that surrounded the parkland until she found a vantage point where she could hide and have a view of the forecourt.

As the hours ticked by, her patience wore thin and, thinking Tadgh's effort to severely poison the household had failed, she decided to abandon her mission. But just as she was about to leave she saw a motorcar hastily drive up the avenue to the house and a man she recognised as the local doctor run up the steps and through the front door. Not long after that an ambulance arrived, and the staff were helped into the ambulance. It drove away and was followed by the doctor in his motorcar with Pierce and Clara.

As Constance made her way back to her own motorcar, she felt dazed as she realised that Tadgh's poisoning of the well had worked. In his attempt to drive the Armstrongs from their home he had provided her with the opportunity she had been waiting for. She could not risk going into the house when it was still light, in case she might be seen by Prudence or one of the other farmworkers who might be lurking around. Tadgh had said the poisoning of the water would result in the household being in hospital for a few days. Whatever about that, Constance was sure they would be kept in the hospital overnight, so she would wait until night-time to make sure there was nobody left in the house and nobody had returned to it in the meantime. There were always lights left on in the hall and the landing upstairs at night so, if the house was in darkness, Constance would know for certain there was nobody there.

She returned to Seymour Hall, had a couple of stiff gins to boost her nerve and waited until after midnight before she set off. Parking in the same hidden spot, she then made her way on foot to the house in the half moonlight. She was filled with relief that the house was in total darkness, indicating there was nobody there. The curtains also remained open, a clear indication that nobody had returned.

She made her way to the window that she had wedged ealier that day and was relieved to find it open. She climbed up on the window ledge and swung her feet into the dining room. As she dropped onto the floor inside the room she hit off a long-legged stand, causing a crystal lamp to fall to the floor. The noise of the crash echoed through the house. Using the moonlight to guide her, she walked across the room to where she remembered the light switch was inside the door. But when she flicked on the switch the darkness remained. She opened the door, walked across the hallway and tried the light switch there but again no light came on.

She cursed to herself as she realised there must be a problem with the electricity supply to the house. Alarmed, she wondered if this could mean there were people in the house after all. But no. If so, there would be a few oil-lamps lit, at least on the landings to light the way up the stairs. She paused for a moment as she thought she heard movement but there was only silence. She carefully made her way up the main staircase. She shivered as she stood on the landing. The house felt eerie and frightening, being empty and in darkness. But she reminded herself of the formidable situations she had encountered in the past and continued down the corridor and around the corner to servants' stairs.

As she had to navigate in the darkness, she took her time climbing the steps to the attic rooms.

She went to the room where the precious painting was hidden. The moonlight shone through the window as she started to move the boxes away from the knee wall. She took a chisel wrapped in cloth from her pocket. She had brought it just in case the box of cutlery, containing the knife she had used before, had been taken from the storage room. Then, kneeling down, she slid the top of the chisel into the indentation in the crevice and levered the panel off the knee wall.

Reaching inside the space, her fingers made contact with the painting and she pulled it out, taking the utmost care as it was now no longer wrapped in protective brown paper.

She carried it to the bed and sat down. At last, the painting was hers.

She realised she was panting from nerves and excitement. She was shaking so much that she had to take some time to breathe deeply and calm herself. Then she sat soaking up the beauty of the painting until she forced herself to move and complete her task.

She replaced the panel and moved the boxes back against the knee wall.

Then she left the bedroom and carried the painting down the narrow servants' stairs, no easy matter to carefully manoeuvre it down.

Then, as she reached the landing she heard a noise. Her heart nearly stopped as a light shone up the servants' stairs. She panicked as she realised somebody had come into the house through the back way and she could now hear them coming up the servants' stairs. She hurried down the landing to the main stairs.

Then the chandelier suddenly ignited fully above her, and she froze.

"Constance?"

Her heart filled with dread as she turned to see who was there. She didn't know whether to feel relief or dismay when she saw it was Hugh who had turned on the light and was now standing at the end of the corridor with confusion written across his face. She tried to think of an explanation as to why she was standing there in the darkness, holding a portrait.

"What are you doing here, Constance?" he demanded as he walked towards her, his eyes on the painting.

She cursed to herself when she thought that she had only needed another few minutes and she would have been gone.

"What are *you* doing here?" she returned the question.

"Lady Armstrong came rushing to my cottage saying somebody had broken into the house. She was alone here as everyone else is in the hospital."

Constance sighed as she realised that the movement she had heard earlier must have been Clara.

"What are you doing with that painting?" asked Hugh and then a look of realisation dawned on his face. "It was *you* who Clara heard breaking into the house! To take that painting!"

"So? Are you going to report me, Hugh?"

"Why should I not? A thief is a thief."

"Well, there is such a thing as honour amongst thieves. Is there not a bond between us?"

"Whatever else I am, I am not a thief," said Hugh.

"This painting is worth a lot of money, Hugh. I'd be quite happy to share the profit with you for your silence."

Hugh shook his head in disgust.

"What a fucking disappointment you turned out to be," he said.

Constance shrugged her shoulders.

"I never pretended to be a saint," she said.

"I knew you weren't a saint but never had you down as such a sinner," he said.

"If you ever did have any love for me, Hugh, you won't tell anybody about this. It will destroy my life."

"Maybe you should have thought about that before you tried to rob something that was not yours," he said. "And, worst of all, from a woman who believes you are her friend."

At that moment both of them froze as they heard the front door in the main hall downstairs unlock.

"Please, Hugh, I'm begging you not to say anything," Constance hissed as she bolted back down the corridor.

"*Clara!*" came a shout from downstairs.

Constance recognised Pierce's voice.

Hugh looked at Constance at the end of the corridor as she made a pleading face to him.

"What the blazes are you doing here?" demanded Pierce on seeing Hugh standing on the landing.

Hugh was stunned into silence as Pierce came bounding up the stairs to him.

Constance dashed around the corner at the end of the corridor.

"I – I –" stuttered Hugh.

"*While the cat's away the mouse will play!*" shouted Pierce. "*Where is she? Where is Clara? In my bed where you were fucking her?*"

"No – no! She's in my cottage –"

"*Ahhh! She does like to go slumming, my wife!*" said Pierce, consumed with anger. "*So, all the rumours are true – you are fucking each other!*"

"No, I swear I never touched her!"

"*I thought she was reaching for the bottom of the barrel when she went to Johnny Seymour's bed – but you! She's now sleeping with peasants! She has the morals of an alley cat!*"

"I swear, Lord Armstrong – you've gone this all wrong."

Peeping around the corner, Constance saw Pierce, consumed with rage, confronting Hugh.

Hugh stepped forward, palms raised placatingly as he said, "Listen to me – I can explain why I'm here."

Suddenly Pierce leapt at Hugh, giving him an almighty push in the chest.

Hugh fell backwards against the banisters and toppled over them.

Constance heard the horrific thud as he landed on the hall below.

After that, silence.

In shock, Constance watched Pierce stand on the landing, looking down at Hugh. He stood there for what seemed an eternity before he slowly walked down the stairs.

Constance was shaking uncontrollably. She knew she had to get away from there as quickly as she could before she was discovered. Still holding the painting, she made her way down the servants' stairs, crept through the kitchen and escaped out the back door.

Clara listened in astonished horror as Constance concluded telling her the sequence of events that led to Hugh's death.

"Your husband killed Hugh, Clara. It was an accident, but he still killed him," said Constance, wiping tears from her eyes.

"But – but then it was you who were having an affair with Hugh all along when everyone thought it was me!" said Clara. "It all makes sense now – when Asty said she saw my motorcar outside his cottage – it was the time you borrowed it!"

"It started as just a little bit of fun ... but it became much more. He's the only person I ever truly loved and now he's dead – thanks to your husband."

"*Thanks to you!* You've been manipulating us all and it resulted in Hugh's death. Even after he had been killed you still had the presence of mind to continue to steal the painting!"

"I did not. I hardly knew what I was doing. When you come from where I do and led the life I've led – you don't even think, you just act. It's called survival."

"So why did you bring the painting back here?"

"I couldn't deal with the guilt. I couldn't make money out of Hugh's death – I couldn't live with myself if I did. So, I thought if I came back for the ball I'd get the opportunity to put the painting back and be rid of it."

"I see."

"But it's a wonderful painting, Clara. It clearly shows he loved you."

"I know. I could not have it anywhere that Pierce could find it as it would remind him of that," said Clara.

"There's really not that much difference between us, Clara. We are two women who just followed our hearts."

"*I am nothing like you*," hissed Clara.

Clara did not give a damn about the painting any more or even Constance's criminal behaviour. All she could focus on was learning that Pierce had pushed Hugh to his death, even though it sounded like it was not intended. But if he could do that and pretend everything was normal, what else could he do? After killing so many people in the war, she believed another killing meant nothing to Pierce. He had been that damaged. And now she could believe he was responsible for the attacks on her during the year.

She suddenly remembered why she was there in the house.

She was being delayed from making her escape.

Chapter 56

Molly O'Meara was making bread at the kitchen table when her husband walked in from the next room. He had that look on his face that she had become well accustomed to. He had it during the Civil War just before he was due to go out at night to plant a bomb or conduct an ambush. Molly knew her husband was a fiery man. When he believed in a cause or felt somebody had done him wrong he would do anything to win or avenge himself. But she had never seen him as angry as she had since Hugh had died. He held the Armstrongs responsible, and he had told her he would not rest until he got revenge. He was holding a bottle in his hand, and she feared she already knew what it contained.

"What's that?" she asked.

"Paraffin," he said.

"And where are you going with it?"

"I'm going to Armstrong House to do what I should have done months ago. Síle told me the house will be empty for a few hours after three o'clock, as all the staff are going down to the village to feed the hunt food and drink. She has left the window into the ballroom open for me."

Molly wiped her hands on her apron.

"Is it safe for you to go up in daylight?" she asked.

"Didn't I just tell you there will be nobody there!" he snarled. "Even Prudence will be at the hunt and not hanging around. I might not get this opportunity for a long time."

"But setting fire to the house, Tadgh – won't everyone suspect it was you that did it?"

"Let them think what they fucking want! They can't prove anything, can they? Nobody proved it was me who did the other things during the year."

Molly conceded that this was true. Tadgh had certainly become an expert guerrilla fighter during the Civil War and it served him well in his campaign against the Armstrongs during the year. He knew the Armstrong estate like the back of his hand and could slip in and out unnoticed. Nobody had seen him go into the stable that morning and put the chestnut burr under Lady Armstrong's saddle that sent her bolting and nearly killed her. Nobody had seen him in the woods that day down by the lake when he had attacked Clara with stones. And when he gave Síle the weed-killer and instructed her to put it in Clara's perfume bottle nobody suspected him as they thought he could not have had access to the house. And nobody in their right mind would ever have suspected poor simple Síle of doing such an act. Síle, whose father was a close comrade of Tadgh's during the Civil War.

When Tadgh had put the dead fox down the well at Armstrong House he had told Síle not to drink the water but pretend to have the same sickness as the rest of the household and go home to her family so not to arouse suspicion. As it happened, Mrs. Fennell had sent her home in any case. Tadgh knew how to look after his own and he expected complete loyalty from them too. Síle was still a loyal and trustworthy informant.

"I should have done this months ago instead of messing around trying to frighten Clara Armstrong away. She's tougher than she looks. We should have known from the War of Independence the only way to get rid of the Armstrongs is to burn their house down. Even when I put the fox down the well and they were all carted off to hospital it didn't scare them away."

Molly nodded her understanding.

"And that bitch is responsible for Hugh's death. Sure, now we know why Hugh was so besotted with her and turned against his own family for her – didn't Asty tell the truth when she said Clara Armstrong seduced him and was sleeping with him? Isn't that what he was doing that night in Armstrong House when he died?"

Molly knew Tadgh was grieving so badly for Hugh that she could not dare to mention that he was as responsible for his death as anybody else. If Tadgh had not put the dead fox in the well, causing everyone to be in hospital that night then Hugh would not have been in Armstrong House and suffered that fall which was still a mystery to everybody. But, what had been a campaign against the Armstrongs to drive them away and claim their land had now developed into a vendetta since Hugh's death.

"Be careful – come home safe to me," said Molly as she approached her husband and kissed him.

He kissed her back and then walked out the front door. As Molly watched him go she knew he had to do what he needed to do.

"Mrs. Fennell's bacon sandwiches washed down with tea and whiskey – scrumptious!" said Philly Scott as she munched on her sandwich.

The hunt had gathered on the green in the Armstrong village and the riders were gratefully being served refreshments by Pierce's staff.

"I say, where's Clara gone?" Philly asked.

Pierce looked around but could not see her.

"She's always such a laggard – we probably lost her along the way! Hope she is alright!" said Philly.

Pierce thought back and could not remember seeing Clara for the last part of the hunt.

He remembered how strange she had been the previous night and that morning.

He walked over to Prudence and pulled her away from the crowd.

"Where's Clara?" he asked.

"I would say she's halfway to Dublin by now," said Prudence, looking at her watch.

"What do you mean?"

"She knows everything, Pierce. And before you get mad at me it wasn't me who told her."

"Knows about what exactly?"

"She knows all about our plan. She found out we knew she was an heiress before you reconciled with her – and also that your suicide bid was staged to get her back."

"Who told her?"

"That I don't know but she confronted me about it last night. She made me swear not to tell you until she was gone. So I thought good riddance to bad rubbish and agreed!"

Anger flashed across Pierce's face as he ran to his horse and jumped on.

"*Let her go, Pierce! You really are better off without her!*" Prudence called after him.

"I don't know why but I feel better now you know everything," said Constance.

"I'm glad your guilty conscience has been somewhat alleviated," said Clara sarcastically.

"So, what are you going to do now?" asked Constance.

"I have not decided," said Clara.

"You could tell the police, but I'll just deny everything and since the painting is here you can't accuse me of stealing it, can you?"

"And I guess you wouldn't give testimony about Pierce killing Hugh either?"

"Of course not – that would be admitting my guilt, that I was in the house taking the painting in the first place. Revealing the truth will not help anybody. Really, Clara, you don't need the scandal of that coming out about Pierce, do you?"

"No," sighed Clara. All she wanted to do now was get away from Pierce and Armstrong House and reporting anything that she had just learned from Constance would only keep her there and tied to Pierce indefinitely.

They suddenly heard shouting in the house.

"Clara! Clara!"

"It's Pierce!" exclaimed Clara.

"Well, that's my cue to leave!" said Constance. "I've done what I came here to do – return your painting."

"Good luck with your next fraud," said Clara spitefully.

Constance gave her a salute, half smiled and walked away.

"Clara!" shouted Pierce as he searched downstairs.

Clara looked down at the portrait lying on the bed and then turned and quickly left the room. Constance had delayed her and now she would have to face Pierce, but she was determined to continue with her plan of leaving that day. She could not bear the thought of spending another night under the same roof as him.

When she reached their bedroom, she quickly finished packing and then buckled the straps of her suitcase.

The door opened and Pierce walked in.

"Why did you leave the hunt?" he demanded.

She turned around to face him.

"I'm leaving you, Pierce. This time for good. I know everything – the fake deeds, the fake suicide attempt and that you knew I was going to be an heiress before even I did."

She wasn't sure if the expression on his face was anger or shock.

"I know other things too – about the night Hugh died and that you pushed him," she said. "I never want to see you again and will file for a divorce as soon as I arrive home in London."

There was no doubt her revelation about Hugh had turned his expression to complete shock.

"And for your information, I was not having an affair with Hugh. That was Constance." She watched him absorb that and wondered how he would react.

He didn't disappoint.

"You can't leave – today of all days! What will I tell our guests?" he demanded.

"Tell them what the hell you want," she said, taking her suitcase from the bed. "You have what you want from me – you've had my money to rebuild your precious house and farm. And I hear you are going to even get a windfall soon with the compensation for the burning of the house. You'll be just fine without me from now on. I'm sure Philly Scott will be more than happy to keep you company with her endless procession of lame horses for you to tend to if you get lonely."

She walked towards the door, but he blocked her way.

"You're not going anywhere, Clara!"

"Why do you even pretend you want me to stay! You don't love me – you really never have. You don't even like me!"

"You've made a disgrace of me once by leaving me and I won't allow you to do it again!" he said angrily.

"And that's all this marriage ever was to you. A show for other people. I am just some trophy that you like to show off. Well, I'm tired of it and I'm tired of you. I should never have come back here, but I'll never be fooled by you again – I promise you that." She pushed him out of her way.

She opened the door and walked to the top of the stairs.

Pierce followed her.

"I admit I have deceived you, but I just wanted you back," he said.

"You wanted your old life back and I was just a means to getting it for you," said Clara as she walked down the stairs.

In her bedroom, Constance could hear Pierce shouting loudly as she hastily packed. She could not wait to get away from there and as she opened her bedroom door she could hear her hosts were now arguing in the hall downstairs. She didn't want to face either of them, so she opted to leave by the back way.

She hurried to the servants' staircase and down the narrow steps until she reached the small hallway which led to the kitchen. The windowless hallway was being lit by an oil lamp resting on a side table. As she hurried through her suitcase hit off the table, knocking it over. The oil lamp fell to the floor. Constance swore to herself as the paraffin in the lamp spilled across the rug on the floor and caught fire from the lamp's flame.

Constance ran to the kitchen, filled a large jug with water and threw it on the rug, but it did not extinguish the flames. She made another couple of attempts to douse the fire with water but it continued to burn. She began to panic as the fire started to spread to the wooden servants' stairs.

As she heard Clara and Pierce continuing to shout at each other upstairs, she ran through the kitchen and out the back door and from there to her motorcar. She threw her suitcase in the back, sat in and drove quickly down the avenue as fast as she could.

"I actually just feel pity for you at this point, Pierce!" said Clara. "Because you will never be happy and you can never be happy. You are a shallow man who is beset by insecurities that you hide behind by putting other people down. The only reason you like me around is because you can belittle me in private and in public, thinking it makes you look superior. I deserve better than you – I always did but I really did love you. But I don't anymore. I really don't – and for that I am truly grateful."

"You can't survive without me, even with your money," he said.

"We shall see. I think I can't survive with you, so I have no other choice. But I'm glad I never really trusted you when I came back here and you will never know how much you have lost because of that – you will never know."

Clara had started walking towards the front door when she heard the sound of crackling. She turned to see smoke coming up from the servants' stairs at the end of the hall.

"What the hell is that?" demanded Pierce as he rushed to the end of the hall. Then he jumped back when he saw flames shooting up from the little hall at the bottom of the stairs.

"It's a fire!" he shouted.

He disappeared down the stairs. Clara dropped her suitcase and ran to the staircase.

As she looked she saw Pierce was attempting to get down the steps, but the fire was too strong.

"Pierce! Stop – it's too dangerous! We need to get help!" she shouted.

Pierce reluctantly backed up the stairs and Clara raced to the telephone and rang for the operator to contact the fire brigade in Castlewest.

Smoke started billowing up from the basement as Pierce tried to think what he could do to extinguish the fire. But as Clara looked on she remembered how quickly the fire had spread during the previous one there that she had experienced. Suddenly the fire had reached the hall and the panelling on the wall became inflamed.

"Pierce, we have to get out of here!" shouted Clara as she opened the front door, grabbing her suitcase. Pierce was still at the end of the hall and began to choke and cough.

"*Pierce!*" Clara screamed which prompted him to rush along the hall and out the front door as he gasped for air.

"I'll go to the village to get the riders from the hunt to help!" said Clara. She rushed to her motorcar and began to drive to the village where she hoped their guests would still be.

As she turned out of the forecourt Pierce stood in front of his house as the fire began to take hold.

Tadgh O'Meara was making his way through the trees that crossed the parkland beside Armstrong House. This was a relatively easy mission to carry out compared to ones he had conducted during the Civil War. All he had to do was open the French windows to the ballroom that Síle had left unlocked for him. He would then throw the paraffin he had brought on the curtains that hung either side and light a match. It wouldn't take long for the house to catch fire and he would be home in time for tea.

Tadgh suddenly stopped abruptly in his tracks as Armstrong House came into view. He could not believe what he saw. The house was already in flames.

Darkness had fallen and the fire still burned. The riders from the hunt along with locals from the village formed a long line from the well at the back of house, passing buckets of water to each other to try and put out the flames. At the front of the house, the fire brigade from Castlewest were doing their best to do the same.

Clara stood in the forecourt as the memories of the last fire came flooding back. Nearby Pierce stood in a trance as he watched his house being destroyed. Clara almost felt sorry for him as she knew Armstrong House was the only thing he had ever really loved. But she did not go to him. The fire spread an orange glow in the sky above and across the snow on the ground.

Eventually Clara knew it was time to leave. Armstrong House was no longer her home or her problem and neither was Pierce. She walked to her motorcar and started the engine. Then she drove out of the forecourt to leave forever. As she drove down the avenue that final time the fire from the house continued to glow behind her.

Chapter 57

Present Day

Having learned from Sergeant Cantwell's police file that he was co-operating with the the Royal Ireland Insurance Company over the fire at Armstrong House, Kate checked if the firm was still in operation. She found that it was and they advertised themselves proudly as one of the country's oldest insurance firms. Learning from Google that many of the older insurance companies kept records of policies and claims from the 1920s, she sent Royal Ireland an email requesting if they had anything on the Armstrong House fire in December 1923 and if their policy would allow her to view it for research purposes. Kate imagined Pierce had put in a claim if Sergeant Cantwell had been assisting the insurance company.

It was evening and Kate was alone at the house as Nico was away for a week with work and Cian was staying overnight at a friend's house. Kate wondered how long it took for Clara and Pierce's divorce to be finalised once she had left for England. She also wondered if there might be any details in the divorce records that might show if Clara was the co-owner of Armstrong House.

Sitting at the desk in the library, she checked whether it was difficult to get a divorce in 1920s Ireland. She was not surprised how draconian the laws had been then, with divorce not even permissible under the new constitution of 1922 in Ireland. Clara and Pierce would have had no option but to pursue their divorce through the English courts where she was by then living. Kate discovered the law in England had changed in 1923, allowing both a wife and husband to file for divorce on grounds of adultery, where previously only a husband could file on these grounds. Still, even with this change, divorce was very much geared to protecting the husband and his assets. Kate rolled her eyes when she read there was even an 'alimony panic' in the 1920s, fearing wives would be trying to take their husband's assets. The press inflamed this panic and the term 'gold-digger' was used often. But the reality was most wives received little compensation after divorce and as Clara was an heiress in her own right, Kate imagined she had no claim over anything Pierce might own, including Armstrong House. Royce Charter's claim would have to depend solely on Clara being on the deeds before they separated. As adultery had to be proven in the proceedings, Kate hoped there might be some indicator of Clara's alleged affair with Hugh O'Meara in the divorce petition.

The National Archives of England and Wales held the divorce files granted between 1858 and 1937 and they were available online. As divorce was still very much considered a scandal and few were granted, Kate found a record of Clara and Pierce's divorce with relative ease. It had been granted in 1927 and the petitioner was Lord Pierce Armstrong with an address at 17 Monkstown Terrace, Dublin. He was seeking a divorce from his wife Clara on the ground of her adultery and desertion. Clara's address was listed as Oak Trees in Kent. Pierce painted a horrendous picture of Clara in his divorce petition, stating that he had endured the indignity of an affair she had with the well-known artist Johnny Seymour while he was away fighting the war in France. And that after an initial separation, Pierce had given his wife a second chance and welcomed her back to his home, Armstrong House, in 1923. But that Clara had continued to prove to be a feckless and disloyal wife who had deserted him after a fire occurred at their home in December of that year. Clara had made no defence to the proceedings and accepted full culpability for the breakdown of their marriage. Kate could only imagine what this would have done to a woman's reputation back in the 1920s. Kate continued to read the list of grievances Pierce had against Clara which began to sound very petty. Clara remained silent throughout.

As an actress Kate had learned to read between the lines. She could read a character she was playing more from what they didn't say than what they did. Pierce made no mention that it had been Clara's money that had rebuilt the house after the first fire. Neither was there a mention of putting her on the deeds of the house. As Kate reread Pierce's petition he sounded a very difficult and controlling man who was very bitter when he didn't get his own way. Kate felt it was Clara who had given her husband a second chance not the other way around. And by paying for the rebuilding of the house, she had done everything she could to make the marriage work a second time. Tellingly, Pierce made no mention of the alleged affair with Hugh O'Meara. Since Pierce was throwing everything including the kitchen sink at his wife during the proceedings, Kate was sure he would have also stated her affair with Hugh if she had indeed had one as rumoured. Kate concluded the gossip about Clara and Hugh was untrue, otherwise Pierce would have gleefully broadcast it in court to sully his wife's reputation further.

Afterwards, Kate went into the drawing room and put on some music – the theme from *Chinatown*.

She walked out into the hall and looked at the area under the landing where Hugh O'Meara had fallen to his death over a century before. She wondered what had really happened that night – was it a dreadful accident or had something more sinister occurred?

She went and opened the front door and looked out at the sun setting over the lake. The house had experienced so much history – often painful. She thought about Nico's great-grandfather, Lord Charles, who had been shot there. She thought of Pierce and Clara and how they could not find happiness there. And, as she looked out at the lake, she thought of her first husband Tony. It was true what she had said to Alex the day of the wedding. Kate did not dwell on her past – particularly her past with Tony. She had been a different person when she had met him – a star of sorts and he had been a hugely successful magnate. Even with all that, she had been looking for something more in her life to give it meaning. When Nico had put the dilapidated and fire-damaged Armstrong House up for the sale, she had remembered it from growing up in Castlewest before her family emigrated to New York. She had persuaded Tony to buy it and he had used his vast wealth to restore its former glory. That's when she had got to know Nico as he had been the architect they employed to oversee the project. As she allowed herself to remember Tony, she recalled his larger-than-life personality. She had often wondered if she was just another acquisition for him, but they had been happy for a while even if she felt she never really knew him.

Now she allowed herself to remember how Tony had been killed there in the speedboat accident. As his empire had been crumbling at the time, people had said it was suicide. Kate could never say for sure. Tony's assets had been sold off to cover his debts after his death and she had to leave her beloved Armstrong House. Then, through a twist of fate, Nico had managed to buy it back during the property crash at a knockdown price due to the sale of a portrait he had inherited from his grandfather Pierce – a portrait of his first wife Clara by the famous artist Johnny Seymour. And, as Nico had helped Kate through her grief, they had fallen in love and Kate had ended up in Armstrong House as its mistress.

Gazing out over the lake, she allowed herself to cry for the first time as she remembered Tony's laughing jovial face. She suddenly missed him very much. She had felt very lonely since Alex's wedding day. Nico was so solid and down-to-earth that she always thought that was what she loved most about him after her years of marriage to a man like Tony whose personality was as unpredictable as the Irish weather. But now she wondered had she misread Nico's coldness as dependability. Maybe he was not so unlike Pierce, the grandfather he never knew.

Kate went inside and locked the front door. As she walked through the house she began to think Nico was right. It might be time to leave Armstrong House and its memories to start a new life.

Kate was at the island drinking her coffee and going through the morning post. There was a large, padded envelope addressed to her and when she tore it open she saw it was from the Royal Ireland Insurance company. The covering letter told her that following on from her recent enquiry concerning a fire at Armstrong House in December 1923, they were forwarding the enclosed record of the subsequent claim. She knocked back her coffee and began to read the findings which had been authored by an insurance investigator named Ernest Pitchfork.

17th of May 1924 – Claim No. 67345 – Lord Pierce Armstrong for Fire at Armstrong House

Following a fire that occurred at Armstrong House, County Mayo, and a claim for compensation made by the owner Lord Pierce Armstrong, I was charged with investigating the circumstances and possible arson. This is my final report.

The fire occurred on the 12th of December 1923 and caused much damage to the west of the house, leaving it uninhabitable. The local fire brigade was called roughly 4pm by Lord Armstrong himself. The firemen were assisted by the members of the local Hunt Club who were in the vicinity that day. It took many hours to control the fire.

I started my investigation once Lord Armstrong made his claim for compensation in January 1924. I spoke firstly to Sergeant

Cantwell of the Castlewest Garda Sergeant Cantwell who strongly suspected a local farmer named Tadgh O'Meara had started the fire, as it was known he wanted to want to drive the Armstrongs from the area. But I could find no evidence of Mr. O'Meara's involvement and his wife Molly insists he was at home with her all day.

I interviewed Lord Armstrong at his new home in Monkstown on 17th of February 1924. He told me what had occurred the day of the fire. He and his wife Lady Clara Armstrong were alone in the house as the staff were all in the nearby village, attending to the local hunt which had taken place that afternoon. Lord and Lady Armstrong were in the hall of the house when they saw smoke coming from the servants' staircase at the back of the hall. When Lord Armstrong went to investigate, he saw flames coming from the small hallway at the bottom of those stairs and, though he at first tried to deal with it himself, he realised it was beyond his capabilities. At this point his wife called for the fire brigade by telephone. He left the house with his wife who drove to the village to get help from members of the hunt.

Lord Armstrong has since petitioned for divorce and his wife Clara now lives in England. After much persuasion Lady Armstrong agreed to an interview and I travelled to her home in Kent where I understand she now lives an almost hermit-like life. Lady Armstrong confirmed her husband's version of events and said that there was no reason to suspect foul play as they were the only two in the house at the time the fire started.

I asked Lady Armstrong if she was a party to this claim for insurance compensation and she said she was not, as she was not entitled to be since she is not the owner or on the deeds of Armstrong House. As she is now being divorced by her husband, she said she wanted nothing more to do with her husband or Armstrong House.

I then interviewed the staff at Armstrong House. As they had not been present during the fire, I did not expect them to be able to offer much information. However, the family's cook Mrs. Fennell broke down during my questioning and admitted that she had left an oil lamp lighting in the small hallway at the bottom of the servants' stairs. She said she had been in a rush to get to the hunt to serve them refreshments and had forgotten to put it out. As both Lord and Lady Armstrong reported this is where the fire originated, it is my conclusion that the fire was started by this lighted oil lamp and that the lamp either fell or malfunctioned, causing the fire.

Signed

Ernest Pitchfork

Kate felt lightheaded as she reread the line which said Clara was not on the deeds of the house. This was the evidence they required to establish that the deeds Royce Charter had were fake.

Before she could even register it further the doorbell rang, and she rushed upstairs to answer it. She was surprised to find Barry O'Meara standing there, a big smile on his face.

"Morning, Kate. Hope you don't mind me dropping by?"

"Of course not! Come in, Barry!" She beckoned and showed him into the drawing room.

"I got the deeds for our farm that you were asking for," he said, opening a file under his arm. "This is a copy of them from our solicitor."

"Oh, great!" said Kate as she sat at the bureau to read them, a little nervous of what they might reveal.

"As I said, it's all there. My grandfather Tadgh bought the farmland from your husband's grandfather Pierce back in 1925 and our family have owned it ever since."

Kate opened the relevant pages which showed only Pierce as the previous owner of the land, with no mention of Clara.

"Is it any help?" asked Barry.

"Absolutely! This confirms Clara was not an owner of the estate or else the sale could not have gone through to Tadgh without her being listed here in the chain of title!"

"Well, I hope that is the end of the trouble for you," said Barry.

As Kate smiled at him, she remembered Sergeant Cantwell's belief that Tadgh O'Meara had intimidated and attacked Clara in order to drive her and Pierce away so he could claim and buy the farm. As she looked at Tadgh's name on the deeds acquiring the land in 1925, she felt a surge of anger that his campaign had worked, even if he had not been responsible for the fire that finally drove them away. The affable Barry clearly had no idea that his family's wealth was built on ill-gotten gains.

As Barry rushed off to see his new-born grandson, Kate knew he could not be held accountable for his forefather's actions. No more than Nico could be held accountable for his.

Geoffrey Conway confirmed that the sale to Tadgh O'Meara in 1925 proved Clara had not been on the original deeds and that Clara had confirmed herself in the insurance investigation that she was not an owner of Armstrong House. He wrote to Royce Charter's solicitor in London explaining this and that the deeds they possessed were clearly a forgery. Kate was surprised but very relieved when Royce's solicitor wrote back, accepting this fact, and said that they were dropping their claim.

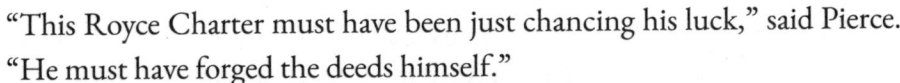

"This Royce Charter must have been just chancing his luck," said Pierce. "He must have forged the deeds himself."

He and Kate were seated on the terrace outside the drawing room, enjoying a bottle of wine in the evening sunshine.

"I don't think so. Royce's deeds did look as if they were authentic and from the 1920s. I would like to believe he was just trying to rectify the past – and Clara's past."

"Anyway, I hope we never hear from him again."

"We never did learn how he was related to Clara," mused Kate. "How did he get those deeds in the first place? I've learned so much about Pierce and Clara and yet there are still unanswered questions."

"Well, we know what happened to Pierce. He bought the house in Monkstown."

"Clearly from the compensation he got from the burning of the house by the rebels and the sale of the land to Tadgh O'Meara. He would have been quite well off because of this – otherwise I imagine he might have been destitute."

"And he eventually got a job as a clerk for the British government, based in Dublin," said Nico, "which led to a job in the British embassy when one finally was established there."

"Do you know if his second marriage to your grandmother was happy?"

"It was such a short marriage. He was in his late forties when he married her and then he was killed soon after in the Second World War. I remember my grandmother saying he was a complicated man but she could not resist him, and he used to tell her she reminded him of Clara."

"How strange he married a woman that reminded him of the first wife he professed to loathe!" said Kate.

"It certainly is. Perhaps on some level he loved her despite all."

After a short silence, Nico leaned his head towards Kate.

"Thank you, Kate," he said.

"For what?"

"For getting to the bottom of all this and resolving it. I am truly grateful. And I really am sorry how I acted the day of Alex's wedding. I didn't put you first and that is unforgiveable."

"It was Alex's day, it's understandable," she said, feeling her voice croak.

"We both know that's not an excuse, and I promise you it will never happen again," he said. "I don't know how you put up with me sometimes. I know I don't show my emotions as much as I should but as the song goes – you are always on my mind."

She leaned toward him and kissed him.

"Maybe we just spend too much time in each other's company in this big old house. Maybe you are right and it is time for us to move on. Make new memories somewhere else?" she suggested.

"I have too many good memories of being here with you to want to be anywhere else," he said.

Kate's phone bleeped and she picked it up to read a text from her agent, causing her to suddenly light up with excitement.

"The actress who got that part in the series I auditioned for has walked off the set and they want me now!" she said excitedly.

"That's wonderful – that is if you don't mind taking her place?"

"Of course I'm going to take the part! You know I have no problem with being second choice," she assured him with a grin.

Chapter 58

Kate was kept very busy with her new role in the television series. She was thrilled to be back working regularly and fitted her home life at Armstrong House around filming. Their lives at Armstrong House continued as it always had, but Kate felt they were more at peace after the disruption of the wedding and the interference of Royce Charter.

Even though his claim had been proven invalid, Kate's natural curiosity as to how Royce was connected to Clara remained unanswered. She thought about Clara a lot. Picturing her in her unhappy life at Armstrong House and how she felt it was worth a second chance. She felt dissatisfied that she still didn't know what happened to Clara after she left Armstrong House that final time and it played on her mind that the insurance investigator described her as leading a hermit-like life in Kent.

During a break between filming one day on set, she tried to find any reference to Clara in the years after she left Armstrong House in the British census online. But her heart sank when she discovered all the English records of the 1931 census were lost in a fire that occurred in 1942. Then the 1941 census had not taken place due the Second World War. Kate thought it sad that there was no record of the people that lived during those those decades. But it was also strangely apt as the people of that time were known as the Lost Generation – Clara's group who had lived through the First World War – and the Silent Generation, their children who lived in the shadow of the next world war. It seemed appropriate that the 1931 census was lost and the 1941 census was silent. How unlike both those generations were to her age group, Generation X, or Alex's age group,

Generation Z who documented and posted what they had for breakfast, lunch and dinner. It seemed to Kate that Clara's Lost Generation were so much more dignified.

When Kate had to go for a week filming in London, her curiosity got the better of her. She still had Royce Charter's phone number from when he sent her the photograph of the Hunt Ball and she had been tempted to phone him to try and meet. She knew Nico would kill her if he knew what she planned to do. But as she always thought, what Nico didn't know wouldn't harm him. As the filming drew to a close she plucked up the courage and phoned Royce's number.

"Hello, Kate," he answered, and she felt a little unnerved but relieved that he had saved her number.

"Hi, Royce, I'm sorry to disturb you and I'm sure you were not expecting to ever hear from me again," she said.

"On the contrary. I was very much hoping you would contact me. In any case, I would have contacted you eventually."

"I'm actually in London and I wondered if you would like to meet for a chat?"

"Very much so. You're more than welcome to visit me at my home in Kent," he offered.

Kate hired a car and drove down to Kent. She found the address that Royce had given her. She felt nervous as she found the house, which according to the name on the gate was called Oak Trees. She suddenly remembered this was the address given for Clara in the divorce proceedings and became even more intrigued. It was a lovely old house with beautifully kept gardens although the privacy it might have once enjoyed was now gone as it was surrounded by housing estates.

Kate parked the car. She walked up to the front door and rang the doorbell and soon after Royce answered.

"We meet again!" he said as he stood aside for her to enter.

"Indeed, we do!" she responded.

As he led her into a sitting room they exchanged pleasantries, and she sat down when he indicated she should sit on the couch.

"Tea or coffee?" he enquired.

"Coffee would be lovely," she said.

He left the room and returned in a minute or two with a tray bearing coffee and a plate of shortbread biscuits.

He sat on an armchair facing her, lifted his cup of coffee and said, "I really do apologise for intruding into your lives in the way I did."

"Well, we did get a bit of a shock to hear from your solicitors in the way we did," she confessed.

"I was just trying to get to the truth. Once I realised the deeds I had were fake, I withdrew and felt sorry that the matter had arisen at all."

"But where did those deeds come from and – and who actually are you?" she asked.

"The deeds were found in the possessions of my grandmother Clara Charter after she died," said Royce.

"Your *grandmother*?" exclaimed Kate, nearly dropping her coffee.

"That's right, Kate – my grandmother was Clara Charter and my grandfather was Pierce Armstrong."

"But – but they never had any children! The only child Pierce had was Jacqueline, my husband's mother!"

"Not so. I'm afraid. When Clara left Pierce after the house burned down, the first time in the War of Independence, she was pregnant with his child. She gave birth to my father James in 1922 – here at Oak Trees, which was her grandmother's Louisa's house at the time. Pierce did not know and he never knew. Only her grandmother knew and Clara lived here for the first few months with her child."

Kate was astounded. "What? She had his child?"

"Yes, she did."

"But why did she keep it a secret?" demanded Kate.

"Because she didn't want Pierce to be involved in their son's life. She had seen how damaged he was, how damaged all the Armstrongs were, and she feared her son would not have a safe life with them. Her Grandmother Louisa agreed and made Clara her heir so that she would be financially independent, to look after the child."

"But she went back to Armstrong House after their son was born! And even paid for it to be rebuilt and she never told Pierce! Why?"

"She went back for two reasons – Pierce had pretended to try and kill himself and she was consumed with guilt. But mostly she felt she had to go back for her son's sake. She felt she had to give Pierce a second chance, to see if he had changed as he had promised. To see if she could trust him enough to allow him to be around their son, my father James. Also, her son was the rightful heir to Armstrong House and the title of Lord Armstrong. She didn't want to deny him that if she felt it was safe for him to live there."

"So that's why she gave the money to rebuild Armstrong House after the first fire." Kate nodded her understanding.

"Yes, she was rebuilding for her son. not for her husband. And during those months when she was living back there, she left my father in the care of her parents who she had told by then and a wonderful housekeeper called Mrs. Wilkins. Her parents had moved here to Oak Trees temporarily, to look after my father. She travelled back here to see him as often as she could. As well as the fact she had to wait to see if she could trust Pierce before she told him about their son, it was not safe to bring the child to Armstrong House at the time, as the Civil War was raging. She knew Pierce would insist she brought James there regardless, if he knew of his existence. During her second time at Armstrong House, she came to see Pierce had not changed in the least. He was the same brutal, selfish man he always was. He had just pretended to be somebody else to win her – and her money back."

"So after the second fire she came back here to Oak Trees to her son," said Kate.

"Yes. And she did everything to continue to prevent Pierce from learning about James. She knew if Pierce ever learned of their son's existence he would take him away from her – out of spite if nothing else. He destroyed her and her name in their divorce case."

"I'm aware of that. I read the court papers on the divorce and no doubt Pierce would get custody as she would be seen as an unfit mother," said Kate.

"Clara's name really was destroyed but by then she didn't want anything to do with the high society world she had grown up in anyway. She knew if she brought her son up in that world, word would get back to Pierce about him."

"So she lived as a recluse in this house, rearing her son," said Kate.

"Yes, but my father James had a very idyllic and happy childhood with Clara and her family. He went on to be a doctor, got married and had two children – me and my sister Amanda," said Royce.

"And that's the woman I met years ago when I returned Clara's items that I found at Armstrong House! I knew she was related to Clara, but she never said she was her granddaughter!"

"You must understand that Clara warned us all to stay away from the Armstrongs as they were dangerous and damaged. Neither my father nor my sister and I ever used the surname Armstrong. When my father turned eighteen Clara did give him the option to make his existence known to Pierce but then Pierce was killed soon after in the Second World War, so my father just got on with his life."

"What made you suddenly make contact with us after all these years?" asked Kate.

"I had got to an age when I was looking for something to give my life a new meaning – a fool's errand really," he sighed.

"I understand how you feel. I also once turned to Armstrong House to give my life meaning," said Kate, remembering her first marriage.

"I suddenly started thinking about the side of my life that I had never known anything about and been kept away from. As my father was Pierce's eldest and only son the title of Lord Armstrong is rightfully his and should not have become extinct. And I by rights should be Lord Armstrong."

"And so you are! Do you plan on claiming the title – nobody could deny you that as it is rightfully yours," said Kate.

"I don't think so. I think the title is rather meaningless without Armstrong House, don't you? The two go hand in hand."

"I agree. Well, my husband will be intrigued to hear all this. You are his cousin! You must come and visit us at Armstrong House so we can properly get to know you – as long as you don't try to take it from us again!"

"I would love to, and I promise not to stake any further claim!"

"How long did Clara live?" asked Kate.

"She died in 1973. She was a wonderful grandmother to me and my sister when we were children. We loved her very much."

"I'm sure you did. And I'm so glad to learn that Clara was surrounded by love for the rest of her life. She deserved that. Though, it must have been lonely for her being on her own, having been so unlucky in love."

"I wouldn't quite say that," said Royce, smiling. "She wasn't lonely because she did have a friend. Everyone needs a friend, Kate."

Epilogue

1927

Clara sat in the gardens of Oak Trees watching Cosmo play with her son James in the sunshine. She felt she could finally relax as her divorce from Pierce had been granted. It had been a turbulent few years, trying to be free of the man who had ruined her life not once but twice. And her one concern through it all was that Pierce would never learn of the existence of their son James. She knew Pierce would take him away from her and as he had destroyed her reputation in court he would get full custody. She could not bear the thought of James being brought up by Pierce. She knew his life would be destroyed. Once she had left Armstrong House and moved back to Oak Trees, she had been content to live a life of isolation. She was shocked when Cosmo had shown up one day, unexpected and out of the blue, to find her playing with James in the garden. She had pretended that James was a friend's child, but he looked so much like Clara that Cosmo knew straight away that he was hers. She was afraid that he would reveal to everybody that she and Pierce had a son, but she knew deep down he would never be disloyal to her.

She often contemplated what her life would have been if she had accepted Cosmo's proposal rather than Pierce's back in 1912. But then she wouldn't have James. She wondered why Cosmo had tracked her down but really she didn't have to ask. He loved her. He had always loved her. She always knew it but never quite grasped just how much he did, until he had shown up that day. She insisted he forget about her and that his future would be limited with her. She couldn't show her face in society after the divorce and, besides, she had now decided to dedicate her life to bringing up her son in obscurity. Cosmo said he couldn't stand the meaningless life he led in London anymore and he couldn't imagine anything better than just living in obscurity with Clara. She had turned him away. When he showed up again and again, she kept turning him away. Not because she didn't want him to stay but she felt he would be so much better off without her. Cosmo told her he had spent years trying to find somebody to make him forget her and he had given up hope that anyone could. He now understood why she had gone back to Pierce as she was desperately trying to make the marriage work for the sake of their son.

She tried not think of Armstrong House anymore, but it never really left her mind. People said she had been destroyed from her experiences there and from Pierce. They said she had gone mad and was a hermit who never left the house. They said she was a sad, broken woman who could not hold her head up as her reputation was in tatters. Clara didn't mind them thinking that as it made people leave her alone and she could be left in her contented little world with just James and Cosmo.

Mrs. Wilkins came out into the garden to take James in for his tea.

Cosmo walked across the lawn, joined Clara on the veranda and gave her a kiss before sitting down beside her.

She reached out and held his hand and gazed out at the gardens.

"You're lost in your thoughts again, Clara," he said.

"I was just thinking how much James adores you," Clara said.

"Well, then, he has bad taste like his mother!" joked Cosmo.

"I certainly hope that doesn't prove true as he goes through life," sighed Clara.

"I wondered, now that the divorce has come through, would you like to go abroad to celebrate? A trip to the Riveria or Italy could cheer you up after the whole ordeal."

Clara turned to face him.

"No! I really don't want to go anywhere," she said. "I have everything I want just here."

"Are you sure?" Cosmo asked and she could see he was still insecure about her feelings for him.

"I couldn't be surer. I have James and you and I promise you that you finally have me," said Clara. "Thank you for giving me my happy ever after."

The End